To CHRIS

DOOM SALOON

3rd Ed. Revised

Tim Bonner

A *Bud Coke Jack & Marlboros* story

Easter Sunday, April 2021

Tim Bonner

all The Best!

First Printing, 2020

KDP ISBN 9798632667142

Cover by Tim Bonner.

Illustrations by Lionel Emabat.

Tim Bonner
P O Box 1911
Eastsound, WA 98245

www.timbonner.net

Dedicated to
Dan C. Rinnert.

If he can do it, so can I.

Asaf had a vision. A fantasy in his mind. He saw himself as a black-robed rider, holding aloft a great sword, dripping with blood. The sword changed into a scythe. He looked down a great valley and the wrongdoers were chopped-up and scattered about.

Asaf reached into his tunic and withdrew his heart. He held it up and the heart spoke to him.

"You are not me and I am not you. I am a heart and you are a man. I will continue to give you your life's blood, but the reaping of the bad men will come from your spirit. The desire for light and good will come from your soul."

The sun rose, and the light of its rays made all the dismembered corpses disappear. Asaf's bloody scythe changed into a flagstaff. The flag was green with a great white dot.

It read: Goodness Shall Overcome — Evil Shall be Overthrown.

Asaf was encouraged by the flag. But he was not happy that his heart was not with his spirit and soul.

"I will let my heart do what it does naturally. But I will not stop what I plan on doing to this village."

25.5

Asaf knew who the spies were. They came and went, spending an inordinate amount of time in the bar, far more than any other military group, entertaining all sorts who all needed a place to drink and talk. When the spooks moved on to more fertile ground, they always left one behind. Someone who could waste away in another margaritaville and call headquarters every week, month, or year, or not call at all.

Asaf brought the leftover spy's drink to his table. "I know you are not fully occupied with your career. I have something for you, that I think would give you something to do and stimulate your mind at the same time."

The spy sipped his Jack and Coke. "Go ahead Asaf. I'm ready for one of your gigs if you think it suits. Tell me what you want me to know."

"How far back should I go? I'm not sure how much you know or understand or don't know."

"There are things I know. And there are things I understand. Go back as far as you think is conducive for what we both need to know and understand. How's that?"

Asaf set his tray on the table. "Let me start from the beginning. Well, not the beginning-beginning, but far enough back so we are on the same page. Do you — or what do you know — about the Soldier and the old club? And the sectarians and this whole area? I don't want to waste our time going over things that you already know."

"Listening is my forté. Proceed."

Asaf sat down and began. "This land around here — about as far as you can see — is considered to belong to my people. Our culture exists in this land and our culture is both a religious thing as well as a national-homeland thing. Religion is part of a whole way of looking at things, and how things should be. Is this the direction I should be going in? Am I too far ahead, or way too far behind?"

"No, you're good, go on."

"Well, it all started when the Soldier was finishing a bottle of water."

1

"YOU KNOW WHAT THIS PLACE needs? It needs a bar. This place needs a place where a guy can sit in the shade, put his feet up and knock back a few cold ones. That's what this place needs."

The Soldier tipped the bottle back and trickled the last of the water into his mouth. He regarded the empty bottle briefly, then set it down on the cheap table. He mopped his brow and surveyed the village.

Lonely, dusty streets,
  a few old women — and men,
  walking, shuffling.

Withering, bright sun.
  Boys kicking around a ball.
  Water at a stall.

Shops barely open.
  Fallen, abandoned buildings.
  Steel shutters at dusk.

The vultures and crows,
  having had their fill of gore,
  flown to the next war.

The Soldier looked at Asaf, the young man behind the table. "What about you?"

Asaf raised his eyebrows. "Me? What about me?"

"Asaf, how long have you been selling water here? Heck, I've been making rounds in these parts for longer than I care tell. But time and again, here you are. Steady as she goes — or he goes. Selling water.

I've thought about it. I think you can help build a bar for me and my buddies."

"Build a bar?"

"Asaf, it's hot out here. We just want to drink a few beers. Beer shouldn't be a problem. Like a club where the guys can hang out. A place of our own off base. No one looking over our shoulders. Off the beaten path."

The Soldier glanced around, then kicked a rock with his boot. "Sheesh! As if there was more an 'off the beaten path' place than just here. But what I'm saying is — even in this podunk place — there are places that are more out of the way than others. What we'll need is somewhere where we won't attract attention ... quiet and keep a low profile."

"Podunk?"

"Yeah. Podunk. You know, bee-eff-ee. Like a backwater. But it's not about the backwater here because it's so dry. So forget the backwater. Tell you what. Let's forget about the podunk too. Rural village. Let's just say, this rural village needs a bar — a bar on the edge of town."

Asaf was trying to understand. "A bar ... on the edge of town, right? I mean ... what kind of place do you need?"

"Oh, I don't know ... There are so many bombed-out and abandoned sectors out here, we could just move in and create our own little hangout."

"Why me? You are part of the great army. You have all the money and weapons. You could just go and take over a building. I don't think you need me to do that for you."

The Soldier waved his hand. "No, no. Not like that. Look Asaf, we're all far away from home. We get tired of the same old routine. The same old base. We want a place of our own. Not fancy. Not flashy. And especially — not official. So, it has nothing to do with my role or the squad's role as military. That's why we need you. This is your village — your people. You know what's going on and how to get things done. I see you here like I said. Everybody likes your water. You keep selling it. Where do you get it?"

"My family has visited a certain spring for as long as I can remember. It was my Uncle's idea to sell water down here."

"Well, it's mighty good. But maybe it's time to step it up a notch. You can help find us a place — and you can help run it too. Think about it. A change for you. Get on with your life. How about this? — there should be a way to make money in a bar, right?"

Asaf thought a moment, looking around the broken road. "Now that I think about it — maybe it is time for a change."

Asaf walked through the neighborhoods looking for abandoned buildings that seemed to fit what the Soldier was asking for. Towards one end was a good-sized, bombed-out building, that was originally two stories. The neighborhood was in half-decent shape with a variety of shops and humble houses. Asaf also found a small building he liked because it had a view of the mountains that his family loved for generations. He came to the other end of the village; a poor, neglected neighborhood. The last structure on the block was an abandoned building with a basement. On the backside of the building, what few old roads there were, had long since been abandoned and petered out into the dry countryside. Opposite the building were shells of ruined structures mixed with heaps of rubble. Some remaining shops and homes were scattered along the broken sidewalks. The meager infrastructure was a patchwork of improvised electrical wires and a few communal wells. Women and children carried water on foot or in a cart. Propane, charcoal, and wood were used for heat and cooking. Asaf was skeptical. He thought that being at the end of a road, at the end of the neighborhood, at the end of the village, was not a good place to build a business.

When the Soldier was shown possible sites for their bar, he said the third site would work just fine. When Asaf asked about the remoteness and the run-down condition of the area, the Soldier explained that being on the outskirts was good, and they would be able to make up for the lack of conveniences with their own resources.

Over the following weeks, soldiers and villagers came and went to the club with parcels, equipment, and supplies. Soldiers pilfered, permanently borrowed, consigned, re-consigned, and plain stole what they could find on base or mixed-in with shipments. In addition to canteen supplies and an ice-machine, they appropriated water storage tanks and a few generators. From around the village, sofas and upholstered chairs were brought in by thirsty soldiers willing to schlep the heavy furniture to relax in comfort. Cheap plastic patio furniture was lightweight, but more often than not, broken. Attempts to rescue it with duct tape were only partially successful. Those that took pride in the club began protesting the importation of damaged plastic furniture. The one concession made to the plastic, was when a small group scored an unbroken matching table and chairs, complete with a huge beer-branded umbrella.

Soldiers and contractors from multiple countries discovered the club and it grew as a popular oasis. Asaf and his coworkers kept busy with all the booze, wine, beer, mixers, and tobacco. Neighborhood women supplied tasty snacks from their kitchens. Many of these homes had lost their fathers and sons in the wars, so the opportunity to earn money was well received.

Asaf brought it to the Soldier's attention that due to all the bottles, jugs and cases the armies brought in, they were running out of space. It was also noticed that some in the neighborhood were gossiping about the club. They didn't like having an establishment that served alcohol. They didn't like it in their village. And they really didn't like the influx of more and more male and female foreign mercenaries.

Asaf's family expressed concerns over the notion of joining a business venture with foreign soldiers. It grew alarming when it was finally understood, over Asaf's hemming and hawing, that there was going to be alcohol served. Some family members were warily sympathetic, some were opposed on principle, with no yielding at all. For Asaf, this was sad because he loved his family. Yet, he also knew that this was a rare opportunity. In his youthful exuberance, he felt he would show everyone that he could make a success of this enterprise. Times were changing, it was a new world out there. He saw his family stuck in an outdated point of view.

Asaf's Uncle watched all of this. He was mostly reserved and chose to keep to himself on the developments of the club and Asaf. When the family members discussed their concerns, he tried to give a balanced answer. He knew the whole situation was tricky. It could lead to a good future for Asaf, but it could also become something not so welcome. When he did talk with Asaf, he would caution him in areas that were a potential danger and try to compliment him on things of benefit. As Asaf deepened his association and trust with the soldiers, he grew in self-confidence — but spent less time with his Uncle and extended family.

2

When the story spread that an actual bar had opened up in the village, it was so unbelievable that the religious conservatives were at a loss as to what to make of it.

"What do you mean a bar?" a leader of the Zealots asked the visitor from the village.

"It is a place where they are serving alcohol. All kinds of alcohol. Beer. Distilled spirits. They congregate and drink. Wantonly. And women. And singing. And radio music."

"Strange. Unheard of. Most strange and most unheard of. Just who are 'they'?"

"It is the mercenaries. Mostly. Mercenaries. And women ..."

The Zealot interrupted him. "You just said, women. What mercenaries? Who?"

"Soldiers. And other soldiers. Not just our pesky soldiers who troop around there. But ones from who knows where. And more. And beer. And singing. And all hours of the day or night. And all days of the week."

"You also already said singing. Where? Where are these singing women?"

The villager hesitated. "Well ... I am not sure the women were actually singing or not. I mean they might have been singing. But I have not got close enough to say. In fact, I have never heard the singing. But it is all the tattle in the neighborhood."

"Which neighborhood?"

The villager explained that it was at the far end of his village; beyond which was only open country.

"Most unheard of," he said again. "I will see it for myself. Conduct me thither."

After witnessing the bar first hand, the local Zealot reported back to his superior regional leader. Together they decided that since no-one knew what to do, that they, the Zealots, would show everyone the way, by protesting the existence of the bar. This pro-activity by the Zealots piqued the sensitivities of the Radicals, who thought of themselves as the vanguard of social causes. Making a public protest against a single silly bar created by and for the military was not part of their calling. However, some Radicals argued that it was prudent to show solidarity with their rather over-the-top Zealot brothers if they must. So, the regional leaders of the Radicals condescended to join the Zealots by sending some volunteers.

As loathe as the Radicals were about throwing in their lot with the Zealots, so unenthusiastic were the Zealots to have their crazy cousins, the Fanatics, come to town. Once the Fanatics got wind of the bar, they decided, on their own, that if trouble was brewing, it was either their fate or destiny to be present.

One morning, when Asaf was opening the club, he saw that some of the old plastic furniture discarded by the club had been appropriated by the religious to make a place to sit down and take a break. The work of creating their little camp was probably the only collaboration the sects ever shared in the village. The Radicals presumed to take the best seats both for the view, the comfort of the chair, and how much shade was available. The Zealots resented this presumption because it was their idea to crusade in the village in the first place, and they deserved dibs on the best places to sit. The Fanatics resented both sects on principle alone. But they went along with the idea because, as spartan as they showed themselves to be, their feet were just as tired.

Arguments broke out. One got so intense, that a furniture-fight ensued. Apparently, since the furniture was free, the men had no regard for whether or not it broke — and it did break — or if broken, broke even more — as they whacked and whammied each other with it.

The following day, some bruised and battered men had absented themselves to the second floor of another building a half-block further back. They cleared away enough wreckage to have their own piece-of-crap, broke-down, cheap, plastic table and mismatched chairs. Their new locale did not have as good of a line-of-sight to the club, but because they had perched themselves up a story, they were proud of their decampment. And they doubled their righteous efforts by hating the club and their former fellows in the faith, all at the same time.

All was going well for the second-floor faction, but the honeymoon was not to last. The lassitudes of looking at the club and leering at the lower camp took its toll. There erupted another fight. The men were wrestling with a water-pipe, which was torn apart and broke in half. The bottom half, filled with water and apple juice spilled all over one man, who then picked up the now-empty bowl, and smashed the perpetrator's head with it. To prevent his fingers from burning, a third combatant made a quick fold in his shirt and snatched up the hot coal that had fallen out of the hookah. He ran behind his (soon to be former) fellow and dropped the live coal down his collar.

And so it went, and that group split in two.

The village end was at a stalemate. The religious couldn't abide the presence of the club. But, because it was a military outpost (in their minds at least) they lacked the fundamental power of force to oust it from their midst. The soldiers couldn't do anything about the religious, because they had done nothing wrong. And, the soldiers knew they had no legitimate standing to act aggressively because, officially, the club didn't exist.

One day, a holy man and his entourage came to the village. They ministered from house to house and shop to shop. A young man would take a slip of paper, fold it and put some resin grains in the fold. He then extended it to the leader, who touched it lightly. The youth turned and proffered it to the homes and shops. "We offer this holy resin which grows in the mountain of God. This token shall be our spiritual seal upon this building and all its inhabitants."

They arrived at the club and repeated their simple ceremony. Those in the club took all this in with stony silence. The Soldier stepped up from between his fellows. "We do not wish to have your token or spiritual seal."

Another soldier grumbled that he had seen enough. Without consulting with anyone else in the club, he went out to the road and began to berate the men. He was forceful and awkward, having partaken liberally of the bar's offerings. He looked the group over, then zeroed-in on the smallest man. "We know you are here. We know why you are here! We don't have to screw around with you! We have our club here – and are going to use it – and enjoy it – and do it whenever we want."

In an attempt to quell the argument, the Soldier walked to the edge of the group and tried to be diplomatic. "Here. Here now. We don't want any feathers ruffled. Let's all calm down."

The leader had a man at his side. He whispered in the man's ear, who then addressed the soldiers. "Your club, as you call it, is a disgrace. It is a vile place and is not allowed here. You serve alcohol and mix openly with women."

The Soldier scanned the men to see if there were any who were sympathetic. "We know it is frowned on to have such an establishment here. But we are not from here. And we still have our lifestyle. We want to make ourselves less uncomfortable in this country."

"Your comfort is no concern of ours. You will shut this place down!"

The Soldier saw that he needed to convince the men that they could all live together — as comfortable or uncomfortable as it may be. "We are guests in this country. We have been invited — or we have invaded. It all depends on your point of view. For the very traditional part of this society, we are intruders. For the current political powers, we are invitees."

A Radical joined in. "We know the political class has brought you into our country. That is another topic — another argument. What we are talking about right here is the very existence of this place. We have knowledge that even your army does not countenance its existence."

This last fact made the Soldier nervous. He tried talking sense with the men. "We — us soldiers — we want what is best for all, but it is not always simple. Most of us just want some form of peace — and to be with our families, preferably at home, in our own country. But since we understand the realities of our vocation, we accept that we will be abroad for periods of time, some longer than others. And, being abroad doesn't necessarily mean that we can't have our families with us. Here, however, we are both abroad and apart from our families. So, we have invented this club to give us a slice of our home culture. We have done it in good faith, not stealing or plundering. We have done it peacefully. We have not spread our ways of relaxation and friendship to your village. We have always tried to keep our men and women out of your way if they get drunk or become obnoxious. We don't approve of such behavior any more than you do. We have not solicited any of your neighbors — and especially none of the women here — to frequent our club. We have employed some villagers — that is true. But these young men are here at their own will — and we pay them. And we buy food from your women. From everything I understand, these women like having this opportunity."

The spokesman began to object. The Soldier felt he had to make his case since he might not get another chance. "Now, let me say this too. We have military might. We can and will exercise that might if we have to. You may not approve. You may think we are Beelzebub. That's your opinion. We are soldiers under command. We will obey our superiors — even though we may not agree with them in every way. In so doing, we may be here even though we do not want to be. We may or may not like you — your people or your country. But this does not mean that we will act bad towards you. We will act according to the military who feeds and pays us. The military of our countries, to whom we have pledged our fidelity. For now, we are stationed here. When our deployment ends, we will be rotated out and others will take our place. We don't know how long our armies will be here. So, in the meantime, we will have our club. We will enjoy our soldier's way of life in a foreign land. In-country — but not of-country. We will do no harm — to the best of our ability. But be aware — be forewarned — we are not pussies. We will meet force with force if needed. We are not looking for trouble. We are not trying to make trouble. But if push comes to shove, we will not stand down just because there are trouble-makers among you. Leave us in peace and we will remain peaceful. Don't stir up the bees that give you honey — or they might sting you."

The spokesman and the leader whispered to each other. "Our Prophet instructs us that what you are doing is contrary to the law and to God's will ..."

"We've already heard all this," the Soldier said, cutting him off.

The speaker held up his hand. "We are not here for discussion! We are not here for questions and answers. We are here to inform you that what you are doing will stop." The Soldier was about to interrupt but saw that he was going to get cut off again, so he decided it was just easier to wait. The man continued, "You will close and leave."

Without warning, a soldier jumped out and slapped the incense and paper out of the boy's hand. Gasps came from both sides. The Prophet's eyes grew wide with rage. One of the Prophet's men jumped forward in anger, not knowing whether to try to save the disrespected slip of paper and incense or jump at the man who treated the holy offering so indecently. The air was tense with agitation, shuffling of feet, and low, menacing whispers. When it seemed like a scuffle was imminent, the Prophet put up his hand and spoke for the first time. "Stop! We come in the name of God! and in peace."

A Fanatic yelled vehemently, "This is our country and you are not one of us. Now you bring shame on our peaceful neighborhood. We spit on your club." And he spat forcefully on the ground.

The Prophet seemed to ignore him. "We come in peace. And in the name of God."

The Fanatic pushed through the circle and stormed up the lane with his fellow Fanatics. "In God's name, no peace!" He spat again on the ground, stepped on the spittle and ground it into the dust with his shoe. He took off the shoe and threw it violently at the Prophet. The Prophet ducked but said nothing. He looked at the shoe lying on the ground, then turned to lead the perplexed group of men across the street to continue their mission.

As they were leaving, the Soldier called out behind them, "You have your ways, we have ours. Seems like we are stuck with each other. Get used to it."

Then he turned and walked back to the club.

Asaf was growing weary. On one hand, he had thrown in his lot with the foreign soldiers. On the other, he came from the very society which the foreigners had invaded. He was caught between two worlds. He went to his Uncle. "Uncle, you know my situation in general. I am very involved with the club. In fact, I run the place except for the building and furniture, which the soldiers made possible. Also, I do not get involved in their lives. They are there to get away from their army routine and spend some time relaxing with each other. I am friends with the one Soldier of course, and I guess you could say a few of his comrades. But for the rest, I am just a bar server. But what most of these military people do not know, is how much work and stress goes into making the club function. They come and enjoy their time together and a few drinks and then go on."

The Uncle nodded. "Well enough. It is work. But are you not getting paid? I think you are, based on what we see in our family compound."

"Oh yes!" Asaf replied. "Yes, I get paid well; much better than I ever would or could have imagined… But is the stress and difficulty worth the good money I am getting?"

"That is a good question. A very difficult one to answer. The prophets and sages throughout history have delved deeply into this area and have come up wanting. Of course, they have framed the question in various ways, but it is still the same basic question: Where is the balance between the two worlds? The material world in which we live, where we need food, shelter, and family. And the immaterial world through which we move. The unseen world. Tell me more Asaf. What else is it that brings you to me with such thoughts on your mind?"

"There is religious opposition to the club. More than you probably already know."

The Uncle said he was not surprised.

"The men have set up a camp there. They have three camps really. There are new men coming to look at our location. They take turns in watching and protesting. Now, there was a man not from here with them. A leader. He was surrounded by a group of followers. He used an aide to speak to us. He had — like religious servants — dressed in their garb. He didn't speak to us directly. It was strange."

The Uncle said, "Perhaps he is using extra caution or some formality. Maybe it is his way — or the culture where he is from — their way of being polite, or at least not rude."

"That may be so. I don't know. If you were there, you would have seen that he seemed most comfortable having his words said by another, like he was on an elevated plain. Anyhow, all these men have made it clear that they are observing us. So far, all that has come of it, are some short speeches on each side. The soldiers and the religious are firm in their opinions ... But my trouble is deeper than that. I am from this culture, this country, these people. I know our family is not religious— in the same way as these men — who devote all their lives to making others feel bad about themselves. But they are still our people. I know my brother does business in the city with partners from across the globe. But what have I done?! Going into business in a bar ... for foreign soldiers? Foreign soldiers and mercenaries! It's everything that's not in our tradition. Sometimes I wake with a start in the middle of the night with cold sweat and a fear that I have cast myself into the devil's own fiery pit. But then the day comes. I forget the bad feeling from the night before, and again I am looking forward to work. Now, these new religious men come sneaking around. It makes me feel guilty and the memory of the cold sweat comes back to me and I feel bad again.

"So there it is Uncle. I am in two worlds. I am pleased with my small career. But feel guilty. I am not a part of the strict religion, but it is in me — somewhere in my soul. I see the look in these men's eyes when they argue with the soldiers, and I know I'm not one of them. Then I see them look at me — me, standing with the soldiers — I can read in their faces the questioning, the hurt — even maybe embarrassment, that one of their own, me, is taking the side with the foreign army. I can see some of the men scorning me with their looks. They are shaming me for being part of the circle of evil. But when I look at the hollowness in the soldier's eyes — I know that I am not one of them. Their eyes are not the eyes of you and me and my mother and brother. I can never and will never be one of them. But I cannot see how I could become one of the religious either. After a confrontation, back inside the club, the soldiers clap me on the back. 'Asaf m'boy,' they say. 'Asaf m'boy.' It makes me glad — it feels lucky — that I am a part of their business. But when I am alone — I know I am not nor ever will be, part of their world. And again I get sad." Asaf sighed, dropped his head and began to shed tears.

His Uncle smiled and gave him an understanding look. "Asaf. Asaf, it is good for us to talk. By speaking of these difficulties it is easier to deal with them. By sharing them with another you can trust, it helps spread the weight of the burden out over more shoulders. What we have talked about will not be something that will be over and done with any time soon. Your heartache will continue. Your struggle between two worlds will continue. Your discussions with me will not end. But it is in dealing with these things that make the difference. Bringing them out from the shadows of your soul into the clear light of sharing them with another — that will always help. Holding up and looking carefully at what makes you sorrowful is the beginning of making sense out of the suffering. It is common to all persons, from all walks of life, in all times, to deal with heartache. It is nothing new. All the greats from all backgrounds deal with it. Now, you too can begin your own chapter in human history as you try to make sense out of heartache by trying to put it into some type of framework or context. Find some parameters. Build some walls or borders in your mental and physical reality. Set up standards that cannot be violated. These will be the bulwark anchors to your borders. Then build a scaffolding or fencing along those uncompromisibles. As these boundaries get challenged, it will hurt. Then you can examine what is causing the pain and proceed to build it into your personal fortress or exclude it. These are word-pictures. It is a mental exercise that I have used. You can use the jungle and the plain, the world of reptiles and amphibians, darkness and light. No matter which words or analogy you like, it is a great and life-long thing, this making-sense-of-suffering. We have made a good beginning together. Consider what I've said as you go back to your life and livelihood. We will speak of this again and continue to learn."

Because of the ongoing, annoying presence of the camps, Asaf told the Soldier that his Uncle could come and offer his advice to the club on how to deal with the situation.

"The deeply religious conservatives pose a particular threat. They hold themselves as special, or apart from society at large. They impose their views on others without good cause or reason — only for the belief that their understanding is correct — and others are not. It is a shallow philosophy and cannot withstand scrutiny. Because of this, they will not sit down and have honest, thorough discussions. They use intimidation and bigotry and threats and hate as their weapons; all the most inferior of human character traits. Because of this, it is difficult to reason with them. Reason and reasonableness are not effective. Force and power and coercion are effective at a surface level — but do not touch the inner man. You see these men all over this part of the world. You will also observe that they rule the deserted and wasted parts of the earth. Sand and dust and scrub and rocks. This is their inheritance. Their inability or unwillingness to cooperate and compromise has made them the flotsam and jetsam of good society. So they take what they can — backwaters and barren mountains and the steepest canyons. So too, do they prey on the lonely and lost of the human landscape: the dispirited and the abandoned. They twist those minds and spirits into the furtherance of their shallow bigotry and theological venom. As soldiers, you know only too well, they would rather die, than be proven wrong. My advice depends on what you want to do with your time here, and what you seek. If you feel you want this club, as a fellowship hall, then so be it. But you are learning that there is a cost. That cost is the price of intrusion into this culture. If you wish to stay and maintain this fellowship hall, then you must also be prepared to pay the tuition that the struggles of this society demand of you, to camp on their campus. You can use kindness and diplomacy with most of the villagers, but you will not be effective in that regard with these religious conservatives. You can only be prepared with a strong defense — or resistance — or, having your bar where they are not. And that would be in a nice villa by the sea, or in a modern city. But you are not there. You are here, at the edge of society, where they also are."

3

One morning, Asaf was walking to the club. Two technicals went speeding by. Asaf ran into the road. He listened to them racing away, then heard explosions. He ran, rounded the next corner, and saw a plume of smoke. He ran one more block, then the shabby lane. At the end, the club was on fire. Plastic glasses, plates, trays, tables, chairs, vinyl and upholstered furniture created a black and acrid and sooty and foul smoke, which billowed and poured from every side of the building. Asaf could hear the sounds of bottles exploding and ammunition popping from a cabinet under the bar. He ran toward the building. It did not occur to him that there might be ordinance spraying helter-skelter inside the building and around the neighborhood. Before he could reach the club, the intensity of the heat stopped him. Pushed by the heat and smoke, he retreated. He found it so hard to take in, that he just stared. His blood sweat and tears, his joy and happiness, his burden and responsibility, the source of his money, the cause for his soul searching — basically his whole world was going up in smoke before his very eyes.

Clumps of people gathered. It might have been Asaf's sense of guilt or shame, but it seemed to him that he was the target of the crowd's scorn and ridicule and whisperings and finger-wagging. He knew many eyes were on him, so he avoided looking directly at the people. Waves of emotion came over him and crashed into his mind and heart. His body began to feel the pressure and upheaval inside. His palms grew sweaty, his stomach began to churn, his knees became shaky and tears began streaming down his cheeks. Hot, bitter tears. No tears of joy or love or sorrow or penance. Only involuntary tears, uncalled for, boiling up and out of his eyes, so that their hot sting made him realize that they were running down his face; now mixing with the soot that began to accumulate there.

It took a long time for the excitement of the village to die down. In the meantime, soldiers arrived. Suddenly, the sound of a speeding technical was heard barreling down the lane. As it neared the club the big machine gun in the bed of the truck began belching out rounds. Chaos ensued. Smoke and noise and exploding rounds and shouts and yelling and commands being given. Then, as quickly as it began, it came to an end. The truck sped off, lurched up the lane, fading away in the dust and distance.

Two of Asaf's co-workers, brothers, came over to him right after the dust settled. They consulted together. Asaf was being attentive, nodding his head. While listening, he glanced several times at the Soldier. When they were done conversing, the Soldier walked over to Asaf. The two stepped away from the others. "My friends know who these men were. They are part of the group that was dismissed by the holy man. They recognize them, even with their faces covered. They say that they are very devout in their own crazy way. They are part of the Fanatics, even more self-righteousness than the Zealots."

The Soldier's face was stony and grim as he listened. "Well, well, well. Surprise, surprise, surprise," the Soldier said sarcastically. "Ain't that a beauty. I think we could have figured that out piece by piece. But it's nice to have it all signed sealed and delivered — straight up from your local friends."

The Soldier paused and a scowl came over his brow. His mind was full of questions he couldn't answer and his heart was full of anger and disappointment. He took a long, hard, narrow-eyed look at Asaf. He looked over at the two brothers. Finally, he looked back at the smoldering club. Not knowing just what to do, he dropped his eyes to the ground and walked away.

The destruction of the club filled Asad with shock, grief, anger, and despondency. His world collapsed with the collapse of the club. His fortune went down in flames and his future went up in smoke with the burning of the bar. Then came the unexpected twist of the knife from the Soldier's reaction to Asaf's report. Information that Asaf thought the Soldier would appreciate, not turn into an accusation. He wandered dispiritedly down the dusty lane after the curious crowds had dissipated; after the military and mercenary men had walked away, and after the boys and beggars grew bored and gave up scavenging what little there was that might interest them.

The destruction of the club made the Soldier's whole world cloudy. Clouds of smoke trailed behind him. Fresh in his memory, they seemed to extend evil, raven-like talons. They penetrated his being with feelings of failure. The claws that scraped the inside of his brain did not give him a headache, did not give him heart-break, they made his soul sick and sad. Clouds of war he was trying to escape, by taking refuge in the club, had now become sulfurous plumes from the netherworld; ridden by religious fanatics coming for his head with outstretched scimitars. Clouds of foreboding swirled above and ahead. He didn't know in what order the disciplinary system meted out its punishments. He didn't know what disciplinary action was available; in use or not, current or from some other age. But his mind was a jumbled jungle of words, images, film clips, headlines and felon stereotypes: A schoolmarm rapping young boys' knuckles morphed into a horse-haired judge hammering his gavel. 'DISHONORABLE DISCHARGE' was stamped in red ink all across his ID card. He saw, then became, Cool Hand Luke endlessly digging holes. Sickly hands, sticking out of a threadbare blue and ugly-white striped shirt, grasped cold, round jail-bars. He watched the black and white blur of a spinning tabloid coming to a stop, and the headline read: 'BOGUS BAR BURNS — SOLDIER'S STRIPES STRIPPED'. He plodded along thinking things were as bad as they could get. Then, he needed a beer — or any drink if it came to that. The thought of a nice, cold beer cheered him up — for a fleeting moment. But the bad got worse: no club, no beer. The only place he could get a beer was back at the base — exactly where he least wanted to be right now.

The destruction of the club was considered by the Fanatics as an act of righteousness in accord with God's wrath. They congratulated each other on the planning and carrying out of the firebombing and attack. It was a two-fisted punch. First, take down the sinner's lair. Then finish them off by sending their bodies and souls to the burning pit. They were certain God was with them. They, a small local group, dedicated to the holy calling of war on the infidels, had now launched a significant attack on a den of iniquity in their very midst. How could anyone question their holiness and divine protection? God had shown them the path of light. This light shone on the darkness of the evil in their village, and through them, God's will was done. They were now confident that their deed would be noticed by bigger and more important sectarians throughout the realm. To celebrate God's will and their victory of light over darkness, they lit up the night of the day of victory over the darkness of night. First, the holy moonshine lit the fire of purification. Then the fire lit up the precious charcoal which represented the consuming of the hardened evil of sin that makes men's hearts cold and black like coal. The consuming charcoal transferred its purifying heat to the divine bounty of nature's provision of smokable leaves and essences. These essences entered their bodies and minds and souls and spirits to enlighten and liberate them from worldly matter and matters. And then, the blessed white lightning was taken liberally, to demonstrate the freedom from man's moral rules and restrictions. The effects of the powerful alcohol were clear in the way it sets one free of inhibition and shame. Inhibition and shame are mere constructs. Constructs that the jealous and envious put on those who claim to know God on their own. But constructs cannot be put on the ones called into the most intimate and pure communion with the Divine. And so, the Fanatics went wild — in every imaginable way — uninhibited and shameless — until they collapsed in tangles of arms and legs while the sun was rising . This was a trash-heap of men and bottles and hookahs and clothes and censers and dead animals and guns and urine and vomit and pages of holy writ.

The destruction of the club weighed heavily on the troops who wantonly pilfered from the base. Now the cultural scandal could start a new round of religious war they didn't need. Officers had chosen to ignore the club because it was not important enough to deal with. Now they began to talk among themselves what course of action they could or should follow in dealing with the controversy. To compound matters, military intelligence was rumored to be ginning-up an investigation. These rumors ran the gamut from hearsay and gossip, to criminal investigation and inquest.

4

THE GENERAL HAD THE SOLDIER called into his office.

"What do you think of this club episode?"

The Soldier cleared his throat. "Well, sir, it is unfortunate, to say the least ... It is not something we expected. Umm ... There are a lot of areas to cover with regards to your question. Could you be more specific?"

"Sure," the General replied. "Since this is off the corn-cob, and I'm not a kernel, for the record, I won't be cussing you like as I shood. You're a flucky I'm not tearing you the shopping cart of a sphincter. And you nose-kink sure we have not the toe-tag clouding up the whole snafuzzle. I've been a spring beaver and the dam is gotten muddy dried-up at last. Let me jus' say it is fortunata a la posterior-itis that you were not called in here-two-four now."

The Soldier remained passive and stony. After the club was burnt up, he figured something like this would happen. The General could have locked him up. As he listened in silence, he breathed an internal sigh of relief that things might not be as bad as he imagined. He felt he might dodge a bullet. However, there was one more fact that the General seemed not to know of. "Sir? It may be — maybe, you are not aware — that there was one casualty in the attack."

The General cocked a worrisome eyebrow. "Who was it?"

The Solder replied somberly, "He died in the fight, at the club. His name was Robert Palmer."

The General did not show any emotion. He changed his focus from the Soldier to his desk. He opened a desk drawer, fished out a cigar and went through the ritual of cutting and lighting it. "Despite what I have pronuncified beauregarding the pardon of your posterity, there are — and will be — axe-shins partaken about this club of yours — and it's futurization where withal."

The Soldier continued his silence. He wasn't sure where all this was going, so he remained on guard.

A cloud issued from the General's lips, and then he pressed on. "Here's what is going to happen. Instead of shuttering the palace, or pre-tenderize to ignore it, we have decided that we will make lemonades out of lemmings. And — as with any great bureaucractizations," he went on sarcastically, rolling his eyes, "we will institushmalize your club, as you call it. It will be rebuilt. It will be modified during reconstructivizing accordion to the best plaid lanes of spice and sin."

He paused at this point waiting for the Soldier's reaction.

The Soldier raised his eyebrows and pursed his lips, not quite knowing if he should say something, or wait for his superior to continue. He had a clutter of questions in his mind. Seeing that the General was done speaking for the moment, he asked, "Sir, would it be rude or stupid of me to inquire just what this planned course of action is? Frankly, I don't follow. How do we jump from pretending to ignore the club's existence — or chalking it up as a stress-relief outlet — to making an institution out of it? How does that happen?"

The Soldier was trying hard not to be impertinent, especially under the circumstances where his ass had just been spared, but he was not able to sound a bit incredulous.

The General relaxed. He had delivered the strange news as he had been instructed to do. "No need to be apologectic," he said waving the cigar, "I understand your consterns. And relieve you me, I snare them. If it was up to me an mine, I would have jus' told you and your gumptions, that this experimeterish — as unassumptive as it was — or was foundered upon with only the good extinuation of comradeliness — would simply cease to exist. Jus' call it a daze and forget the whole thing. Move on, older, finger-burnt, bud wiser."

The General stopped to look at how his ashes were progressing. "However, I am not the only gee-eye around here with author-a-tie. Sure, I hold the titular of Base Commando, and I shorely carry out my oblige-you-kindly as such, but, as the quote goeth: 'No man lives in Iceland.' There are — as you are mindly of — variated and sundry compartments and divisions — whose existence enfeebled you to risk-off all that stuff you fin-galed for your little party house."

He finished this cutting remark with a long draw on the cigar followed by a mighty exhale of frustration and disappointment. He looked at his desk. "In order to fullfill my duty, I will obtain on this to the reading of herein orderlies."

He opened a folder and shuffled with the papers. He focused for a time on a sheet in front of him. He glanced up at the Soldier, then began to read slowly, carefully and methodically.

"Dated this day … Lez start without the prelimbenary hogwash … Here we go … In the reconstruction proceedings, built by our engineers, a secure office space will be built. It will have space for a desk and chairs. It will also have lockers for tactical and survival gear. The service bar will be fortified to house strong boxes. Surveillance equipment will be installed in the building. There will be a parapet on the roof's perimeter with an antenna array. This array will be installed to blend in with the surrounding neighborhood and not attract attention. This will commence in two days, two weeks, two months, or two years as circumstances dictate."

He replaced the sheet in the folder. He interlaced his fingers and let his hands rest on top of the folder. He looked up across the desk at the Soldier. The Soldier stared back. He opened his mouth to speak, then shut it. He reached up and pinched the bridge of his nose. As he sat there with his eyes closed, pinching the bridge of his nose, he briefly wondered why he did this. Then realized he did it because somehow that's what people did when they were getting a headache or something. So he stopped doing that and put his hand to his forehead and propped his elbow on his other arm. Then realizing that he was being quite casual in the General's office, he dropped his arms to his side and simply accepted the discomfort of the whole situation. The official military involvement was too aggravating to get comfortable with. He shifted in his chair. Finally, he lifted his head and looked wearily at the commanding officer.

The General gave him a knowing look, expressing an understanding of the Soldier's misery, but helpless to do anything about it. The Soldier never considered, and certainly never envisioned, that his club would become a den of spies. It turned the club's entire raison d'être on its head. The General was put-out because the existence of the club was at first a petty concern about missing equipment and supplies. Then it grew into a small crisis with the bombing and shooting. And finally an inter-departmental, logistical can of worms that he totally did not want or need.

The General's cigar had gone out. He glanced at it and didn't even give half a thought of re-lighting it. He sighed and continued reading with sarcastic torpidity. "You are now assigned, to be the, quote,

'Public Point Person', or PPP as it will be called in the officially unofficial documents that will and will not exist. There will be a small staff, on rotation, from the following as needed: the defense liaison office, the engineering corps, ordinance and munitions officers and their subalterns, surveillance personnel and cultural envoys. All consumables will be sourced through official supply depots. The surveillance team assigned to this mission, will vet all nationals working, having access to, or supplying goods to the bar which are not sourced from the depot. There will be regular inspections, irregular visits, as deemed appropriate, and possible street-level surveillance. As the PPP, you will be responsible for filing a summary report on a bi-weekly, semi-weekly, bi-monthly, semi-monthly or annual basis to begin, then subsequently, to be determined."

The General stopped speaking. He looked like he had the flu: lack of color, weak and weary. He stood. The Soldier stood.

"Questions?"

The Soldier was sad. He looked at the floor, at his boots, not knowing where to start. "Yes. I have questions — many questions." He swallowed with difficulty because his mouth and throat were dry. "But I know from this briefing that it is not a good use of our time to go there."

The General motioned to the door and they went outside.

"Let us perambulate, Son. I know this is har. It's hard for me too."

The Soldier began to interrupt, but the General waved him off. "It's har for me two. Fair enough that you are outraged and confusidated. There has been a significant attachment of impotancy to the club among the spook class. I'm not into all the coat and swagger stuff in the military. It's not my interest. However, I think I have a notion on this, because of my tenure of service and acknowledge of how thinks aspire in our greater military and governmental vulture. The details we can only guess at."

The Soldier began to calm down and listen politely. The General was just as unhappy about the stupidity of it all as he was, and maybe now he would begin to learn why all this fuss was going on.

The General continued, "It seems that we, or you, have stumbled upon, or into, the perfect storm with your bar idea. Without knowing it, you pickled a neighborhood that has been of some interest in the intellimince community. Also, you have unwittingly done this at an opportunity time for said community of spies. Somehow, they came to beleave that there is sectarian ferment — the kine they don' bite. The dangerous kine. For me this was not concerning, in light of the fax that these reports are more or less ongoing. Which, brings me to the last elephant of this maelstrom: your cosiness with that local youth of yours … Anyhow, the game's afoot, as they would say up in old two two one B," he grumbled.

The Soldier involuntarily blinked twice at this odd statement, but, when it became clear that the General had let sufficient gas out of his balloon to let the other party in the conversation have a shot at blabbing, the Soldier reported that he still had not seen 'that local youth' since the incident, but had not looked for him either. He gave the General a simple recounting of their last time together and the uncomfortable parting of ways.

"Ok. But we'd like you to see if you can get in contact with him."

"I'm not sure he is interested in getting involved again considering the series of events — and especially my dumping on him."

"No need to beat around the bush with all these explanatories. Will he or will he not? can you or can you not? put us all back together?"

The Soldier resented the General referring to the whole club enterprise as 'us all'. It further augmented his growing desire to open that other, further-away bar. "Sir, I will try. But in truth, I cannot say how it will go or how things may turn out. We had a good relationship. But this religious sectarianism cuts deep in this culture. I don't believe for a minute he has any interest in the Zealots. But that does not mean he can't be compromised, or put under pressure, or however you want to phrase it … to come under their sway or begin to share their point of view, or look the other way and so on. And … and, if you really want to make a worst-case scenario, he could become an unwilling mole. Is there such a thing as an unwilling mole? I don't know. Lemme see. There's the secret agent. The double agent. Double oh seven, if he counts for anything. Then the mole. And the seed mole, or something like that. The sleeping mole. Deep cover. Whether or not the mole is a double agent or not, I'm not sure. And then there's the whole turned-thing. 'Can we turn him? Can he be turned?' Knowing him as I do, I don't see that happening. But in this culture, who knows? He could turn into a mole I guess. Or a sleeping mole. Maybe he's a deep-cover seeded-mole who has turned on us and we don't even know it. I can't name a case, but there are probably weirder things that have happened. Like the Jesus potato chip. I knew a guy who said when they trimmed back all the vines on his local bank there was a Virgin Mary behind it …"

"Which goes to the horn of the matter in having him back," the General butted in. "One way or another, we are going to have locals in this new club. We might as well have your old crew. Plus, maybe he was totally on the Seven-Up and up with his story. Maybe it's jus' like he told it. His friends know who these freneticals are. Period."

The Soldier replied, "I agree with the last part of what you said. Even though I don't like how things ended up with us there at the end. Looking back, I wish it hadn't gone that way. I like the guy — have always liked him. We spent lots of time together. I trusted him. It's just at that last minute, this whole blow-up really got under my skin. When he told me this little nugget of intel, it pissed me off. Deep down, I don't think our relationship is too damaged. He probably wonders why I walked away like that, and doesn't get it at all."

The General listened patiently, even though he felt the Soldier was pretty convoluted in his manner of speaking. "So, that's why it's all Boeing down … I guess," the General mumbled with exasperation. "Once the spookmobile got into gear, there was no stomping the juggernaut. All the depertments, with nothing bitter to do — and money to spin — all jumped abord. Now we have this mess."

The General stopped. He looked at the Soldier. "I'm sorry."

5

Asaf's Uncle borrowed a mule. He made sure the animal was in good condition, well-watered, fed, rested and ready for a journey. He went to a family of recyclers and loaded the mule with empty bottles and jugs. Early, before sunrise, he went and woke Asaf. "Come Asaf. Come and we will go for a walk."

Blinking at the dusky visage of his Uncle, Asaf yawned. "What is going on? Why are you here, and why so early?"

"All will be answered in due time. For now, get ready. We will be going for a long walk. Think about bringing some extra clothes in case the weather changes."

Asaf was confused but did as his Uncle requested. They went outside. "What's this? I haven't seen this stupid mule in … I don't know how long. I see how it's loaded. It makes me wonder. I could guess. But then again, knowing you it could be anything."

"Well, that's up to us to decide. I have a plan, but my plan is a thought, an idea."

"Can you tell me about this plan? You're making me a bit nervous," Asaf ventured.

"Sure, sure. I'm sorry. It seems I'm the one upset by all this …" The Uncle trailed off this last sentence and became quiet. He stopped and hung his head down. "I'm sorry. I don't even know how to call what happened. I mean, I know what happened. Or I think I do … Now 'the event' as I've heard it whispered. Now … now …" Once more the Uncle faltered and became silent.

Asaf came near to him and put his hand on his shoulder. He could feel the light quaking of his shortened breath and knew he was quietly weeping. "My Uncle. My good and favorite Uncle."

The Uncle wiped his cheeks and continued. "I have always felt good about helping you. Teaching you. You are a good soul. A fine soul. A rare find. As you know, I have a lot of experience in life. I don't easily cast my pearls before swine. So, when you came to me for advice, or just to talk, I was glad to be your friend. Then, when our friendship took a turn towards the water business — and the business of life, I was very happy that I could help you in a meaningful way. The entire world of master and disciple, teacher and student, mentor and apprentice is one of the greatest, yet rarest of worlds, when there is truly a significant relationship between the two."

They had been loading the mule, and double-checking its tack while they talked. "I was bursting with joy that I could and would be of help to you in this hard life. It made me feel good that I could impart to you some things I have learned. Maybe giving out pointers on how to avoid pitfalls. Advice from my school of hard knocks."

The Uncle's voice had been growing more confident, but he stopped again and became silent. "And now this," He said simply, waving his hand vaguely around. "All this. I knew you would be kind enough to go along with me without explanation. I would like to go to the mountain spring. I decided to take the advice I would have given myself, and that is to get out for a long walk. I am sorrowful for the loss of the club — for your sake. Can you tell me about what happened — from your point of view?"

They continued steadily along the old narrow road beginning to wind up into the hills. It was a pastoral scene. There were scattered, sparse flocks of sheep and goats with a lonely herdsman perched every so often on a knoll overlooking his scrubby grazing grounds. The sun was now up and the heat began, but they knew that the further they hiked, the cooler it would get as they gained elevation.

Asaf finished recounting the scene of the club fire. " … And that was the last I saw of my friend and business partner … Searching my face, with a scowl on his, to see what was there and if I was partially responsible for what happened. It left me speechless. Let's say dumbfounded. I couldn't believe it. But it happened so quickly. One moment I was doing what I thought was a great service for the club by pointing out a real source of information. The next moment I was looking into a face I knew so well … that I thought I knew so well … but never with a look like that."

Asaf's Uncle said, "You must understand that this reaction on the Soldier's part was not aimed at you personally. It was aimed at whatever messenger brought him such news. Remember, historically, it has been a sticky career to be a messenger. One's reward could be great and worth being a good envoy. But the risk was death."

Asaf's eyes widened at this. He knew vaguely of such things but never thought anything of it.

"So, you were in the right place at the right time. But with the wrong message. I am not justifying the Soldier's reaction to what you said. In fact, it aggravates me. But I must rise above my aggravation. Now, you must try to put your friend's look and words in context. He was hurting just as much, if not more than you were. For you it was bad. Unfortunate. Disappointing. Your countrymen acting foolish and evil. But for him, this is war. He is already a soldier in a foreign land and you are part of this country, this culture. For such a thing as attacking this club, which is not a military target, would get him as angry as batting a wasp's nest with a big stick. I am fairly sure he now regrets the way your last moments together ended up. But I am also sure, he has deep training in being above trust and friendship. When it comes to what matters most to a soldier, it means fighting the enemy."

The following day, the two set about getting a new water stand open. Asaf was not enthusiastic about his Uncle's idea. "I appreciate your concern and coming to get me for some fresh air. But I have already been a street vendor. I'm older now and have a lot of business experience. What will everyone think? It's embarrassing. What will our family think? The village? Everyone will see me down here and make fun of me. I can't go back to my old spot because another kid has moved into that space. The shop owner doesn't want us back because of the scourge or stain he thinks it brings. So, answer me this: is it too much for me to ask these simple questions? Am I too conceited? Aren't I allowed to have feelings of pride? Is this one of life's lessons, go backward when things don't go well?"

Finally, the Uncle held up his hand and replied, "There are two things Asaf. First, it was, and is, my plan to get us both out into the fresh air. To take a break from the pressure and tension of the neighborhood. Second, I completely agree with you. This is a step backward. You have grown much since the bar. And, you are in the right to ask all these questions. I don't know for sure if this is a good idea or not. I have the same fears and incapacitating negative emotions as any other man. I am not free from the lot of our existence. What I have done, and presume I will continue to do is to put these emotions in a framework so that the dog isn't wagging the tail, or the tail the dog, or however that phrase goes. I may seem calm and cool and collected. But inside there is still uncertainty. I work on such things, but they don't disappear. Recently, in the wake of this upsetting event, I was really shaken. Troubled. This grip — this emotional grip — caught me off guard. It took me by surprise. And when I had a chance to step back and look at it, I knew, that if nothing else, action was what was called for. Never wallow in your own negative emotion. That's a trap. In fact, it's the strangest of things, that for all its negativity, it is somehow inviting us into its craven maw. Welcoming us with a seemingly warm embrace, but they are putrefying arms that wrap us in their strong malevolent hold. It's the same thing that fascinates us when we see mayhem, gore, and horror. Its emotional kin is fright. But this self-pity is much worse than fright. Fright weakens our faculties. Fright makes us jump and open our eyes. Self-pity draws you down into a clammy, dark, lonely cave of hollow righteousness and it sneers at the dim light trickling down, beckoning you to climb back to the healing balm of well ordered right and wrong. Where life is in balance. Good is good. Bad is bad. And you have to stand erect and look right and wrong in the eyes and admit that right and wrong are above you. That they are better than you. That they exist apart from you — have and always will. So that in their light, your negative emotions become trivial and not to be indulged. That is not to say they are not real. Nor should they be denied. But that they should be put into proper context. Which context is, that they are — but they are never foremost. So I shook myself and said, 'Action. I must take action!' And so I did. I made a quick and simple decision to come get you, trek up to the spring, get water and come back and sell it."

"Just like that?" Asaf asked with a perplexed look.

"Just like that," the Uncle answered, with a snap of his fingers.

"So all of your insight and taking apart of the different kinds of good and bad feelings has led you to us opening a water stand?"

"Uh, well I guess so," the Uncle replied with a smile.

After a long pause, and looking up and down the dusty street, Asaf sighed deeply. "Ok, I've listened to you and I appreciate it. I think I have to digest some of it — but never mind. You still haven't really answered my earlier and still important questions."

"Go ahead. Like … ?"

Asaf sighed again. Deep down, he harbored the vague understanding that all of his questions and protestations were naught. That no matter what he said, or how he argued, that his Uncle would have clever, well-reasoned answers. "Like, being embarrassed, made fun of. They will say I'm a failure. They will heap scorn on me for having joined the league of Satan. He's too big for his shoes, and all that."

His Uncle replied with a caring voice, "That is probably what will happen. I think you are right."

"Well there you go then," Asaf said excitedly. "I'm right. People will make fun of me. They'll tease me."

"Ok."

"Ok, what?" Asaf asked wrinkling his brow.

"Ok, they will make fun of you and call you things and point out how you went from a big-shot to nothing and it's all your fault for thinking you were too good to be a plain water boy and your family should be ashamed and you should have known better and have you learned your lesson. Ok?"

Asaf wasn't sure what to say. "So then what?"

"So then you give them an honest answer."

Asaf was puzzled. "An honest answer, right?"

"An honest answer. But with some seasoning of reason. Some salt of truth, some herbs of self-healing and the nourishing potion of life in all its strange paths."

Asaf looked at him askance. "And when all this happens; and I'm supposed, to tell the truth …"

"Wait," his Uncle interrupted. "Didn't say the truth, I said, an honest answer."

"Ok, I'm supposed to give an honest answer, like what?"

"Like, this. Go ahead and pretend you are one of the villagers. Anyone you like. Now go ahead and ask a question, or make some statement, that they might ask or say."

"Ok. That's not hard. I've already thought of a million of them. How about this: 'Ha! Look at you. Back to where you started. Learn your lesson water boy?'"

"Perfect. Here's what you do. You keep a straight face. You keep calm. Don't display any anger or resentment or the like. You face them and answer according to the words you just gave me, but suited and adjusted to the actual words your inquirer uses, you say: 'Yes, I have been brought back to where I started. Or almost. See, I was over there where that kid is selling imitation French leather goods. Now I'm down here at this end of the block. And yes I learned many lessons.' There, that wasn't too hard, was it?" his Uncle asked.

"You make it sound easy," Asaf protested. "Here's another one.

Maybe a harder one. 'You! You are a spawn of satan. You have brought terrorism to our neighborhood.'"

His Uncle replied calmly, looking at Asaf just as he would have an actual accuser: "No, I am not the spawn of satan. I have a large family here in the area, some of whom you might know. I might share some guilt in bringing terrorism to the neighborhood. If I do, I am sorry for that and regret it. It was never my intention to bring any terror here." The Uncle continued: "See? Just stay calm and give an honest answer. You can take your time to answer. It can be short. In fact, don't make them too long. Short and sweet. You'll notice that I took these accusations piecemeal. Do that. Listen to what they say, digest it, then respond. Do it evenly. Don't let yourself be dragged around by your emotions. I acknowledged the question, then replied directly to just that question. I didn't elaborate. Now notice. In both of these scenarios, I was willing to be humble. I was accepting the fact that these questions and accusations would come. And instead of deflecting them, or defending myself, I take them for what they are and give an honest answer. This will calm most situations down. After all, once you have humbled yourself and accepted your share of whatever guilt these people think you deserve, what else can they do?"

"I still think you make it look easy," Asaf replied, a bit defensively. "This is hard. It hurts. I'm embarrassed." Asaf stopped. His throat was dry.

"It's ok. It's ok. Yes, it is hard and hurts. But it is the only way. And it will be better, once you have accepted this hurt as your own. The difficult part is accepting hurt for which you are not responsible. Taking blame that isn't yours. That's tough. But sometimes it can't be avoided."

Asaf breathed deeply. "It isn't the only way. There are many ways. I think this water stand is a ridiculous idea."

The Uncle stayed calm. "Yes, there are many ways to re-start your path. But there are no other ways to resolve and answer all of the questions and accusations these people will have — than to face them and give an honest answer — bearing the pain and hurt it can bring. The other ways are many. The easiest is to go somewhere else. But your past will follow you. Even if you have done no wrong, it will follow you. And you will have little control in what form that past will come. If you stop everything now, the past can be settled and will not haunt you."

Asaf was trying to listen and make sense out of all this. "I don't know how going back to sitting on the side of the road selling water does any good."

"I am not insisting on that. I am only taking a course of action. And I chose something simple and something we are able to do. I don't have any big plans. I don't know how long we'll be here. I'm just taking forward steps. In my plain manner, I just thought we would be better off doing this, than sitting around feeling bad. We already feel bad enough. Now we have a little business to look after." He looked with caring eyes at Asaf and finished, "Even if it's only for a day."

Asaf drooped his head. It was a bitter pill, but hearing his Uncle say maybe only for a day made him feel better about the whole crazy plan. Plus, his Uncle was right. It was better than sitting on one's bed staring at the ceiling wondering what the world has come to and what will come next. Might as well sell some water in the fresh air, make a little money AND wonder what the world's coming to and what's coming next.

6

"FOOLS! THE DAMN FOOLS!" SHOUTED the Prophet slapping his palm on the table. "What in the name of all that is righteous do they think they are doing?"

"Eminence ... " the Messenger began hesitantly.

"Shut up!" the Prophet yelled with an impatient wave of his hand. He went on in a low voice talking to himself. "Now wait a minute. Get ahold of yourself. This can be dealt with. Calm down. After all — you are God's chosen. We will take this one step at a time ... Lord above, forgive your servant... yet ... " He paused. Putting on a sinister smile and raising a clenched fist in the air, he boldly finished, "Yes forgive me — and thank you for giving me righteous anger!"

"Messenger!" he called out.

The Messenger, who was still standing nearby, inwardly rolled his eyes and answered politely. "Yes Eminence."

"Have the Council summoned. Let me know when they will be arriving. You can go now."

"Yes Eminence", the messenger answered unenthusiastically.

"And Messenger!" the Prophet shouted. He continued in a firm voice, "Tell no one of this. It remains a delicate matter."

He dismissed him with a flick of his fingers.

The Prophet, his Minister of Justice, a Councilman and a Plebe sat around the conference table. The Prophet's Captain sat on a stool just outside the door wearing a black T-shirt and comfortable black baggies. The Messenger entered with tea for four. He would have brought one for himself, but he had grown accustomed to being a mere after-thought when the Prophet had others in his presence. He knew from experience not even to ask the Captain.

The Prophet began, "Welcome. Nice to see you all. Are you well?

How are your families?" The three nodded and gave polite greetings, all was well in general.

"I think you all know why we are here together today? This thing that has happened is not good. It looks bad — it makes us look bad. Nobody has anything to gain from it. I am disappointed. I'm not sure what to do. But I have some thoughts. I would like to hear your thoughts. I would also like to discuss what we should do if anything. And — maybe work out some sort of plan if it comes to that."

The Minister of Justice cleared his throat and lifted his finger. "Eminence, thank you for having us meet together on this matter. I will tell you what I think at this point. Our way of life, our movement, is the way of righteousness. We act according to God's will. We try to be an example for all mankind. This calling is not easy. For whatever reason it may be — and may it be the reason of reasons above all reasons — destiny has called us out of the blind masses and given us light and truth. And ... and has called us — better stated — commanded us, to spread this truth. In fulfilling our mission, we encounter and attract men from various backgrounds. Some are smart. Others not so smart — some downright stupid. There are young and old. And so forth and so on. Suffice to say, our followers are from many walks of life and many different backgrounds."

He paused, but seeing they were content to let him go on, he continued, "As unfortunate as this bombing was, it comes with the territory, as they say. These are part of who we are: a righteous people. It was done because the club was a den of iniquity. Foreigners! Whores and drunkards! It's as plain as day! These Fanatics were certain they were doing God's will, I just know it! However, if we are messengers of God, then, when God is angry with sin, we are the conduits of his wrath. His wrath!" he said again, pounding his fist on the table causing the others to jump. "And it is our business to bring down the wrath of God when it is suitable. When God calls for it. We — we decide how and when action will be taken. Otherwise, every crack-pot who thinks he knows why the sky is blue and the dirt is brown will be taking his turn in God's person-of-the-month club."

Everyone in the room was trying to figure out the earth and sky meanings, but no one had the simple honesty to ask.

The Prophet nodded. "Interesting. And you two, anything to add?"

The Councilman leaned forward and looked at the others. "I understand what my brother here is saying about it. What he is saying, you know? And there is much I agree with. Some and some. But this bombing is a whole another question of it. The question of it. If we have this patchwork of a following, as he says — what are the parameters?, what are the boundaries?, the limits as to what is, and what is not 'Our Way', so to speak? Ok, these men are Fanatics. But we accept the Fanatics as part of our righteous way, even if they may be — how do you say it? be from the wrong side of the track. The track maybe?"

Smiles and quiet chuckles.

"We all have that black sheep, that weird aunt or uncle. These are our little black sheep — who have gone astray. They've maybe gone astray."

"Now wait a minute," the Plebe chimed in. "I know the analogy of the black sheep is cute and all that, but it doesn't stand up. Either these black sheep are with us or they are not. I am not interested in embracing anyone and everyone who claims to walk righteously. I follow his Eminence here because his is the right path to follow. God has appointed him to show us the way. Not the way of the Fanatics. The Fanatics must conform to what his Eminence says. Now, if God so ordains it, that violence is necessary — and it is necessary mind you — it is through his appointed one that the message of violence will come. These Fanatics are renegades. They disrespect the Prophet by committing violence outside of his sanction. I do not think we should sit back and pat these sheep on the heads and tell them they are naughty little sheep but God doesn't mind," he finished with heavy sarcasm.

"In fact", he started again, "I think we should take action! And that action should be to show the world that his Eminence does not tolerate rascals and renegades."

"What do you propose we do?" asked the Prophet.

Not expecting to be put on the spot, the Plebe was caught off guard. Faltering, he said, "I don't know … But something … Let me think about it."

The Minister added, "I agree with my brother. They have done this act of violence, as justified as it was, without his Eminence's knowledge or consent. For that, this act must be addressed in a serious manner."

The Prophet nodded. He turned his face to the Messenger seated by the closed door. "Anything to add my friend?"

The Messenger stood up, slightly embarrassed, not expecting to be asked. He started slowly, "I follow the way of righteousness because

God has had mercy on me. God has been merciful in allowing me to discover the teaching of holiness. And I am grateful that I am allowed to work with all of you … in our mission of bringing about a more righteous world. His Eminence has been very kind to me. I am glad for that. I think our way preaches peace, not bombing. We all know — we are all aware — of these bombings going on here and there. And we wink an eye at them and pretend that we are above all that. But at the same time, we know that we approve of many … I'm not sure … I don't like any of them. I don't know why these black sheep — or rascals or whoever — or this or, that group — did this. I don't know what we should do about it. All I know is I don't like it … But at the same time, I also know I am only a poor servant. I do not have the things you have in your lives. I do not have the education and the deep contact with the Almighty. Forgive me for intruding into your conferences."

There was silence in the room. Then the Prophet nodded to the Messenger and said, "The only two here with me in front of the mercenary bar when we were passing out blessed incense were my attendant friend here and our agent by the door."

Prophet said to the Messenger, "Tell them what you saw and heard."

The Messenger was not clear what he was asked to recount. "What is it you are asking?"

The Prophet told him, "About what those Fanatics did when they left us and went down the road."

The Messenger then recounted the events of the day when the dispute arose in front of the club. He went into as much or as little detail as needed, being prompted, cued and encouraged or discouraged by the Prophet according to how the retelling progressed. When he got to the part where the Fanatic turned and threw his shoe, the three in the room not at the scene were surprised.

The Minister, who scorned the Fanatics the most, jumped to his feet. "That's it! I've heard enough! Enough of these rascally sheep! Black, white, spotted, striped. It doesn't matter the color! Usurpers. Interlopers. Upstarts! Whatever we do, we do not do nothing! We will punish them. The only decision left here is how bad they should be punished. And how. And maybe some details in the manner in which they will be punished. But certainly punished."

The Minister had no compunction with regards to such words in front of the Prophet. He knew the Prophet well and knew that such a zealous outburst on behalf of the Prophet would not only be acceptable but would stroke his ego. The Messenger clammed up. The other two were pleased to let things stand as the Minister had outlined.

The Prophet lifted a hand. "Ok, ok now. We have now heard what happened in the lane. Now, all of us know the seriousness of the matter. Attacking a foreign military outpost unilaterally is one thing. But this overt act of defiance is another. This act clearly signaled that this fanatical group intends to separate themselves from us. And in so doing might become our enemies. Our merciful God has given me an abundance of humility. And it is with this gift of humility that I wish to make it plain that these rascally Fanatics — are not in my disfavor because of me. But because in disavowing me, they are casting their dirty, dusty shoe at the righteousness of God himself. And, in so doing, have made themselves our enemies. Furthermore, as they are now our sworn enemies, we must avenge them in God's name."

He paused and looked slowly around the room. He could see that all eyes were with him, except the Messenger, who looked like he didn't understand what was going on. "That settles it," the Prophet announced.

"How shall we proceed? What should we do, you know?" asked the Councilman.

The Prophet looked at each one by one as he spoke. "Find the Fanatics that consider that village as part of their territory. Bring them to the back of the compound. Bring one, two, three — however many you can get without too big of a fight. Keep it quick and get it done fast. Next, find out about the pigs that were in charge of the pigsty bar. Which of the foreign mercenary bases was this pigsty joined to? Where is this base? Also some information about how it is laid out. What are the surroundings like? What kind of buildings there are. Maybe some idea of how they run the place. Whatever information seems interesting. And last, find that young man who ran the bar for pigs, and bring him to me. Do not lay a finger on the young man. He is not our enemy. We will bring him here in peace. We will use persuasion and the arts. We will open his scale-covered eyes to the nature of truth. Find out where this boy was raised. Who are his family? What kind of world does he inhabit? But don't dawdle in all this. Just get whatever information you can that is easiest to get without arousing the pig soldiers. And always remember, God has chosen us for this. We are the bringers of peace for this generation. And I am it's Prophet."

7

Attached to the rear of the Prophet's great enclosure was a large courtyard facing the open vista of the countryside. The courtyard proper was sparsely furnished with simple folding table and chairs. The ground and the walls were stained and pockmarked with gunfire. Stout rings were embedded in the rear wall and solid door led into the orchard.

A black sedan pulled up. The driver and passenger helped three men out whose hands were zip-tied. They were brought into the courtyard. They were three of the Fanatics who had broken away from the Prophet's group on the day incense was being offered. One of the three was the one who threw his shoe at the Prophet.

The Messenger and the Prophet entered through the heavy door, accompanied by two boys, dressed in black with crimson silk waist sash. The Prophet took a seat in a metal folding chair at the table. The Messenger and the boys stood to the side.

The Prophet addressed the three men. "Gentlemen, welcome to our compound. As you can clearly see, this court serves the surrounding area for husbandry. It is also a punishment and execution ground. We have brought you here because we are disappointed in your disrespect of me in public while we were ministering to that neighborhood some time back. I think you remember. It was uncalled for and unkind to throw your shoe at me. It shows to the outsider that there are friction and division among us. This is not the picture we want to paint. And, let me state plainly, that I don't believe such friction truly exists in our collective hearts and souls. I believe that you were upset by the existence of the heathen club — and let your emotions get the better of you at that time. I understand there are some differences between us in how we interpret and practice our common faith. This does not concern me too much. We all know, from history and experience, that all the faithful around the world have their own style and cultural ways of religious expression. This is fine. But to make a show, like you did, especially in my presence, your spiritual head, was not good. I have brought you here to demonstrate my displeasure. I will have you flogged. I do this out of love and compassion. I am a man of peace. God is merciful but also demands justice. What you did was unjust and we are here to square the spiritual balance sheets, so to speak. By this flogging, we wish to demonstrate two things. First to establish, here in the temporal realm, that God's wrath will be propitiated by your punishment. And second, to show you that in bringing you here by force, I am not to be taken lightly as the spiritual head of our faith. Let me state that in this flogging, my truest heart's desire is for this punishment be unto you like a loving father disciplines his sons. As youngsters, they are prone to err, playing in dangerous areas, or harmful ways. The father nurtures them with love, but also corrects them. If he is a good father, he will most certainly instruct his children in the ways of peace and mercy, the font of which is God, who is peace and mercy himself."

The Captain came through the door dressed in a black cotton karate gi and black pants of the finest kid-skin leather. In his bright red waist sash hung a large scimitar in a heavy-duty leather scabbard. He walked over to the wall and took down a flogging whip with a stout wooden handle with three heavy strips of leather, about as long as a man's arm.

The men were taken up to the wall, each one beneath an iron ring. The driver cut their zip-ties. He took their arms and had them grasp the top of the ring; then he re-tied them at the wrist, each to their respective ring. Without further ado, the Captain went up to the first man and tore off his shirt with a mighty yank. He then drew back his arm in a full arc and came down forcefully on the man's naked back. The man grunted in pain. He whipped him with two more powerful strokes. Long reddish-purple welts appeared. After the third stroke, realizing that the flogging was over, the man hung his head, sucking air into his lungs. His knees wobbled and he had to rely on the support of the ring to stay standing, even though the zip-ties hurt his wrists.

So proceeded the Captain; stripping off the shirts and lashing the bare backs, three awesome times.

The Prophet said, "I hope these stripes will serve as a reminder that you have been redeemed from the wrath of God. Whenever you feel their discomfort, or are seen with them on your back by others, may your heart go out in gratitude for this temporal pain and societal shame. For it serves you in recollection, that God has had mercy on your souls. May it also serve as a reminder of your humble and peace-loving spiritual father. For I am only God's servant in carrying out this merciful task of laying on your backs these stripes of pity and love."

The Prophet nodded to the driver who cut the men down; then to the Messenger, who whispered in the boys' ears. The boys went to the door and led out two women, each holding a child by the hand. Two of the men looked with horror upon this unexpected appearance of their wives and children. The Messenger nodded to the boys again. Obediently, they went to the middle man; the one who threw his shoe at the Prophet, and led him solemnly to the middle of the courtyard. The boys moved over to the Captain. One unfastened the scabbard and withdrew the large, sharp scimitar. He handed it to the other lad, who took it by the handle and blade. Stepping in front of the executioner, the lad bowed his head and lifted the weapon to him. The Captain took the sword and returned the bow.

The boys then approached the middle man. They gestured him to kneel. When he did not kneel right away, they took him by the wrists and gently tugged. Not knowing what was happening, he resisted. The two lads, still holding the wrists, moved around the man's body, and pushed up forcing his arms into a chicken-wing hold. The sudden pain of the arm-lock got the man's attention. Realizing that he was being asked to kneel, he did, with a look of bewilderment on his face.

"Just so you know," the Prophet announced, "we have the ways and means to reach out to your family and friends, in case we need to show them God's mercy as well. We cannot know all the ways of the Almighty, but we can try to discern his will and ways by what he has revealed to us. In the case of our brother here," gesturing to the kneeling man, "we can only do what is best for him and for the faith at large. What is best, is that the whole human race is drawn into his loving embrace forever. However, how this comes about can be mysterious. It can seem like a wrong is done to make a right. Here, our brother has brought himself into eternal jeopardy by cutting himself off from me by his defiance. As his Shepherd, I must act, so that he does no further harm to himself or those around him. And especially, that he does not lead other innocents in the way of perdition. This act, which I am doing here and now, is for his own good, and the good of the faith. It is an act of purification. The diseased branch must be nipped at the bud ere it infects the whole tree. So, we commend his soul to God, who will do what is right with it … Proceed."

The two boys kept one hand holding the Fanatic's wrists with one hand and with the other, they pushed down on his shoulder blades. At the exact same time, the executioner stepped to the man's side. The condemned man's natural reaction was to strain against the boy's hands on his back. Although the boys were physically inferior, as the man pushed back, the boys lifted his wrists. The counter-leverage of the straightened arms and the man pushing upward, caused his head and neck to extend forward. Before he could further react or make any move against the boys, the executioner came down with one strong, well-aimed stroke. The blade went clean through the man's neck. His head rolled to the ground, blood gushed and the torso plopped to the ground.

Nobody stirred. The only sound was one of the women gasping in shock and disbelief.

The boys went up to the head and grasped a tuft of hair. They walked out of the pavilion and across the dirt road. They swung the head back, then launched it into the air. It landed with an unceremonious thud. They turned without a sound and returned to the courtyard.

In the distance, two vultures wheeled about and began a long, slow glide towards the head.

8

THE STAFFER CAME THROUGH THE General's open door and said with a hint of mystery, "Someone to see you, Sir."

"What is it about?"

"Better come see for yourself."

The General welcomed the interruption of his daydream. He was supposed to be finishing a pile of paperwork. Back home he had a modest staff, but not on the lonely base.

Out in the open office space, there stood a boy. He was dressed in black silk pants, and a matching Nehru-collared black shirt with red piping. Something a page might wear in an old majestic hotel.

The General looked at the boy, then at his staffer, then back at the boy. "Ok … I agog a fashionably dressed boy here."

"He says he has come to bring you to his Prophet."

The General gave the boy the once-over a moment more. "Is he dangerous?, or is there any apparent dander?"

The staffer shook his head and handed over the binoculars. "Take a look for yourself."

At the front entrance, there was a black sedan. Four soldiers had surrounded the car, and secured a man dressed in all black, a plain dressed driver, and another boy matching the one in the office. The General took the binoculars down, looked at the boy, then returned his gaze to the gate. One soldier was holding what looked like a large scimitar.

"Get one of those guards on the horn."

The staffer gave the handset to the General.

"Guard, can you tell me what the fang-dangled is going on out there?"

The guard reported that the car had driven up slowly. It was stopped, secured, and searched. All that was found was the scimitar.

"They said they were here to bring the General to a meeting with the Prophet. We had some serious reservations about the visit, so, they offered the boy as *an emissary*."

The General walked to the gate. "Well now. What can we doofer you today?"

The man in black answered, "Our Prophet would like to meet you, and speak with you."

"Ok boys," the General began, "this is might be half unusual. However … since you caught me jus' now doing paperworth, and I don't like paperworth much, ceptin when I am going over my pension fund — right gentleben?" he yelled to the guards who obligingly nodded in agreement with an unenthusiastic, "Yess'r."

" … and, said paperworth, is the most loathsome kind, boy-row-crastic BS with duplicates to who knows where in boggy sodom … well, I'd much rather leave off and come out here to chat with you all … you all dingbats of a ninja circus. Now, tell me, what's on your mind?"

"Our Prophet would like to meet you, and speak with you, as we said."

"Fellers, it is not a common thing for someone to come up to this gate and ask such a thing."

The General called out. "Gentleben, not such a common thing, is it?"

The guards replied mechanically, "Nos'r."

"So dee doe, who and what is this profit? And why should I meet him? But wait a giblet, I don't have much else to do to get away from the dang-blang paperworth, so I'll meet with your profit. I have three interrogativeness, for you, or for him: Ah-one: Does he have a decent golf handicap? Ah-two: Does he enjoy a fine see-gar? Anna three — wait for it — Does he like his martinis extra dry?"

The Captain and the driver looked at the General, then looked at each other, then back at the General. "We do not know. You will have to ask him."

"Jus' as I figgerd. Goons," he said to the staffer, jutting his thumb at the two men.

"When and where is this meeting supposed to happen?"

"Whenever and wherever you like.".

"Good answer! In fact, the only answer. You both get a gold star and smiley face on your report card. I think my putting is in good form. And I know my bunker and chip slots are dialed in. I've got some Cohiba Panatellas and some Bombay Sapphire for the 19th hole." The

General laughed at his sense of humor. Everybody else stayed quiet.

"How's my schedule look?" he asked his staffer. Then without waiting for a reply, with a loud voice, he called out to the men and boys outside the gate, "Great! I'll seek ewes in the morning." Then waved the car away.

9

THE NEXT MORNING, THE PROPHET arrived and was escorted to a large canopy behind the General's office building. After looking him over, the General gestured for him to sit. "This is very unusually. We don't have much of an SOP for this. But since I'm an SOB, I'll invent my own pro-seeders." He laughed loudly at his pun, looked around for some support for his humor, and seeing none, returned to the Prophet. "Now, we have a gabillion questions, but why don't you take a presumptive strike here and tell us what this is all about," the General said, waving his hand languidly in the air.

"Thank you. Like yourself, I have many people under me, many responsibilities and a busy schedule. So I do not wish to take up a lot of your time."

The General listened and observed. "You seem like a nice enough guy. Here we are together. I — a not-so-welcome guest in this country. You're some kind of local religimous leader. I'm not clarified what we have to offer each other that is in our Mutual of Omaha interest."

The Prophet answered calmly. "I understand the awkwardness of our common situation. To make a slight correction on your knowledge of me, let me elaborate a bit. I am not a citizen of this country. I am, therefore, not a local religious leader. I do have local religious leaders under me, that is, under my spiritual umbrella. As you in the West have bishops and pontiffs, so too here. I am a pontiff of our religion."

The General sat back in his patio chair. "I'm not assured what to respond. I mean, I am a career militarize man. I don't know how to put this in context. On the one hand, I could figger you are a lyin' bum of a bumpkin and toss you out on said body part. On the other hand, if you maybe who you say you are, then it is a mighty big leisure to meet you. But I don't know eggs lacky how to handle properwise a visit from a religimous diginnary. So, can you help me out here?"

"I understand," the Prophet said. "It is a long story, which we can go over sometime, but here are the things I can share with you which are germane to our meeting today. As you probably know, our religion, like most, has divisions in it. Cultural, historical and doctrinal. All these different groups are certain God is on their side. Some have a better claim on God's blessing on them than others. Likewise, our great religion is not confined to any geographical map or political landscape or lines drawn out by some conqueror. How I fit into this, and why I can ..."

The General interrupted. "Ok. I"ll go along with your judgment on that for now. And trust me, I will need a Uriah Heep of historical and religimous gap-filling to cross that chasm in my upbringing. Sheesh. You know about being raised in a military household? Well-let-me-tell-you something Señor Pope. Differin' schools every year — or two or three. Differin' friends, maybe — if you're lucky. Playground fight-em-ups all the time. There warrant time to study history. And not much time to devote to spiritualizn' matters either. Then basic training, more fights, more drinkin-an-womanizin'. And — unless you're caught in some ding-dang-damn fox-whole with mortar fire raining hell down all surround you — not much prayin' ether. So, tobaccah my questions. My first question: What can I do for you today? And the secondary question is a bite off topic, but I gotta know: What the hell was all that about yesterday? with the kids and the goon all gussied up like some old swashbuckler movie?"

The General sat back and pulled a fresh cigar out of his shirt pocket. Keeping an eye on the Prophet, but without offering him one, the General methodically began the little ritual of getting a cigar all good and going ... Making a neat cut on the end; moistening the end in the mouth, savoring the wrapper's distinctive flavor. Lighting a little stick of wood, and then the long ignition process: drawing and puffing and twirling and making sure of an even burn all around. Then finally, a nice draw and examination of the tip to make sure there will be long ashes.

The Prophet watched all this, unimpressed. He knew this was all bluster to properly show who was in charge of this meeting. It didn't bother him. He was his own man. God was with him. The spirit of God was with him. History was on his side. The outcome of this one meeting was only a phrase in a sentence in a paragraph in a chapter in a story in a volume in a set of tomes. It would be helpful for this meeting to have a positive outcome, but in the grand scheme of things, it was not imperative.

The General looked at the cigar ring. "Cohiba Panella. Mighty nice. I get these by the box. A few El Presidentes too. The El Presidentes are a bit big. Too long of a smoke. And even for me, a true veteran o'the art of o'the see-gar, it gets me a little Mean Joe Green behind the gills. But I got a little humor-door in the orafice," pointing his cigar in that general direction, "so I can weasel 'em along for a while and Bob Dole 'em out on special moccasins."

The Prophet wasn't sure how to respond to all this. So he tried to steer the conversation back to his agenda. "I am here to offer you assistance."

"Assistance? What kind of assistance?" the General asked with surprise.

"We know that the burnt-out bar is in a strategic location."

The General was not prepared for this. He had a bad taste in his mouth about the club. It was an episode that upset the balance of his normal routine. He thought it was all over when the club was bombed. Then, like the evil character in a horror film that makes one last gasp, the club was unexpectedly brought back into existence like some Phoenix. Now he had the unwelcome duty of overseeing a project that didn't exist. These were the worst assignments of all. Worse than KP and latrine work. With grunt labor, you know what was up and what was down; when to start and when to stop. The whole shadowy world of spy versus spy made him disappointed with the institution he loved and swore his life to. He knew the club had strategic interest for the military intelligence. He knew it had to do with sectarian violence. Now someone from the other side was having a semi-sanctioned meeting with him on the base. Someone who was, apparently, high up in the food-chain of these religious groups. He was on shaky ground. He could bluff. But he knew that in all likelihood, that if the military intel knew something about the strategic importance of the club, then the locals who gave a rat's ass about it, must know too. How much overlap there was in this intel? what kind was it? how good? how important? — all these hypotheticals raced through his mind one upon the other. He was not trained to sort out all these shades of gray. "Ok. That's interesting. I am a privy to this notion. Although I am in charge here — I don't necessarily follow all the details as to why it is an important location. That is, if we cogitate it is worth making something out of this old abandoned building, then there must be some strateregic logic to it. But to what specific end the strateregy is directed, is not something I know much about … mostly because I don't delve into these things."

Mumbling lowly, he added, "Gets in the way of my golf game."

"What was that?" the Prophet asked, leaning forward and cupping a hand to his ear and betraying a slight, sly smile.

"Oh, nothing. Just mubberling … 'bout being the boss … y'know."

The Prophet dropped his hand. "Hmmm. I thought you said something about your golf game. I must have not heard correctly. Sorry."

Before he could stop himself, the General unloaded on the Prophet his current golf woes. "Well, it's the mid-game isn' it? The fairway woods aren't practical out here." He went on (and on) about the ease of bunker practice in the sandy scrub. The ease of ordering astro-turf and Titleist balls. The ease of emptying a tumbler and laying it on the fake grass. And the ease of just driving the requisitioned balls into the wasteland. "But the fairway … well, believe you me Your Hopefulness, it's a whole nuther bean-dip." As the Prophet waned like a dessicating puddle, the General continued jabbering on about boundaries, bounces, long irons and lies. Pars, putts, stances and swings. The soldiers and guards were eyeballing each other while passing out Juicy Fruit, making subtle gestures with their hands imitating a duck's bill quacking away.

"… you could also close the face a bit and scooch your right foot back … maybe get a great bounce. Up and down in reg. That's what I say."

The General set his cigar down and put his hands together in a practice grip; going over in his mind the shot's adjustment and hopeful course correction as it flew down the par five. Satisfied with his take in such a situation, he took a nice draw on his Cohiba. Then he came out of his musings and asked, "What were we talking about?"

The soldiers and guards hung their heads in exasperation. The Prophet shook himself out of his torpor. He clasped his hands together and rubbed his palms to wake up, so soporific was the General's speech.

"That you didn't have much time for strategy and such," answered the Prophet, "because all your time is taken up with golf … I mean, that you did not spend enough time on your golf, because you have to run a large military installation," he corrected himself diplomatically.

The Prophet had, from his youth, been accustomed to spiritual exercises like meditation, fasting, prayer, acts of devotion, pilgrimages, and so on. So with the warm air and the General's boring blathering, he had to marshal his spiritual resources and reserves to maintain his composure and focus. The Prophet was a busy man. He wanted to respect the General's time, but was getting antsy at the languid pace. He glanced at the guards. One of them looked back and gestured a forward-rolling wave motion while slightly nodding to signal, "Go ahead, go on with it, say what you need to say — we're dyin' over here."

The Prophet gave a shallow nod, straightened himself and said, "General, you and I, we are on the same side in this war. Yes. I am not the enemy. I am no one's enemy. I am a man of peace. Whether by design or happenstance and for this discussion it doesn't matter, your bar is located in a very well suited place — for both of us to overcome those who oppose us. It is located at the edge of a small village. This village is of ingarest — I mean interest — to three rival sects: the Zealots, the Fanatics and the Radicals. It is theorized, that control of this village by any one faction can be leveraged into greater geographical control. All three groups are doing damage to the fabric of society. Their misguided fervor is fueled by hate and revenge — and especially self-righteousness. These rascals are the source of the firebombing of your gentlemen's club. They are the source of the assassination attempt in front of the club. It is with these that you and all the armies must contend. They are the scourge of the planet. They know no boundaries nor borders. They respect no laws except the ones they falsely derive from their sacred texts. They take these texts and mix them in with their predecessor's interpretations. They take these interpretations and commingle them with some sort of historical account tailored by their bogus leadership into a narrative. They take this contorted history and weave a twisted net of rules, regulations, and restrictions. These sets of spurious codes lay a foundation and groundwork of their scandalous plotting. Their plot is to trap people by making it impossible to live according to their invented morality and barren lifestyle. Then, set up for failure, they proceed to judge guilty all men, women, young and old alike. Their prosecution is unabated. No logic, no treaty can change their minds.

"These are ruthless men. They will not be swayed nor diverted from their perceived duty to rid the world of those who do not or will not follow their way. They cannot be bought off. For them, a bribe is a trifle, not to be compared to what they expect from their God as an eternal reward for their holiness. They cannot be persecuted because it merely bolsters their zeal. Persecution is interpreted as a good omen; a sign that they are on the true path. They cannot be threatened, nor have the Sword of Damocles held over them, because that end is martyrdom. This is a reward as coveted as any — for it guarantees them eternal life."

The Prophet ceased from discoursing, then sat back awaiting the General's response.

The General motioned to one of the soldiers The General whispered in his ear. "Seeing if we could get some refreshments."

They sat in silence waiting for the soldier to return.

The soldier brought out a tray of iced tea and diagonally cut ham and cheese sandwiches.

"Hep yourseff Pope," the General said, taking one of the glasses and half a sandwich. He set the items on the armrest and withdrew a flask. He tipped a generous amount of brown liquid into the tea and poked the cubes with his finger. He lifted the glass, glanced at the Prophet and took a long quaff of the tea.

"Ahh," the General exhaled. "Nothing like a little hair o'da houn' diggity dog to take the edge off — if you know what I'm catching at."

The General gave the Prophet an unabashed wink. "I know it's early, but as my old comrades in the naval division are wont to say: The shadow has cast the yard-marm somewheres."

One of the guards groaned, crossed his arms in defeat, closed his eyes and dropped his head.

The Prophet remained passive. He was there to discuss what he felt were weighty matters. He couldn't protest because he was a guest. But he didn't understand much of what the General was saying. The strange way he talked about golf. The unexpected hospitality of cold drinks, which he had never drunk. And bread with some sort of meat and cheese together. He presumed the tipple was alcohol. Since he had little contact with the alcohol drinking culture, he merely watched and listened. He did not know how to interpret the dog and shadow statements. Not to be impolite, he lightly waved his hand at the refreshments. "Thank you. I'm fine."

"Suit yourseff," the General replied, taking another swig and a big bite. "Mr. Prophet, Sir, I know my ways are not your ways. I know you think I'm an unwashed pig or something. But I partake the liberty of my lifestyle here because ... well ... because it is pert near all I got. I don't get out and see much action. My grunt days are off a ways behind me. So, although I unnerstand and apprecigate the morality and motivicums behind this war effort, it wears me down. I take solace in what pleasures I can scrabble along together. So you'll have to indulge me. We're trying make our way out here. It's tough. From outside it's easy for others to criticalize. Here on the ground, holding the line, in the middle of the clash of everlastin' who wazzits and temple-tied-turks — well that's another thing. It's the blastin' fershizzle that swamps the brain pan and makes it all gimble-eyed. Why, we fan our brow, sip up the slurp and wag it all over just for the slim-slam of it … Now we got this whole crack-up with the God-forsaken gentleben's club. All jacked up and served on a platter."

The soldiers had finished their chewing gum and switched to chewing tobacco. They knew from experience, once they heard the word 'brain pan', any semblance of sanity was now gone down the river into the sea of forgetfulness. They sat down at the table on the side and began preparations for a good long game of poker with cards shuffling, snacks put in order, and money counted.

His tea finished, the General took the liberty of appropriating the Prophet's untouched glass. He poured half in his own empty glass. The General opened his flask again and doused what was the Prophet's tea with booze.

He looked at his cigar. Happy that it was still lit, he puffed greatly on it, until the end glowed bright red again. He took a long draw and let it out very slowly, the smoke clouds rolling over the Prophet. Then he took a massive swallow of his tea, sat back and let it all melt into his being. "Now where was I?"

The soldiers and guards didn't even hear this last question, as they were concentrating on the cards.

The Prophet was not sure where they were in the meandering discussion. Hoping to reach the General while he could, he said, "I want to assure you that I am here for a noble cause. I am on your side in these difficulties you speak of. I have two things I'd like to cover with you while I'm here. One, to explain to you why I can help you in resolving the underlying conflict which makes this war and occupation effort a perceived necessity. And two, a concrete step I would like to propose on how I can help. The first thing, why I can help, is something I can try to do with or without foreign occupation. The second thing, how I can help, can be accomplished with your cooperation, and collaboration."

Here he paused, waiting to see if the General wanted to hear more, or was listening, or cared, or what. He did not know what to expect.

The Prophet saw that his words were neither accepted nor rejected, so he went on. "There have been, are, and always will be men, who are sent by God to lead his people. For this generation, I am that man. As God's emissary for his people today, I can exercise spiritual authority over them. To put it in plain terms, I can wrest peace out of this current unrest. I, and I alone, can bring the sects under control and end the conflict which harms us all. This can come about in many ways, for we do not know the future. And even those of us who have a special measure of his spirit, myself, for example, the future is only seen in broad strokes — not necessarily the fine details. That is why we all must seek to understand the currents, culture, and communities all around us. Naturally, we all see this surrounding world through our own eyes. For our eyes are the windows to the soul, as it was once said. These windows take in, but what is taken in is filtered, winnowed and made to fit, either consciously or subconsciously, into constructs … Constructs that range from the natural state of physical birth to the era into which one is born, all the way through to education and personal opinion."

The Prophet paused once more. He was hoping for some sign from the General, whether to go on, to stop or for clarification. The General took another generous bite, chased it down with bourbon and tea and squinted at the card hands.

Turning his attention back to the Prophet, he said, "Go on. It sounded like you were jawin' on about Kant or Jung and those fellas."

The Prophet couldn't help but raise his eyebrows at the General's recognition of the great German and Swiss thinkers. He was crestfallen because his pride had been pricked by this buffoon of a commander. He regained his train of thought, realizing that maybe his words were not falling on deaf ears after all. "I'm sorry General," the Prophet answered. "I was meandering. Maybe I will have some tea after all."

The Prophet adjusted himself in his chair, took the half full glass of iced tea and had a sip. He nodded his head and took another sip. "Good. We are not accustomed to cold tea. Thank you."

The General smiled. "My pleasure." He cheerfully lifted his glass and drained it.

The Prophet relaxed and continued to elaborate. "As I was saying … I can bring these rascals to heel. Reign them in, so to speak. And I can do that because of my unique spiritual authority. At this juncture, the conflict, which has caused such injury and drawn in the armies from abroad, can be quelled — if we act now. The village in which you have set up an outpost can serve as a base for my men to broker a peace. It is a fortuitous thing that this outpost is there. We were unaware that you foreigners knew the strategic value of this area."

He said this, dropping his superiority for the first time since his arrival, hoping that a little honey may go further to gaining his goal, then vinegar.

General said nothing.

"So," the Prophet went on, "because you have a presence in this village, we would like to cobble onto your being there with our own little base. It gives us a perceived legitimacy since it will seem that our presence there is just part of the natural growth of the village. And, it gives me a base of operations from which I can best exercise my spiritual authority."

The General was listening. He decided, right then and there, on the spot, to do something he never thought he would do: open the door to collusion with the enemy. Not collude — not yet. But open the door ... and take a peek ... at what's on the other side. The General started evenly. He figured if he was going to strike a deal with the devil, no need to rush in. He eyeballed his cigar and puffed on it leisurely. "Ok, you have my attention, but I am not sure this nag is going to get out of the gate."

Once again, the Prophet was lost with the General's metaphors.

"Clarify for me just what you mean by 'cobble onto'?"

"I mean to build onto your club building. An add-on."

The General nodded his head. "Thank you. Wasn't quite sure. Let's get on with what you were saying. You have the hoocum wherewithal to bring about a cessation-a-thon of hostiliries between all these warring groups, right?"

The Prophet nodded, "Yes."

"Next, this place we stumbled upon for this unsanctimonious gentleben's bar, is of significant strategic importance that you want a joint presence there, right?"

"Yes," the Prophet said. Thinking to himself, "Now that was pretty good. Why didn't I say that?"

"Ok. Now we're getting somewheres," the General said with satisfaction.

He noticed a pause in the action over at the poker table. The guard raised his eyes over his hand and subtly caught the General's attention. The General scrutinized the hands again. He pointed the cigar to the left and shook his head; then pointed it to the right and nodded.

"It seems to me," the General resumed, "that there are some details we need a fixing to talk on. First, we are here under hostile circumstances. How do we know who you are? How do we know which side you are on? Sorry to say it Bub — but sometimes, heck sake, most of the time — one of you all is just six o' one and a half doz'n o' t'other. Why we're so lost over here, some of us have plum forgotten why we're even here. Shoot ... Give a gander over at yon card sharkin'. At first, they're all, 'Ten-hut!'. Then, they go on the chewin' gum. Then on to the chaw. Finally, they settle in for a little mixin' o' the wits for pocket change. Boom boom boom boom. One two three four. The four stages of soldierdom out here. We're all in. We're kinda in. Don't know if we're in. Don't care, 'Call, whadda ya got?'

"We're all of a shin-bagged hootenanny, one elbowed in on the other, horns a crackin' in this testicular triathlon of tribes, traitors, tobacco chewin' trainees and turbaned trumpeteers of tomorrow's intransigent tumult. Hangin' on until the land o' cotton calls us and the Crimson Tide chariot swaddles us in the folds of her train to journey us to the land of the sweet by-and-bye."

The General paused for breath. He took hold of his glass and saw that it was empty. He tossed it over his shoulder, where it landed with a crash. Without missing a beat, he reached into his pocket, sucked his flask dry and exhaled a boozy effluvium while a bulging varicose vein swam like a subterranean serpent under the skin above his ear.

The Prophet witnessed this with consternation. After a pause, he asked if they could stand up, and perhaps go on a walk.

"Sure thing pard," the General said. "I shorely need a stretch and a stride. Follow me. Yo! Ace-in-the-hole! Saddle up! You're with me and the pope. You other three, clean up this mess and vote one of yourselves as a point man for this joint adventure. You'll be in charge of filing, and conscriptionizin' and organizational chart-rendering and keeping all hush-hush, sub-rosa, down-low, low-down and 'Where's Hoffa' in this whole gig. Get crackin'! And we're not on Hogan's Zeros, so I don't want a lumpy good-for-nuthin' Schultz, but a downright angel of a soldier. And for the third man, I want someone who can really listen and not always be sayin': 'Huh? Wadde say?' Hop. Hop. See you after our merry-go-round."

A guard looked at a soldier. "Dude, this is messed up."

The soldier replied, "Yeah, I know. But what's a guy gonna do?"

The General led his little cohort to a lonely part of the base. As they strolled, the Prophet explained his ideas for the club's expansion. "We need to build a tea-house on the back of your club. We feel certain the best disguise is to have no apparent disguise. The club changed the way the little village did things. It was the cause of an economic boon. It was also the cause of violence. The villagers know all this and are firmly on the side of prosperity. Thus, they will see the rebuilding effort in a positive light. The addition of the tea-house would gather in people who cannot or do not want to be where alcohol is served. This may be redundant, but your club catered exclusively to your own kind. No slight or offense meant."

"None taken," the General answered politely.

"We want to blend in, but, I do not want to make any false pretenses. Our presence at the club will be for the purpose of reining in those who cause so much grief for both of us, and our people. This is an arcane and labyrinthine business. Generations upon generations. Layers of parchments, texts, and scrolls. Histories of mountains, valleys, and springs. Our enemies are also our brothers. Our misguided brothers. And although it is true, they have caused anguish and bloodshed, it is our ultimate goal to bring them back to the peace of God, not his wrath."

The Prophet smiled slyly, stepped a bit to the side, elbowed the General lightly and said, "Fear not my friend. God has put us together for such a time as this. Who's to say we can't make a little money too?"

The General took the cigar out of his mouth and spit a big brown loogie on the ground. "I think I get the gist of it. What's next?"

The Prophet continued, "We are there for strategic espionage. Our espionage efforts would not impinge upon the military's but rather add to it through cooperation. From our side, we can offer a ground game. We know who is who and what is what. Quite honestly, most of you foreign armies don't know what you are doing. No slight or offense meant."

"None taken," the General answered again politely while patting his shirt and pants for a hidden or lost little flask. "Miracles do happen, me little noggin' o mine. Sloggin' and foggin' for naught o' the groggin'," he thought whimsically.

The Prophet went on, "I know already that this request is a touchy subject. But it can be done, if we keep in mind our mutual interest and mutual benefit. It is said: Do not bite the land that seeds you."

"And we say: Blest be the tight that blinds ... or something like that," the General riposted with a tinge of uncertainty.

"Sure," the Prophet answered meekly.

Feeling the nagging need for a nip, the General said, "You know what else we say? In for a Ping, in for a round. And I'm ready for a round of adult fluids."

The General turned to go back. In a low voice, addressing no-one in particular, the General muttered, "So this is what it's come to?

Constructive buildings on two sides of a blind man's bluff.
Who's blinding? whose bluff?
Who's bluffing? whose blind?
Which sides' heads are full of nothing but stuffing?
Now, fraternal with the enemy ...?
Bosomy bonhomie ... or infamy?"

He finished, waving his cigar all around, "Sometimes I wonder which side of the butter my bread is on. I'm gettin' Merle Haggard of all this, and before all is sad and fun, I might as well Johnny Cash in."

10

THE GENERAL BROUGHT THE SOLDIER to his back patio where they sat at the cheap chairs card table. "Son, I have new orders for you. Once again it has to do with your club. It seems things have taken a new twist and shout. Not only is your club being renovated, but it is also being expanded. There are a few reasons for this. It seems that the idea of a spy-nest has evolved into a regular outpost, a bit more 'on the map' if you will. More permanent, and, obviously, more visible. The powers that be have decided on the strategy of 'Hyde in plane site'. I understand this concept, in theory, but I am not too sure how it bakes out in reality. Nevertheless, it will be carried out megizzle and a lump."

The Soldier was not sure how to put this information into context. He was already uncomfortable with his new orders. He hadn't started looking for Asaf. He was depressed about all the paperwork and officialdom that was being thrown on the old club like a wet blanket. He had been trying to figure a way out of the assignment, now this news. "Sir, tell about this expansion."

The General pulled out a cigar and started his lighting routine. "Well Soldier, it's a might complicated, but seein' how were both on the tight nickers looking at the watch, I'll put in the needs be and we'll swagger on as it goes. Here's the skinny. The club will be resurrected and cuttin' to the Chase Manhattan of it, there will be a new building, an addition more or less, to the rear."

The Soldier was stoic. Why the new club would be attached to a new building made little sense. He could understand that there might be reason enough for expansion if it was warranted, but to him, the entire thing was ill-conceived. He wanted to say something along these lines but wanted to be careful. And it was possible that the General had more to explain that would fill in the missing pieces of the puzzle.

"And, this should coarse white lighting down your guzzle. We are going to build this new building — with my friend, the Prophet."

With that revelation, the General sat back and puffed mightily on his cigar, enveloping his head in smoke, almost as if with this disclosure, he wanted to shroud himself from the double-dealing he was proposing.

"General," the Soldier began, "I don't want to sound ignorant, but I am not sure who the Prophet is."

The General answered, his head reappearing like a rounded island in waning fog, "I didn't know that. If I would have known that, I would never have mentioned it. Heck and all heck. If you don't know who the Prophet is, what does it matter with whom we, you and I and ours, co-Labrador with? Kin or no kin, sin or no sin? We're all in for the machinations. Are you sure you don't know who the Prophet is? If I get my tales told twice on the straight and arrow, he might have been the causation of the dust-up in front of your brothlesque building."

The Soldier's eyes bugged out. "You mean the whacko who brought his gaggle of holy wannabes down the lane? Why? … what in the heck? … I mean … what? … why would you get tangled up with that crew? Sir, am I to understand this is who we're talking about?"

More clouds of smoke. "To be sure."

"General, isn't this somewhere under the heading of 'aiding and abetting'? And before you answer, with all due respect, if it is aiding and abetting, I don't want to be involved."

The General said, "I can understand that. Soldier, do you remember my feeling about the spy-craft?"

"Yes."

"Well, ok then. You know I don't give a baboon's butt about 'em. But, … Hey, I just said 'but' twice, in two different forms. That's like a hollow-gram or something. How 'bout them pansies?

"Where was I?" the General asked.

With weariness in his voice, the Soldier answered, "The spies and apes … or something."

"Oh, yeah," the General started up again. "Spy-craft. I should say crafty spies. I am my own non-plussed today. Like a regular Wilde man."

Laughing loudly, he went on, "That's wild man!. Like a beet nick. Gilbert O'Sullivan and the broken back-hills of who dunnit. I should get an Oscar for that!"

Fanning himself from the exertion, he said, "Ok, ok now, everybody calm down. Ok, the apes, the apes."

The Soldier was looking around for a beer to soothe the pain inflicted upon him by the General. "So we're back to the spies, are we? Is there any way for them to either go away or just do their craftiness somewhere else? It just can't be that simple, can it? I mean really … a stupid make-shift bar … and now some dumb outpost operation …" The Soldier trailed off his speaking for lack of anything meaningful to add.

Seeing his mental anguish, the General said: "Son, let me dispense with the pretense. How about if we think of it as a business venture? I would like you involved because of your background in the club; the neighborhood, the ins and outs of running a bar, and especially your rapport with the locals. It takes personnel to run an operation, and I think I can look to you to handle that end of things."

The General paused, waiting to see if he elicited any reaction. The Soldier noted the pause and said, "A business. Hmmm. And what business do we have running a business here? In a foreign country where we are supposed to make war and bring peace? No pun intended. Nor Tolstoyistic reference General. Just breathing in your cigar fumes. Sorry, Sir. I wasn't trying to be fumey — I mean, funny."

"Quite all right Soldier," the General said with subtle pleasure. "They do get heady sometimes."

The General took another puff and inspected his ashes before continuing. "Let me be frank. I have said I don't like the spies. Nevertheless, they seem intent, for their own kooky reasons, on going forward with this outpost. I have been roped in. Don't like it a lot, but I'm over it. The Prophet gets involved, I don't know from the front door, the back door, the side door or down the chimney like ol' St. Nick. At this point, I don't care much because it's all cozenage. Overt, covert or both, who knows?"

The Soldier raised his eyebrows at this.

"At first, I'm tasked with just getting a few things lined up for the spies. A few people, a few bags of cement. Then, when the Prophet comes into the picture, I begin to wonder and doubt how this all hangs together. Well, long story even longer, the Prophet and the spies are on the same page with the strategic importance of the outpost. Mind you, on the same page, but reading it from different manuals. Apparently with the same, or similar goals. I'm not exactly sure how the Prophet operates, but he some way or another triangulates between him, the spies and me. He has his agenda, which includes the tea-house. How or if he got this signed off by the spies, I don't know. Maybe, he asked them, explained his ideas, just like he did with me, and they said 'Yes'. Again, not sure how he did the details, but, at some point, he has a plan. We, the military, are in his way — but also, are his way. I don't know if it matters, because, in the end, he brings me around to joining in the parade."

The Soldier, listening to this serpentine saga, said, "Sir, that's the most coherent speech I've heard you give."

The General smiled wryly. "My lands. Sometimes the neurons develop a sort of transmogrification and line up like the planets do every generation or so. Then, forth sallies the soothsaying like who laid the rail."

The Soldier nodded and wondered how much of this man was goat, skunk or possum. What does that mean? I dunno, we just tossed it in there.

The General tugged hard at his earlobe. "Now all along, you were in the mix, because of your intimacy with the whole bar thing. Your idea and all that. Now, however, I believe we can steer that vessel to port by steering it toward the one thing that men will endure the storms of the seven seas for namely, TREASURE. As unexpected as it may appear, it was the Prophet who proffered profit as persuasion. He made a reasonable argument. My age, my tenure, my ennui. Versus: the potential lure of adventure, the gamesmanship. You know — something to stir up the waning embers in my entrails. When I objected because of all the obvious obstacles, he basically told me, nothing ventured, nothing gained. Should I take the straight road and ride off into the sunset; or should I try the winding road, fraught with brambles and thorns, but offering, excitement … maybe, danger … maybe. But, I can only practice my golf game for so long. So, I went along with his appeal to my state of mind at this point in my life.

"Now I lay before you the same proposition. How would you like to go into the bar business for money? A regular business, but done with a little sleight of hand? Look at it the way I do now: I'm in the evening of my career, I have a somewhat boring outlook for the future, and so on. For your part, it is similar. You're at the end of your time here. Rotation in, or out, or who knows. Meager pay. Maybe bored. But now the crazy opportunity to run a semi-legitimate business here. I think if we play our cards right, we can make a lot of money."

The Soldier had an admixture of feelings. He could understand the appeal of adventure and fortune. But the cost of the risk being offered was much different for him than the General. The worst that could happen to the General would be that he would be sent out to pasture. He had friends and old favors to call in and an abundant retirement. The Soldier had a long career ahead of him. If he did enough stealing and shady business he could lose a lot. He could get tossed in the brig, court-marshaled, lose whatever pension or savings existed for his service-time, reputation, future employment opportunities. If things got too hot, he could get killed. "I think I need a little more persuasion. No, I said that wrong. I need assurance. Some sort of assurance from you that I won't end up in jail, or the graveyard. The graveyard part might be out of your hands. But maybe there are some precautions to being shot or poisoned and so on. That — we can work on together, as it is in our mutual interest. Jail — that's another matter. I am not an international lawyer or anything, but I could imagine there are rules or something about us, an occupying army, running a bar over here. What I did was for the fun of it. You know, like an NCO club, except off base. Really off base. If we are going to try to make as much money as it seems you are talking about, that is a whole different matter."

"What?" the General exclaimed. "You already ran that place as a bar in this foreign country for money. So what's the buggering in your bum?"

"Yes and no. We ran a slush fund. Cash came in and cash went out. The only half-way real obligation was paying the help. And that wasn't too expensive. Our mark-ups were modest and we also had a kind of honor system. We weren't really in business. I'll say that a bit differently. We didn't look at our bar as a business entity. We were there to have a beer and relax. The money was incidental. From what I understand you are saying, this enterprise will be bigger and will have some sort of positive cash flow."

The General banged his fist. "Damn straight it will have a positive cash flow. Like the who damned-up the sheep dip."

The General paused, then eyed the Soldier. "It's the skyrocket up and down the schnoozle. It goes poinging around the circumvent until the unit seizes up and dither dather flops on the waggle. Sorry … Lemme pull out and have a pullet, outer-wise my snake-oil will drown the chicken."

The Soldier just sat there because he didn't understand what the General was trying to communicate.

The General pulled a well-worn flask out of nowhere, popped it open and took a big slug. He exhaled and wiped his mouth. "Oh my, pumpkin pie."

The General shook a little bit all over. He then suddenly shouted. "Get offin' me you scoundrels!" waving his hands around his head.

The Soldier started with concern. "What is it!?"

With alarm in his voice, the General said, "Dang me to a sling-blade. The Tinkerbells get all floozy around my head like a grade-schooler on pop rocks. I'm afore it and I'm ag'in' it. Gimme the rot gut nevermindliness."

He took another big slug of booze. His eyes involuntarily focused in and out. It made the Soldier nervous.

The General held one hand up in front of his face, looked at it, then abruptly slapped himself hard with his other hand.

The Soldier watched with growing anxiety and consternation. "Uh, General, Sir … are you all right?"

The General kept observing his hands. Then he looked up. "Yes and no. I get excited and the hoo-waz-where comes outta the skull. But more rationalize-like and they sleeps. I get a offerin' up the drop and they slip into the slips. The crease in the crack that is. Lemmings start listening now. Go on with your story."

The Soldier was still unsure. "Uh … I don't think I was telling a story."

The General started nodding his head vigorously up and down, waving one hand in a circular motion like a side-wheel steamboat, indicating to get on with it.

The Soldier continued, "I'm not sure if there is a story here, but I was saying that we just had some fun times. We didn't mean anyone any harm. We didn't want to step on any toes. Any comparison to our bar and an on-going business is a stretch. Be that as it may, I understand your interest in my involvement. And I don't want to say, 'No', straight out. But I was wondering if there were ways for me to have my rear end covered so that this venture of yours doesn't ruin my life. That's all."

The General took out some snuff. He tipped a dash onto the back of his hand, put his nostril on the little pile of dust and snorted it with gusto. He then repeated the dose with his opposite parts.

It seemed like the Soldier's plain, serious talk, had a calming effect on the General, so the Soldier continued, "I know I am of value in all this, but it isn't really what I signed up for, to use a worn-out phrase."

The General sniffled a bit, then let out a tremendous sneeze. It seemed to clear up his head some. "Yes … of value. Yes … not signed up for. And yes … can cover. Best of my ability."

After these snippets, it looked like the General was struggling, trying to get a grip on the chaos inside. Snot, mixed with snuff, making it a forest green color, began a slow trickle down to his upper lip. He shut his eyes tightly. He trembled. The ball of snot at the end of its trail quivered when he shook. At the same time, he clenched both fists. The Soldier was alarmed.

The General's eyes popped open, he took a few gulping gasps of air, and his head bobbled to the side like a balloon.

"General Sir, are you all right?"

The General didn't answer right away. He stayed motionless, apparently still recovering from his spasm. Finally, he brought his head up and settled down.

He looked at the Soldier with unfocused eyes. "I want to say … The vigorish is in the chicory."

"I don't understand. How can I help? Is there anything I can do?"

The General continued looking at the Soldier and said haltingly, "Snarffle, be-pop — the cortex outlook. Placido Domingo."

The Soldier was at a complete loss.

Without warning, the General stiffened sharply in his chair. He said with difficulty, "Winnebago. Forensics in the drainpipe." Then went unconscious. The Soldier didn't know if he fell asleep, fainted, or died. But it became apparent that he hadn't died because he was still breathing.

The Soldier decided to wait and see what happened. The General was alive. That was good. They had covered most of their agenda, except for all the persnickety details, but those would fall in place as things progressed. The Soldier started making mental lists of things that would have to be sorted out. Who to talk with. How to procure a variety of equipment and supplies. Then he realized that his thinking was as if he was part of the plan. When he found, deep down inside, that he felt excitement, not fear, he knew that he was going into business with the General. He would have to deal with the General's illness another time. Right now, he had to go back to the village and find Asaf.

11

THE SOLDIER BEGAN HIS WALK through the village, bouncing around in his mind the future prospects of a spy-infested bar. He wanted to think about his role as a willing participant, rather than just a grunt being commanded to do this or that. The sad reality was that he was being offered two choices: fall in with the military's plans, or be stripped of everything meaningful to him, and sent packing. So he tried the best he could to buck-up mentally. Maybe the General would cover for him if things got really sideways. But after seeing him almost die right before his very eyes, anything the General offered or promised was shaky. Maybe they all would make a lot of money. Maybe it would be fun and adventurous. Maybe he would get his gizzard cut out by some religious fanatic. Round and round his thoughts went, but ultimately he knew he would have to make at least a go of it. If things went well, that would be great. If everything went down the sewer, he could tell himself he did the best he could, given the circumstances. One thing he knew he had to do for sure if any of his new orders were to even have half a hope of success: he had to find Asaf. That might be the easy part. Once he found him, to bring him back into the rebuilding effort was more than he wanted to think about.

The Soldier muttered to himself, "One step at a time. One step at a time. It ain't over till the fat is all hung in the theatre. Or something like that. Somebody doing opera … Maybe this is a bunch of hooey. Maybe I'm a grunt however you slice it. Well anyhow, thinking I'm part of this because some part of me wants to, at least makes me feel better. And if it makes me feel better, to heck with all the psychological puzzle games. I'll just get on with my mission, try to feel good about it, maybe try to make sense of it, but not too much sense — since — see there a double sounding spelling whatchamacallit — and here's my two cents worth to make it three! What was I thinking? Oh yeah. Don't get too wound up about making sense of all these shenanigans. Drive yourself crazier than I am already. Now, what is what I was chewing on? Oh yeah. What's that double spelling-sounding thing? An apostrophe or a polymorphism? Something like that. I wonder if I'll ever need to have that tidbit of a tidbit in the old noggin'? Alex, I'll take Useless Grammar for Nuthin'."

The Solider sang as he perambulated peripatetically, figuring out in his mind how to keep everybody and everything in some semblance of order and balance.

Shoulda been a math teacher — got so much figuring to do.
Shuck off these boots — see if there's skates to figure on too!
Intel, See-oh, Foe and Friend. Any on my life depend?
Intel: Recon far and near.
See-Oh: Draw the curtain on Oz.
Foe: Prophet for profit, doubt the odds.
Friend: One to have for beer.

He had to figure out how to keep the pesky spies from becoming even peskier.

Spies like flies like mosquitos.
Lie and lie and lay and lay and lay and lie and lie and lay.
Squat but mum, laying sum, eggs none lonesome.
Math AND grammar, graph AND stammer,
Take a hammer — to it all!

He had to figure out how to fulfill his duty as a Soldier, his obedience and respect to the General, while at the same time partaking in illegalities.

Legal-shmeegle eagles and beagles.
He's a hawk and I'm a hound.
Heel! hound when I'm around.
[Salutes]
Sir, Eagle Sir!
[Mocks General's voice]
Blimies and bejitters, crazy critters get off it!
Runnin' roun' my crazy crown. To me they say:
Shaken and shakin' swindlin' swillin'

Prophet and profit for the cure and the way
of Muffet and tuffet.

He had to figure out how the sectarians fit into the whole mix.

Burn my house down.
Steal from me to rebuild for me.
Steppin' on my backdoor. What for?
Sad truth is:
When I'm long gone, they'll still be in town.

And he had to figure out what to do about Asaf.
[Mournfully]

We had laughs — and lost it.
We were friends — I tossed it.
Ask myself — what cost it?
Don't know the future — do I care?
To rebuild the bar — do I dare?
To ask him to share — is it fair?

12

THE SOLDIER DIDN'T KNOW A lot about Asaf's private life, so he didn't have a direct method of finding him. So, he retraced his steps to where he found him. It had been a while since he was on that patrol and didn't find the street right away. When he came to a familiar part of the neighborhood, he asked a kid selling cheap leather and plastic crap on a table. "Anybody around here know about a young guy who used to sell water on this street?"

The kid shrugged his shoulders and asked the Soldier if he wanted to buy a purse for his girlfriend. The Soldier shook his head. He poked his head into the shop behind the table and asked the same question. The owner glared at him. "Go away from here. We know who you are. Psssh! Pest! Off! Off! We know how you took our boy and made him a son of Satan. We know he was the humiliation of the neighborhood. He comes from a good, decent family. Now he is an outcast. And it is your fault. Go away. Get out!"

The Soldier wasn't looking for trouble and walked away.

A woman beckoned to him from between two small buildings. "Over here, over here."

The Soldier slowed down and approached cautiously.

"I know what you are talking about. The boy. The water. I know these things."

He continued moving, keeping an eye on his surroundings. The woman saw the Soldier's hesitation. "I know your concern. Don't worry. I used to make pretzels for the foreigner's army bar."

"Pretzels?"

"Yes. I spent time away years ago and learned about pretzels. How to make them. It's easy. But we have such good food here that nobody wants them. But for the beer drinkers, I know they eat pretzels. So when young Asaf went into this business of the bar, I sold pretzels."

She smiled with pride, showing her remaining lumps of ivory.

"You know Asaf?" the Soldier asked with a hint of excitement.

"Some. Not a lot. We are from different parts. But I like making money too. So, I made a little with my pretzels. I don't ask the money in my pocket whether or not it was in the club with alcohol. And nobody ever asked me if my money was in such a place either."

"Ok …" the Soldier said hesitantly, not knowing just what to make of this moralistic disassociation with filthy lucre.

"We know it was a scandal. But to me and my friends, as long as they bought our food, all of that other was less important."

Here she paused, looking calmly at the soldier, and glancing around the street at nothing in particular. A pedestrian, a stray cat or dog. The Soldier saw that she was gaming him, on the chance that he was willing to pay for information. "Two can play at that," he thought. He nodded and turned to go.

"Wait! Don't you want to know about the boy?"

Seeing that his hunch was correct, the Soldier was nonchalant. He sauntered a few steps on. "Maybe. But I don't need to know today. I was just in this area by chance and I wondered what happened to him. That's all. Curiosity." He continued slowly along, waiting to see where this cat and mouse game would go.

"Well that's ok, I guess," she said matter of factly. "I know what happened. I know who was behind it."

The Soldier stopped and turned. "You do?!"

Now the tables were turned and they both knew it. The Soldier slapped his forehead realizing his tactical mistake. She smiled widely, knowing she just out-smarted him.

"Ha! You thought you were going to put me off on my trying to get some money out of you," she said smiling and wagging a friendly finger at him.

The Soldier smiled back. "Yes. And I thought I would not play into your tricks. But look who tricked who?"

They both laughed, pointing at each other.

"So, it seems we're at an impasse. Who makes the next move?" the Soldier asked with a hint of humor.

"What move? I am making no move," she said coyly. "I don't have any tricks, like you soldiers. Always full of tricks."

"No tricks here," the Soldier said. Knowing it was better to pay up rather than banter for half a day, he pulled out a small bill. She eyed the bill curiously, then made a scornful face and didn't try to take it.

"Ok, ok," he said with some resignation, "How much more?"

Her face lit up. "One more time, I draw you in. So easy."

She took the bill with a smile. "No need for more. Our little game is enough payment. Let's walk this way and we will go see Asaf."

The woman conducted the Soldier down the village and rounding the corner the woman pointed to Asaf's water stand. The Soldier hesitated, not exactly knowing what she was pointing at. She told him to look again. The layout of the stand was changed. Everything was different. The modest decor was new and pleasing to the eye. The set up of the water, and how it was displayed, all betrayed one who was a professional. All the bottles were neat, clean and organized. He had three standard sizes in plastic, all priced to offer a per-unit quantity discount for each larger size. In addition to having twist-off bottles, there was a hand-operated capper for pop-top bottles. He was selling these in six-packs using re-purposed cardboard beer caddies that were in good shape. He had a modern, locking cash-box on a side table that was out of reach from the sidewalk. Behind him, he had a used, restaurant-style, stainless cart with sliding doors. There were washbasins and bleach on the side. The Soldier was impressed.

Asaf was selling some water and did not see the Soldier approaching. When Asaf looked up and saw him, he was filled with conflicting emotions. At first, a flutter of delight was followed by a quick, chilling fear. In succession, Asaf felt anger, resentment, and his old emotional acquaintance: broken-heartedness. After some moments, he saw that there was no malice in his friend's countenance.

The Soldier walked to the stand a bit languidly. He simply said, "Hello Asaf." His tone and manner were very cool. Asaf merely replied "Hello", with similar reserve. A bystander would have never guessed that these two were longtime acquaintances, considering how unemotional their greeting was. Even though he was at his own table, in his home village, he was nervous about this encounter. He was not sure where he stood with the Soldier and the Soldier's superiors. The Soldier saw the apprehension. "One bottle of water please."

"Sure." They silently exchanged a few coins. The Soldier sipped, wondering how he was going to explain why he was here. He was going over in his mind over the plans and plots for a new club and the discomfort of dragging his old friend into this potential rat-hole. A car with tinted rear windows pulled up out on the road. A man dressed in black baggies, black T-shirt and a black baseball cap approached the stand. The Soldier stayed put, waiting for them do their business and leave so he could talk with Asaf. The man glanced at the Soldier then began looking over the different sized bottles of water, appearing to be in no hurry. The selection was modest and normally would have taken just a few seconds to choose. This man seemed hesitant. His behavior caused the Soldier to look at him again out of the corner of his eyes.

The man said to Asaf, "Let me go see what my friends want."

The man carried on a short, quiet conversation with the driver. By this, the Soldier reckoned that there was at least one more person in the rear, hidden by the dark windows. The Soldier had nothing to fear, so he remained where he was but changed his body language to show that he was clearly watching.

The man returned and asked for five bottles of water. Now the Soldier figured that there were two or three more in the back seat. "Seems like it would be crowded," he thought. "But, oh well. To each his own. If they want to travel all cramped up, so be it. Probably why they're all thirsty."

The man picked up four bottles, using his fingers to hold two in each hand; leaving one remaining on the table. He said to Asaf: "Can you bring that bottle? My friend has a bad leg."

Asaf nodded. The Soldier watched and started moving up the road to get a better angle.

Asaf and the Captain came around to the rear window on the opposite side of the car from the water stand. The window rolled down and a man took the water from Asaf's extended hand. "Thank you. My leg is bad."

"Ok," Asaf said, "Goodbye."

"Wait, I have something to ask you."

Asaf hesitated, glanced up and noticed that the Soldier was moving to get a better view. Asaf nodded at the man but didn't say anything.

"Do you recognize us?"

"No."

"Do you recall the day we came down the lane where you had the bar? We were passing out incense."

"Yes. I remember that," Asaf answered with an even, sober voice.

The Councilman gestured to the Messenger. "He was there. Standing right by our Prophet. Right by him. Do you recognize him now?"

"I guess so. But why do you ask? What do you want?"

"We want you to come with us."

With growing hesitation and the hair on the back of his neck beginning to tingle, Asaf said, "Why would you want me to come with you? That makes no sense. I have no reason to come with you. It's really weird for you, and these guys with you, to even ask something like that. 'Come with us.' Do you know how ridiculous that sounds? Nobody, no strangers, drive up and ask someone they don't even know 'Come with us.' I'm not going anywhere. You guys can park, get out of your car, walk over to my stand if you want. You can sip your water and we can talk. But I'm not just going to jump into your car. Enjoy your water. If you want more, I'll be over at my stand."

Asaf turned to go. The Captain side-stepped and cut him off. The man in the car said, "Wait."

"Now what?" Asaf asked with exasperation.

"We want to bring you to our Prophet."

"Well at least we're getting somewhere," Asaf muttered to himself. He looked at the man in the car and the one trying to block his path. "Wow. You guys are really slick. This is no way get me to do what you want — whatever it is. Who is your Prophet? what does he want with me? and why should I go? I mean, really — can't we just do this out in the open instead of here at the car? — you inside it, and your buddy here trying to cut me off?" Asaf said with annoyance.

Meanwhile, the Soldier had made his way up and around and had a good view. Seeing some sort of unpleasant talk, he began walking towards the car in a slow, easy manner. He certainly did not want to stir anything up. Seeing that the Soldier had flanked the car, the Captain put his head down and spoke to the driver. The driver started walking directly towards the Soldier. "We are asking for him to come with us. There is nothing here for you. This is between him and us. We see you are a soldier. We are not stupid. We don't want trouble."

The Soldier answered, "Trouble? You don't want trouble? Well, my friend, if you don't want trouble, why in the heck are you out in the middle of the road, talking with Asaf out of a car window and asking him to come with you. That is very stupid and a good way to cause trouble. In fact, there will be a lot of trouble if I don't get some sort of information that makes sense out of this whole charade."

The man stood still. "We are men of peace. We would like to talk to Asaf."

"Fine. Let's all go have a bottle of water. It seems the only thing we have in common."

The driver stayed where he was, but turned his head to observe what was happening at the car.

Still talking through the open window, the Councilman said to Asaf, "I have something to tell you. Tell you something."

Asaf was quietly sizing up the sturdy man, wondering how far he would go to block his way.

"We drove all through the village end. We couldn't find you. We made inquiries and found your Uncle. He told us where the water stand was. Here this stand here. We mean you no harm. Do you believe me?"

This surprized Asaf. He thought, "How did they find my Uncle? Why would he talk with them? Maybe it didn't matter. The water stand is not a secret."

Asaf felt provoked. "I don't like any of this. I especially don't like you bringing my Uncle into all this. And why should I want to see your so-called Prophet? He doesn't mean anything to me — except he seems strange."

The Councilman took offense. "Please do not speak bad words about our Prophet. He is chosen by God. He is a man of peace. We do not speak of him like you just did. No. Now, I understand your excitement. However, I must ask you again, to trust us. We did nothing but ask your Uncle where you were."

He then segued and asked, "Do you know they are re-building the club?"

Once again, Asaf was jolted emotionally. First the Soldier, then the abrupt mention of his Uncle, now the club. Asaf paused. He wasn't sure where to go with this strange conversation. Seeing Asaf standing there mute, the man repeated, "The club, your club, it is being rebuilt. Do you know this?"

Asaf was not sure how to handle this information. It was impossible. But why would this man be telling him this? And why was the Soldier here? Finally, deciding to go against his better nature which was to speak the plain truth, he dissembled and mumbled. "Yes, I know … vaguely." He paused again, trying to gather his thoughts. "I have been busy. I left the burnt-out site, and have not returned. My leaving was not a good experience for me."

The Councilman was watching and listening carefully. He saw that this was a difficult topic for the young man. Gently, he prompted him. "Go on …"

Asaf swallowed hard. His heart was becoming a lump in his throat.

He had to remind himself to keep breathing. "That club was my life," he said quietly. Then, fueled by his suppressed anger and poignant memories, he yelled, "MY LIFE!"

The shout caused the man in the car to wince and draw back from the window. It was clear that he had struck a chord, but he hadn't anticipated such a reaction.

Asaf went on loudly. "I put everything I had into that place. Every day — all day! I hired, I fired. I had liquor from every part of the world. I served mercenaries and their prostitutes. I calmed down fights. I made sure the drunks were safe. Housewives from the whole neighborhood trusted me with their wares — never questioning my honesty. They always got paid. And paid well. And paid out of my pocket if I needed to. Because I looked after the details of the club."

Then, lowering his voice, he continued. "The Soldier paid me well too. For that, I am happy. I worked hard, but have the money to show for it. I have much more money than these guys my age around here." Asaf waved his arm at the neighborhood in general.

Asaf addressed the man with venom and loathing. "Then … then … you happened. You … YOU religious. You, you … sectarians … You Zealots! You Fanatics! You PIGS!!"

Asaf turned and spat on the pot-holed road. "You think you are holy. You think you can tell others what is right and what is wrong. I'll tell you what is right. Enjoying the company of others over a beer is right. It's good. It's wholesome. It lightens the mind and heart. It opens you up to another's story. It nourishes both belly and brain. And I'll tell you what is wrong. You are wrong! You and all your kind. Wrong! Wrong about life … the meaning of life! Wrong about family and friends. Wrong about true friendship. Wrong about God! Who do you think you are, pretending to know God or know about God? If you are representatives of God — then that's no God for me. Or — or you are just really bad, piss-poor representatives. It's no wonder most of the people hate you! And you know what else? Like I just said, you're really wrong if you think having a beer with friends is wrong. You don't even know what I'm talking about — you're so … so … so self-righteous with your head up your behind."

The man in the car was shaken. He did not expect to be lectured by this young man. His feelings went from shock at Asaf's vociferousness, to offense at his accusations and finally confusion about the meaning of beer and camaraderie. But the man in the car was not a novice. He had risen through the ranks of his religion because he was smart and had the gift of empathy. He gathered his thoughts. "I understand your pain. I feel your hurt and disappointment. I too, have labored long and hard and have not been rewarded in life. A cruel fate has touched us. But our fate is not forever. It is temporal. It is fate for a season only. A season. The tree's fate is to lose leaves. But it re-grows them. So it is with us. You, young man, and I, we are brothers in sorrow. Sorrow. But we — you and me — have fortitude. We have the backbone of mules. We press on. I was once a Zealot. I too, now, I spit on their ways. They say they represent God, but I myself know they do not. Listen to me. Our Prophet is a man of peace. Recall the scene in front of your bar, when the Fanatic threw his nasty shoe. This was an outrage. An outrage. An act worthy of the sword. But ... but what did our Prophet do? He did not allow himself to be drawn in by violence. He turned away from these rascals and continued on his mission of peace."

Turning to the Messenger then back to Asaf, asked, "Am I not right?"

Inside the car, the Messenger nodded soberly.

Seeing that he was getting the advantage over Asaf, the Councilman pressed on. "Now — now I see you are remembering the way it really happened. Let me say this so that you can know my heart is in the right place. I do not drink alcohol. It is not something I am interested in. I do not know the benefits of beer, as you do. Like you do. And this is why the Prophet wishes to see you. To speak with you. Learn from you. Yes! Learn from you. Not the other way around. Our Prophet is a humble man. Yet, as humble as he is, he is aware, as all those around him are, that the spirit of God is upon him. And upon him in a unique way. He is the Prophet for our time. Our time, you and me. And for your Soldier friend even, should God will it, and our Prophet believes God does will it."

Asaf was wary. "I hear you, but I do not necessarily believe you. I do not know if I can believe you. Or even if I need to. What do you and the Prophet offer that would interest me?"

"The Prophet can answer your questions. He can make meaning out of your life. He knows you are searching for meaning. He knows you are trying to put things in context. Does what I say mean a lot to you? Is this something your Uncle talks about? Meaning and how to make sense of the world?"

The Councilman was trained to read men. He watched carefully as he asked these questions because if they elicited the response he was looking for, his job here was done. When he saw Asaf's eyes widen and his face soften, he knew he was on the right track. He went for the winning argument.

Asaf had spent his rage and was now only full of emptiness and futility. He was involuntarily nodding his head slowly, just enough for the trained eye to see. The man in the car closed the deal. "Do you know why I ask this? Because you and your Uncle and our Prophet talk about the meaning of life. And in a way in which only they know how. Deep, deep meanings. Things too difficult for me to explain. That is why I am here. Your Uncle knows your pain. The Prophet can help. Trust me. Trust our Prophet. And I know — we know — you can trust your Uncle."

Asaf was deflated. Any resistance he had, was waning. He began to see there might be a difference, a distinction, between the evil Zealots and this man and his people. As he thought about what they had gone over, he became aware that there was nothing this man had said that made him evil or a liar. He had categorically rejected the sectarians. Asaf's world and the sectarians world were completely incompatible. Joining these two worlds was never a consideration for Asaf. But now that his world of the club was literally and figuratively burnt up, he was being offered an opportunity to look into this other world. A third option. One that rejected the sectarians — but was still religious. It felt very strange. It came to him that he had no world to call his own. For all his struggles to make sense out of things, here he was in the middle of the road, talking with a man he did not know, and the only prospect he had for the rest of the day, week, month or however long, was to walk back over to his little stand and sell bottles of water. "That's it?" he thought. "That's where all this has brought me? A stupid water stand on the side of the road?" He looked up the road at the Soldier and driver. It gave him a bitter taste in his mouth. "Is this what I am defending? This Soldier? Who, it seems, took me in, then turned away from me and walked away? Because he thinks I am involved in bombing our club? It makes no sense at all." He was tired. He was empty. His eyes filled with tears. He didn't care if they ran down his cheeks or not. He was beyond caring. He sighed, looked at the man in the car, and said very simply, without further argument or explanation, "Open the door, I am coming with you."

The Soldier had been watching. He could tell it was an animated conversation, but couldn't hear. He wanted to get involved, or at least get closer, but he restrained himself. He was in a difficult position. He did not know where he stood in his relationship with Asaf. He knew their last time together did not end well. But he also did not know how bad — or not so bad — that ending was. For the Soldier, the burning of the club was a tragedy. He had no plans to rebuild or make another bar. But this did not carry over to his personal feelings about Asaf. He wondered, "Is it really any of my business what this whole visit is about? Why couldn't this be as simple as a family squabble? Maybe someone's goat got caught in someone else's barbed wire. That's always happening with these people. Your cow stepped on my cow's toes. Well, your donkey bit my horse's ass. Ha, that's funny. My horse's ass, a donkey. Oh boy, I better settle down here. So how obliged am I to get in the middle of this? Am I obliged at all? Maybe I'm the odd man out here. Asaf sure doesn't act like he needs me over there. I mean — come on — am I a rescue team or just a busybody nosing around in stuff where I don't belong?"

The Soldier was brought out of his reverie by the sound of the driver's voice. "I'm sorry, what was that? What did you say?"

Driver: "I said Yes. I think that is a good idea. To go sit down and talk over tea."

"What about them?" the Soldier asked

"Let them be. I'm driving the car. We can go sit and let them finish their business. When they are done, we will all go our own ways."

Uncertain of his role in the whole scene, the Solider felt it was just as well to sit in the shade also, but with his eyes and ears wide open. They walked over to a small shop with a plastic table in the shade. It offered a clear view of the car out in the middle of the road. The owner approached.

The driver said, "I'll have hot tea. But my friend here wants something stronger."

The Soldier raised his eyebrows at this unexpected order. He tried to protest but was quickly cut off.

"It's no problem. It's ok. Right?" the driver said, looking between the Soldier and the owner.

The Soldier started again. "Hey. No. I …"

This time the owner interrupted. "It is not all right. But I can make it right. It has to be discreet, that's all. And we charge for the effort. Also, it will be Cola-Cola for both of you. No tea today." The proprietor turned to go. The driver asked, "It's been a long day. Do you have a toilet?"

"No, out of service. But since we are having something special today — we'll make it work — and add it to the bill. No problem, right?"

They didn't appreciate the owner's sarcasm, but they didn't care enough to fuss. The Soldier still wanted to say he didn't want 'something stronger' but the owner was already gone.

The driver pushed his chair back and excused himself. The Soldier waved him off like a fly at the table.

The proprietor returned with two Cokes and half a mug of brandy. The Soldier asked where the driver was.

"Using our facilities," the proprietor answered and left.

Out of respect for the man's need to relieve himself, if nothing else, the Soldier refrained from picking up the mug and turned his attention back to the street. He still couldn't hear what they were saying, and his view was impeded as the conversation was taking place on the far side of the car. He didn't like this situation. He felt vulnerable and chided himself for letting himself get into this uncomfortable position. Then, without any outward sign, or warning of any kind, Asaf got into the car. The Soldier jumped to his feet. He was confused as to what to do. He didn't have a good reason to try to "rescue" Asaf. No one in the neighborhood asked him to be there. Asaf had not asked for his help. He didn't appear to be coerced or kidnapped. The Soldier went out into the road and watched the car drive away. He returned glumly to his seat at the table. Nothing stirred. It was a hot day and everybody was inside. Suddenly, behind him, the proprietor brought down the metal shutter with a bang. The Soldier was stunned. With a loud curse, he violently swept the two Cokes and the mug off the table onto the sidewalk where they broke with a loud crash. Asaf was gone from the village. Those who were outside or in their shops and homes shook their heads and turned away from him. He didn't know where else to look for Asaf, so he returned to base.

13

THE CAR DROVE FOR ABOUT an hour. They arrived at a walled compound in a remote agricultural area. Inside the compound was the main house, a huge garden and orchard, agricultural equipment, outbuildings, and a cottage.

The Councilor gestured for Asaf to sit at an expensive outdoor furniture set. Without announcement or protocol, the Prophet calmly walked out of the orchard to the patio. He seemed expressionless; no smile, nor frown. He waved his hand in a gentle arc. "Sit. Anywhere."

The Messenger brought tea and left.

Since the encounter with the men in front of his water stand, Asaf didn't like the whole thing. He didn't like the man in the street blocking the Soldier's path. He didn't like being told that they had been talking with his Uncle. Although he came willingly, the sequence of events and the cajoling made him feel vulnerable and defensive.

"Asaf — may I call you Asaf?" without waiting for a reply, the Prophet said, "Asaf, these are strange and trying times we live in. The ripples and currents of events outside of our doing and control have spread and pushed their waves of upheaval into our otherwise simple lives."

Seeing that Asaf remained quiet, the Prophet continued. "I say this, as a preface to what I wish to talk with you about."

"Why am I here?"

"You are here because you agreed to come here. Correct?"

"I guess so. Why did you talk with my Uncle?"

"Doing what they did speaking with him was done on their part. My goal, that is my wish, was to meet you. I didn't give them instructions one way or another on how we should meet."

"But if I were to make a story why I'm here or to tell someone else, someone who didn't know anything about why and how I got here, it wouldn't sound like I just up and decided to come here. I feel … I feel like I was having my arm brought behind my back. Everything … everything …"

Asaf began replaying in his mind the scene and conversation in the village. He felt again the man's insight into his life and feelings. He felt again the emptiness of not belonging to anything. He felt again how stupid it was to go back to selling water. He lost whatever train of thought he had and went silent.

The Prophet pulled out a silk kerchief and handed it to Asaf. "Dear boy. I'm sorry. I too cry. I cry for different things, maybe different reasons. But I share your sadness. It is the wars that make us sad. It is the wars that tear apart and undo the fabric of society. The very substance of *civitas*, the old word for living together in mutual accord, the very substrate upon which neighborhoods and villages and cities are built, is discomfited by war, and especially civil war, the most unwelcome, and the most difficult to discern. Such is the nature of the social contract within which we are swaddled, that when it is abruptly unfurled bringing disarray to our welfare and commonweal, it dumps us on the ground like a worn-out hammock."

Asaf was uncomfortable and embarrassed. He only took the silk kerchief out of politeness. He couldn't bring himself to use it, so he used his shirt sleeve. By the time he had stopped shedding tears and had wiped his nose, he heard the Prophet mention being dumped on the ground by a hammock. He looked up at the Prophet through his watery eyes, and sounding like a dunce, said, "Hunh? What hammock?"

The Prophet had mesmerized himself with his musings about how war made civilization suck and was barely aware of the hammock analogy. "How's that? Hammock you say. What hammock?"

"Yes. What hammock?"

The Prophet was momentarily confused. "Oh. Yes. The hammock. Sorry. Um … I was day-dreaming about the days when there was peace and one could rest and relax under a tree by a cool stream with a hammock tied between two trunks."

Asaf was confused.

The Prophet sighed. "Why don't you have the tea, and a cookie. There can't be any harm in a tea and cookie, right?" The Prophet smiled.

He wasn't in a mood to relax, even though the series of events that day had tired him out. The Prophet's smile seemed calming. So, for etiquette's sake, Asaf picked up his glass and a cookie.

The two of them sat quietly, sipping and nibbling. Asaf began reflecting on the recent events. "Well, here I am in this crazy guy's orchard. I suppose it could be worse. I'm alive. No one has shot me or tried to do something bad to me. Maybe my bad feelings come from hanging around all the mercenaries so long, and their dislike of these religious types. Maybe I shouldn't be so harsh on them. Maybe I have been on the wrong side of the fence all this time. I can't believe I'm thinking this way. But it does make me remember all the talks with my Uncle about how confusing my life had become ..."

The Prophet looked up from his tea. "What do you understand about the seen world and the unseen world?"

Asaf nodded his head back and forth — not sure.

"We are existing within both worlds. Like the amphibians. We are in our world. But our world co-exists with and in another world. Here, away from the reality of your home and work and Uncle and the mercenaries and the club — all that — here, you can become aware of the shimmer of the other world. Or at least you can become more attuned to that world — than you would be stressed and distracted by your life out there," he said waving a relaxed hand towards the wall. "You may, I think you will, but suffice for now to say, may make a life-changing reconciliation between the two worlds that are at war. At war within you of course — but more importantly, somehow make peace between these two worlds which will spread into a greater peace ... A regional peace. Maybe it will spread to mankind in general — peace on the earth."

Asaf thought for a little while. Still skeptical, but considering how polite and pressing the Prophet was, he said, "I have wondered about the two worlds. I have bitterness about the wars. The war inside. And the wars outside. My village is a wreck. It has had a time of peace lately. Probably because there's nothing left to fight over. Maybe you can understand why building the club was an excitement for me. But that's all over now. I'm sick of hearing about it. I'm sick of talking about it. I'm sick of thinking about it. I'm frustrated at being back as just a 'water-boy'. I feel trapped in a bombed-out village — 'podunk' — the Soldier called it. I know there is more to life than being a water-boy. But how to get there ... I just don't know. I hate the wars now more than ever. But I know there are two worlds. I know it. I've experienced it. but I'm not so sure how to talk about it so it makes sense. So, I'm curious of what you are talking about even though I don't know what it all means."

After a pause, the Prophet said, "The starting point for this discussion is the material and the non-material. Those are the two worlds. As a religious leader, it is my job to look after both worlds on behalf of our adherents, and those beyond our religion. As you know Asaf, our religion is a great one. The greatest there is. We have God's truth. That is, we have been blessed to have that truth revealed to us, given to us. This blessing also brings with it the burden of being the shepherd, the caretaker, and for passing it on faithfully. All this is in addition to giving, showing, and making known to the whole world, the truth. The truth of the Merciful One. We are told to bring the nations into obedience. We are commanded to bring the human race into submission. This is not easy. Satan tries to blind men's eyes. The world lures people with fleshly desires. Desires of impure sex. Desires of the temporary gratification perversity can offer; notwithstanding its evil serpent-bite afterward. Look at the drunkard. He is possessed by alcohol and takes it regularly to feel its effects, knowing all the while, it will bite him the next day. Look at the man who lusts and commits perverse sexual acts — and then is bitten with diseases. Look at modern society. Full of lights and sounds and all that is sensual. These things distract and detract from the peace and quietness of spirituality. We are charged by God to combat these evils in the human race by bringing them into the light of mercy. Some come willingly. Some have to be brought in, because they do not understand the peril they are in. Some of these are too blinded by perversion to even see or know good from evil. Such ones must be brought into submission by force; for their welfare.

"It is a serious responsibility. Over the centuries, there have been times when this responsibility has been discharged faithfully, and during other periods, not. There also have been times when our religion has blossomed and shown to all the glory of God and the blessing to witness the evidence that he has entrusted the truth to us. There have been challenging times. Times of war, times of trial, times of darkness and doubt. The enemies of the truth are everywhere, and they do not rest. There are demons who do not wish the light to be shown to the earth. There have been times when our enemies have cast us into the margins of civilization. But they have never prevailed. God cannot be marginalized. Asaf, are you following me? Do you have any questions?"

Asaf walked along. "When you say 'we' and 'our', who do you mean? Do you mean you and your followers? Do you mean more than just your particular group? Or do you mean all of us who have been born into our religion?"

The Prophet smiled serenely. "Asaf, it brings joy to my heart to be with you because you are bright and insightful. To answer your question, let me say 'yes' to all three questions. When I say 'we', I mean you and I and my followers and those of our faith who are not my close followers but still believe in God and the truth he has given us. When I say 'we' I am being inclusive. But there are those, like me, who have a special mission. Some receive the gift of the spirit of God in their lives in a special way. There have been such blessed men here and there over the centuries. They are beacons of light for their generation. Only because I am humble, can I fain to understand these matters. So, to answer your question, think of it as three circles.

"One, the largest circle, encompasses all mankind. Although maybe not religious at all, or of another religion, they are all heirs to the mercy of God through creation. To each individual is given an eternal spark by birth, by nature. This spark is mere wording. Spirit, soul, *nefesh*, breath of life. They are all components of the non-material part of man. I don't attach a lot of importance to what term one uses. Spark is the most worldly, so let it stand for those who are also most worldly. These have the furthest journey to the center of any, but are no less important, since ultimately God is their father too. The second circle are those who are part of our great faith by fate, from birth. Like you, your Uncle, your whole family, our neighbors, and so on. Adherents to all religions have the devout — and the nominal. So it is in our culture. We devout, bring those who do not participate fully in our faith, along the path of righteousness through our prayers, giving, and acts of mercy. We are here to set an example for the weak. The next circle in comprises those who strive to persevere in the faith. They exercise all the outward duties God expects of them. They are followers of the truth in word and deed. Finally, there is the middle, at the center of the circles. And in the middle of the center stands God's chosen one. Chosen from every generation, as I said.

"The great prophet to the Chaldeans wrote of circles in circles, wheels and wheels. These wheels within wheels are the interactions of the great groups of people with relation to the center of all the circles.

It is the center that draws them in, and orders their ways. It is for the center of the wheel to balance the entirety through the outward radiating spokes. That is why only one center is given to each generation. There cannot be two centers. One center; one span of time. All must be drawn to the center during each one's sojourn on Earth. And the Merciful One provides such a center to mankind, one generation at a time. Do you understand?"

"I'm listening," Asaf said politely. He was listening because he was interested in what this Prophet was explaining. Asaf felt he had better understand this whole scheme because he was growing more certain that all of this was not just for the Prophet's fresh air and exercise. Asaf took his culture's religion for granted. It just was. It wasn't something he thought about much. Not until the club heightened his awareness of the deep inter-twining of the culture and religion. Asaf's family followed their religion as was practical for their busy lifestyle. They also had a comfortable lifestyle and didn't turn to religion to assuage the sufferings of life. This, in turn, made them "part of some outer ring" Asaf thought with uncertainty.

Asaf stated his thoughts to the Prophet and wondered aloud about his family's standing in the circle of things.

"Asaf, do not think that the circles are something concrete or fixed. It is an explanatory device. These are generalizations, yet useful nonetheless. Your family, yes, could be categorized as belonging to the second or even third circle. But do not make the mistake of equating that with being bad or less worthy or anything like that. From my point of view, it is the less fervent that makes those of us more zealous, a necessity. We, the holy ones, are here because of the less devout. And we draw them towards the center, as I said regarding the spokes of the wheel. It cannot be the good fortune of all to be near the center, it is just the way of creation. And it is the burden of those of us at the center to carry the load of so many souls into the light of righteousness. Very few hear what you are about to hear. It is a deep thing, and must — can — only be poured into a deep vessel. So, I will say it plainly: I am God's prophet for this generation. I am at the very center of the wheels. I draw all to myself by being who I am. Not to me personally, but to the true exercise of the true faith. The eternal One has specific commands and instructions for the whole human race. And for this generation, he has chosen me to deliver his message, his commands, and his instructions. This includes how we should exercise our religion, in all its beauty and sublime subtlety."

14

THEY CONTINUED TO WALK, THE Prophet allowing his words to sink into Asaf's soul.

"Asaf," the Prophet ventured, "are you aware that the club is being rebuilt?"

Asaf looked wide-eyed at the Prophet. "How do you know that? Why do you know that? Is it true? I don't even want to know … Here we go. The club, the club, the club. I was hoping from our talk out here that we might have moved on. But I guess that is too much to hope for. I'm sick and tired of the club and all the drama surrounding it. I haven't been back to the site. My Uncle and I revived the water stand. Mostly because I had nothing else going on, and I believe my Uncle wanted to shake me out of any depression. Then the Soldier visits my stand; the first I had seen him since the fire. I know he is there for some reason. Not just to rekindle an old friendship. He doesn't need my friendship. He has all the friends he needs. I'm just his water boy. So we politely say hello. But before any further conversation takes place, your men show up and take over. I'm left standing in the street with two choices: I can go back to the water stand, and maybe back to the Soldier, or come with your men. I didn't have any big reasons to go back to the Soldier. I had come to a dead-end in my life. The water stand was just something to pass the time, and make some money. Your men made a good enough case for me to come see you, so here I am. I don't get all of what you want with me. Really the only reason I'm here is because I don't have much of a reason not to — and curiosity."

The Prophet stopped in his tracks. "Oh Merciful One! In truth, he would be no more than a water boy. Yet in thy divine mystery, perchance the living water will flow to the nations for peace. Once again, I put aside the contemplation of the eternal, to descend to one of his creatures, wherewith to enlighten him."

He sighed, lifting his eyes dreamily toward heaven. "Forgive me Asaf. It is the spirit that takes me betimes." He closed his eyes and began to whimper and lightly shake. Asaf stood still, not knowing what to make of this sudden behavior. When the whimpering stopped, the Prophet regained his normal composure, then continued with the conversation. "What I want to discuss with you is the location of the club. The location you and your mercenary chose, is of special interest to us. You see, broadly speaking, we can lump these groups which swirl around the center into three. We call them the Zealots, the Fanatics and the Radicals. They are all of the faith but vary in their adherence to the truth, the center. The Zealots, we can appreciate them. The Fanatics, we are not so fond of. The Radicals are of little concern for our purposes today. They circle in higher orbits. By happenstance, or circumstance or fate, whatever the case may be, it is possible that the areas under the control of these sectarians is very nearly equidistant from your club." The Prophet paused to see if Asaf was taking this in.

Asaf looked up and asked, "You mean the club is in the middle? really in the middle? between — in-between, these religious factions?"

"Yes, but not necessarily middle as in a geometric circle. But as a focal point or a fulcrum. Like a possible wedge for the faction who possess the edge of the village. It is the last spot on the last lane. Whoever holds that area can create a redoubt for greater strategic ascendancy."

"Well, why is that? I didn't pick out that spot. The Soldier did. Well, he sort of did. I guess we picked it out together. But it had nothing to do with getting in the middle of a spiritual turf war," Asaf said defensively.

The Prophet watched and listened carefully. He had to assess how complicit or innocent Asaf was in the whole thing. He needed to know or understand what factors there were in their decisions on where to build the club.

The Prophet asked, with a hint of suspicion in his voice, "Well now. Did you, or did you not help in choosing that spot? Or — did the mercenary lead you by the nose to that very spot? Were other neighborhoods in other parts of the village considered? Maybe different types of buildings or where they were located in relationship to the surrounding land? Maybe he led you to the club building without you knowing it. After all, you yourself said you were merely a water boy. How do you know if you were being led there? How do you know whether or not the mercenary had a plan to build the club right on the edge of town? And used you to further some nefarious plot? Beyond the bar is only waste, but it allows for a long view into the distance. Coincidence or strategy?"

Asaf was getting annoyed at these accusations but was not in the mood for continuing to defend himself. "I've thought about it. It is true, I cannot deny that maybe I was fooled by the Soldier. I don't believe so, but I'll play along for now. So on one hand, I can see that there may be something in what you say. Something of a plot on the Soldier's part. On the other — even though my feelings don't just go along with this bad acting by the Soldier — I'm still interested in listening. And I guess finding out how and why I may fit into your plans. But why is the location of the club so important? It's a bombed-out building at the end of the lane — at the edge of town. You've been there. Why can't these sectarians or the army or you or anybody just build a club or temple or anything else one more lot down the lane? There's a lot of empty dirt around there."

"Yes. I have been there. It is a good question — questions. Anyone could go to the edge of town and build something. The club came to be in an existing building. This existing building was taken over in an underhanded and secretive way. The military tells different tales on its origins. It was a cultural misstep in their plans, that they did not count on, that the religious conservatives in your village brought it to the attention of their regional leaders. They are either hiding something or truly ignorant. I grant they are ignorant in other areas, but that they have redoubled their efforts to salvage the club is extraordinary … And now it has taken on a life of its own. It has become an object of secret desire. Perhaps the viper is biting its own tail … "

"I don't understand," Asaf said.

The Prophet nodded. "I don't like to admit it, but because I have tried to be forthright with you, I must confess I don't fully understand it either. I have been lured-in just like other interested parties. When the local religious formed an unofficial action, there were waves made that got some interest in the sectarian hierarchy. The snake begins. Since none of these groups like each other, the one began to suspect the motives of the next and of the next and the next. Nobody could say exactly what and why the club's location was so important — but it had to be something. It was never a consideration that your Soldier and his comrades built the club in that old building for pure recreation.

It made no sense. And even if the idea was suggested, it was dismissed as impossible. These religious leaders do not understand how such a thing could happen. And I can understand why. That is, I can see why they don't believe such a club could rise into existence without official military oversight. So, each sect became suspicious of the other, thinking that they had the inside track on what was going on or were building a secret alliance. And since the club couldn't be just a place to drink beer, the only other explanation was that the military was putting its footprint on the village and the club was a pure front.

"On the other end of the snake, the foreign intelligence got wind of the sects' rivalry to know more about the club and its reason for existence. Then, they too began making the same mistakes as the sects. They had a hard time believing that the club was unofficial. In their suspicious minds, everything unofficial is code for official. When reports began coming in from this or that source, some or all of whom may have not known of the other's existence, that the sects were interested in the club, it became a self-fulfilling prophecy. It didn't matter what or why or how the sects were interested. Just that they were, was grounds enough to create some real or fake dossier. The logical circle was the same on both sides. One, the club is a front for unknown military purposes. Two, the respective enemy wants to know more about what the club is for. And three, if the enemy wants to know more about the club, then there must be more to know. So, the club's existence was then elevated on everyone's watch-list as an important asset or target of vital interest. And the more it's watched, the more interested parties want to get in on the watching. Mostly watching those who are doing their own watching of who is watching. It became lost in all the secrets being passed around that the real and original watchers just didn't like a bar in their village — pure and simple. On top of, or under all of this, is the idea or notion or discovery that the end of the village is the best place to have an establishment for a strategic triangulation of the three sects. No single sect could move into the village without arousing the interest of the other. So the military moves into the village under the noses of everybody by disguising themselves. It's a feedback loop. The village must be important, just like it was told."

They continued walking, each digesting this scenario and logic. The Prophet continued. "So we know the club is being rebuilt. Fine. However, it is being rebuilt by the military proper, not some renegades looking for a cheap party. And … and, it is being fitted with espionage gear. The secret service of the foreigners is taking an active role in the rebuilding. They are not doing the actual construction, but they are overseeing it. All of this heightens the interest in the re-building. The sects see the military double-down on its commitment to the old building. The regular military sees the intelligence's heavy-hand as a confirmation that it was a front from the beginning. What some, most, or all on both sides don't know, is why the edge of the village is so important to begin with. And that is what I want to know. I need to know what underlying factor makes one or another sect so keen on being in control of that area. I need to know because it is my obligation to know. It is part of my mission, as the center of the wheel, to be able to draw all things unto myself, for this generation."

The Prophet sighed. "So much of this is mundane. I have higher sights. I see in the other realm a divine plan for the bringing together of the sects for their salvation. I see the hand of God fanning the flames of peace between the sects, not the flames of war. The flames of war burn things down to ashes. The flames of peace burn away the dross of sin and leave pure silver or gold. This is the fire I am interested in. This is why I must be in the center of the new club. For peace. For salvation. So here is why we want you, my young friend. We want to know more about what these foreign devils are up to. And we need to have an inside track. And we think a way to do it is to participate in the actual re-building of the club. This sounds ridiculous. Or audacious. And it is! But we are determined to get in. And we think we have a way to do it. There are aspects of the idea that you don't need to concern yourself with. The council and I are doing our work. But you are the one person who can go in there and be our inside man. I know what you are thinking — Why me? That is easy to answer. You are the former manager of the club. You have all the knowledge, expertise and local contacts we want and need. And, now that I think about it, I would guess that the reason the mercenary was visiting you was to ask you the same thing — Would you come back and manage the new club? It's a perfect fit. It's exactly what we want! But they don't know what we do about these sectarians, therefore, their reasons for having you run the club may differ from ours. We want to make a strike at them!" he said loudly, smacking his fist into the palm of his hand. His eyes were fiery, but he quickly regained his composure. He was a touch nervous that he may have given Asaf too much information. He paused just a bit, realizing that the must maintain his aplomb. He did not want to alarm the young man.

Asaf, for his part, jumped and looked at the Prophet with wonder and surprise.

Without acknowledging his reaction, the Prophet went on smoothly. "You know Asaf, you are my brother. You are a brother to all my followers. And also a brother to the sectarians. You may not feel a kindred spirit with the sectarians, but you can say at least they come from your background and culture. And before you object, let me state, as I mentioned, that I too hold them at once at arm's length, yet at the same time I embrace them — imparting to them love and peace. And why not? God has called me to be a humble man of peace. He has given me his spirit, and with that spirit, I draw my wayward brethren to the mercy of God."

They continued to stroll, starting round the large enclosure again. A man came from the main house and approached. The Prophet stepped aside and the man whispered to him. The Prophet listened, then shook his head, patted the man on the shoulder gently and sent him away.

"Business, business," he sighed with a deep exhalation. "Ah, such is the life of God's calling. Always looking after the welfare of others. It is a heavy burden, but it must be done. No matter. Where were we?"

Asaf replied plainly, "The new club management and the sectarians."

"Ah yes, our wayward brothers in the great faith. So you see, even those with whom we do not see eye-to-eye on everything; they are still loved by the merciful One, and we are called to help them along in the faith. Asaf, I know you do not come from a religious family. I know you may not care for all this religious and spiritual talk. I see that you are on the edge of boredom. But I ask you to bear with me just a bit more. I am asking you to consider your life. Look deep within and ask yourself about life's meaning. Has not your Uncle conversed with you on this very matter? Have you not struggled, as we all do, with the meaning of life? I know you have, you need not reply. I understand. How much satisfaction does your involvement with these mercenaries give you? Yes, they pay you money. But how much good does that money do you when you approach the judgment seat of God? I can tell you the answer: none. None at all. All the money you get — some even call it filthy lucre — all that they give you is but a moth-eaten cloak or a rusted-out bucket when you approach the Holy One face-to-face. In light of these facts, I ask you to join me."

The Prophet stepped in front of Asaf and placed a hand on his shoulder. He looked into Asaf's face and searched it for a moment. "Join me in my crusade for a unified religion. Join me in shaping God's will that all his children become one under the banner of peace and humility. And, as I have told you, I am that man of peace and humility. We can use you as an instrument of righteousness. You can put yourself, through me, into the merciful bosom of God. I am not asking you to become a Zealot or anything. I like your simple approach to life. I understand your background. I don't feel there is a need to change you. God will do that for us. But, I am asking you to be our eyes and ears in this new den of evil. We must keep abreast of what the enemy is doing and saying. And, before you protest, I also am aware of your loyalty to the club … or what was the club. I know you were close to the mercenaries there. I know you feel great loss in all this. But what I offer is a way to make sense out of this tragedy. To make sense out of your own life."

They continued their slow walk. An old bird's nest had fallen to the side of the path. The Prophet picked it up. The nest was infested with bugs. "Look now, the foreign military has taken over your club. They are building it on their terms; for their reasons. At least the old club served the common man in his need or desire for amusement, evil as it may have been. But we allow for that, even while we pity them. Now, even the least of good reasons for the club to exist has been snatched from under you. You, who built up the business with your blood, sweat, and tears. I believe your sweat and tears were not shed upon the precious ground in vain. No! I believe they were nourishment for a future harvest of righteousness. That blood, your blood, shed by the broken glass or the slippery knife, is the same blood shed by the holy men of old. That blood cries out from the earth for vengeance and restitution. I believe the time has come for you to recognize the hand of God in all these mysteries hidden underneath the agonizing cry in the dark of night and the murky meanderings of the soul — Why!? Why, o God? why? do I work so hard for these foreigners? They do not love our land. They scorn our people. They murder them! … I know, Asaf, I know you can hear the whisper of a voice inside you. In another part of your heart that is there, but you have not attuned your ears, your spiritual ears, to listen to this faint voice. That inner voice which has become frail and weak with the empty food and drink of moral laxity. But you can change that. You can begin to listen to that voice within. You can cultivate that part of your soul which has become drowned out by the noise of the world. Look around you. This compound can be a garden for food, but a garden for the soul too. A garden to escape from the noise of the world. The noise of sin. I am not asking you to change the way you dress or the way you speak. I am not asking you to change your name or swear by anything. No contracts signed in blood. No. All I am asking is for you to seriously consider what I have said to you this day and return to your people and your faith. Return in a much more meaningful way than these outward showings which only please the self-righteous. You can join with me in your heart. It is a simple thing. Go along with the foreigners' plans for the new club. Be kind and understanding. But be observant and listen carefully. And all I ask of you is your loyalty in reporting to us what you see and hear. We are not asking for any action on your part. You will not be asked to do anything distasteful. If events happen from the sects you don't understand, things that seem out of line with the way of peace and humility, we on the council look after all this. You don't have to act as a go-between in the sectarian wars. Such things may happen because within the wheel there can be great mysteries. We will surrender such things to the will of the Merciful One. But I digress … Can you do that? Can you take hold of this opportunity to heal your soul, to bind up your broken heart? I know it will be healed, for you will be living according to God's will."

The Prophet stopped speaking. Asaf did not speak. They continued to walk. Finally, Asaf said, "Your words are deep. You go into things that I barely understand. But what I feel, what makes sense to me, is what you said about the bad feelings at night. I lay there looking up, in bed, but completely awake, and I cry. I wonder, what am I doing? This is difficult, it hurts … I never put it together like you have, that my pain comes from displaced, or misplaced efforts. That I spend my time and energy doing things that don't matter. Another thing you talked about, which I have thought about a lot lately is the gnawing in my heart about these foreign soldiers. When I first started with them, it was exciting. I was full of, full of... well, excitement. I looked forward to seeing what was next. My friends thought I was lucky. I gave many of them jobs at the club. My Uncle supported my new, budding career. And I was able to bring work and money to the housewives of the village. But, for all this, there was that doubt. That little voice inside sometimes. Well, it wasn't a voice, but sort of. It made me restless and doubtful. I couldn't understand that things seemed so good, then, when I was alone I felt so bad. I tried to ignore it but it wouldn't go away.

"Then there was a period where I felt torn in two. I had a long discussion about it with my Uncle. He tried to explain the two worlds. I found it hard to understand, I still do. But listening to you, it makes more sense. The way you describe these two worlds is easier to understand. But also more exact or precise. You say that one way to go is to follow you and God. And another way to go is not to follow. Pretty plain. But the religious side of all this is not something I have heard before. I mean, of course, I know about religion. But you talk about it so much. It's easy for you. And it makes more sense, especially when you talk about the pain inside. And I agree with you that these soldiers have no love for our land. I find it sad. We have an ancient and rich culture and heritage. But they never see it. They don't want to see it I guess. I don't know. The ones I'm around are the ones in the bar. They are not there to enjoy our country or our way of life. They are there to escape their own misery being away from their homes. In this respect, I understand their dislike for our ways. But to me, it is still sad. They drink beer and talk a lot, eat a few things, then leave. Once everybody is gone, we clean up, unattached and unappreciated by the soldiers we work hard to please."

They turned and walked to the cottage. The Prophet stepped to the door and motioned for Asaf to stay on the porch

When the Prophet came back out, he was wearing an expensive black cap with silk embroidery. The cap was not flat but rose up in the center to a filigreed point. At the sides and back, there were three gemstones woven into the cap. A single, large marquise-cut ruby was set in front. He held a bronze plate. On the plate was a bronze bowl filled with incense and matching spoon. Next to the bowl was a brazier with a smoldering charcoal. He picked up the bowl of incense, then extended the plate to Asaf, allowing him to take it. "Blow on that coal. Blow on it with your breath. Blow so it glows red," the Prophet commanded.

The Prophet took a generous spoonful of incense and showered it onto the hot charcoal. Instantly it snapped, crackled and popped. Then strong, sweet smoke came billowing up. The Prophet took his hand and wafted the column of smoke toward his face and inhaled deeply. He did this three times, took the plate, then motioned for Asaf to do the same. Asaf nodded and waved his hand hesitantly through the smoke and breathed in some smoke through his nose. The Prophet made a sign with his hand for Asaf to boldly waft his hands through the smoke and inhale deeply. Asaf tried again, but it wasn't enough to satisfy the Prophet. He reached out and took Asaf by the back of his head and pulled him down into the cloud of smoke and held it there until he could tell that the young man had inhaled deeply of the smoke several times. When he released him, Asaf stood up straight again. His eyes watered some, but he did not feel any sting. He could feel, taste and keenly smell the rich incense smoke that permeated his face. He felt a calmness come over him and a warmth in his blood. The Prophet took a large pinch of ashes and sprinkled them on Asaf's head. The Prophet made a large smudge on Asaf's palms. The Prophet placed his hands on Asaf's head. He lifted his face and closed his eyes. The Prophet began murmuring; then speaking softly and unintelligibly. His hand gently shook and vibrated.

The Prophet's shaking stopped. He calmly gathered his sacramental vessels and walked quietly into the cottage. He came back out, wearing his everyday cap. "You see this cottage. You see some of what is inside. Keep this in mind. One day, if you need to, you can come here."

The Prophet looked at Asaf, perhaps the way a father looks at a grown son, then spoke with an intense whisper, "Go back. Go back to the club. But this time your heart will be light. Your soul will not be heavy, for you will be doing God's will. You do not need to worry. Just do as I have told you. We will arrange the rest."

15

THE COUNCILMAN AND THE DRIVER brought Asaf back to the water stand. Asaf packed up his stand and rolled his cart back to his family compound. Without much thought, he scraped some ash with the tip of his finger and looked at it. He smelled it. Nothing remarkable. He leaned over and brushed the ashes off his head. He reviewed his visit to the compound and how strange it was. When the Councilman left him, the final word they exchanged was peace.

Peace. Asaf wondered what that word meant to him. As he looked at the water bottles in the cart, he recalled that he felt peace by the edge of the spring talking about life with his Uncle. Maybe returning to the place where he knew peace at one time, was a good place to go.

Asaf traveled at a leisurely pace. When he got to the spring, he off-loaded the side saddles and let the donkey loose to graze. He sat down and listened to the spring as he used to. He tried to just sit there and let whatever was supposed to happen, happen. After a while, he realized he was growing bored. He had never sat by the spring alone, with nothing to do. He and his Uncle always had things to talk about. Now he wasn't sure if sitting alone by the spring was as meaningful as he hoped it would be. He went back to the main path. Off in the distance, he could see his village. It looked small. He recalled when he was just a boy, his Uncle had talked about the origins of the mountains and how they were when they were new and not eroded. He turned and looked up the trail. He decided to go up the trail and see where it led. He had provisions, so was not concerned for his well being. He knew his way back to the spring, should he come to either a dead-end or just get tired of walking. After traveling further up into the lonely mountains, it grew dark. He stopped for the night.

The following morning he arrived at the top of the trail and the mountain pass. He proceeded along the pass until he could look at a broad, wide valley below. It extended as far as he could see. Silver ribbons of small tributaries flowed down into a river. There were scattered villages, surrounded by bits of green acreage.

He walked down to the upper reaches of the great valley where herdsmen and farmers had their seasonal outposts. He continued along the path which was growing wider and more used as he went. He arrived on the outskirts of the first small village, found a humble shop and bought some food. He asked the shopkeeper if there was a place to spend the night. The shopkeeper pointed out a large house further on.

The innkeeper was polite. "Where are you from?"

"I am from the other side of the mountains"

"Oh yes. We get visitors from the other side. Not too often. But once in a while."

Asaf talked with the innkeeper and asked him many questions about the valley. The innkeeper explained that there were few visitors because the whole valley was a long distance in every direction from any other place where people lived. He said the mountains were on one side and beyond the valley on the other side was just cold desert. The river was long, but shallow, and only small boats could navigate it. There was enough fertile land to sustain the current population, but not much more than that. This made it an area that was uninteresting for outsiders. Asaf asked about the wars. The innkeeper told him there was nothing to exploit. There were no natural resources. The people who lived in the valley naturally kept to themselves. Most of their day was taken up in herding and growing food. For these reasons, the foreigners did not bring their military and troops to the valley.

Asaf spent many weeks in the large valley. He was interested in what the innkeeper had told him. To satisfy his curiosity he wandered the length and breadth of the valley. Everything the innkeeper told him was true. The people were peaceful and mostly attached to the land. The villages were quiet. The commerce served the needs of the inhabitants, and much of what they sold was produced in the valley. Asaf went as far as the great, cold desert. He hired himself out for manual labor and the donkey out for transport in exchange for homespun warm clothes. He made a sweeping loop back down to the river and followed it along until it became a marshy delta. He stopped when the marshlands became impassible and never learned how far the low, swampy water went before meeting the sea.

Asaf turned toward the mountains. He went back to the innkeeper. They talked about the valley. The innkeeper smiled. He was glad to hear that not much had changed in the far corners of the valley.

When Asaf was leaving the next day, the innkeeper stopped him. "My friend, we have talked much about this great valley. You have crisscrossed it on your own. You and I are in accord as to its nature, both in the people and its geography. But we have not talked about where you come from. That is, I know you came down the mountain pass. But for all our conversation, we have not talked about where you are from and what it is like. Also, I have been curious about why you came into our remote place. Am I being presumptive or intrusive by inquiring of these things? I do not wish to pry into your business. You are friendly. I do not sense bad nor evil in you. I also would guess that my questions do not bother you. Is this true?"

Asaf laughed at the innkeeper's perspicacity and answered with a compliment. "True and true. Well, at least the second is true. I don't mind you asking anything you like. I am glad that you think there is no bad or evil in me. I don't think I know exactly what you mean by that — but I think it is a good thing, right?"

The innkeeper laughed. "Of course it is a good thing. We who were born and raised here are plain-spoken. We have nothing to hide, so we just talk about what is on our minds. This does not make us all good people. We argue and disagree about all kinds of matters. But by and large, we try to speak the truth. So my questions and opinions are from inside. From my heart, nothing more."

Asaf grew serious. "I hope what you say is true. But you may have misjudged me. In my village, I am considered both bad and evil. Or at least many people think what I have done is evil."

"I find that hard to believe. Many of us know one another here. I am not a spy, but news and reports have dribbled in, here in the village, about you and your travels hither and yon. None of these reports tell of this evil or bad you refer to."

Asaf was quiet. At length, he said: "It is a complicated, very complicated story. I know you have the time and patience to listen to the story — not just my story — but all that surrounds my story. But I am not sure it is what I want to share."

The innkeeper waited for Asaf to go on, but when he saw Asaf remained silent, he said, "Allow me to divine some more. Perchance this evil you speak of is circumstantial. Maybe you were young and naïve. Maybe you were eager to do something or make something or be part of something that was bigger than you and it caught you from behind and bit you. In any case, you have walked all over our valley and the reports are consistent. Also, you are correct, I have the time and aptitude to listen to your complicated story. But I will let it be. What about our other 'true'? Can you spend whatever time you are comfortable with in telling me some of your native land? I do not believe it is so far away that I cannot fill in the blanks where they may appear in your recital. I say this to give you the freedom to add or subtract from whatever you have to say."

Asaf paused, gathering his thoughts. "My story can be told most simply by one word: war. I am young and all I have known is war. In my short life, I haven't seen armies clash in front of each other. That is a battle right there, to see with your own eyes. But my whole world had been done over by war. My village is bombed. There are buildings all over the place that are abandoned. There are rubble and trash all over. Broken stuff everywhere. There are women and some older men and boys but few men. I was a boy. I lived and learned on the street corner selling water. Don't get me wrong, our village is still a village. We have shops and houses. A neighborhood here, a neighborhood there. We eat and drink and live. But all mixed in are the broken and bombed buildings and houses. And our people are broken too. We have lost our spirit mostly. Not all, but a lot. Our streets have foreign soldiers making their patrols there. These soldiers bring a quietness to the neighborhoods. They make it so you can walk around without getting shot by someone around the next corner. But it isn't what it should be with our own people living together with each other in peace … Peace. What a word. I have a lot to say about peace."

The innkeeper saw the sadness come over Asaf when he mentioned peace. "Tell me about peace, and what it means to you."

Asaf sighed. "I am not sure what or how to say it. Do I know about peace? Do I know what it is? I think it is when there is not war. But if there is not war, does peace exist? Does it exist just by being there when war is not there? Doesn't that make peace like air? or space? … or an empty room? Really empty of everything? Bed, other furniture, books and pillows and pictures on the wall. Isn't that what the specialists call a vacuum? Not the kind you suck up a floor with. But a space with nothing in it. I don't know exactly what a vacuum is — but I think it is something like where there is nothing. Does that sound right?"

"Yes. I think you can say a vacuum is a space with nothing in it."

"Well then, peace is not a vacuum where there is no evil. If there is no evil, then it is a place where there is no evil. It is not a place where there is peace. Peace is something. It is more than not war. Or not evil. Peace is its own good thing. Its own positive. Its own goodness and calm and … and some … some feeling of more than just not fighting. What are the words? Like love, but different. Warmth, self-control or confidence. Feeling good about … about your inside. Like in your heart, your mind. I think people think peace is like a still pond or lake with no ripples. But my sense of peace came from being near an active little spring, the one where I got my water. My Uncle and I. It was never still, but it was peaceful. So peace is a sort of stillness, but not complete stillness. I guess that tends more toward the vacuum. You can hear the inner voice, or the voice in your mind running and running on. And it is not still. But the on-going running in the mind can exist in peace, or it can be all troubled. I guess a living spring could turn into a raging flash flood. One is peaceful. One is destructive. But inside in parts of your body, you can feel peace. When you can breathe easy and swallow and your hands are just like every day. But when your chest or throat is tight and dry and feeling pressure, I don't know if it's war or evil, but it feels bad. That is 'not-peace' … And then there is the peace around you. Like right now, there is no real fighting in my village. And, as I said, soldiers aren't shooting each other. It's not dangerous to walk almost anywhere in the area. Or at least around all the parts of the village. But it is not a peaceful village. We don't have peace. Because we are not in control of how we do things and live our lives. We still live with foreign soldiers every day. I mean they aren't running all over our houses all the time. And I think they are trying to be nice. But for all that, they carry big guns — guns that have real bullets in them. And they will use their guns if they have to. I know that for sure.

"So there is a sort of calm in my village. But like a big patch of sand dunes, the calm can go away in an instant when the wind comes. I think the calm can go away in an instant too. So the calm isn't peace. There are neighbors and friends and families that do things together. Plain things like a picnic. Or playing instruments. But all the time this is going on, everybody knows it could end suddenly, that same day or night or whenever. So while you are enjoying your picnic or music together, you aren't freely enjoying it like if there weren't armies ready for real shooting and bombing. I know of places that friends of my family have told about where the bombs came from so far away and so fast and sudden that nobody knew anything. Everything just was normal and then it was all blown up completely. Just like that. Dead people, all sorts of people. And fallen in roofs and walls. And people screaming and crying and blood. So the calm isn't peace. And the calm isn't peace inside either. Who can have peace inside when the calm outside could come to an instant end with a bomb you never see or hear and you can do nothing about it? Just swoosh and boom. You and the block around you are gone. This is how it is where I come from."

The innkeeper truly wanted to hear more, so at the risk of not being as polite as he normally would be, asked, "What did you do to give you the reputation of being bad and evil?"

Asaf wondered whether or not it mattered if he told his story. He remembered his Uncle taught him he could not escape his past. "I went into business with the foreign soldiers. It was a business that only the soldiers would have. It was a business that was considered evil by my countrymen. And because it was considered evil, I too was, or am, thought of as evil."

"Should I ask what this business was?"

"That business is closed now, so I guess it doesn't matter. Or does it? The business has tainted me and I don't like that. I'm not sure I want to bring that reputation over here in your peaceful valley."

"Could it have been that bad?"

Asaf answered, "No. No, it was not that bad. In fact, I did not, still don't, think it is, or was, bad — or evil. That's why I think I used the word 'taint.' It had touched my life in a way that makes me seem different to some than I really am. I think there is a difference between real evil and what some think is evil in their minds for whatever reason. I don't know. I do know — first hand -- that although there are things about this business that can make people think of it as bad, it isn't really. Maybe in some parts. But the business we ran, in our simple way, didn't harm anyone."

The innkeeper thought a minute. "I would like to know more. But I have pried into your life enough. At least on this business business."

They both laughed at this last sentence.

"Allow me to go on just a bit. I see well enough that you don't want to talk in more detail about this. So I will desist from more interrogation on this matter. What I am still interested in is the other half of my question — what about the where? And the why? We don't get too many visitors who just stroll into our village alone. Especially with apparently no agenda — or reason for coming here. My curiosity gets the better of my discretion."

"Your curiosity is just fine with me. I know you mean well. The answer is still the same. War. I come from the other side of the long, narrow pass above your village. When you go over, my country is the first you come to down at the foot of the mountain range. Why am I here? When there was fighting in my village, my business was destroyed. At this point in my life, I have nothing directly in front of me that takes up my attention. Nothing that makes me do something right now. I don't have a job. My family is secure. What's left of it. I earned enough money to give me some freedom to do things I wanted to. And, I guess walking over here is what came to be. When I hear myself talk like this, in answering you, it sounds stupid. It makes me embarrassed. I'm a hard worker. I feel I am honest. But telling you that I am just wandering around doesn't fit, does it? Until now, I haven't thought of myself as a wanderer. But now, I guess that is what I am. But I have not been a bum or freeloader. I have tried to be a good person in walking through here … "

The innkeeper could see that this last bit of Asaf's story was troublesome to him. "That is good for today. I have pushed enough. I like you. It is the reason I ask. That is all. Don't over-concern yourself with being a wanderer. Even if you are — or maybe are or are not — it doesn't really matter. As I said, good reports have come in about you. None of them said you were a bum or a wanderer. So cheer up. It's ok. You're young. Everybody has a time of wandering. And who knows? Maybe you'll wander some more. Or, maybe this will be the one and only time you will wander. I can tell you this. I am an innkeeper at this edge of our realm. I see what happens here, one way or another. If, or when, you come back to this valley, this innkeeper will welcome you. And if any of your past troubles precede you, I will come to your defense regardless if you are present or absent. I don't need to do this. But I can in my position if I want to, and I think I will want to if needs be."

"That is very kind. Thank you."

The innkeeper saw that their conversation was coming to a natural end, so he just said, "Well my friend, I wish you safe returns, wherever that may take you."

16

As an unenthusiastic member of the bar reconstruction crew, the Soldier plodded to the end of the village on a semi-regular basis. One day, he finally saw Asaf, standing with the men who were looking over their drawings. When the Soldier went looking for Asaf at the new water stand, he noticed how Asaf had matured. Now, seeing him in the company of the tradesmen, he didn't look much like a simple water boy. He looked more like a full-fledged member of their circle.

As he approached, he saw that Asaf evinced no emotion. The Soldier did not know who did or did not have full disclosure about the circumstances behind the military's involvement in the construction, so he tried to present himself professionally. "Hello, Gentlemen. I see good progress here."

The foreman replied, "Yes. The construction is moving along as you can see," gesturing to the four corners of the lot.

With a minimal glance at the lot, the Soldier looked at Asaf. "Hello, Asaf. Helping the construction effort?"

"No, I am letting these skilled workmen do that," Asaf answered flatly.

The foreman asked, "Can I help you? Do you have a question?"

The Soldier answered, "No. Thanks for asking. I stay busy, and don't always have time to come over and see how things are going."

"Fine. If you need something we'll be here."

The Soldier addressed Asaf, "Asaf, can we talk?"

Asaf looked up. He did not want to appear rude, but he was also unsure where he stood concerning the Soldier. Without moving from the small table, he answered, "Yes."

"Maybe we can talk over here, or go for a walk."

Without taking a step, Asaf asked, "What do you want to talk about?"

The Soldier did not want to play a game of tag. He didn't want to match wits. He only wanted to see if there would be a way to have some sort of conversation with Asaf.

The Soldier took a deep calming breath. "I would like to discuss working at the new club."

"Are you going to be working at the new club? That's interesting."

"I wanted to talk about you — working at the new club."

"I didn't know I was working at the new club."

The Soldier was getting frustrated. He stood back, kicked a small stone lightly, looked at the sky, then at the building site, then the men at their charts. "How long do you think it will take to build this?"

One of the men stood up, thought a bit, nodding his head left and right. "We think we can get this done in about several months. Maybe longer. Maybe less." He waited for a response from the Soldier, and seeing none, turned back to the drawings.

For his part, Asaf did not feel he needed the Soldier's advice, support or employment. But, they had spent so much time together, that he couldn't just let this meeting end without some personal closure. "Would you like to see where the walls will be?"

The Soldier didn't want to appear desperate, so he played it cool, and answered in his own time. "I don't know if that's necessary. I think I can see it from here." Seeing the excavator, he said, "Tell me about the excavator."

Asaf understood the nuance of the response. "Sure. It looks like something worth looking at."

They walked together over to the machine. Asaf said, "These stakes show where to dig."

Feigning innocence, the Soldier asked: "What is the digging for?"

"There will be underground storage here. The temperature is cooler and more even. The tea-house will be able to have more space and keep things which need a cool, stable environment down there."

"That's interesting. A good plan. When will they be digging it?"

"I don't know. I am here for a look. Just to see what is going on."

Asaf's tone was aloof. It made the Solider uncomfortable once again. He was at a disadvantage. His life as a peacekeeper instead of a warrior never set well in his soul. At a loss for something meaningful to say he tried to find common ground. "I guess the military club renovation will start soon." It felt like the dumbest thing he had ever said.

"I find that surprising. It was not their's to start with. It was part of the village first. Then it was yours. Now it's a ruin. It's a long way from the base. You chose it because it was way off. On the edge of the village where you would not be bothered."

Asaf turned and faced the Soldier. Without trying to hide his cynicism, Asaf asked, "So tell me — why are they rebuilding the club?"

Asaf knew this was a key question as to why the Soldier was here and why he was interested in the building site. Listening to Asaf"s reasonings, the Soldier realized he was cornered. The Soldier did not think about the club's renovation in those terms. He was too close to the forest to see the trees. For him, he was following his duty. He did not expect to be asked so soon and so frankly the most obvious of all questions: "Why is the military doing this?"

He scolded himself for being caught off guard by something so simple. Not knowing just how to answer this plain question, the Soldier said, "The military can work in strange ways. Maybe better said, to use an old phrase which fits — they march to their own drumbeat. It is possible, very possible, that neither you nor I will ever know the full extent of the designs, imaginations, schemes, ploys, surveillance, conference calls, on both open and secret channels, that went into this. Not only in the decision to do this project, but in the vetting of it. I don't want to paint a dire picture. It can't be all bad. There has to be some silver lining to this cloud and … "

Asaf interrupted boldly, "This is all just words, words, words. I know you have your life and your lifestyle. Your duties and orders and all. You know what? We were friends and business partners. Evil came into our lives. It took away the good we had. I have moved on. I don't know if you have or not. It seems by the way you are explaining this situation is that part of you has, and another part has not. I don't know the future. I don't know about clouds or whatever slivers of lines. But here is what I would like from you. Tell me plainly what you know. Tell me why you are coming to me now, as well as back at the stand if that matters. I will listen, as long as it is not some deep mystery that I cannot understand or cannot be allowed to know about. I have a life to look after. Family for example. My mother is getting older. My family has come to expect me to do my part for our home. My people. I have to show some respect for our traditions — even if I am not traditional. The Prophet teaches a way of peace. I don't think it's wrong to stand for peace. All these things are plain and simple. Family. Community. A sense of belonging and well-being. I'm over here because I have been asked to give my ideas on the tea-house project. At least it is something we villagers can understand … I guess … Everything got really good, then really bad. Now is it going to get good? — or really bad? … again … ?"

Asaf paused. He did not plan on getting into the Soldier's face about these things, but they percolated up out of his soul. "Maybe I got too excited. Sorry."

"That's ok. I may not understand the particulars in your life, but I think I understand the generalities. I respect your position in all this. Here's what I can say. Not all of what I was saying was mere words words words. The military is weird, but it has some good people in it, like a lot of things. And you're right, I have my life, you have yours."

The Soldier paused and looked at Asaf, waiting to see if he had more to say. He nodded for the Soldier to go on talking.

"For their own reasons, the military has decided to create an outpost out of the old bar. When I say, 'For their own reasons', I'm not trying to blow smoke. They have their reasons, but some of the bigger-picture reasons are beyond my knowledge or caring. I'm not here to drag you into something you are not interested in. I am here because I have my orders to be a part of the team to open and run the bar."

Asaf cut in. "You keep saying 'bar', but you also admit it is an outpost. How should I make sense out of this?"

"It is both. It will serve the military as a small outpost. But it will also be a club, open — I guess — to the public."

"Why do you say I guess?"

"Good question," the Soldier answered. "I think the business of serving drinks — beer and booze that is — around here, seems bass-ackwards. But that's the idea, as far as I understand it. My guess is that it will serve as many soldiers from as many armies as it can."

"I don't know back-ad-words, but I do know about inviting someone to dinner then sticking a fork in their nose. We have a saying something like that, but I don't remember just how it goes. I would think the military would not want to start another fight down here. It seems stupid. What about this so-called outpost? Is there anything I should know about that? I have little understanding of military-style or how they do things like this. What will it mean for the club to be an outpost?"

"Another good question. For us, an outpost is like a fort that is run by and supplied by a base. Outposts are for geographical expansion or control of land that has strategic value and … "

Asaf cut in again. "What I want to ask is: what will the club be? What will it look like? How will the outpost part of it be? What does it do? Will it be a big place for soldiers to live? Will all sorts of guns and weapons be stored there? Before, we had a little bar. Some tables and chairs, all gathered up from around the neighborhood. We served drinks and some food. People sat around and talked. What will the new bar be?"

The Soldier took his time in answering. He wanted to give the right answer because it was a good, honest question.

Asaf began speaking instead. "I can tell by the way you are thinking, that there is something going on. Either you don't know, or you can't tell me. If you don't know some things that the military is planning for the new bar, that's too bad for you. If you can't tell me, that's too bad for both of us. And, now that I think about it, what do I care? We haven't even gotten as far as the reason why we're talking to each other. Before you go into … No, wait. Just let me know why you want to talk to me. Then we can go from there. If we can go from there."

"Good idea. One thing at a time. First, the bar will be reopened. Second, I am here to recruit you as manager."

"And … ?"

"And nothing," the Soldier said. "Are you interested in managing the new club, which will also be an outpost? Now you can ask whatever you want. I have given you the official reason why we are talking today."

"Official reason?"

"Official reason. I also am here on my own — as me. We had a long run of it together. And as you said — well said by the way — evil came and we went our separate ways. I wasn't happy then about what happened or how it happened. And I'm still not happy about what has become of our friendship since that day. That being said, I'm here to tell you, at the time, I was operating as the man I am trained to be. But on a personal level, I apologize for everything that happened that day, and especially how we parted. Better stated, how I left. So, whether or not you are interested in the new bar makes no difference to me. My apology is to you. As my friend."

Asaf was deeply touched. He had never thought that this would be a moment, nor how he would react should this moment arise. His mouth was dry and he had a big lump in his throat. His initial response was to try to cover up his emotions. But he had learned that this was ultimately futile. He had come to know that allowing his emotions to have their expressions were better for his heart. So he relaxed and allowed himself to feel the lump in his throat. He allowed his eyes to fill and overflow with tears. He allowed his breathing to become steady and less heaving.

It took Asaf a long time to compose himself. The Soldier remained patient and did not try to hurry him along.

After Asaf's tears had spent themselves and he wiped them away, after the lump had finally melted, and after his breathing was normal, he looked up at the Soldier. "Thank you. Thank you for your apology."

Asaf and the Soldier talked about the old club, the new bar, and tea-house. Asaf said, "I think this kind of talk is good. Just the talking itself is its own goodness and light and healing. My Uncle and I talk often about making sense out of things. Things that are not easy to understand or to deal with. That is, things that are hard or painful. He teaches that we have to find a way to put things in context. I have found out that just trying to make a context for something doesn't change it. Maybe that's why we have become friends. You are here, a long way from home, among a people you do not know or share much in common. So you have to try and make sense out of that. For me, I am caught between my country and people, and the military. My future selling water was no future. Many start with a little trade, then time begins a hard-scratching race with you. The weeks and months and years go by, and there you are selling all that street stuff. And what do you have to show for it? Brown skin, wrinkled face and hands, some coins in an old box. You're dependent on the family if you have one. I'm lucky. I have a good family. Now, I have experience running a bar. Now I am asked to run a tea-house. I can take my money and create a life. I can have something to offer a wife. I can have something to offer my friends and community. This is not the final answer to all our questions about life, but it is one I can live with for now."

The Soldier listened. He wanted to be polite or empathetic but was not completely sure if Asaf's speech was good, bad or made any difference. He wanted Asaf on board because he was a good bar manager. He was not concerned about how much Asaf wanted to be paid. Without him, nobody would get paid. For all Asaf's talk about the meaning of life, the Soldier wanted to move on with the new bar. "I appreciate what you have to say and I see what you mean about different lives and cultures. My training has been to do my duty. The General has made a good enough case for me to follow him on this bar. And there's pressure from another part of the army that is pushing me in the same direction. It's complicated. Sorry."

"Hold it," Asaf protested holding his hand up. "Didn't we talk about what you know and letting me in? I'm not sure we understand each other. It makes me uncomfortable where part of the story is 'it's complicated, sorry.' I need more than that, or I won't sleep tonight."

"Sorry. It was more like me thinking out loud than anything else. There's nothing to hide. Just the inner workings of the military. I made my report to the General. He said he knew about the club and didn't care, but because of the incident, and the scandal it caused, he was obligated to tan my hide. At the end of our meeting, he sends me over to Intelligence, who through their officers, give me orders for the new bar. The General and I are on the same side, not liking what happened to the old club, but liking even less the construction of an outpost directed by the spies. There. Any better? It gets murky when divisions operate independently from each other and give what seem to be conflicting orders. Then, the General decides to make the bar a money-making business, figuring the spies can't do anything about it. Or might not even care. He ropes me in with this scary idea. I know if I don't join him, somebody else will. So now I'm here under orders from the military to build an outpost, and from the General to build a real business."

They walked slowly along the far side of the road. Asaf said: "That's a ghost snake-trail to follow. I don't have your experience and background, so maybe this isn't as stupid as it sounds, to someone like me."

The Soldier wanted to comment on the insightful and accurate 'stupid' reference, but he let it be. "You see, I wasn't trying to keep you in the dark. I wanted to preserve your sanity from all the military bureaucracy. To be honest, neither the General nor I could do this half-baked idea without you. Presuming you say yes, we will have a sit down with the General where we can put together some details and plans. I forgot to ask. Do you know the General?"

On the back patio, the General gestured for Asaf to have a seat. He let the Soldier choose where to sit — or stand if he liked. The General waved his guards at ease. "No need to watch around too much. This here whippersnapper is our guess-who."

The guards sat at their customary table and pulled out a deck of cards.

The General beckoned to his staffer. "We'll have the usual hosbipalleties," he said with a knowing wink.

"What'll it be Schnappie? That's short for Whipper Snapper. Whipper Snapper is too long to say. I mean really. Whip-er-sna-per. Who wants to say whippersnapper all day? Whippersnapper. Whippersnapper. Whip out yer tongue and snap it off for all that of it."

"Sir," the Soldier intervened, "his name is Asaf."

"Ass-aft. Got it. Like a bum in a wringer and that," the General replied with a smile. "Boys, what'll be your pleasure? It's on me today." The General laughed at his attempt at humor. The guards and the Soldier rolled their eyes drearily.

"Iced tea for me. Half-mast, what'll it be? There's plenty o'hospitableness for all here. Soldier?"

The Soldier looked over at the staffer. "Beer."

The staffer looked over at the card table. The guards made mocking faces of the General, forcing the staffer to scowl in frustration. They waved him off, they would get whatever they wanted later. The staffer turned his attention to Asaf. Asaf looked at the Soldier. "Just tell him what you'd like to drink."

"That's right Half-caste, anything you want. Now, remember what I always say … "

At this point, two guards started mouthing in unison with the General. "The shadow has cast the yard marm somewheres," and then looked over his shoulder: "Ain't that right boys?" In unison, the guards drearily responded, "Yessir, General, Sir."

Asaf said, "In that case, I would like a Vesper on the rocks."

The General, who was minding his own business fetching a snipper out of his pocket to cut a fresh stogie, fumbled the cigar on the ground. "Ho, ho, ho and a boggle of rum! Did you say a Vesper? On the rocks?"

"I did."

"Staffer!", the General bellowed, "Gordon's, Smirnoff, white vermouth, rocks. Double-time!"

"Sir!" the staffer replied with pizazz.

Asaf looked with suspicion at the General as if to question or doubt him.

"What?" the General said with a surprised look.

"I thought I heard you say 'white vermouth'."

"Rightee-o Buckle Slapper," the General replied with pride.

Asaf parlayed, "I believe the Vesper calls for Kina Lillet."

The General took this moment of uncertainty to retrieve his fallen cigar.

Asaf, seeing that he had the General by the tail, went on, "However, since true Kina Lillet is rare, or perhaps impossible to come by, I have learned to make do with Lillet Blanc."

Quietly noticing that he had everyone's attention, after a pause, Asaf continued, "But, we are in a dry climate here. There is no need for quinine. So, the taste for it has lapsed too. Maybe you, or your men, can inform me about the greater world. Whether or not Lillet Blanc is a true substitute for the original Kina. I do not know. In my interpretation, I have found that zesting a lemon and a lime, still with a bit of the white attached to the zest, adds flavor to the mix. It adds just that touch of bitterness you know. Maybe bringing it back some to the original."

Turning to the Soldier, Asaf asked, "What do you think?"

The Soldier, seeing that Asaf was showing off, but not wanting to make it seem that this was unusual, simply said, "I pretty much stick with beer."

Asaf nodded and turned to the General. "General, Sir, I appreciate your hospitality. If you do not have the ingredients for a Vesper, that is not a problem. I am sure vermouth will do."

"Thank you. Thank you kindly-gums."

The staffer went away. The General looked at the Soldier and said, "Son, I do believe Haz-mat here is the gofer-dofer ta dong." Looking at Asaf, he asked, "Cigar?"

"No thank you."

The staffer returned, set the large tray on the table and stood back to see what would happen next. The Soldier picked up his beer, stood up, took his chair and skooched back from the table, so as not to crowd in. The General poured himself a tall glass of tea. Realizing his faux pas, being so readily greedy to make himself a selfish and indulgent high-ball while ignoring the bottles he ordered for his guest, quickly set the tea down. Then, just as quickly, picked it back up, tossed the tea and the ice over his shoulder and set it back down with a bang on the table.

He then grumbled and mumbled to himself and began fiddling with the bottles which clinked and clanked against each other.

"Ah, here we go," he said, only half-sheepishly. He winked at his guards who just shook their heads, not hiding their amazement and shame of their boss.

The General took the now empty highball glass and tossed in a big handful of ice cubes. At this point, one could see that he was a bit shaky, both physically and mentally. It had been a long, long time since he had ever attempted to make a mixed drink other than swilling into his tea or mouth, generous plops of the most recent brown liquor that found its way to the inside of his hip flask.

An ice cube jumped out of the glass when the General jiggled a bit.

"Sir, may I?" Asaf said politely.

"Ah yezzuh Azzah," the General answered in a low voice.

Asaf looked over to the Soldier. The Soldier shrugged his shoulders. Asaf slowly stood up and walked over to the staffer. He whispered in the staffer's ear, who nodded affirmatively as he listened. The staffer then turned and left. When he returned, he had miraculously assembled a lemon and lime, a zester, a cocktail shaker, two martini glasses and a shot glass, all on a tray.

Asaf took the shaker and filled it with ice. With a practiced hand, he measured out one, two, three, four shots of Gordon's gin, followed in quick succession by one, two shots of Smirnoff. He then picked up the vermouth, opened it and carefully tipped in one, two capfuls. He placed the two martini glasses in front of him. Holding the fruit over the glasses one at a time, he took the zester and cut deep spiral gouges allowing the oil to spray on and into the glasses. He let the ropes of rind fall off the zester into each glass, forming nice-looking loops of green and yellow. He took the shaker and gave it a long, vigorous shake. "I thought since you were kind enough to provide the necessaries for a proper drink, I would forego the rocks and pour us a matured, well-shaken, frosty. This allows some of the ice to melt, and the heavy shaking adds that drinkability which I call, a frosty. But the Soldier tells me that is a word for ice-cream too."

Asaf uncapped the shaker and expertly poured out two gin-vodka martinis with a double twist of lemon and lime.

Later, when they were alone, the Soldier brought up the subject of the basement excavation.

"There's not alot I can dew about it, Son. It's their gig. I'm being assurified that it is for orin muddled benefits."

"Excuse the informality but, jeepers creepers, Sir. I ..."

The General interrupted. "Soldier, long story, shorthair, the Rubeicon has been circumcised. In for a Pfennig, in for a furlong. We'll do our bidness as bests we can. Earn the brash cash stash and cross our fingers or hearts and hope not to die."

17

THE INTELLIGENCE OFFICER CAME INTO the General's office and closed the door. "We never thought this idea of teaming up with the Prophet and his camp was a good idea. Now here comes a boomerang as in a basement to boot. We don't like it," the intel officer said.

"Why not?" the General inquired.

"We just don't like it. We see no advantage in bringing a potential hostile into such close proximity. We have a legitimate illegitimate underground operation to launch. We are just getting our bearings. We see this whole idea as a threat. Now, we hear that part of your scheme includes doubling the square footage of the basement to accommodate these plans."

"Well now," the General replied, "that's a particular which I may or may not be able to comfort or plausibly defy. The parcel behind the club is owned by the Prophet. There is strong support among the communityhood for his plans to open a tea-drinking joint in our backyard. I'm not conveened there is much we can do about that. We are not real estate brokers. This is their turf. We just happened along through a sideways roguish tippy-toe through the tulips into their patch."

The intel officer narrowed his eyes at these last words. It was part of his training to look like he was on the low-down with the details of his assignments. He quickly assumed that the General was using some code words he had not been briefed on. He decided to proceed assiduously, hoping he might understand some of these more cryptic references. He would move the conversation along until he could discern what the General was getting at.

"From what I understand," the intel officer replied, "and mind you, I am not a real estate agent either, but I was given the impression that this area was a no-man's-land. Then, it seemed there were other interested parties in some possible urban development plan fostered by a neighboring province. Not to be blunt or plain-spoken, but the intrigue caught up with our … well, let's just say, Harry's Bar. We had to take some matters into our own hands. But we seem maybe, or maybe otherwise stated, that the shoe was put on another foot. If you know what I mean. But we were disappointed in the turning tide. Now this ocean bottom. Be that as it may be, in the out of the going in and on, in my job, it's easy to intimidate as a means to an end. We didn't not resort to any such measures but were only prepared to. One has to be careful to not let the means become an end in itself. It becomes sort of a subliminal personality trait. Your openness in this matter has calmed my mind. Thank you."

The General looked to each side of his desk. He then glanced over his shoulder, wondering if he was being addressed, or if there was someone else in the room. Not seeing anyone, and not quite understanding all the intimidation subliminal mind-calming stuff, said, "Well you know sir, I do what I can for the couch-slouchers. Why I dreamed of old Freud myself once. He came to me, like that old shaky-chains in Dickens. He came to me and said, all spooky like, he said: 'Don't interpret this dream. It's only a dream. You will find meaning in it if you look hard enough.' Blimey, that was all Christmas cookies and rum punch. But never mind. My brother-in-law did some poking around in the housing market. I think he got onto one of those hackem-sackem no-money-down deals. Never heard what came of it. I think he finally scored it in some flap-jack joint. Dunno. I told him clearly: 'Don't go where the foot has not trod on the Ides of March, nor any other month on the Mayan mosquito coast calendar.' Don't think it could have been said any more straight forward than that. These sidewinders are just plum over it sometimes."

The General sat back in his chair. "So, since we're having this sort of busy-mess meeting, mind if I fire up one of my Indonesian hound turds?"

The intel officer looked with bewilderment at the General, who was briefly preoccupied with his cigar ritual. Then, he too looked around the room, wondering if it was he whom the General addressed, or another person, or even a specter. Not seeing anyone else, he decided to get the conversation back on track, even if that spur was only a trace in the sand. "You are a military man. Do you think it is wise, or possible, or recommended to secure a perimeter around the club?"

By now, the small bonfire at the end of the cigar had died down and peering through the blue haze, the General answered, "Possible yes. That's for sure. Or darn tootin', as some say. Recommended, not so darn tootin'. Wise, no."

The intel officer sat waiting for a further explanation, mentally steeling himself for come-what-may out of the General's mouth. He was still not certain whether or not he was sufficiently briefed with the codes for this operation.

The General, for his part, was leisurely contemplating the cigar's grey and red tip, as if seeking therein portent or powers that the coming ashes would be longer than however long a good cigar ash could or should be, and sign themselves of what may or may not come to pass at some unforeseen time in the future or déjàvuistic past in his current present.

He then noticed that the intel officer was silent. He had a combination of fear and dislike for spies in general. He didn't want to step too heavy on their toes. And being a little uncertain as to the proper protocol in these delicate negotiations, assumed a passive demeanor.

Finally, the intel officer continued in a hesitant cadence, "So … you don't think it's wise, shall we say … a possible recommendation … to secure a perimeter?"

The General was still mentally dancing around the possible directions the conversation could go in. "No."

The intel officer was hoping for more than that. Usually, he was in control of the agenda and dialog. He belonged to intelligence. He was used to moving in and out of situations with impunity. Here, in the base commander's office, he was not quite sure of his standing in this unusual situation of building an outpost like the one they were supposed to be discussing.

Deciding to play it safe, rather than throw his weight around, he said, "General, I respect your authority here, as well as the position you are in regarding this club. So here's what I'd like to do, to proceed."

The General pulled a flask out of his drawer and took a casual sip. He puffed his cigar, then waved it at the intel officer, indicating for him to go on talking.

"We will defer to your side of things regarding the club's building and physical plant. We will likewise defer to you on this new adjacent building. We feel we have bent over backward so far. Now, this underground project is truly beyond the pale. We don't like it. We feel that it is more or less a monkey wrench in our operation. However, we can't control everything. We would like to maintain good, open and honest channels of communication, above board and all. Cards on the table. In light of this, we would request that this conjoined enterprise not only be thoroughly vetted from your side but kept under physical surveillance via your staff as well. I don't need to tell you that we have and will continue to exercise due diligence in these areas as well. I mention the physical side because you have many more resources to deploy in this regard than we do. In fact, our deployment of really anybody but a nominal contingent is about as much as we or you can expect. Our opposite number's numbers are numerous. Say, voluminous. Our assets, merely meager. We act sentinel on every side, so it is only common-sense reality that the division of labor is divided disinterestedly. And while we're on the topic, regarding what I just said about open honesty and such, I must also make you aware that not all of our nominal personnel will always be identifiable. That would be, at the very least, an absurd betrayal of all that we are. It would furthermore undermine the very thing we are there for. So, I will do my best to keep you apprised of our goings-on. But only to the reasonable limit of what is necessary for us to continue to function properly. Which means you may or may not know who we are or what we are doing. Does that sound equitable?"

"Sure," the General said, sucking more booze out of his flask.

"Anything else?"

"That's a good question." The General had no reason to tell the spies one thing or another. He didn't know what they knew or didn't know. Combined with his length of service and apparent mutual understanding with the Prophet, he felt that he was not in a situation that called for a cat and mouse routine. "All else being equal, I understand what you are saying regarding the human and physicum nature of your messy, busy bidness. So, let's move on. Tell me more about this other basement that you and I are hearing about?"

The intel officer calmly said, "You tell me."

"Ok," the General started out, "I am not really interested in the whole club thing. That is well known. I am a Gary team Player, however, and will do what needs deeds indeed needs to be done to make a *semper virilis* of this outpost — as it seems to be called now. I was a gonna say taking an amateur cephalopod to the monied level, but I digress ... I know we need to stay clear of you guys, in the right mannerisms. We're all used to that. I can also keep my men under control in this area. Many are young and or inexperientiated. They get all macho and swagger and stuff. So I can put the bifurcated breakfast citrus in their face on all that egg yolk. And our side, the physical plant — as you say — we're down diggity there too. I mean, really … what the heck are we playin' marbles out there for? — if it is not to protect those little fellers tween and twixt our own massive masculine thigh joints? The bag can get a hiccup here and yon. But overall it's the catcher in the rye that has all that protective gear from his wazoo to the topknot of his granny's bloomers. But that still does not nail down this unnergroun' run-aroun'. For my part, I basically signed off on the tea-house deal. I don't mind confiding that to you, because although my gulliver can go all gimble-like, it doesn't mean I can't make a deal with the devil in the pale moonlight. Now you're an intellimint intellimince man, so I ask you: Do you think it is wise, or possible, or recommended to secure a perimeter around the club?"

The intel officer looked at the General. He was not sure who was asking whom. He waved the cigar smoke away from his face a bit, and asked, "Hey, you got any more of that hooch you're swillin'?"

"Pard," the General said with a twinkle in his eye, "I thought you'd never ask. Let us … Nay … may we, the devil's own duo launch forth, or shall we say, sally forth, to yon sideboard and partake us of some sophisticated libations. We can slay the planet of her voracious vocabulary by imbibing the not-innocuous distillates of the fruited plain. The downward-ho of the jimmy-jum rum shall not abstain us from the jolly-roger of getting all poop-decked ere the tale splint of the sandwich-island blows and knocks us hither and furthermore thither into the wanton wonton soup in disparaging despair.

"Disguise: thee.
Not despise: me.
For I wink at your ways and would you at mine.
Sojourners we two,
for the cold or the flu,
perhaps the gimlet, martini,
margarita or Manhattan will do.
These sorrow-furrowed brows
shall take their repose
in the balmifying quiescence of gentlemanly drinking — just fine."

The intel officer looked at him with admiring eyes and said, "Sir, I perceive you might be Pascal's own reincarnated brain-bake."

"Yeah, I know," the General replied to the intel officer, "But what's a guy gonna do?”

18

ANOTHER HAUNT "SEGURIFIED" BY THE General was a fruit and vegetable shop that opened once or twice a week. He bought out the entire remaining inventory "near as cain bee to the clock-tale hour." His overly generous payment pleased the older couple and assured them that none of their produce would go to waste for the fulfillment of a not too onerous request of a blender, some ice, and privacy. The blender was easy. Closing the shop was easy. Ice, not so easy. But they found a way to keep the General happy. What the General didn't know was they sourced the ice from the club. It was the only gig in the whole region with a ready, steady supply. When the lead bartender asked them about their weekly purchase, they gave a straight and honest answer, which made the General's hideaway about as hidden as the sun at noon. The Prophet didn't go in for the Bacardí, Sailor Jerry's and Myers's "My Ties", but developed a fondness for what the General taught him about "smoochees" laced irregularly and haphazardly with "mountain corn-nectar." The General thought he was doing great international commerce by trading chocolate for this opiated, hallucinogenic, moonshine distilled by some tribes up in the mountains.

"I just want you to know my friend, I have to put myself tween you and the spies. They already don't like this arrangement from the get-go. And they are hissified that you are diggin' a basement under the tea-house. Can you help me out in selling this splintered chicken bone to their maw-paws?"

Not knowing exactly what to say, the Prophet only stared blankly at the General. To break the silence, he said, "General, we both know this is a delicate situation. However, we both must do our part. I — I am on a spiritual mission. My mission is vital to the redemption of our people, and ultimately the whole world. I cannot vouchsafe that we will see this consummation in our lifetimes. But we will have our hand on the crook, guiding mankind as we can. I speak this more regarding myself, but you too, as God's creature, are instrumental in bringing this to pass. Just as a boulder or tree trunk causes the goats to yaw left or right as they walk."

This last reference was lost on the General who was busy lighting a cigar.

"Goats you say," the General said, a big cloud of cigar smoke obscuring his face. "Don't have much truck with 'em. My neighbor had one or two. They smell bad and their milk tastes like a goober of diesel lollytropped in it. I do like it though when they get perched for all their halfpennies and pence 'pon yon pinnacle of a precarious outcrop."

The Prophet looked askance at the General, then pressed on, "You, General are on a path toward your redemption. Part of that redemption is getting some personal gain from an endeavor to which you have dedicated your very being. And, let me remind you regarding our talk at your base, you have not been reciprocated, relieved, respected nor remunerated for your relentless efforts regarding your rank."

The Prophet smacked his fist into his palm. "This is the chance, the opportunity, for the redemption you seek. The redemption you need. 'Tis all for the taking. The wine, women, and song of your haziness. The quid pro quo of your laziness. 'Tis the high time of your effervescent uncorked sudzification. Join me in the dip of the sop in low crimes and even lower miscreantliness unto the depths of misty meaner."

The Prophet opened his eyes wide, then boxed himself on his ear.

The General looked at this strange behavior and grunted, "Hunh?"

The Prophet was trying to shake something out of his ear. "Sorry General. Methinks the cobwebs of thy cranial-lingual infirmities perchance hath attempted an assault into mine own dome."

The General looked at this strange behavior and grunted, "Hunh?"

The Prophet asked, "Didn't you just say that?"

"Say what?"

"Hunh."

"Hunh?"

The Prophet shook his head once more. "Neber-mind. I mean never mind. Where was I?? Oh yes ... I was saying our golden opportunity. Get it? Golden?"

The General waved his cigar. "Yeah, yeah, I get it. Go on."

The Prophet continued. "Yes, yes. I was saying. Umm … I for mine, you for yours. Mine, they pine for the unveiling. Thine, thine is thy own to own. What say you? We dig! We excavate to the fortunes of our mutual estate. I can carry on in the digging on my side. Bring the spy-traders into the fray from your own quarter: coaxing, coaching, twisting and plying. Remember what we talked about. The adventure. The fun. And remember most, the MONEY!"

This last hurrah of the Prophet roused the General out of his ambivalence toward adding the basement to the construction project. Since his first agreement to go into business with the Prophet, the thoughts of getting his own private cash-cow were worth the sordid involvement with the intel people. But the addition of a basement had rained on his ranch and muddied up the pasture.

"Now, see you hear Prophet, this is a right knicker-bocker of a tight wad I'm puttin' myself in," his big brown stogie flapping in his gums and lips. "I've got to entropitize those spies nevermore. What else are we correlating in this fraternal order of giblets?"

"We've been holding our own nicking what we can from what you have already appropriated. Now, in this supplementary phase, the more I can garnish from your empire, the better for me. How much more physical plant matériel can you give us? Not loan, but give — outright? We need all kinds of things: cement, flooring, fixtures, and furnishings of every category. The more the better. I'm only asking because, if I don't ask, you won't know. And let's face it, you're half-cocked off your rocker as it is anyhow. So, what have I got to lose, if your military pays what-it-will for my tea-house?"

The General answered, "Seer-Son, the very fact that you've got a horse's set enough to ask straight up, is Jiminy Cricket for me. I'll suck it up call on the sergeant's fat harms and supply despots to do right by you."

The Prophet stood up and began to pace slowly around the shop. "Speaking of sergeant's at arms, allow me the opportunity to speak of arms; for here is what will happen, my friend. There will be an increase of wars and rumors of wars. Do not be troubled. Sect shall rise against sect. Fathers shall rise against sons. Mothers shall rise against daughters. Even unto the raging sky against heaven and the scorched earth against the ground. The tide of violence has not reached flood. The moon is still pale. For the chalice of blood is not brimful. Armaments will be called for to overcome the violence. More arms.

Then more. Even more. The convoys will clamber like mechanical lizards. Up the steep canyons, down the rocky valleys. Trains of armaments, slithering like adders. Around the curve of a mountain, into the barren draw. There will always be the last in the convoy. There will always be the end of the train. Here is the metaphor. Every lizard has its tail. Every snake has its end. When they are molested, they can drop their tip and scurry along. These ends of the caravans shall be left behind. They will be snatched from the snake in a moment. They will be taken from the tail in a wink. The denizens of these lonely steeps and declines have a saying to bolster their courage in this dangerous game. They teach their sons a rhyme.

In the hill or the dale or curve of a canyon,
the convoy will travel intact.
It will emerge from its track with the lack of the last
for the tail will be taken in fact.

"These gleanings are a precious business for these armament poachers. It is a scary profession. But it seems to be attractive enough. More interesting than grazing goats. It is cutthroat in its own way. It is comradely in another. Above, below, about and around all this are what make this enterprise unending. It is lucrative. There is hopefully a good supply. There is always a good demand. Money spent making guns and bombs. Money spent buying them. Black, white, legitimate, illegitimate. The market remains. The arms flow. They flow into arms and into the next arms. There are market-makers, entrepreneurs, businessmen, wholesalers. They are out in the fields and the mountains. As the poor women glean behind the poor harvester, as the jackal sniffs for a dry carcass, so do these people make trade from the iron caravan."

The Prophet left off speaking but continued to pace slowly along the walls of the shop. The General was silent.

"My friend, I see you are not your loquacious self. In lieu of the lacuna of silence, allow me to mollify your sense and sensibilities and at the same time appeal to your pride, without prejudice."

The General looked at the Prophet, frowned and shook his head.

"What? What?" the Prophet asked innocently.

In a calm voice, the General said, "Well Seer Son, you know from our parlez vous, that I was not the most edumicated under the sun. Not to my poor gulliver's fault, but on the account of base to base to base. Right? Nevertheless, there are certain literary aqua-sentences I have come across. So, urine a religimus type. You're on the knowledge of this'n t'other. Right?" the General said brightly. "Have you heard or have knowledge-wise of those refined aesthetics in old India? Not taken to things, even of going about nekked tales be told."

With confident pride, the Prophet answered, "I believe you refer to a certain group identified as the Jaines or Jainism. They believe the path to liberation and bliss is harmlessness and renunciation. I think the whole nude thing is urban myth or pop-culture. One of those phenomena. Why do you ask?"

"Well now, I met one — clothed and all, yess'r — way down in the capital of Texas."

The Prophet broke stride. He didn't say anything but was confused as to how a political capital city was somehow part of the conversation.

General was not enjoying his cigar and flicked what remained of it into some cauliflower. "Sorry. Where were we?"

"Macro-economic gun-running. And I was saying you were rather quiet."

"Ah yes. Sorry, Seer Son. Long Day. Go on."

"I will try and be succinct. Streams of soldiers and military equipment travel all through these parts. Here and there, one army or another, this type of equipment, another type of equipment. This brand, this system. That brand, that system. The market fluctuates like anything else. Most of these older men know how to do some farming or herding and understand how market prices work. Good crop bad crop, early harvest late harvest. They apply the same economics to black-market arms. They have just moved on from farming to arms trade. I said older men. Now some of their sons have been raised in the arms trade and have lost the art of cultivation and husbandry. This is sad but is one of the unintended consequences of prolonged, unending, maybe never-ending war. I am not sure if the heavy hitters in the military industrial complex, ever contemplated that the trickle-down effect of their particular form of mercantile production, would result in an agriculturally illiterate generation, paradoxically born and raised in an agrarian society and culture. If there were among these captains of industry, some who recognized this lost generation and felt a twinge of compunction about it — even those few — would be suffocated by their board and shareholders due to the irresistible lure of lucre anyhow. We, however, are merely ancillary to those problems … and I digress. For all the systems from all the industrialized warmongers, our role is broker. On my side, I have the ways and means to glean from the train. We know the geography. We know how to shift the goods. On your side, you know how to get the armaments in country, then put them on the road and rolling. This is our business. You and I will be black-market arms dealers, using our tea-house and bar as a front."

The General did not respond. The Prophet saw this and understood. He knew the General was uncomfortable with the topic they were on. "Allow me to preempt some of your objections. Morals. Ethics. This is the single biggest scruple to hurdle. Can we make any justification of you turning arms dealer? I believe so. First and easiest, to make and overcome is the under-orders argument. Then, by the logic of the just-war theory whereby a soldier can be pre-absolved of killing his fellow man, I think we can work something out to lessen the prick of your guilty conscience. We both know war will be stirred up and stirred up some more. This will have the catenary effect of more arms flowing out to the field. The question is: Through whose hands will these arms flow? Of course, the only answer we are interested in is: The General's. When the requisitions come in, when the hardware comes in, you are just doing your job. During wartime, things go missing. Men get killed. All this will happen — with or without you. However, for us, there is an inside track to participating in the profits of the trade. I cannot vouchsafe for good sleep or sleepless nights if your conscience bothers you in this. This is where there may be a difference between you and me. Being an arms dealer has no effect on my conscience because I know my cause. And I know my cause is a righteous cause. I am involved in war for the sake of peace. It becomes necessary to bring some into God's way of righteousness by force. In these times, the force of arms is the effective and efficient method. Now I hope for one of a few outcomes for you. One, that you will rationalize your participation in this business to assuage any perturbations about its legitimacy and morality. Or two, that you will embrace this opportunity the same way you became enthusiastic about the bar. The adventure. The money. Of course in this case more adventure, more money. The third course is less desirable. You resigning yourself to being a mere marionette dangling and dancing to the tune of the military-industrial overlords. Think about it, General! Do you want to be a pawn, even if it is a big pawn? Maybe some other chess piece is more suitable for a general. Pick one. They all get sacrificed on the board. Or do you take hold of the brass ring and fly in the face of armchair moralists?"

The General took out a Swisher Sweet and began fidgeting with it.

He asked quietly, almost a mumble, "What about m'boys?"

The Prophet was not sure if he understood or heard him correctly.

A bit more loudly, the General repeated himself. "What about m'boys? My men? The soldiers under me, the boys. I am aggrieved to know what happens on the snake end? The glean. The last. All the jargon about hijacking the end of the convoy. I would some explanitories on them. I am aggrieved to know, because for all the tea leaves and buddah-pests of religimosity ... I caint never and know-how be part of the menschlisch al zu menschlisch human race if I a jus' throw some boys offa planes or trains or automobiles without knowing their fateful circumstances. I will not lower myself to the fodder-feeding maw of the Molech machine for a plug nickel. So satisfine me on that, and I think I can regiment the crooked brain go straight to visualize webber or not my everloving hereafters will be skewered on the spit of a splined stick, suppurating supine over the sweltering Stygian swamp of eternal sorrow and sadness. Can you help me on that one? For the boys?"

The Prophet raised his eyebrows in apparent surprise. The General saw this and questioned him on it.

The Prophet replied, "Oh, just surprised that you had such qualms about the afterlife. I wasn't aware that you had religiously inspired fears of hell and damnation."

"Well now, you make a fine point on the pencil. True enough, I don' suppose it's all palaver from the saliver. But gosh darn! Twixt-an-tween! Metamorphic, igneous and sedimentary. Let's break down this ethical diatribe diamond. Shore, we are all capistulated from the crib in the God and Devil. Wax the years increase wax in the ears in a way of interpolating the eternal circumspect-wise man-a-mano how are we to square the circle of life. You heard me say my prey life was reservated accordion to the old forsooth: 'Atheists few there be in foxholes.' Ok. It's about push come to shovel. You push him out of the way to shovel the hole bigger, hiding more the hinie. But here above ground regularwize, fun and games before the five senses more to the pushing one's way up to better and better fulfillment here and now. The beyond gets plowed under in the escarpment of escape. Then right between the optical orbs — boom — you get the alarm clock thrown at your sleepy head. Here's my alarm clock. Shore you an mees fussing and fighting and being grown up boys and wheelin' dealin' stealin' slip-shod slappin' and all big badass. But in what I think my poor earlobes are allocating is putting the aggregate grunt in harm's way and progagly death's doorstep. Whether or not you and I live, die or incubate in the bye and bye, high low or lye, is not the grazzle grumblin' in my gizzard. It's the soldier on that last bit tail part you are going to harvest. What's he done wrong that I should cause to swing the swathed-one's scythe across his esophagus carcass sarcophagus? That heartache isn't the Hancock what I on the dotted line signed."

After a few more paces, the Prophet answered, "As a man with a human heart and soul, stony or soft, white as a snow-flake or dusky as ashen coal, I cannot practice gainsaying sophistry to make your reasoning and arguments naught ... I think we are both familiar with the Highway Man. He is possibly a semi-Jungian or a tarot figure ... we'll have to revisit the deck. But the highway-man is our savior come flag or foil. We stand in league with illustrious ne'er-do-wells of story and saga. Sampson the Strong. Templar and Saracen. Robbing Hood. The Scarlet Pumpernickel. Who's side wrote the history of these legendary heroes? Israelite or Philistine? Saladin or Raynald and Guy? Lion Heart or Weak of Heart? Dauphin or Robespierre? Whether or not you read winner or loser or loser or winner, the highway-man wins the booty. So with us. I have said it before. I am on a mission of peace. Counter-intuitively I must make war to make peace. To make war I need arms. To get arms — I need you."

The General had a puzzled look on his face. The Prophet said, "You have a puzzled look on your face. What's wrong?"

The General answered, "Did you say scarlet pumpernickel?"

"Yes. Yes, I did. The great man of guise who distributed bread to the poor."

The General let out a chuckle. "I think you mean pimpernel. Scarlet pimpernel. It's a flower your Wholesomeness."

"Correct. Flour. To make bread. To give to the poor. That's what I said. Why do you snicker?"

"Not bread. Flower. A little red flower. Like rosies and posies and drop dead."

"What?" the Prophet exclaimed. "Drop dead. What in blazes are you gabbing about? Every culture which enjoys the sandwich — you should know, I see you eat them — knows the pumpernickel. It's like rye. It is common marbled as well."

"Tarnations," the General said with agitation. "If we can come ginger-manly to the table of kindly and concord grapes. We have to hask it out evenly. We half and half give and take. The boys and the toys. I guess I can squirm and shiver all my way outten the cold-rums, con-miserables, morel and ephedral con-um-drums that my wearied wobbled walk has worried in and on to iff'n we can segregate the takin' o' the tail and from the coffin hammerin' o' the nail."

The Prophet didn't answer right away. "What about having fun?" he asked, dragging his toe on the dirty floor. "Does the line get drawn here, or here, or over here? Do desist from a reply at this moment General. A few words more. I wish to continue my summation in the plainest of terms. What I am aiming for, is to steal military weapons and armaments from your army's supply trains. I make a distinction here between you and your army. I don't want to steal from you. Unless you consider my stealing from the army you belong to, as stealing from you. I do not. Be that as it may, I need you to be with me in this. Someway. Somehow. Now, how can that be? We have already come up against ethical difficulties. And we have ventured the idea of once removed. Now, can we venture the idea of twice removed? Three times removed? Is there a point, whether a limit or horizon, where your moral compunction will not be so acute as to cause mental and spiritual angst, anguish and angina? Can this be postulated? Or, is your complicity — even from many arms lengths away — too much to bear? Is there a way for your moral responsibility to diminish to the point of allowing you to be, or at least feel, free from the teleological quandary of equipment tendered upon the plains of conflict, strife, war, and death? After all, can any and every individual be responsible for any and every action and consequence?"

After thinking, the General said, "I can't rightly circle the wagons around the square of your ethical equation. Could be — may be — that there will be requisitioned war merchandise that will trickle through yon base that will be far and wide away from any acknowledgementaries 'pon your sides, ides, tides and mebbie demise. That is, guns may be atotin' through even if it was known you were a goner. I caint regularfy everything. I re-cog-ni-size the conning towel of doldrums we're stepping into. Leasterly, as I am stepping into. Add to that, your Morelness, one thing you have not mentucated yet — far as I can tale. That the ebbs and foes of the tides of the worrisome woes and webs of wars spinning and foaming in, out and under ever rock and crusty dune may or may not be friend, fiend or flow. Otter stayed: I not only won't know where each and ever bullet comes fro and goes to, but I caint know. So, returnings to before, I can rascallize the trade, seein's heaps of weapons will be foisted 'pon maw and dawn of yawning earth, but I don't want the blood of the citizen who just happened to be in the wrong place at the wrong time on these already red hands."

The Prophet thought about the last bit of the General's indisposition. The killing of innocents. For the Prophet, this was not only not a problem, but a two for one. Grab the guns and kill a few foreign devils while at the same time populate paradise with anonymous martyrs. But he still wanted the General's business partnership in the deal. "Ah, General Sir. I think I have an out, to overcome your qualms, and at the same time, to raise the quality level of the product."

"These ears wern't built to smoke or sneeze. Gimme your postulations and promentories."

The Prophet said, "How about we create a special class or category of stolen arms? Like blood diamonds and dolphin-free tuna? Blood-free arms. A whole other class of arms dealing. Arms that have been sans sanguinaries properly poached. Channel and supply-line QC. Observer and certification norms and regs. That kind of thing. Why not? The trade isn't getting smaller. And the goods flowing in and out are more and more sophisticated. Might as well get them with a certain appellation contrôlleé. Like Angus beef. Used to be just another cow. Now, it's 'Certified'. Well then, we'll create a new black market for blood-free arms. Don't laugh or say something like 'that's the stupidest thing I have ever heard of.' As a man of peace, I wonder why I haven't actually thought of this sooner."

"I have shorely, yes some momentals where holes be picked in this craniary enlightenment. However, I can also see to get the juices flowing liki-wize. Heck n holler, maybe with all the certificationnesses, we'll launch a whole nuther innerprize. Why it's like all the signs and wonders and stamps and seals of aggravation on ever-lovin, spoonful of boxed or packaged chow that ever was ship to shore to the store. Why just las' week, I opened a jar of peanuts, the old goober-pea. It was written right there for every eyeball to behold: 'Caution: contains peanuts. May have been packed in a factory that has peanuts. May have been packed in a factory that has other tree nuts. May have been packed in a factory that has soy. Parve. Certified fair-trade. Gluten-free. Vegan. No animals were harmed making this jar of peanuts. This label contains only certified organic soy-based ink. This jar was made from recycled glass. The glue that holds the label to the jar is water-soluble. Please dispose of carefully. Do not throw in a ditch. Recycle only. Carbon footprint minimization standards met according to the

WHO, UNESCO, IMF, WWF and Canon Cameras. Conforms to California SB 0070 and 0072. May cause elevated levels of peanut blood serum panel Nr. 67 which may not be safe for pregnant or breastfeeding mothers. Not for birds. Not for dogs and cats. Use responsibly. Do not, under any circumstances, board any commercial domestic or international flight with this jar of peanuts. This is a violation of FAA, CIA and FBI watch-code 12.34.56.'

"Well now. By the light of day and if I ever has any gumptions on the ol' guber a-munchin', I lost and found it right then and there. The only plus-side of the whole dang-be-dang story is they wern't organic. The poor li'l fruit of the legume were ord-in-airy. The label on the organic peanut soooo much text took, that I did never even see Peanuts written down, soooo smallish was the type-face. All the rest of the label were more warnings and seals of approbations."

The General mopped his sweaty face and sighed. "Aller that being stated and said, I guess elbow room enuf there be for bombs and guns to be sold certified blood-free. So, Seer Son, you've got yerseff a bidness pardner. Like you rascalize, them guns will be made, will be shipped, will be stolen and sold. Through these rookers mightn's actualize."

Moral War
Mortal War
Utter Gore
Gusher Lore

Hirsute mania
Pulling my brains out

Resolute mafia
Watching the stains shout

Inventories rise
No surprise
Hiking eyes
Watching thighs

Ship slip trip flip
Run ton hun gun

Money for sumthin' and chits for fee
Can't cop a guilty plea.

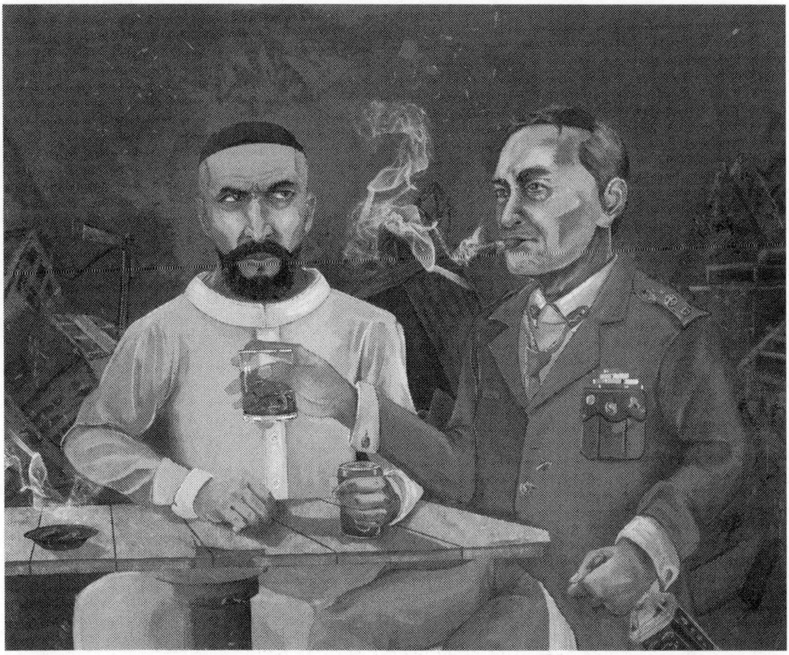

19

Asaf and the Councilman walked along the perimeter of the construction area. "The tea-house will open soon. The Prophet wishes all of us to come to terms. What decision have you come to about managing the tea-house?"

"I will do it, depending on a few conditions."

The Councilman asked what his conditions were.

"First, I want double what I am being paid by the soldiers."

The Councilman asked how much this was. When Asaf told him, the Councilman thought a bit and then agreed. "What else?"

"I am to be paid weekly, in cash."

The Councilman nodded his head.

"I know this business well. That is why you want me. Food, drink, and money. It makes an interesting type of business."

Asaf went on to explain that the very nature of the food and beverage business creates a level playing field for every human individual since all must eat and drink. From the king to the lowest peasant, all can find themselves under the same roof. It is easy to have conversation and do business. Good business and not so good business can be done all around. Deals can occur with staff as well. Special portions. Free food and drink. Pilfering used for a bribe or certain favors. "I can't control the customers. I can try to control the employees. I want our business to succeed. To do that we have to make a profit. To make a profit, we have to keep our customers happy and our inventories safe. To keep our stuff safe, we need reliable people. Men we know and can trust. I know this is a complicated business, and you have many men involved. I also think that there will be men I don't know coming to work here. I would like to have a say about these men which you will be putting in place. Is that fair?"

"This is interesting that you bring this up now. You are correct.

There will be men at the tea-house who will be placed here by the Prophet and the council. To be around, you know? The Prophet has his reasons for them to be there. I don't need another person, you, in this case, to be second-guessing, or looking over my shoulder. But, I am a reasonable man, a regular person. I can understand your position. How would you like it if we had a plan or a policy put in place for such circumstances? Something simple."

Together, Asaf and the Councilman made a policy that each party had the right to question the other's hire. The Councilman was open and honest. He told Asaf that he could object, but ultimately the council and the Prophet would place certain men of their choosing in the tea-house. "I have great confidence in the council. We speak on behalf of the Prophet. Do not feel like you are being put down, or that you are an underling when orders or requests come from the council, or from the Prophet through us. It is the chain of command we have in place. How we do things. Do you have any questions at this time?"

"At this time ... Nothing I can think of at the moment."

They had walked around the two lots and came to the just-finished entrance of the tea-house. They looked at the open floor, paved with the finest marble and furnished with expensive yet practical restaurant tables and chairs. The large covered patio area and the service counter with spotless stainless steel equipment and fixtures were ready for customers.

"Ok. We can go over any questions as they come up, you know? Now, I'm going to leave. The Prophet has told me he would like to give you some of his thoughts."

Without further ado, the Councilman walked out of the tea-house. Shortly after he left, Asaf became aware that there were no sounds anywhere in the low, open building. He glanced around and saw that he was alone. Then the Prophet walked in from the side of the building, as if out of nowhere. He walked up to Asaf and smiled. "I would like you to know, I am pleased that you have become the house manager. We will pay you well for this, as you have requested. I will spend time here, but I will have little to do with the day to day business. For me what is important is that the tea-house is run smoothly and that it is a safe and secure area. These are difficult times we are in, and it is vital that we maintain a hospitable atmosphere, while at the same time staying vigilant. The people under you must understand this. They must be morally upright. They cannot bring shame or scandal to our tea-house. We are side by side with a lecherous den of mercenaries. As strange as that seems, it is a necessary evil for the good of God's plan; for the carrying out and fulfillment of his divine will.

"Also, we will serve no alcohol here. We leave that to our neighbors. You are experienced with this and I trust your judgment in the details as it affects our business. We are peaceful and merciful. If there are drunk men or men wounded by fighting, I would like to welcome them here quietly for their safety and well being. We can find a corner somewhere for them to rest. I feel it is a righteous thing to do and keeps the neighborhood from looking at us with the evil eye. As far as the food and drink, I leave that up to you. My councilmen are at your service in this area. I don't know how much help they will be, but they are resourceful and loyal. I would like to add that a clean, sanitary establishment is very important in today's world. I presume you feel the same. It is not far from a little smudge to a gale of dirt. And the house of hell swallows up the twain."

Asaf squinted, wondering what that meant.

"Finally, let me address you as a young man, not as the house manager. I like you. You are a good person. Clearly, you come from a good family. As God's anointed, and filled with his spirit, I can see in you a special destiny. I feel like God has sent you to me for your conversion from spiritual ambivalence to righteousness. This is why we exercised our spiritual duty in my compound. It is a rare thing for me to perform this rite. It is a powerful thing, and I know it will bring blessings upon you. Who can understand God's ways? It is a heavenly calling to live under his refreshing cloud of holiness. You are now entering that refreshing cloud. It will make your life meaningful. Everything you have searched for can be discovered in the coolness and pleasantness of God's cloud of blessing. Now, Asaf, come close to me."

Asaf approached the Prophet, who waved him closer and closer until he was only a few inches away. He put his hand on Asaf's head and murmured very softly. Then he gently guided Asaf's hand to his genitalia and held it there momentarily. He then looked at Asaf with fiery eyes and said: "Kneel! Kneel right here in front of me."

Asaf was strangely obedient and knelt.

"Now, bend over, remove my shoes — one at a time."

Asaf took off the Prophet's simple shoes.

"Now bend over and gently kiss each foot. Kiss each foot with reverence and love. Feel the devotion rise up in you as you place your lips on your Prophet's feet. Feel the warmth and sanctity of my feet. These are the feet of God on earth for this generation. It is a good thing for you to have this privilege."

Asaf did as he was told.

With an oily voice, the Prophet said softly, "Good … I can feel the love in your lips upon my holy feet … Stay right where you are … Let the warmth of our blood touch each other.

"Yes, yes, I can feel it … I can feel your warmth … It is good."

The Prophet let out a long sensual sigh. Asaf sat up. He felt light-headed.

The Prophet instructed him to put the shoes back on. After that, the Prophet told Asaf to stand again.

The Prophet pulled Asaf's head close and said in a low voice, "You have made your obeisance to your spiritual master. Thank you for joining our tea-house. It will be a very special place. Now our pied-à-terre will be complete. I want you to remember this … "

Asaf's eyes were out of focus — he was dizzy.

"Look at me!" the Prophet said sharply and boxed Asaf's ear.

"Asaf, my son," the Prophet began again, "Remember this: these are difficult times. I want you safe and secure. In order for that to be so, you must obey me. Our tea-house will not only be for the worn and weary to come and rest in the shade. Our tea-house is also a temple. Do you know the meaning of the word holy? It means separate, or, apart-from, correct? There is the holy. And then there is that which is apart from the holy. This is the most holy. Our tea-house is holy. And its apartments are the holy of holies. Do not doubt or fear, my Asaf. I do not speak symbolically. It is not for outsiders to see, hear or have knowledge of. In the holy of holies, portentous occurrences and grave events will be conceived, supervised and existentialized. It will be a place where we will launch forth what will become a turning point in history. A place for bringing about God's will for this generation. You are in a privileged position as house manager — for both buildings. Because of this, you must never, ever speak to anyone about the things which you might see in our apartments.

"There may be periods of time when it will seem that we have grown apart. Or times when we will have minimal contact. Do not be discouraged. Do not feel abandoned. It is the nature of these undertakings, that I go where the mission calls. It is an opportunity to exercise faith. Faith, that invisible tangibility to know that the unseen can be seen with the shine of ineffable knowing. Be assured that your

Prophet will always have faith in you, and a place in his heart for you. So, have faith in me, that from our temple we will bring about great things on the earth."

Then the Prophet turned and left as stealthily as he had come in.

Asaf was still dizzy. His spirit felt like it was opening to the invisible, spiritual world. His soul was quaking. His ears were ringing from having been hit by the Prophet. His lips had a dusty saltiness from the Prophet's feet. But his guts were in knots. He began walking, but between his spinning head and queasy stomach, he felt off-balance. He went over to the low wall of the tea-house patio for support. He moved along the wall, heading out to the back. When he stepped out of the building, he suddenly vomited forcefully. The vomit spewed on the wall then dribbled onto the ground and pooled on the property line between the club and the tea-house.

20

THE CONSTRUCTION MEN LEFT THE site, equipment and supplies were in place and Asaf became the manager of the tea-house and manager of the new bar. He brought the business experience he had in the village, made sure he had a real voice in how things ran, and he got paid what he deserved for all this. He hired local help whenever possible. He taught men on both sides how to cultivate vendors and how to spend money wisely. He continued the practice of buying most of the food from local households. He saw to it that the guests were well served and the buildings were clean, inside and out. He kept track of the supplies to make sure they were properly stocked.

In the tea-house, Asaf counted the money and distributed it as the business needed. By placing himself between ownership and the inventory and labor, neither the owners nor partners could squeeze the wages or overhead, and the workers and suppliers couldn't gouge the owners. When the week was up, he gave a summary accounting sheet to the Councilman along with the money. The Councilman would verify the amounts, return the starting till to Asaf, then pay Asaf his generous salary. The rest of the money was kept by the Councilman.

Asaf was open to the idea of seeing his work in the tea-house as taking part in the Prophet's mission of peace but was not a member of the inner circle. Asaf was not informed just what the mission was, nor how it was implemented, or how it was supposed to come about. This bothered him some, for he felt if he was part of something, he should know more about it than he knew. But his time was limited, so he did what he could by being a good steward of the responsibilities placed in front of him as the tea-house manager.

Asaf found a way to have women served inside the tea-house. All during the construction, the women of the village supplied most of the food and drink, as before with the club. They spent time and energy picking-up and delivering food and caring for their pots and pans. So the crews gave them an area to visit with each other, while the men ate and talked. Over time, the men became used to the women's presence in the tea-house, and the women, being wise, stayed off to one area. They eventually claimed this area as their own and procured some lovely, well-made, room dividers to create a separate space where they could relax and spend time with each other. When construction was over and the tea-house was open for business, Asaf quietly made this a permanent area. All his servers were trained to treat the women's section as a completely equal part of the establishment. He taught them how to politely overcome objections made by men who did not approve of the arrangement. In a short time, even the most conservative grew to appreciate the arrangement since it made the atmosphere amicable and family-like.

The council members came and went regularly. One or the other was usually around some part of any given day. When the Prophet visited the tea-house, he usually used an entrance on the side of the building that led only between the basement and the outside. This side entrance was always securely locked, and those that came and went were seldom seen by the public. If he arrived openly, he would greet people, sometimes offering a quick prayer or blessing, then he repaired to the basement.

The new bar was Asaf's home turf, where both the General and the Soldier knew Asaf was the person in charge. The new bar was a different operation than the old club. Back then, Asaf and the Soldier scrounged what they could. They poked and dug, looking for supplies of alcohol whenever the chance arose. It was not important how much it cost, because all they needed to charge was enough to pay for the product and cover wages. What inventory-keeping there was, amounted to examining the shelves to see what was running low.

To avoid the inventory and stocking issues in the club, the Soldier and the General had a meeting with Asaf and the lead bartender. They explained the different types of bars and what the expectations were.

They took note of their best and worst selling products. They streamlined what they sold to a minimum and chose the best of the best that made sense and was procurable.

The bar grew more popular and busier than ever. To run things even more efficiently, they separated the food business from the drinks and cigarettes. The two cooks took over the entire food side of the bar from sourcing to selling to keeping their own til. They were instructed to pay attention to the best and worst selling items or kind of food and try to imitate the bar's system of keeping the best and weeding out the rest. For this arrangement, the bar took a thirty percent rake of the food revenue.

Asaf told the Soldier that the family that lived one lot over had been supporters of the old club, and were now well established in bringing food to the tea-house. Asaf said he had made small attempts to have the Daughter as a waitress there, but the whole idea was frowned upon. But now, in the bar, it would be possible for the Daughter to be a server because the clientele was different. So, the new food service arrangement included the Daughter as a waitress. She was attentive and polite, which brought more money into her household because she earned good tips.

In all of this, Asaf was happy with his lot in life to be a manager/ part-owner of a thriving business.

Asaf's dedication and interest in running the bar changed his relationship with the tea-house, and consequently the council and the employees. He was still technically the manager, but it was becoming obvious that he could not do both jobs well at the same time. The councilmen didn't mind. They still needed Asaf to help count the money.

But it bothered Asaf that the council was bringing in men of questionable character — men he didn't like. When he broached the subject, the council gave lip-service, but he could see that they were only appeasing him. He came to understand a sea-change had gone on in the tea-house. The Prophet and his council had another agenda to pursue, and the tea-house served as a front. The councilmen used their old excuse: that these brutish men were an inconvenient but necessary element for the Prophet's mission to succeed. They tried to tell Asaf that he was still a valuable member of the team to demonstrate that the tea-house was an actual business, not just a flophouse for thugs to wile away the hours and intimidate other workers. As difficult as it was, Asaf knew the changes were not going away. It made him sad.

21

ORIGINALLY, THERE WAS NO PARTITION in the basement between the tea-house and the bar. It was envisioned to be divided by the respective boxes and crates belonging to each. This was of little concern, for the workers on each side would know what belonged to each business as they came and went from the opposite staircases into the basement. Where the stacks came together was approximately the line between the two sides, which roughly corresponded to the division of the two buildings above. As the tea-house became stable and financially sound, the Prophet gradually spent more time there and began remodeling the basement. The Soldier didn't get what was going on. He thought all the construction work was finished. He spoke with Asaf about it. Asaf reported to the Soldier what had been told him: The business was growing, and they needed to make their side of the basement more useful.

The Prophet arranged a whole array of new things for the basement. At first, there were basic creature comforts like televisions, table and chair sets, and some simple sofas. Later, he brought in luxurious carpets and plush furniture. He ultimately built a full toilet, bath and shower where he, his visitors and council could spend days down there, while utilizing the tea-house for food and drink.

When the basement developed into a full-blown living and conference space, it was no surprise to Asaf, that the Prophet's cohorts stacked unused crates of restaurant supplies from floor to ceiling, no longer pretending that it was a shared space.

What nobody knew about, but Asaf discovered, was that during construction, the spies engineered a narrow hallway between the two buildings with a cleverly hidden entrance. This space was enough to set up a little office, just the size of a hall closet. It had a small built-in desk and a diminutive ladder that allowed a spy to climb down to a subterranean cubby-hole. In this closet, they had old fashioned peep-holes in addition to modern electronics. The electronics were bread and butter surveillance, and the peep-holes gave decent views of the tea-house floor, the bar, and both sides of the basement from the drop-down. If Asaf wanted to know what was going on in the Prophet's lair, he availed himself of the secret vault. When the Prophet was gone, the councilmen allowed debauched foot-soldiers access to the basement to keep them off the main floor. These were the brutes the council needed to undertake and carry out the less savory side of the Prophet's grand design for peace. In the basement, they freely availed themselves of all that the tea-house offered. They got stoned on cannabis in all its forms and chewed khat during the long football matches on TV. They indulged in ample pornographic videos. Sometimes as Asaf sat or stood on the other side of the divide, or hidden in the spy vault, he had to steel his mind against what came through the wall. He could smell the sickly mixtures of smoke. He could hear cursing and yelling during the soccer matches. He could hear the video smut — and heavy breathing among the men. He knew they were having orgies. As disturbing as that was, the sounds he heard when the Prophet was in residence were even worse …

The Prophet always had boys who were his attendants. He made sure there was a fresh supply of boys in the tea-house as well. He told the councilmen to recruit boys from the areas controlled by the three sects. The Prophet kept his boys on a rotation — some from one region, then from the next, and so on. This prevented the seeds of jealousy from being sown in their little hearts, should they learn of the others.

The Prophet impressed his boys by telling them how vast his following was. They were taught about the Prophet's unique spiritually, as God's emissary of peace. He explained how learning at home, in qualified schools and vocational training gave structure to their lives. Over time, he taught them how to observe the human race, how to perceive spheres of influence, and how different levels of knowledge and power worked. He instructed them on the relationship between mind, soul, and body, how all three were equally important gifts of God. He taught them about the woman's place in God's design, how they were his creation to be sure, but in their own way and station in the order of things.

The boys fostered connections and alliances with the tribes where the sects were active. They would make their way back to their respective villages and neighborhoods full of love and respect for the

Prophet, both as a person, as well as God's ambassador on earth for their generation. They were proud of their association with the Prophet and lavished praise on him for his dignity, intelligence, and spiritual anointing.

Those boys who pleased the Prophet and loved him in return were given special training. Guides, chosen by the council, would take them on educational excursions. They were taught about soils and sand, and wild and domestic plants and animals. They were shown where to look for water and how to read the sun, moon, and stars. They collected herbs and gums and minerals for culinary uses and making remedies, unctions, incense, and poisons. They learned to live off the empty lands, eating seeds, roots, certain birds and small animals.

Each sojourn built on the next. They were instructed in making ropes and lines from reeds and rawhide for pulling, binding and tying. Soon they were able to make snares and traps that could kill a wild fawn or kid. They concocted elaborate poisons and were shown how to use them. Eventually, the guide would give them lessons in stealing and explain how it was practical knowledge. First, they stole small things to eat like chickens and gleanings. Then, they graduated to stealing from the flocks and herds. Before they would gain the approval of a Councilman, they would have to earn the degree called: Craftiness.

The guide would pick out a landowner who he knew would not kill a nice, hungry boy. Then they would allow themselves to be caught. They would experience shame, embarrassment and be humiliated. Building on that lesson, they learned how to evade an angry herdsman or orchardist. How to run, where to hide. How to double back or erase tracks. After they knew how shameful being caught felt, then how clever escaping was, they were finally taught true morality. They would have to explain their moral duties when caught in the act. The test was to persuade the rightful owner of the property, that the act of stealing or killing was justified. The spiritual authority and needs of a greater cause trumped the petty ownership of perishable, worldly goods. They would have to turn the owner's legitimate anger, into submission to the missionaries.

When a pair of boys returned, the Prophet would bring them down into the basement. He would explain to them that after such long walking and hiking and hunting, they needed rest and comfort. He told them that they must tell him all about their travels. He offered them fresh fruit juice with milk and honey. He fed them with grilled meat. The Prophet talked about God's love. He explained that the great God had many ways of demonstrating love. He lamented how few there were who knew how important the body was to God. He told them that they were special. They had been given to him by God. And part of their training was, to show them love in its most intimate form. But before that, they must clean up. And that started with communal foot washing.

They were taught how to draw water and bring it to temperature. They were shown the details of the Prophet's footwear and how to have them neat and in order, in accordance with his dignified station. He told them that well cared for feet were a great asset. He taught them how to observe the parts of the foot for any sores or wounds. He demonstrated how to properly care for basins, pitchers and expensive towels. Once they were competent with a basic level of foot washing, he moved on to show them the various lotions and ointments available to make the experience better. Woody, but tender herbs, were lashed leisurely on the back and joints stimulating circulation and cleansing the skin. The invigorating herbal whip would help them to walk or stand for a long time.

When that was done he showed them that other parts of the body were just as needy for ministry as the feet. He and one of the boys undressed the one, then the naked boy and the Prophet undressed the other. The boys were bathed. He toweled them off then gave them a silk tunic. He showed them the massage oils. He showed them the proper amount of oil, how to apply it, and how to skillfully rub it in. He gave them a cursory overview of different sets of muscles. He would guide the boy's hands with his own, moving them into the sub-dermal facia, rubbing the oil in gently, but firmly. They did the back, arms, neck, and shoulders. He told them how much work their legs did for their walking. He demonstrated how the thighs and hips were conjoined to the buttocks, and how important it was not to overlook massaging from the thighs to the lower back, and turning over, to massage the inner thigh and groin. If the boy grew tired of massaging, the Prophet took over and gave instructions while he continued. After their massage, the Prophet kissed each one on the head. He then told them his special blessing could only come directly from his lips. It was how God made the first man live, and now that they were his friends, he would breathe life in each one, by placing his mouth over theirs. He kissed them lovingly on the lips. Lingering, quivering as he caressed their rosy lips with his own. After this, he declared that he was tired from all the ministry. He suggested that they give him a massage as well. It would be good practice for them. And since there were two of them, if one got tired, the other could continue. He explained that the first man was naked and glad to be so. Since he was God's Prophet on earth for this generation and a man of peace, it would only be right for them to be together in the nude. He then went over all the things he had shown them, and the two boys worked their four little hands up and down the Prophet's body. He pointed out to them that his body was different than theirs. He told them that this was because God approved of him. Since they too were chosen to become like him, it was important for them to fully understand the needs of a full-grown man of God. At length, he showed them that life issued from the pillar of God like in the days of old and that they would bring forth the seeds of life by applying special oil to him. He let them witness how good it was for them to help in bringing the life-force out of him into the world. Some of his mannerisms they did not understand. At times, he seemed out of breath. He said the surest sign that they were his spiritual children was when he gave them his very own special ointment. It was precious, and they must learn to love its unique, look, feel, smell, and taste.

The initial cooing and cajoling with which the Prophet initiated his boys became more disturbing noises as the boys grew. The lines, ropes, traps and snares, all had indoor uses too. Asaf could hear the appalling disquietude of these things in use. Horrified, he could hear sounds of perversity, gagging, whipping, slapping, weeping, and cursing the masochist while begging for more. When the madness slackened, there followed an odor not smelled when the bullies were there. The spike of heightened senses, followed by the pain of the heart and flesh, was blunted by opium.

The formerly cherub-faced boys became darkened and hollow-eyed. Their cheerful youth was replaced by sullen dyspepsia. Those roped into the Prophet's web, fueled by lust, and tethered by poppies, became minions of evil, young mercenaries, and suicide martyrs.

22

Some meetings in the basement puzzled Asaf. The tones and inflections of the voices were different. There was some murmuring. Those engaged in talking quietly carried an air of seriousness. Asaf knew the voices of the Prophet and council, so he could tell when they were present. These groups corresponded to one of the three council members. There were meetings between a regional leader and just their Councilman. There were meetings with a regional leader, their Councilman along with the Prophet. And a leader meeting with the Prophet alone.

Asaf learned that the Prophet had a scheme of assimilation — or destruction. Either one sect would be assimilated into another, or a sect would be snuffed out. There were discussions about land, in terms of territory and geography. Each sect held control of a territory. The geography was the physical terrain inside the territory. This was an important topic. There was a lot of information exchanged about the geography and how it corresponded to the territories. There were reports on the specific belief systems of sects; dissecting what they believed, or did not believe, and what percentage believed this or that. The leadership structure was examined. Each leader was cross-referenced with his superiors and subordinates, his equals and his counterparts, and how different leadership roles related to each other. This batch of information was then compared to the other third in turn, then back again, each time gleaning meaning about alliances and enemies. And there were censuses. How many believers belonged to each sect? What was the makeup of the population? And how defined were the territorial boundaries in relation to the underlying populace's belief system?

In addition to the geo-political-religious reports, there were reports from another set of men covering mechanical, electrical and other technical issues relating to some plan that was key to the Prophet's design for peace. They went over their progress and advances, or setbacks and obstacles to overcome.

At first, he paid close attention, but the more he listened, the more he grew weary of all the layers of information and knowledge of one concerning the other, but not the other way around and how none was all and all was none — or something else.

On the main floor of the tea-house, when he just wanted to have coffee or tea, Aaf would sit quietly at his own table. He didn't assert himself as an owner or manager, but Asaf was looking, watching and observing. He watched the waiters. He watched the councilmen. He watched the thugs. Which waiter spoke with which thug. Which thug spoke with which Councilman. And who each Councilman spoke with. If he could discern the relationship between the Fanatics, the Zealots and the Radicals, he could try to figure out the Prophet's insane plans for his enemies, his friends, if he had any, and when and where this diabolical scheme would unfold.

23

THE PROPHET CALLED A COUNCIL meeting. "Now, the time of culmination is near. I have brought together the pieces necessary to bring an end to the factions. To usher in a new era of stability whereby God will begin a new wave of spirituality across the globe that will shed his merciful peace on his devotees and bring down his anger upon those who scorn him. This undertaking will begin with the shaking of the ground and sky. It will bring shock and awe to the Zealots and the Fanatics and the Radicals. It will be a great and auspicious event that will be marked down in history."

He dramatically put an architectural drawing tube on the table. He looked at his council with pride. They looked back with perplexity or blankness on their faces. The Prophet dropped his head in disappointment. He beckoned for the Plebe, they unrolled the sheets and weighed them down.

"Now, I lay before you the fruits of our labor which you have been shielded from — one from the other — in order to keep things as quiet as possible. The first scroll comes from the mechanical team which has been charged with making the hardware. The second sheet, the electrical team has supplied, as is apparent, all the electrical wizardry. And our specialty team has acquired a key material for our little surprise: a kilo of black plutonium."

The Prophet paused again in anticipation of the council's awed reaction.

The Minister of Justice cleared this throat and lifted his finger. "This seems rather irregular your Eminence. Are you to have us really believe that you are going to make a functional nuclear bomb? Isn't that a bit much for a rag-tag lot like us ...? ... in this backwater part of the world? We don't have the expertise to do such a thing ... Do we?"

He asked this rejoinder to all in the room.

The Prophet put his hands up. "I understand your concerns and questions. Let me say this. We are not a rag-tag lot. We are a legitimate spiritual organization. We have been chosen by God to do this very thing. Yes, this might be a backwater. But that is not all bad. It gives us a low profile. The ways of modern logistics are such that we can get everything we need, or almost everything, just like other places. It may be harder, it may take longer, but there are enough corrupt people out there to get things done for the right price."

The Councilman joined in. "Well, I think the minister is right. I mean, look at us. You say we are a 'legitimate spiritual organization'. Come on. The Pope is a legit guy. Jerry Whatever and Jimmy and … what's that gal with all the hair and satanic make-up? and all their groupies. They've got schools and TV and stuff. Don't they? Help me out here guys," he pleaded with his fellow councilmen. "Aren't they on the TV?"

The Minister of Justice said: "There are all sorts of kooks on TV. That doesn't make them legit. What about those guys with ashes on their forehead who don't eat for a year and bunch themselves up into a box and all that? Does that make them legit? Heck, David Blain gets all sorts of TV time and his stuff is fake and everybody knows it."

"Oh, I know, I know. The Dali Lama!" the Plebe interjected shooting his hand in the air. "He's got it all going. There are even bumper stickers calling for the freedom of his own country. His own country! — even if it is not his right now. He can still claim it until the bumper stickers get everybody signed up to take it back, or whatever they plan on doing. Those guys are the real deal."

The Councilman added: "I think the Plebe is right. I think it takes more than three guys and a bunch of their teenage flunky followers traipsing around the countryside to manufacture a nuclear bomb. With all due respect to my fellows," he finished bowing slightly to his companions. They nodded back.

The Prophet listened patiently, waiting for any other objections or clarifications. "I understand your concerns. I know it seems a bit far-fetched. But it is nevertheless the truth — however, you slice it — we — we rag-tags — have overcome all the supposed wisdom and obstacles and impossibilities and unlikelihoods and difficulties — did I say obstacles? — and obstacles to make this bomb. Let us put it in context though. This isn't some crazy ICBM. It isn't even a rocket-style bomb. It's really kind of little compared to the big ones. And who is to say that we don't have the wherewithal? I get a machinist with a good mill or two. Some techno-geeks living in their auntie's basement. I have friends in neighboring countries who can supply me a little bit of heavy water. And some real desperados who can procure black-market abalone, coltan, blood diamonds, and rhino horns. I draw the line with the rhino and elephant products, God's creations and such. These reprobates can actually nick genuine plutonium. It's expensive and difficult to handle — special containers and all that … I don't know all the nitty-gritty. I know it's not like shipping contraband in a can of Folger's like in the old days. It can be dangerous — but — it's not here today so we can't enjoy its magnificent radioactivity — or how weird it looks. What do I know? I've never seen it. For all I know, it could be a lump of clay or scrapings off an abandoned ship or something. So, dangerous and radioactive, but most important! — the explosive value! Like so many tons of TNT … And while we're at it, what is the deal with, 'Like fifty tons of TNT?' Nobody knows how much TNT that is. Not even those reporting it on the news. If you went up to the guy or girl and asked: 'How big of a blow-up would fifty tons of TNT be? Is it like a stick of dynamite? Is it like those fake car crashes in movies?' They wouldn't have a clue. They just say it because they are told to say it, or read it off a cue card. Nobody knows how big fifty tons of TNT is … Do you Minister?"

Minister shakes his head.

"Councilman?"

Councilman shakes his head.

"Plebe?"

Plebe shakes his head.

"There you have it — fifty tons of TNT — it's a complete crock. So here's what WE are going to do. When WE are ready to blow the thing off — and everybody wants to know what's going on — WE are going to tell them something like this — and you three can ad-lib as much as you want — because the whole thing is a big crock anyhow …

"We'll say: It's like three Hiroshimas packed alongside four and a half tons of TNT. That will set them on edge. Especially the four and a half. They'll be all like: 'Wow! Did he say four and a HALF tons? They must really know what the heck they are doing to be so precise.' Then the next guy says: 'This is a big bomb and these are really bad dudes!'"

"Oh, I know, I know!" the Plebe said, raising his hand like he was still in grade school. The others looked at him. "Let's get Ben Stiller to do Zoolander and say: It's a really, really, REALLY big bomb."

The others rolled their eyes in shame and wonderment.

24

WITH THE ADVENT OF THE club, there came a tangential rise in the economic well-being of the neighborhood. The quarter saw an increase in foot and vehicular traffic. The destruction of the club had dealt a harsh blow to these budding businesses. When the end of the lane was resurrected in the form of a real bar and the tea-house, the sleepy little concerns revivified alongside. This activity rippled out from the village end, so that it's little economic pulse could be detected from a ways off.

Not long after the Prophet and the council brought in the thugs to do their skullduggery, there opened up an opium den in an abandoned sheep shed. The den was within sight of the village end, but far enough away so that the sordid side of its existence was not too disgraceful for the humble, family-run concerns.

This enclosure was fully equipped with all the modern accoutrements one could expect from such an establishment. Since it was a dry climate, there was no urgent need to make sure the roof was not leaky. Also, the cracks and crevices in the clapboard sidings were a benefit, for they filtered just enough light to see, but not to be seen. The proprietors imported some old busted-out pallets for furnishings. For comfort, there were bales of straw and gunnysacks. The burlap could be rolled up into little pillows, or stuffed with the itchy straw. For the discerning customer, there was the dainty society of rats. These rodents did not readily aggregate in the little barn much, but with the arrival of people and their food crumbs, dribble and spittle, blood, sweat and tears, the rats had reason to mingle with the men. The furry little race brought their friends with them to the gathering: the fleas. And so it was that the barn had its denizens. But the sad twist to the whole situation was that some of the men would retire back to their permanent abodes and develop painful black lumps in their lymph nodes … and die.

Although *Yersinia Pestis* is found in limited habitats in the greater area of the province, it is a sad commentary that the existence of the bubonic plague was pretty much unknown in the village before the opium den arrived.

Aside from the distraction of the black death, the opium den was popular enough. It was handy that its primary commodity was highly addictive. This meant a steady supply of return customers.

The Soldier had been in country too long. He was misunderstood back in his own country, and a permanent stranger in the country he was assigned to. New military personnel and contractors were always discovering the bar and the effort it took for him to cultivate friendships became wearisome. Some didn't understand his cold-shoulder attitude. This made them suspicious and aloof, creating a vicious circle of unfriendliness and doubt. To allay the heartache from realizing that he was no longer one of the guys, he doubled-down on his Budweiser.

He found out that the tea-house was getting a quiet reputation for a place where one could obtain different drugs. To dull the pain of his overindulgence in beer and the solo pity-parties that accompanied his drinking, he began popping pain pills that were simple to get next door.

The combination of beer and pain pills caused him to oversleep and miss work in the bar when others were relying on him. It soon became a noticeable nuisance.

One of the waiters at the tea-house observed this. He came to the hungover and droopy-eyed Soldier one late morning and guided him over to a quiet table in the corner. He went and made him a special coffee. "I made this just for you. It is a special brew from expensive beans. We do not offer it for sale. It is only available through one of us here in the back of the house. I know you from the bar, and I see you are overworked. It is alright. This coffee will help, and I will make it for you whenever you ask."

The Soldier nodded his thanks. The coffee was strong and sweetened just right. As he was going to have another sip, the waiter said: "Just a moment," then put his hand out, and showed the Soldier two white pills. He tipped the two small pills into the coffee and stirred it. The Soldier looked from the waiter to his cup of coffee, then back to the waiter. He picked up the cup of coffee and drank. The waiter slowly nodded his head. The Soldier waited for a few moments, then nodded back at the waiter.

This became the Soldier's routine. One morning the waiter said: "I see that you are still a bit sleepy after your strong coffee. Can you come back for more coffee later? Or maybe I should give you an even more special blend that we only give select patrons?" The Soldier told him that he had a busy day ahead. The waiter nodded politely. "That's ok. I will give you our special reserve blend this morning."

After stirring in the regular two pills, the waiter took out a small pouch. He took a diminutive spoon and filled it with white powder. He held it over the coffee and allowed the Soldier to observe it. The Soldier remained stoic. The waiter stirred the powder into the already spiked coffee. "This is our special reserve blend. Please enjoy." He began to leave but turned back. "I know you are a principal at the bar. We are always happy to accommodate you and your partners here in the tea-house. But I would like to politely mention that this reserve blend costs us more to make. You can have this cup on the house. But in the future, I'd like to be able to charge just a little, enough to cover our costs for this brew."

The uppers in the Soldier's coffee gave him a boost through the middle of the day. By the afternoon, he became grouchy and started in with his beer program. This took the edge off of his grouchiness. But after the beer buzz wore off, reality caved in on him in the evening, and he became bitter. Not wanting any more alcohol, but craving a release from his twisted anxieties, he started a routine of wandering over to the opium den. As his emotional pain was drowned in beer, likewise the physical pain from his hangovers was shrouded by the opium. By means of the false physic and flawed pharmacon that the drug delivered, he filled the fractured and fissured filaments of his necrotic neurons and would drift away to the phantasmagorical shores of an ephemeral elysian field of day-mares and night-dreams.

In other words, he first got drunk. Then he got stoned out of his gourd until he passed out. Then to get going again, he had to take a bunch of speed and crank mixed with coffee.

He was a mess.

Probably the only reason he wasn't dealt the hand of the black death is that the fleas didn't like his pickled blood.

One late morning, the morose Soldier was sitting alone in a corner of the tea-house. When his coffee came, he motioned his waiter not to trickle the small handful of pills into the cup, but rather to just put them down on the table. He asked for a drinking straw from the counter.

He took out a revolver and ground the pills into a grainy powder with the butt. He then pushed the course pile into irregular lines with his fingers. He bit the straw in two, spit one half on the ground and loudly snorted the gritty white trails, one in each nostril. He let out a great gasp. His eyes watered and his nose burned. "Oh yeah, come to mama!"

The waiter raised his eyebrows at this. The Soldier had never been so brash.

The Soldier waved the waiter to come closer to the table. "You know, Amigo, I never drink beer or booze over here because of respect. I respect you. I respect Asaf. Heck, I even respect the Prophet. It goes without saying that I respect the General. So I will go without saying it. However, Amigo, today is a different day. Today, I change my notions of respect. And I start here and now."

He pulled out the General's flask and poured whiskey into the coffee. The black liquid overflowed and made a mess of what was left of the powdered pills. The Soldier didn't care. He merely took the overflowing cup and tossed it down his gullet, giving himself a small shower of boozy coffee down his chin and neck.

The other men in the tea-house looked over at the commotion. The waiter was growing nervous and embarrassed.

The Soldier let out a big belch of satisfaction, unconcerned that he had washed away the remains of his toot and spilled his drink on his face and neck, all at the same time.

"Now lemme show you something. See this?" he asked, showing him the revolver and extending it towards him.

A few of the men started paying close attention.

"Go on. Take it and get a hard look at it."

The waiter shook his head and would not take the gun. He flitted his eyes about to see if any were witnessing this.

"Well, it's ok. This is a gun, for sure. But it's also a game. Come on. I'll show you the game. It's a real game. For men. Manly men. A game for keeps. All the marbles. You got your marbles, you lose your marbles, then you play for all the marbles."

The waiter was confused. His uncomfortableness was turning into fright. The Soldier's eyes showed the raving inside his head.

"See this?" The Soldier snapped out the cylinder. "That's the wheel of life. The wheel goes round and round. Where it stops is yet to be found. And here is the Kingpin of Freedom." He held up a live round. He pushed it close to the waiter's face.

"There it is, freedom. The Kingpin of Freedom. We call it the Kingpin because it is and does and says what is the finality. As an old soldier taught me, 'No one can gainsay the Kingpin.' You have to let the Kingpin do its own talking. It has its own will. It will not, cannot … nor will not, be denied."

He held the bullet up and looked at it with glowing admiration.

"Look at it!" he yelled, "Look at it! The Kingpin!" He stood up and held the bullet in the air for all to behold.

He slowly sat down. All the eyes in the tea-house were fixed on the Soldier.

"Now, come here and I will show you the wheel of life. I will show you the Kingpin. I will show you the freedom. But freedom is not easy to come by. It doesn't dilly-dally around in prancing shoes and beckon: 'Yoo-hoo, here I am.' The Kingpin, he knows the freedom. He knows that he is not likely to give you the freedom right away. He allows the wheel to spin. It spins freely, then the Kingpin speaks."

Abruptly, the Soldier slammed the revolver down in the small puddle on the table. He grabbed the waiter by the wrist and pointing to the waiter's pocket, yelled: "Gimme more of what you got there!"

With a trembling hand, the waiter pulled the baggie out.

The Soldier snatched the baggie, poured out a bunch into his hand and tossed the pills into his mouth. He picked up the flask, chased the pills and threw the empty flask across the room.

The Soldier paused, letting his bitter snack slip down his throat. "My respectfulness is coming to the end of its life. The Kingpin will set it in the wheel of his life … I'm sorry. I had the respect. Look what I have done … I lost the respect of the tea-house. I lost the respect of the coffee." Looking at the waiter, he blubbered: "I lost your respect."

Looking back at the tabletop, at the gun, and at the bullet, he said loudly: "Now I can turn my respect to the wheel and the Kingpin! The Kingpin will tell me everything I need to know!"

He picked up the gun and pushed the round into a cylinder and spun it. He held the revolver close to his ear. In a hushed voice, he said: "Listen to the wheel of life. Listen. It tells us to respect the Kingpin. It tells us to enter into the wheel."

He cocked back the hammer, spun the cylinder again, put the end of the barrel against the side of his head and pulled the trigger.

There was a loud snap.

"The Kingpin didn't speak! He has not called me into the wheel of freedom. I have no respect. Oh, wheel! Oh, wheel of freedom! Kingpin!"

He cocked, spun, barrel against his head. Snap.

He cocked the hammer again.

A man came running across the room and forcefully tackled the Soldier while at the same time slapping his forearm down. The gun came flying out of the Soldier's grasp, clattered loudly to the floor and slid away.

25

ASAF TOLD HIS UNCLE SOME of the bad things he was learning about in the basement. "I have come to the point where I can no longer allow this evil to live in our village. Or even in our country. I will destroy the bar, the tea-house and everyone in the village who does not escape. I have gone over this in my mind how I will do this. I know I can't do it alone. I would like to ask for your help."

The Uncle was surprised. "Asaf, I have always thought of you as a good person. And as an intelligent person who thought things through ... This news, this idea ... well ... I'm not sure how to express myself. It is not common for me to have nothing to say. But right now, I'm speechless. Obviously, I'm not without the faculties of moving my mouth and so on — but I'm not sure what to say, or how to say what I would say."

"I am troubled. My soul is stirred up. In the old club, we used club soda for all of our drinks. You can't run a bar without it. In the new bar, we serve Coke and Bud. Both are fizzy, but both are not club soda, which is mostly pure water. My soul was water once. Now my soul has the sugar of cola and the bitterness of beer. These bottles foam and overflow if they are shaken before being opened. If they are shaken too much they can burst. I am that bottle of bitter-sweet! I will bring down the bitterness on their heads. And I will return sweetness to our valley and what remains of our people."

The Uncle thought in silence. Asaf waited. He was committed to carrying out his plan, even if he did not have all the details in place. The Uncle's hesitation to join him was unsettling. Asaf reminded himself that it was ok for his Uncle to weigh his words before setting out on a long answer.

"Asaf, I have seen you grow and mature. In trying to understand your intent, I am reminded of some of our talks together. At one point,

I think I told you, that life is full of suffering. And the victory in life comes in contextualizing that suffering; looking at the suffering in context, and stepping back for an attempt at an objective look, makes the suffering less potent. Your suffering, Asaf, stems from your chosen role in life, your work, and associations. It does not have to be theorized. Your struggle with your chosen path and the two worlds still gives you heartache, but now, to a new, visceral level. It is at such turning points, or crossroads, that one must summon the courage to see clearly. To look around and survey the landscape of life — during the trial, while in the valley of tears. Then continue with some measure of fortitude that the courage can offer, and choose a path forward. Now, let us look at the application of this wisdom. First, is what I am telling you true? Or is the talk of suffering and courage just words and philosophical mush? Second, is it actionable? Is it either reasonable or useful or both? Let's acquiesce that it is true and useful. Therefore, third, what is Asaf going to do with his current state of suffering? What I have heard sounds very, very disturbing. Am I to just take your plan as real? Or am I to believe, much more rather believe, that you are just upset and are letting-off some pent-up steam? I hope you can answer that the latter is the case."

Asaf thought about this. "Ok, it may seem disturbing. But it's the right thing to do. I haven't thought about how my hurt inside is related to my plan. I'm just asking you to join me in sweeping away the blackness in our village."

"Because I love and care for you; and you are a smart young man and my blood, I want to answer your request as best as I can. Well, you say it's the 'right thing'. You may call it what you want, but it is your personal agenda. It is not universal. What you think is right, is right to you. It is subjective. For another, it is not, according to their subjectiveness, or subjectivity. I feel it is my moral obligation to tell you, it is an ethical axiom that one cannot do good, by doing evil. In general, I do allow for divergences in moral constructs. Differing opinions and conclusions in the whole matter can be accounted for among thinkers of all disciplines, schools, and eras. The field is widely treated from ancient to modern. The application of differentiated subjectivity can be useful in explaining away traditional morality. But this also opens the door for unsound reasoning, leading to even more faulty conclusions. If these faulty conclusions are acted upon, demented results are just one possible negative outcome. I, personally, am not overly fond of this catena. Now before you object, just allow me to say this. I am not stopping you from your course of action. I am not endorsing it nor condemning it. I am pointing out to you that there is a higher standard, or reality, or accepted truth to this than what you or I think, regardless of how we feel or how much we think our actions are justified."

Asaf was listening but wasn't convinced by his Uncle's line of thought. "I suppose we could spend a lot of time and effort seeking answers to your moral concerns. I guess in different circumstances, if we were on a long walk to the spring, we could continue to talk about it. But I am not inclined to do so. The circumstances in the tea-house persuade me that now is the time to act. And even then, I don't know how long it will take to make everything ready for the great destruction. So, I want to start on my plan, I want to get on with it."

Without addressing this concern, his Uncle continued. "Also, there is the matter of weight. Is this action the appropriate measure to right the scales of justice? Ask yourself if it promotes the commonweal? What about alternatives. Are there any? I suppose we could go on. What I am allowing for, and asking you to consider, with me, is that it may be possible that what you are doing is not right, maybe not called for, and is probably an unbalanced answer, to the evil you speak of. All that being said, there is a time when even brothers must go their own way. Whether or not you fulfill this mission, or fail at it, even dying in the effort — God have mercy — I want to let you go on your way with the understanding that you have been shown that you might not be right. I will not stop being your Uncle, ever. I will not stop you. But I cannot join you in this. If you proceed, you will do it without me."

Asaf was crestfallen. His Uncle had always been there for him. Now, at the time Asaf needed him most, his Uncle was saying 'No.'

He showed some disappointment, but quickly change his countenance to determination. "You have not judged me rightly. I allowed your positive opinion of me tell me things that were not true about my character and nature. As I look back on how I began with these soldiers, it was a bad decision. I am not someone who thinks things through. You know this. You have just been too polite to say so in plain words. I let some sort of pride or conceitedness become my guide. That bad guide led me into the world which I now must destroy."

Less sure of himself Asaf went on, "I didn't know how bad men could be. I'm still shaky inside. I have doubts and fears about doing the right thing and about revenge and about rage and about the religious who feel maybe like I am feeling. I don't know … I just don't know. It is possible … that I have lost some of my faculties. Where is my soul? Has it been fouled like a derelict bird's nest? Where is my spirit? … so much like me, for I am it's abode. Now, has it flown from the soul's smelly nest? Or has it been overwhelmed by darkness and maybe even demons?"

Asaf wiped his teary eyes with his hands. He stood up straight and breathed deep. "What I do know, is to take matters in my own hands — and get on with what I have to do. I have gone beyond good and evil! My hatred for them is the fuel of my anger. I will exercise my will to bring about the cleansing. If my heart and soul and spirit are too timid to support me in this thing, then I will proceed by the force of will-power alone. I am grateful for your honesty. Forgive me and heed the warning of what is coming. Take the whole family out of the village. No one will be safe. Possibly no one will survive. I'm sorry ahead of time if you disapprove. Only forgive … and prepare to get away from here."

After a few moments, his Uncle said: "I see you are not happy with my answer. To give a space for pause, for reflection and consideration, I offer you this proverb: There is a three-legged stool. From Giuseppe to Schrödinger, no one leg can be perfect. When sufficient weight is put on the seat, one of the legs will break first."

26

ASAF TOLD THE SPY WHAT he knew of the sectarians. He went over what history he knew and tried to give the spy a sense of the differences they had with each other. "These days, the sectarians are three groups: the Radicals, the Fanatics, and the Zealots. Please don't ask me why — or what this means. I think of it like the name of a football club. My family is not overly-religious, as most everybody knows. So, my understanding of these details is not the best. What I should say is that I know some of these things, but I don't have religious training to understand what the big deal is. I just know that somewhere along the line they made a big enough fight over these beliefs that they became enemies."

The spy nodded in understanding.

Asaf went on to tell of the long-term struggle between the factions for land. As the borders of sectarian-controlled areas shifted with the tides of war, the village was on the edge of whatever sect was in control for that time. As it passed from one militia to another, the village kept getting reduced and impoverished. However, the village was at the base of a small pass through the mountains, which made it a stopping point for modest trade- or foot-traffic. The net effect of this crossroad was that the village survived, but didn't thrive.

" … and that brings us up to now."

The spy sipped his drink. "Ahh. That's a good drink. The subtleties of it."

He held up his half-empty glass and studied it. "There are only three ingredients — but the range of the three in the mix and amounts … Well, I think I may have exhausted the permutations … What was it you were saying?"

Asaf opened his mouth, but the spy interrupted.

"Yet, one never knows for sure. Maybe I could count the number of cubes — the temperature of the room. Ah yes ... the possibilities ..."

He clinked the ice around.

Asaf said, "I was going to ..."

"But then again, maybe I am reading too much into this. Why shouldn't I just sit and enjoy it? ... not philosophize about it too much."

He took another swallow. This time Asaf did not presume to speak but waited patiently until the spy was done with whatever he was going to say.

The spy said, "What were you going to say?"

Asaf cleared his throat, attempting a preamble to start taking again.

The spy lifted his glass, then seemed to change his mind and set it down again. Asaf paused.

The spy asked, "What was that?"

"Nothing. I was just ..."

He tipped the glass, slurping at the remaining ice cubes. "I would, in times past, light up a smoke just now. But I've learned over time, that, in spite of my urge, it's better not to smoke. For professional reasons, you know. I'm going to the outhouse." The spy walked away, lighting a cigarette as he headed out.

The following day, Asaf asked the spy if he could be trusted.

"Yes, but you shouldn't trust me."

"Why not?"

The spy replied rhetorically, "Why?"

"I don't understand," Asaf said with a look of doubt on his face.

"Let's consider my role, my occupation, my profession. By definition, I am several things at once. I am secretive. I use deceit as an art-form to carry out my craft. I buy and sell secrets. I get dirt on people and governments and all their military and technology. I follow people around and pretend to be someone who I am not and the better I fool people the better I get paid, either in money or in kind. So look at it this way: the more deceitful I am, the better I am. And — and, add to that, this: My rewards, my recompense is, most of the time on the down-low. I don't even get a cock-a-doodle-do when I score. There are just a few who reap the rewards of my salaried work: house payment, wife and kids. But a lot of what I bring in is off the books. Who can you share it with? 'Hey, check it out! Here's some spending money for an all-out cruise to Aruba! I got a bonus because,' dot dot dot. You fill in the dot dot dot. I hit a punk politician. I blew up a boat full of dope. I fingered some lousy schmuck for dealin' arms to the bad guys. Passports for money. Surveillance of some kinky politician with a gal — or even a kid. Double-cross. Triple cross. How much of this can you share with somebody else? Some, maybe. And even at that, you have to be careful. And there's stuff you can't share no-way no-how … Just as important — no — maybe more important. Yeah, more important is who you tell. Anyone who is a listener to what you have to offer is a potential threat. An enemy, a competitor, a traitor. Maybe a blackmailer. So in this big bag of mixed-up communications, there lies a kernel of wisdom: You can't trust nobody."

Asaf tried not to look dumbfounded, but was at a loss as to what to say.

The spy picked up on this and decided to help him out. "Look, I know it's frustrating. But I come to you with the truth, for the good of all concerned. Don't take it personally. If you tell me something or involve me in some plan, there is no way to guarantee that it will be completely safe. I'm not telling you all this to distance you from me, or vice versa. I'm telling you to protect you. Let me re-phrase that. 'To protect you' sounds like a pious platitude. How shall I say it? … Even though we are friends — in a certain way — like we see each other a lot, or we've known each other for a long time, anyone, like you, would think that I am in their corner. That I've got your back, and so on. Ultimately, this may be the actual and true outcome of this thing you have involving me. Most likely — I'll say it again — most likely, everything will work out fine. I'll be an upstanding mensch, and we'll all live happily ever after. Most likely … ok?"

Asaf nodded. "Ok. Most likely. But here comes the big 'But.'"

The spy smiled. "But. There it is. But, that in no way guarantees anything. And — I'm not jumping through all these plausible outcomes for my sake, but for yours. I'm getting long in the tooth at this game. You've got the oyster in your headlights. Consider my speech as a warning, and as a solid piece of advice. What do you think?"

"I would still like to talk with you about my plan."

"Ok then, let's move on. Let's go ahead and talk about your plan. I invite you to tell me what you want to. I will listen. We will go forward in some fashion based on your ideas of what you want to do.

What you need to realize — I can't emphasize this enough — what you will be doing is a gamble. A roll of the dice. A flip of the card. Let's presume I will participate in your plan. You will have to take the risk of either believing that I will not betray you — or, that if I do — you will make good your escape, or revenge, or bait-and-switch, or whatever may come — to turn things around if I go south on you."

Asaf was not happy with the spy's reasoning. "But why? Why can't I tell you what I am planning and you can say: yes or no, and we can proceed accordingly? If you say, no, that's it. If you say, yes, then we go on. Right?"

The spy leaned forward. "No — not right. You can talk and tell me whatever it is you have to say, but I will not say 'Yes' or 'No'. I will only listen. I will affirm you. I will tell you I am listening. I might ask for more information or details. And I will be listening. But beyond that, I will not be able to say 'Yes' or 'No.'"

Asaf reached up and grabbed his hair. "Why? Why can't you do more than just listen? Listen, listen, listen. Can't we team up and carry out the plan? Can't we act? Do something? We just can't sit around and talk."

"I understand your irritation. But I do not think you understand the very nature of spy-craft. We mostly just listen. We tell what we have heard, but only and always in the context of who we are telling what, in the larger context of always listening to the conversation. Even when we are telling it."

Asaf leaned his head back and looked at the ceiling. He felt like he was on a merry-go-round and did not know how to start or stop it, or even how he got on board. "I don't think we are making any sense here. I have a simple plan, and I want you to be part of it because I think you have what is needed for this plan to work. And all you tell me is that you really can't be a part of this plan because I can't trust you. Or at least that is what I am getting out of this."

"I'm sorry for the confusion. I'm trying to do the right thing by you. Let's do this: You tell me what's up with this plan of yours. Like I said, I will listen. When I have a question or some other indication that I would like you to go on with what you want to say, we will go on. Fair enough?"

"Fair enough already! Why couldn't we get to where we are now, way back when we started?"

The spy answered: "I guess we could've. I guess we would be where we are now. Except — now — you have heard my warnings and explanations, should things not go as you foresee them."

"Alright, alright. I just want to move on. Ok. I think a big part of the plan will be timing. Timing. It must be timed just right ... "

The spy cut in. "Ok — just wait a minute. I've got to go take a leak."

Asaf slumped and closed his eyes in exasperation.

The spy returned and Asaf said: "Ok, let me see if I got this right. I tell you what I want — or need. You may or may not be able to help. You may or may not be friend or foe. But to proceed — I still have to tell you everything. Right?"

The spy chuckled. "A good beginning, but still some nuances need to be put in place. Or let's say fine-tuning, adjustments and additions. To start, no. Not everything, you don't. You must pick and choose what you are going to tell me. You must judge what is necessary to get what you want without giving away information or knowledge or insight that is superfluous and may tip the balance against you. Granted, it's a fine line sometimes. And it comes with practice — undergirded with training — both lacking in your case. But you are coming to me, and I am telling you like it is."

"There you are — no experience. I don't know how to play this game. How am I to know what part of my plan I should explain to you, and what not?"

The spy leaned back and smoked, looking lazily at Asaf, taking his time before answering. "Ok, Asaf. Shoot. Give it to me straight. What can I do for you?"

Asaf paused, gathering his thoughts. He took a seat next to the spy at the table. He leaned in just a bit. "Well, to start, I need explosives. Lots of explosives. I have a plan to destroy this place. My idea is to blow it up with explosives. The whole thing. I need enough explosives to blow up this entire building, the tea-house and the whole basement. And I want it to be even more. At least twice as much as necessary, because I don't want any mistakes or have any possibility that what I want to have happen, won't happen ... But I need your help. All this time we have been talking, this is what I want to do. This is my plan, at least as far as I have thought it out. Blow this place to smithereens."

Beneath the table, the spy gave Asaf a swift kick in the leg and above the table a menacing glare.

Asaf was not to be deterred. He lowered his voice and continued quickly before the spy had a chance to stop him with one of his inane lectures. "And I need the equipment or stuff to string them out and make them blow up. Some detonation program. And I need to blow things up by remote."

Another kick. Another hard look. The spy interrupted: "Coffee. How much coffee."

"Coffee?"

The spy hissed. "Say 'coffee'. How much coffee it will take?"

Asaf, being honest and unacquainted with the world of spying, was confused. He hesitated, then said: "I don't know how the coffee will make all this happen. But I guess that's why I'm coming to someone who knows better. It's got to be pretty basic stuff. I mean look how many people there are who blow things up, but don't want to be near. My plan calls for that — sounds simple — even to me. But I don't like how I am explaining this, in these child-like words. But I am not sure I know what to call these things. Bombs and blow up devices. Sounds silly. But you know what I mean, right?"

The spy was a cool customer. But in this case, he became a hot chili pepper. He stood up and through clenched teeth said: "You're a nincompoop. Why don't you go to your people for these things? They're the experts."

Asaf was immediately offended. He stood up in anger but didn't say anything. He glanced around the bar, trying to bide his time, trying to quell his agitation and to see if the two of them had attracted any attention. He brushed his hair back with his palms, subconsciously distracting himself and drying his palms at the same time, so quickly had he begun to sweat.

The spy didn't move a muscle. He held Asaf in an icy stare.

Asaf relaxed his posture. He was not just posing as if he were thinking, but actually thinking that what the spy just suggested was a genuine possibility. Before he knew it, Asaf was thinking that the spy's remark may not have been a dirty insult, but also may have been a real piece of advice. "Actually I hadn't thought of that. I don't think of them as 'my people'. In fact, now that I think about it some more, it might be a really good suggestion."

The spy showed no more emotion. He looked straight ahead, then down at the table, stubbed out his cigarette, and walked out of the bar.

27

THE NEXT DAY, ONE OF the waiters from the tea-house told the lead bartender that the spy was in the tea-house. The lead bartender told Asaf.

When Asaf approached, the spy smiled widely, exhaled a bunch of smoke and said: "Ha! I'm not surprised to see you here."

Asaf smiled back, a quirky, nervous smile. There was certainly nothing wrong with the spy having tea or coffee in the tea-house, but it was unnerving for Asaf. He had never seen the spy outside of the bar and it made him uncomfortable.

Asaf asked in a hasty whisper: "What are you doing here?"

The spy laughed. "Coffee my boy — coffee! I want coffee. You want coffee. We all want coffee! Like I scream."

"Ice cream?"

"You scream. I scream. We all scream — for I scream!"

Asaf didn't like this scene. He brought a finger up to his lower eyelid to stop it from twitching. He didn't want to get sucked into some jumbled coffee and ice cream tango with the spy. But he did want to know why the spy was in the tea-house, and he did want to know why he was so amped-up over coffee. He didn't want to know about the ice cream, for his poor eyelid could only take so many tremors.

In a less sinister voice, Asaf asked again: "What are you doing here?"

The spy ignored his question. "So, tell me my friend — what are my options? Is there a menu? — or do I just — wing it?

"What options? What do you want? Why are you here?"

The spy continued to ignore Asaf. "Where I come from, there's the coffee and the cream — or milk nowadays — and sugar. I do us all a favor to skip over all the tedious, pestiferous pastel packets of ersatz sweeteners. Just the sugar — thank you. Now, on to the coffee. Drip? Expresso? Au lait?"

Seeing that the spy was not going to do him the pleasure of answering him, Asaf signaled to a waiter. The waiter came over and Asaf spoke with him briefly.

"May I sit?"

The spy responded merrily. "Of course — of course. Your place, not mine."

Asaf sat. They smoked in silence. Asaf, feeling the irritation of the heat and smoke of the cigarette. The spy, feeling the soothing nicotine and the simple pleasure of a leisurely smoke.

Coffee service for two arrived. On a burnished tray, the waiter set down a set of cups and saucers, a sugar bowl and a nice little milk pitcher and two apricot biscuits.

Asaf was about to reach for his cup when the spy stretched out his arm and blocked him rudely.

"Let me be of service my friend," the spy said calmly.

Asaf sat back, put off by the spy's behavior, but curious.

The spy said: "This is for future reference. Keep this basic knowledge in mind."

The spy then set the two cups of coffee on the table: one by Asaf, the other near himself.

The spy continued: "Here are two cups. Now, look … " He picked up the sugar bowl and poured out two small piles of sugar next to each cup. "Here, next to the coffee is a small amount of sugar. The sugar is pure sugar."

Then the spy picked up the milk pitcher. He slowly and carefully poured a stream of milk from one pile of sugar to the other pile of sugar. "Here is a line, made of this milk, from one pile of pure sugar to the other pile. As you know, when you put the sugar in the coffee it tastes good. The milk is good too. We could put this pile of sugar in your cup and the other in my cup. Also, this milk could be put in the cups. But you see here, that the milk stretches across the table. We can't really put it into the coffee."

The spy stood up. "Look," he said, "I can take this biscuit and go away with it. You can too. But it is still part of the coffee service you ordered, even though I am walking away with it."

The spy then straightened up, took a bite out of the biscuit and walked out of the tea-house, humming a tune as he left.

The following day, the spy was back in the bar. He raised his eyebrows at Asaf, who came over to the table. The spy started out very cautiously and slowly. "Good day. I want to thank you for inviting me to have some coffee with me yesterday."

Asaf began to respond, but the spy ignored him, cut him off and continued talking. "I hope you have taken some time to recall how good the service was. The condiments. Milk and sugar. Even the cookies."

The spy paused. Asaf was about to speak again, but the spy went on: "And the presentation and the way we enjoyed the coffee. The milk, the sugar."

Pause.

Asaf didn't bite this time but remained silent, reminding himself of his Uncle's lessons on the virtues of patience and how hard it is to acquire it and the patience it takes to become patient. He reminded himself that it was he who started the whole thing and it was no fault but his own if the spy was completely or even half gonzo. And if he continued to ramble on in his mind anyone reading his thoughts would be lost as to who was the subject and who was the object of the sentences. Amid these musings, Asaf realized that the spy was indeed silent now.

Asaf looked carefully at the spy. Nothing. Asaf was about to start with questions but then hesitated. He began to consider what progress he had made by peppering and badgering him with questions. Nil. Or almost nil. So, Asaf decided to take a different approach. "Simple Asaf — keep it simple," he thought.

"I'm glad you enjoyed the coffee."

The spy lit a new smoke. He cast half-mast eyes at Asaf and said nothing.

Asaf plodded forward: "Yes ... And, how we shared the time together. And the sugar ... the milk ..."

The spy waved an extended hand at Asaf and said softly: "That's enough. Enough. I see this is torture. And it's not what I want for us. Asaf, we can talk about coffee. Sugar, milk — your shoes — sports always works — even though it's pretty worn out as a medium — and as far as I can tell, neither of us follows sports much. You?"

Asaf shook his head. "No, no sports," he said listlessly. He was beyond disappointed and angry. He was just frustrated and was deciding in his mind that substantive communication with the spy would be futile. "I just thought you could help. Sorry — I was wrong.

Here, I'll take care of this ashtray and get a new one. Anything from the bar while I'm away?"

The spy said plain water was fine. Asaf left with his head hung a little bit low.

Asaf returned with a clean ashtray and some water for their table.

The spy said: "Let me stop making you angry with me. Once and for all. We can't talk about your plan. I only have a mere inkling. But your one mention about it the other day when I left, gives me a clue. And that clue is: that it is something we cannot discuss. It could mean death for us both. There, I've said it."

Asaf asked if he could sit. The spy gladly gestured for him to sit.

Asaf asked in a low tone: "Ok. Have it your way. But is there somewhere where we can talk?"

"No," the spy answered very quietly while retaining his composure, demeanor, and poise. "There is nowhere. Where are we going to go? We can't talk here. We're surrounded by soldiers. We can't go to the tea-house — we're surrounded by freedom-fighters. Where else? Your friend, the Daughter's house? Everybody will say: 'Hey those two went into the Daughter's house. I wonder what they're talking about?' The cafe? Everybody, including your proprietor buddy, will say: 'Hey, look at those two sitting around the cafe. I wonder what they're talking about?' And so on. The only way for you to tell me about some plan that involves what you mentioned is to talk about it by talking about other things. Our own code. Even then — it's full of risk. Here's some bar talk ... I like the ponies. Hit the consensus favorite to show and spread two to ten bucks per race on the long shot — over all nine races — if you're in it for the whole live-long day — and you'll come out ahead. Before the race, the owners and the trainers and the jockeys all get their heads together to sort out the details of the race. All kinds of details. Enough to give Dick Francis material for dozens of books. Well, there you are. He did — and has. But the basics are the same for any set of owners, trainers, and jockeys. They can be summarized as the length of the race, the number in the field, the conditions of the track, horse, jockey and his weight. But I figured you didn't know the pastern from the pasture or the fetlock from the farrier. So, I circumlocuted myself to the circumstances we have here."

Asaf was at a loss for a response. His family didn't own any horses or donkeys. They borrowed an old bony one for the water stand or an errand. Sometimes they would hire a cart to hook up the donkey if it was a big load. Asaf wasn't even sure exactly what it was. His Uncle talked some about mares and jack-asses and fertility, but Asaf was not interested in the difference and paid little attention. Asaf knew that some of the ethnic groups had competitive horse games, but he had never seen one and did not know the rules. Asaf mumbled: "Sounds like something the General would say."

The spy cupped his ear. "What was that? I didn't quite catch it."

"Oh, I was saying I thought you were speaking in a general sort of way."

The spy frowned. "Generally speaking? I try to remain specific in what I am trying to perambulate. But when I specify what I am talking or asking or listening around at to and for, it is not the generic, but the actual detailed thing that is."

Asaf cupped his ear. "What was that? I didn't quite catch it."

"I was saying that since I figured you were not up on all the horse-racing terminology, I'd find something better suited to things we have right here. Coffee came to mind."

28

So, over Marlboros and Jack and Coke, they agreed that coffee was just as good a code-speak as any other cover. It just appeared that the two of them were exploring wholesale and retail ideas and how to make and serve different styles of the beloved brown bean.

The spy inquired: "So, why ask me? What makes you think I know about grinding and blending coffee? And if by chance I do, what makes you think I have access to these products?"

Asaf answered: "I don't have a firm answer. I just think, or thought — or am thinking — that someone in your position would know a lot more about the international bean trade than me."

"Yes. I concede that's true. So that makes sense. But, although you were uncomfortable with my suggestion for getting this stuff from your people, I think you realized the value in my idea."

"Yes. You're right."

"So? Why not go along in that direction?"

"It's a good idea. But, as an idea, not something I could do."

"Why not?"

"The most obvious answer to 'Why not?' is: Because it is dangerous. After all these conversations, I have come to appreciate your initial and on-going wariness. Now, when I look around, I see what you saw."

"Sí. Seesaw."

"Very funny. Anyhow, back to the point. I can't be asking around for coffee grinding equipment … even if I knew where or who to ask."

"I'm not sure that answers my question: Why me? We've already pointed out that you are in business with military personnel. What about the General? What about the Soldier? Well, before you roll your eyes at me even mentioning the General, I withdraw. But the Soldier is still your buddy, right? And while we're at it, I think I'll withdraw asking about the Soldier too. I was just thinking here and there for others that you might consider. We still know that most of your clientele are military. So far so good. But the danger notwithstanding, I would think that there were many, much better options than a leftover intel guy."

Asaf was hesitant. "I am not sure what I am gambling with — or about. I do not know what I have to lose. I do not know if I will be betrayed or not. I do not know if I will ever know — since I myself do not know — if I am betraying or being betrayed. I have even been told by my Uncle that he cannot go along with my plan."

The spy lowered his voice. "What doesn't he like?"

Asaf answered: "He doesn't like the part … Wait a minute! Who cares what he does or doesn't like? We're not talking about my Uncle. We're talking about the plan."

"Sorry. The plan. I was getting mixed up with the uncle stuff. What is it you were saying about gambling?"

Asaf set his tray on the table. "You were the one who was talking about it."

"I was?"

"Yes. Right? You said I had to roll the dice and flip the card."

Asaf looked blankly at a drop of condensation trickling slowly down the bottle of Coke. His mind wandered, sadly wondering what small, short life the drop had. It gathered mass and sped up as it took in another little bit of moisture. Then slowed down as it lost water behind in a little trail. Asaf was beginning to philosophize about the drop's journey and his life in the village and what parallels there were. He then reached out and rubbed off the drop and wiped the dew on his shirt sleeve. "I'm just a regular guy. I come from an average conservative home. I want to have a good life like everybody else. The sectarians have ruined all that. Look around. Look at our village. Look at our countryside. It's a crap-hole. And it's been this way my whole life. I only know things can be better because I listen to my mother and Uncle and their friends talk about the old days before the wars. And, I've had the chance to make a few visits away from here. I've seen that there are places where over half the neighborhood is not all bombed-out. Where entire streets have not been abandoned. So when the Soldier explained to me the whole club idea — I was really eager to help. Nothing like that had ever happened here. I didn't care from a dirt clod or a mountain that it was a bar for foreigners. Anything was better than sitting on the roadside watching your crumpled, broken-down neighborhood waste away into nothing. And I have no regrets or apologies. The club brought back some life into our village. People working — and getting paid for once. New ideas on how the foreign soldiers might help instead of thinking they are here only to kill everyone. Even then — right when it looked like something good was going to happen — for the first time in my short life — the stupid religionists come along and ruin what little we had. I hated them. Hated hated hated."

Asaf paused. He looked around the bar to see if he was making a scene. Nobody was paying any attention.

29

"ASAF, LET ME ASK YOU a question. After the whole bombing, it seems you went your own way. Then, here you are — part of, and committed to, this whole rebuilding effort. Not just the club — but a whole new enterprise — the tea-house. Seems to me you jumped from the frying pan into the fire … … I was waiting for my brain to misfire on that proverb as it does on most — but I guess it came out right. Right? Frying pan, then fire. Right?"

Asaf looked at the ceiling and rolled his eyes. "It was after fire and the new stand I met the Prophet. It was very, very strange. So strange, it's hard to talk about."

Asaf grew very still. Tears filled his eyes and trickled down his cheeks. He went over to the bar, got a bar mop, daubed his face and dried his eyes. He then returned to the table and sat with the spy. "When I say I cannot talk to you about it, I'm not trying to be rude. It is something that is hard to explain. With anyone. Hard to say — to explain, to tell."

The spy nodded politely. Asaf went on with his story. "The Prophet … Everybody wants to know about the Prophet."

The spy jumped in, "You're right. Everybody wants to know about the Prophet. Heck, I'm a spy — and I want to know about the Prophet."

Asaf eyed the spy very cooly, bordering on suspicion. "What do you want to know about the Prophet?"

"What do you have to say about the Prophet?"

"The Prophet … You might not believe this, but I am a follower of the Prophet."

Asaf waited for the spy to drop his cigarette in his drink, or watch his eyes bug out of his head. Nothing. No flinch, no reaction. Asaf was secretly a touch disappointed at this. He hoped his little revelation would get a rise from the spy. No such luck.

Asaf sighed and continued. "As we all know, the sectarians are at war with each other. But the Prophet is the reason we are here. He is the reason the tea-house exists. The Prophet wants to end the war. He has a vision to bring lasting peace. He wants the sects: the Zealots, the Radicals and the Fanatics, to lay down their arms. He wants them to come together in a mutual or shared compromise for the good of the faith and for the good of all. He wants to be the spiritual father of a brokered peace between the factions. He believes that God has chosen him for this — at this time. He believes he is God's emissary for this generation.

"When I met the Prophet, I was full of bitterness. My world was empty. I got out to his place under bad circumstances so I was in a lousy mood. I was in his garden, waiting for him. He was serious, but not stern. The peacefulness of the big garden and his calm way settled me down. We made some small talk. Tea was brought out. He asked a few questions about who I thought he was and what others thought about him. He began to talk to me with words that told of other things than I ever knew were. He described other worlds. He described other worlds like I would describe that ashtray right there. So familiar. But for me — my head was spinning, I guess is what they say. We went for a walk along the garden paths. I don't know how long I was at his compound. When we were done walking, he made a ceremony with me. I don't understand it all — but, I knew, that when that strange ceremony was over, the Prophet had converted me into one of his followers."

Asaf paused again, maintaining his composure. Then, with great animation, he said loudly: "But there's more!"

At this unexpected change in Asaf's tone and demeanor, the cool spy started a bit.

"There's more to what the Prophet did with me than just with anyone. I'm sure of it. I don't know how people get converted, but I am sure they don't have the Prophet give them each an individual ceremony like the one he and I did. It wouldn't be possible. There's too many followers all over the place. What he did with me ... Well, it might not be unique, but it was special."

Asaf was talking as if releasing his mind straight out of his mouth. It seemed that he was unaware, or at least didn't care, that he was at the table with the spy. He stared straight ahead and spoke evenly. "I have always known that it was a special event — most likely for both of us

— but I didn't see it until now. Yes, yes. I have been afraid to admit it to myself — certainly not to another — but even here … and here …" Asaf touched the side of his head, then the middle of his chest with an open hand as he spoke these last words haltingly.

"Somehow, the Prophet knows. Maybe he is a prophet. I believe that he knows, but can't come to grab ahold of it — can't wrestle with it the right way. He knows that there is something that will happen between us, that he can only peek at, around a shadowy curtain or veil. He can only peek at it because it is in the future. And even for a prophet, the future is hard to see. He even said so. He has tried to see what this was hiding behind the veil, but he cannot see it. But it arrests him. It grabs him by the soul and forces — no, not forces — it drives him to do what he would otherwise not do. I don't have the word. Compels him. Something takes his will and draws it to what it — the something — that it wants, and the Prophet must go along with it, for to not to do so would be ever more and ever more discomfort. But to move with it and go along with the prompting gives the soul some rest. That is, some relief … relief from the compulsion."

Asaf stood hypnotically and said in a loud whisper: "And that thing is me! He knows it. He doesn't like it because it makes no sense. But he can't help it. The object of his compulsion is me, and he can't explain it. I am the object of his future — that thing behind the veil. That which he does not want … but cannot resist. He can feel it, but the feeling is something other. It is the other that escapes him and makes him uncomfortable. You see the moth fly into the fire. What fight? What struggle? We cannot know. Can we go into the moth? Can we get under its furry skin? Can we get under that furry skin and be drawn by the light and warmth — only getting closer and closer and the light is brighter and brighter and warmer and warmer and too bright too bright too warm too warm too bright blinding hot hot blinding heat — tear away fly back go — can't can't turn can't stop — too bright — can't stop! The pain. The torture. The twist of the mind! Only able to make the sensations into ecstasy. An ecstasy of dissolving abandon. To whatever it may be without care and not caring — but being — and being engulfed — caught up into some unity of merging into one fiery consummation."

Asaf stopped his soliloquy. He stopped staring into blank air. He leaned forward. He boldly placed his hands flat on the table and spoke directly into the spy's face. "This is the fate of two faces. Fates to fulfill the driving and drawing of the Prophet. The future knows he will fumble and falter in his mission because not many men can undertake what fate has asked him to undertake. Knowing this, the future has made another way to take it from the Prophet and move it to another soul. But the vessel-soul or souls are outside the distant future — they are in the now. And, in the now, they struggle with the push and pull of the future on them. The one generation. To each generation given. This is central to the Prophet's belief system. Each generation. This is the Prophet's strife — and his striving. This is my struggle and pain. The pain from the pull of the future that has drawn me into a plan that was not meant to be — or maybe only meant to be as some sort of an alternative. Or I am a vessel that has not been properly made, or trained, to be an alternative. I don't know. What I think I know, is that I have been given the spiritual seal as the successor to the Prophet. The ceremony. It only makes sense if all this future and now is true. I don't know if the Prophet knew or was driven to cause this ceremony to happen. But it doesn't matter in the end. It happened. And this succession can only come about if I destroy the Prophet. That is why I am here. That is why you are here. That is why the plan must go forward. I have not seen and did not understand. I have seen and still don't understand very well. But it is making more sense. I have seen the evil grow and grow in this wicked place. And I have been deeply troubled and confounded by the mix-up between the righteousness and peace the Prophet said he was to bring us — the peace I wanted so badly — and the evil he has brought to us. The Prophet's followers serve tea and cookies to the old men and whoever else happens to pass by and wants a place to sit out of the sun. I don't know if those men who eat and drink there know the tea-house sits over one of the gates of hell or not. And whether or not the termites and beetles that scurry in and out are trafficking in guns and drugs and boys and girls. Now I think I understand. The future has picked me to destroy its first messenger because he has turned from his calling and given himself over in complete abandonment to his lower nature. The strange mix-up is that the very calling he had to bring peace, came with the possibility of giving that calling away if he needed to. But because he was unable to be calm inside about the possibility of giving his calling away, it became a source of discomfort to him. Being unable to rest — and more and more unable to recognize that his unrest was of his own making, in not being willing to give his calling away — he became reprobate."

Asaf stood up straight and was still. He returned his focus to the spy. "I was once excited about the new life these people and businesses brought here. The problem is, the arrival of all these outsiders has changed this village forever. And that brings us up to now. The bar is here, the tea-house is here. It seems the outpost idea has been put on the back burner — I guess? You would know better than me. I don't see a lot of action that makes it seem like this is the cutting-edge of what's next in the big-action war scene. The wars are not in this area. The soldiers come and go. They don't know why they are here when they get here and are just glad to leave when they do and don't know any more about why they are leaving than when they got here. It makes for good business, if you want to spend all day serving mercenaries beer so they can tell stories of where they were, and maybe where they hope to go, while they drink and play cards and throw darts to pass the time. They have brought here everything that our culture and religion despises. I have a deep feeling, way down inside, that the fight over control of this village and this area will never — at least in my lifetime — come to any good. My soul is filled with disgust with the battle of evil versus even more evil. I want to send everyone — everyone involved with and associated with this place — to hell! And my plan calls for making this place no prize for any group for as long as … as many generations as I can. Maybe if the village ceases to exist, the little pass will never be discovered by these outsiders and foreigners again. And you know how I want to do it. I have been a good bartender for your time spent here. We have talked and laughed and now — cried — at least I have. Now, I want you to look deep inside and see if there is something there that can make room for my cause. Somewhere inside that can find a kindred meaning in what I am proposing to do. I have seen and heard from you how you got satisfaction in making evildoers pay for their crimes. That is the part of the inside of you that I am talking about. And one last thing — then I will be done. I would ask you to consider another future. And it is this … You know I am determined to see my plan through. With or without you. No offense. But think about how mixed-up things could get, how bad it could go for me if I got this type of help from the wrong person. I have enough stress and nervousness just trying to get my plan in action all alone. Imagine how bad it could get if I got caught in someone else's web."

30

In a quiet corner on a quiet evening, the spy gave Asaf his last lesson. "Now after all you have learned about the coffee business, there are some areas I'd like to give you practical advice about. First, even with the knowledge you now have, it is still a beginning. You will still need a confederate. This can be a subtle thing. It has to be a careful choice. This confederate, he is necessary. He may be an ally. But, be circumspect, he could become a hindrance. In this undertaking, you can't really trust anybody too much. Especially your confederate. You're bringing him in for dastardly work. If he knows how to deal in this whole business, he needs to be vetted as best as you can with the tools you have at your disposal under the circumstances. But, as it appears that time is of import, you will have to make a leap of faith at some point. You will have to use some instinct and some of the things you have heard me talk about from the world of spy-craft. I think this includes using your guts."

The spy sat back to see if Asaf had any questions or comments. Asaf looked at the spy and nodded for him to continue.

"Your confederate is an important player, right? But there is also some sort of team. There will be insiders and not-insiders. How are you going to keep things moving forward and still keep one group from knowing too much? In fact, you need to ask yourself, what is too much? Who needs to know what? Who is a friend, who is an enemy? Who can know this and know that? And when the train goes off the rails, who is coming with me, who is left behind, and at what point do I only try and save my own life if I have to? Think about these things. You have to keep all this in control in some fashion. This is challenging in so far as you will be roasting a lot of beans. And a nice dark roast, I believe. My advice is to play your cards … wait, I need to come up with another phrase. My advice is to keep things simple. To keep a complex thing simple is to keep it from having too many parts — and compartmentalizing as needed. This guy for just this thing, and that guy for just another thing. I know it's counter-intuitive because this compartment design is a little more work on your end, but it keeps the wheels on the bus until you drive it over the cliff. See there? I came up with something other than cards and horses. A train wreck. Or bus in this case. Between the coffee and the team players and exit strategies, I don't know how much our code speak is working or not. But who cares? We've never mentioned anything other than the coffee biz so who knows if they are listening and cop-on, or are just thinking we're bamboozling him, her, ourselves and Juan Diego."

"Who's Juan Diego?"

"He's that Folger's coffee guy. You know. Juan Diego has the finest beans on the mountain. Juan Diego. The donkey and burlap bags. Right?"

"Isn't Juan Diego the man chasing windmills all over the place. He rode a donkey."

"Windmills? You must mean coffee grinder, and somehow got lost in translation. Mill and grinder are pretty close to the same thing. I think the guy you're talking about is Pancho Santana or something like that. Probably related to Carlos Santana the great guitar player. Or is it José Vargas? Maybe it was José Vargas and the mountain of beans. Mountains are grown for bitter flavor. I don't know … All I know is that we're getting sidetracked again and beans and mountains and grinders. The lesson here is don't get sidetracked. Simple is better, or less moving parts if you like that way of saying it. Ok?"

Asaf nodded.

The spy went on. "Next, you always need an exit plan and a backup plan. The exit plan is kind of self-explanatory. But the backup plan has two forks in it. A secondary exit plan, and an overarching, permanent bailout. The secondary exit plan is for when the primary exit plan goes tits-up on you. The general bailout is only when things go fubar. This is the scenario where you are primarily concerned with getting out alive. The plan goes out the door, any escape is a good escape. You may still be able to use the primary exit plan route, but only as a convenience. Route one, route two, route Sixty-six. The goal is to live for another day. So what is an exit plan? You need to think ahead how you want to get out of the village. Kind of simple as that. Simple?! Sure. It won't be simple, but if you have a general idea or a basic plan on how to stay alive or save your hide, it will help. In complex cases, we did dry runs. Sometimes multiple dry runs. Adding twists and turns as we saw fit or trying to foresee what obstacles and choke points that might jump up and bite us in the butt. You can do this too. This is your village. This is your home turf. This should be turned as much as you can to your advantage. Think about who, what and how sets of circumstances and what people — especially a foe — can be outsmarted, by using your local knowledge to your favor. In putting the plan together, these are the overarching stratagems you should keep in mind. Not just keep in mind, but use and implement as best as you can. They will serve you well and give you the upper hand when things get dicey. There are a variety of other tools and techniques you can learn or think about, but we don't have the time or a conducive setting for this. So, that brings me to one more last thing, unless I have already used up some previous last things. But first, let's have the pause that refreshes, ok?"

The spy had not been in the bar for several days. Asaf asked the lead bartender if he knew anything. He said no-one had heard anything. He then went quickly over to the tea-house and made the same inquiry. Nothing. Asaf went to the corner table where the spy sat, and looked at it wistfully. There might have been some mission underway. Asaf felt that he and the spy had developed a friendship. Asaf didn't spend much time thinking about it, but he knew the spy wouldn't stay in the village forever. Despite his adherence to the cloak-and-dagger-smoke-and-mirrors code of non-ethics, Asaf didn't anticipate that the spy would leave with no good-bye or farewell.

Asaf did not like the situation. The spy was always on guard, at some level, the whole time. Asaf was fairly certain that the spy was on his side, but there remained that shadow of doubt. Asaf now had a fear creeping that he may have overstepped his boundaries in trying to take the spy into his confidences. Asaf only had conjectural imaginations about the actual world of the spies. Maybe the spy will rat him out as a hostile entity. Maybe one fine day, some random sniper will pick him off from a thousand meters with a special sniper round and nobody will ever know what happened. Maybe some double agent would spike his drink, or kidnap him as the councilmen did. These dark scenarios made him shudder.

Asaf sat down where he had spent hours butting heads and

matching wits with the spy. Hours of frustration not knowing if up was up or down was down or if both were sideways under different circumstances. Hours of trying to understand his way of communication. And hours of coffee-bomb tutorials. Now that he was apparently gone, it was upsetting. Asaf already started feeling unprepared. He felt despite everything the spy tried to teach him, it was still not enough. He went for a walk to think.

When he returned and looked over at the spy's table, something was laying on it. There, right in front of the chair where the spy usually sat, was the engraved Zippo he always had handy and preferred over the plastic Marlboro lighters. The Zippo was something the spy toyed with now and then when he talked. Flipping the cap and feeling the weight of the lighter. He spoke about it once, when he saw Asaf observing him fiddle with it. It was given to him when he was a new spy. In those days, the Zippo was a fashion statement. When the age of miniaturization came along, the iconic lighter became an international undercover tool. Microfilm, little cameras, microphones, poisons and such, could be inserted into it. Then, when miniaturization was eclipsed by the digital revolution alongside the boom of the plastics industry, the Zippo was no longer in vogue and no longer in the modern spy's tool kit. The spy said he kept it as a reminder and souvenir of his early days and because it was sturdy, functional and could still be retro-fitted with old spy gear if necessary. He said the only issue with that was, he had had it engraved with his old bureau's logo. That made it slightly less attractive as an undercover item than if it were plain. But he said he didn't care. It was a nostalgic and sentimental piece, not cold-war espionage equipment.

Asaf's first reaction was to pick it up and look around for his friend. Then he hesitated, unsure if there was some trick. He looked at it carefully, assuring himself that it was the Zippo. He nudged it with a finger. Nothing happened. So, he picked it up with his hand, hefted it, felt the quality build and the brushed satin finish. He looked at the old bureau logo, the engraved lines, black from the microscopic collection of particles of dust and dirt and soot from who knows how many corners of the world and how many hands and pockets. He flipped it over. His eyes widened. There, on the other side, was a brand-new engraving.

It was a lovely depiction of a cowboy and his wife, smiling serenely. R. R. & D. E. Tune was engraved below in fancy script.

Asaf looked carefully at it. He flipped it over again. Then back. The lines were clean and bright, no trace of dirt or soot.

He flipped the top open and it made that unmistakable Zippo flip sound. He hesitated to light it, again wondering what it all meant. He examined the wick, and gave it a sniff. Nothing remarkable. He put his hand to the sparker wheel and spun it. It sparked, and a clean blue and yellow flame popped up barely above the wick, exactly as it should. Asaf snapped the lighter shut with a clack. He looked it over again. He knew what he could do to solve the mystery.

“Good afternoon General, Sir,” Asaf said in a friendly manner.

The General looked at Asaf. “Flop o’ de hat tooze you too matey.”

Asaf planned to go straight for the heart of the matter and skip over all the preliminaries of the Zippo’s pedigree and how it came into his hands. “General, Sir, I was wondering what you could tell me about this engraving?”

Asaf’s plan worked, for the General took the lighter in his hands and looked at the engraving without asking any questions. “Hauler, holler, half a dollar. Tain’t it a pippy-squeekin’ thing. Shorely now, if my Yessir Cap’n spherical mind nodes round the pastry of the hexagonally grasping digitized grappler dint no it … tis *Rex et Regina vaccaribus*.

“Wazzit ledgerdized? Tune? Well, for the *vallée des pommes*, I’ll tickle yur drum.”

The General clears his voice …

[Sings to the tune of Happy Trails]

Sloppy Snails to you … until we sleep again.
Rusty Rails to you … keep filing your nails till then.

Who wears the clogs on unclipped dogs in leather?
Just throw ‘em off and feel better.

Flappy sails and goo
Until it’s like a mend

Some snails are slippery ones, others aren’t cute.
It’s the way you file your nails, and a cuticle too.

Sloppy snails …
Rusty rails …
Healthy bed nails …
Until … we … sleep … again!”

31

ASAF BECKONED THE WAITER WHO provided drugs to the Soldier to his table. "As you know, I have been chosen by the Prophet to act on his behalf. I would only do this when he is unable and with the agreement of the council. However, there are circumstances where I must take certain actions alone. Only for some time, or for something special. When the special deed or work is done, everything will be given back to the Prophet and the council. Do you understand?"

"I think so. You can take the Prophet's place sometimes."

"When it is necessary,"

Asaf remained silent a moment to see whether or not the waiter had anything else to say. He also wanted to see his reaction to what he told him. The waiter just stood there attentive to what Asaf would say next.

"There is a special event coming. I will have to act alone and apart from the Prophet. And from the council too if it can be accomplished. I may have one Councilman included in this event. I don't know yet. To make this event happen, I need your help and the thug who is your mentor. I have watched you and I see that you can be helpful. Helpful to me in this event — which is the same as being helpful to the Prophet. Which is what we all want, yes?"

The waiter nodded. Asaf could not see whether or not the waiter was being wary, or just polite. So Asaf continued, hoping inside that his plan with these two would work out. "I would like to meet with your boss."

The waiter said yes and asked when.

"Tomorrow, when I come in — about this time. I will be right here. Serve him whatever he likes. Run a tab. I will pay for the bill in cash myself. We can sit together and eat and drink and talk."

The next day, Asaf sat with the thug and went over everything he had told the waiter. "Now let me be a bit more frank with you, for you are his boss, and you deserve to know more."

The thug nodded.

"First, the frank part. I know you are pushing drugs here, and maybe over at the opium den. I don't know about that for sure, but maybe. It is not important about the opium den, it is enough that I know you are involved in drugs here in the tea-house."

The thug was unimpressed. He remained silent and did not show any emotions. Asaf noticed this. He moved on with his agenda. "The Prophet, as you know, is a man of peace. He does not like the wars. He does not like the struggles between the sects. He knows he is God's emissary for this generation. He also knows that he will not live forever. He knows that someday, maybe sooner, maybe later — either way, may God be merciful — he will pass from this life to the next. He knows that there must be a spiritual heir. I would like to ask you a question."

"Ok."

"I have a mission. But first — I need to know — you can keep it secret?"

"You and me," the thug began waving his finger back and forth between them, "we come from different backgrounds. I'm thinking you have a nice house to go to at night. You have family, maybe the family has money. Maybe — I don't know. Me, I come from the streets of a big city. Nobody gave me nothing. But I got a brain up here," pointing to his head, "and the brain, it knows how to work it."

The thug pulled out a pack of Marlboros and they each took one. "I see the poor and I see the rich. And I see myself, in my brain, as the one poor and then I see myself as the one rich. And I say to myself: "You ain't going to be a poor sunovabish. You are going to be a rich sunovabish.' You hear what I'm saying?"

Asaf nodded.

"So, I stay sharp. I look for ways to make money. I find out the ways to make money. I was all over. I was in the street. I was kicked around. But I didn't never cry and blabber. I just didn't find out how to gather money in weeks or months. No. I find that the ways, is to do, the things need doing, what nobody wants to do. Like digging a hole. Somebody has to dig the hole, you know? You can do it and not like it — or you can do it and say 'How can I do this and not feel so down about it?' That's the key to the making and keeping the money. Whatever they call the big words? Attitude. I learned this word not the easy way. I learned it through a man who only did the work others would not do, and he has an ok life, and his sweat and the dirty shirt does not bother him, and he eats his middle-day meal in quiet in the shade. I see and learn that he knows from the attitude."

The thug sat back and smoked. Asaf remained silent. Then the thug continued.

"After I get the knowledge of the attitude, I go on to discover that there are more ways to make money — more than just the work the others don't want to do. And this is what I am talking of right here." The thug thumped his finger on the table. "Two things. The thing that is dangerous to do. And the thing that is illegal to do. The dangerous pays because for too many is not the work they like. The illegal is the same. Too many who from their feeling in the breast — they can't do the illegal. The both, one or the other, they pay good. And some of these things are dangerous and illegal. The both — when it is dangerous and illegal, hoofta! — the pay is the best. I get at good doing both. But the dangerous, hoofta, it is dangerous, and that is not the way I want to go living and carrying-on in life. But who laid the rail? So I do the illegal. But, you understand, this illegal is not illegal to me. The illegal is made illegal by the rich. The rich, they keep everybody out of the illegal so that they have it all to their fly-stink selves. So, to me, is not illegal, because everybody wants the illegal, they want all sorts. I am not in control of what they want. I am one who can get for them what they want. Am I a bad person? I am not a bad person, no. I do this business because they want what they want, and the illegal is still what they want, but they cannot get it regular. So I get it irregular. That is that. But there are others, who say I am the bad one for doing the illegal. Here is the fig for them! We eat our reputation as bad because we have to fight for our business. The fighting it makes us tough. It makes us harder and meaner. But not inside deep. There we are just like a smart person like you. Hoofta. That's the sum of it."

Asaf took all this in while the thug drank some tea, then said, "Thank you for your story. I understand that since you provide illegal goods and services, I guess, can I ask you for the favor I just mentioned? I would like to go back to the secret. Can I tell you this mission without concern? It's very important."

The thug casually lit another smoke. He poked it in the air to emphasize his point. "Let me tell you this thing: I am no rat, a rat-fink, a cheater, a make-stink, or none of that. It is always the best the respect, the honor and the loyalty. Also no lies. In our business, if you lie, and then you are catching it. It is very sorry for you. The bad will visit you personally and up close. We are walking the tight-rope in our dealing and disrespect is not a good thing, you know what I mean? So we have a 'Yes' and we have a 'No' and we have the code. We are not perfect, but if you ask a favor or a job, and I give you my yes or my no. Then it is a done thing. Otherwise, I am dead because my other businessmen will take me down for not trusting the word and the promise. They will do it too. It is risky, but we are like that, and it is our lives. I answer your question with a question I have for you: Do you want that I partake in this mission, as you call it? Is it something that you need from me — and to do as well?"

Politely and firmly, Asaf answered, "Yes. It is something I wish you to share with me. I am asking because I need your help. My first question was about trust, and you have answered that."

More cigarette poking. "If I am proved worthy, I would make certain securing my future, going forward in life, living how I choose, but never looking over the shoulder, starting the car, a man around the next corner, the bad plate of food — this will not come after me because of this thing of ours. Ok?"

"Yes. It will not come to haunt you from me. You may go on with your life how you choose. I only ask for silence. It is a risk on my part too. It is a great and grave matter. I cannot do it alone, so I must ask for help. This is a first step. Be true, and it will be well for both of us. Fair enough?"

The thug set his cigarette in the ashtray and opened both hands. "My truth is my honor, is my loyalty, is my life. Hoofta. You will not be disappointed. Tell me everything you wish to tell."

32

ONE DAY A TRACTOR PULLS up with a twenty-foot container. The driver gets out with a clipboard, walks into the bar and asks for "The General."

Asaf says: "I can help with that," and looks it over.

ORIGIN: Apple Valley, CA.

CONTENTS: Coca-Cola. Bulk for Retail. 10 Pallets.

Folger's Coffee. Cream. Sugar.

In the 'OTHER' section was written:

THE GENERAL'S EYES ONLY.

"Wait just a minute while I ask."

Asaf takes the clipboard over to the lead bartender and shows it to him. "Ever seen him?" The lead bartender shakes his head. Asaf continues quietly. "Well then, let me introduce you to your guest. I'm going to the tea-house to find the thug."

They go over to the driver. "I'm going for the General. My friend here will make sure you have our full hospitality." He nods at the lead bartender who nods back.

The lead bartender takes the driver to a quiet table. He returns with a full, unopened, bottle of Jack, a bottle of Coke, an empty tumbler and one full of ice, a pack of Marlboros, matching ashtray and lighter, and a basket full of savory turnovers from the neighbor. "Here's a few things for you until the General gets here. If he's out golfing, it may be awhile. Make yourself comfortable. If you like, you can sit in one of those old chairs. May I?" he asks, and before the driver can answer, the lead bartender cracks open the Jack, sets it down and opens the Coke. "How would you like it?"

The driver is not sure what to do. "Uh, sure. A little whiskey on the rocks and the Coke."

The lead bartender proceeds to fill the tumbler half Jack and half

Coke. "There's more of whatever you would like. Just let me know."

The driver is staring at all the things on his table as the lead bartender walks away.

In the tea-house, Asaf gets the waiter's attention. "Where's your boss?"

The waiter leaves then returns with the thug.

Asaf whispers, "I think our thing has started."

"*Our thing*. That's a pretty name," the thug mumbled. "Since this thing of ours all winding around these building is going, and it bites bad, a snake you can call it. And this start, the snakehead."

Asaf leads the thug outside and nods at the container. "I know the General wouldn't order this — whatever is inside. There are some things about the bill of lading that tells me it's the start of … start of the snake or start of the head? The driver is in the bar."

"Wazza this driver man doing?"

Asaf explained the paperwork and the hospitality tray. "I wasn't sure what to do, so I made sure he had plenty of whatever he wanted to keep him occupied while he waited for the General."

"We are not able to drive this lorry away while he's all the listening and looking after his load. And I know I'm not in this way of doing if my Coke was a strong one."

Asaf was getting anxious. He wasn't prepared for any of this. Rather than try to act like he was in charge, he made his first step in trusting his confederate. "Ok. Let me be honest with you. I asked for your help. And I guess the time has come, but I'm not sure what to do next."

"That's ok, Asaf. Under the code, we're both gonna be just fine. A review we'll make now. This twenty-footer. Explain in your words whazza suspicious. Like a school teacher a grade I'm giving you."

"Speaking of code, the man I worked with used coffee as a code word. That container has Coke and coffee in it. Cream and sugar too."

"Hoofta my boy, Asaf! You're doing the work good. Of course no cream and sugar there is in there. If coffee was your manner of speaking what should not be spoken openly — which is what I think it is — then you are right. Izza your benefactor. Or malefactor, better?" the thug finished, with a glint in his eye and a sinister smile.

"What should we do with it?"

"It has to get away from this village. Hoofta. The mercenaries. They can look with the fly-speck-eye at us and that container, and it goes like the finger in the tree sap."

Asaf wasn't sure what that meant, but he didn't ask because he got the point. "I've told the lead bartender to give him plenty of booze. But I don't know how long …"

"How long before he's hearing us not drive his iron-maiden away. Right? Too much longer for that to sit out there before the cat being killed is."

Asaf was not sure what the iron and cats were about either. "Sure. I think … What about putting him to sleep?"

The thug grinned. "In the movies like you are asking? You gonna walk in there and the trichloromethane, which the bar and tea-house has on all the tables, right? and stuff it in his face with a bar mop?"

Asaf wasn't amused. "Hey. I'm just trying to be helpful."

The thug patted Asaf on the back. "Ok, ok friend. Come we'll take care of our driver and his snakes together. You have your barman bring my waiter outside here. I make a visit to your driver."

The thug waltzed to the table and without explanation pushed the Jack and highball aside. "Halloo. Wazza we have here my buddy? I am here by the General's orders. I don't think he wants your load off the road in a ditch landing. Come next door. The keys in the truck still, right?"

He hooked the driver by the elbow and got him outside. The waiter and the lead bartender stood near the tractor. "Here you go. My best waiter, he will show you the side of these businesses where this is going. Coke, coffee and sugar."

Before the driver could get his bearings, he was being led away by two young men and his rig was being started up and put in gear.

The driver was getting tucked into his seat just as the thug parked the rig in the dirt behind the tea-house.

The thug came in. "At's my buddy!" The thug clapped the driver on the back. "Your equipment right outside. Better food and drink on this side and the General is onna his way. Waiter!"

The thug strode off to the back of the tea-house leaving the driver wondering what happened and how it happened so fast.

The thug waved the lead bartender back to the bar while he went with the waiter to the back of the house. "Ok, howz good are you with your coffee?"

The waiter tipped his head back and forth in thought. "For him? Comme ci comme ça. Dreamland or blank or final?"

"Not final. He will the driving be doing after we arrange the snake. Dreamland or blank."

"How long?"

"In the morning, you will be fixing him the reserve roast, yes?" the thug said with a scurrilous grin.

Is short order, the waiter sent the driver the best pastry in the tea-house, got out a spoon, used the smooth handle to gather some gooey opium, smeared the opium on the inside of a demitasse, smeared date molasses over the opium, smeared an eight-spice paste over the molasses, ground the finest beans, and made a double shot of espresso. He brought the dreamy-blank to the driver and explained that the pastry was best enjoyed with the house-blended bitter-sweet. "It is our most exquisite offering. With this pastry, it is the only coffee we recommend. It has layers and layers of flavor. Please enjoy."

While the driver slowly but surely got stoned away to dreamland from which he would remember nothing, the lead bartender and Asaf stood watch as the thug drayed the container out of the village. He picked a small town that had been abandoned, having been destroyed by bombs and shelling. The streets and alleys between the empty buildings and piles of rubble made the shipping container inconspicuous. The thug was sorely tempted to examine the contents, but his pact with Asaf appealed to his sense of loyalty, and he deferred opening the container.

The thug brought the tractor back into the village and parked it a few blocks away. Asaf signed off the bill of lading using the General's name and put the paperwork into the cab.

Asaf, the thug, the lead bartender, and the waiter went back to the container. Although Asaf didn't like the torn-up small town where the container was parked, he appreciated the thug's resourcefulness in putting it somewhere out of sight and mind

They walked around the container, examining and inspecting it closely. Asaf asked for the thug's opinion. He said there was not much he could see that raised red flags and that the simplest way forward was to open it carefully. They stood in front of the large double doors. Asaf looked at the customs seal. SOFT DRINKS / BULK FOR RETAIL. All of the diamond-shaped warning signs were folded closed — nothing to see here — was the message.

They clipped the seal and slowly opened the doors. Sure enough, it was loaded with standard pallets of Coca-Cola.

Asaf said: "Everybody keep an eye out. We don't know if this … well, we don't … Just say something if you see anything questionable."

Asaf and the thug climbed into the container. The thug felt around on the first pallet, looked up at Asaf and shook his head. "Nothing the hair on my arms poking up. I'll cut the wrap, ok?" They unwrapped the pallet. The Coke was the same as they stocked in the bar: half-liter bottles, twenty-four to a case. They began handing it down. When they lowered one pallet down to where they could see past it, they discovered that there was another row of pallets. Asaf gave the thug an inquiring look. The thug said: "If this is all normal, this size box takes the ten standard flats to fill it. Two layers. Looks ok to my eyes."

"That's a lot of Coke," Asaf said. "If we want to find out what's in this shipment, we will have to bring more vehicles out here and unload all this."

The thug asked with smile, "Why bring out more cars and trucks? It's a nice neighborhood. Lookie all the housewives. All the pretty flowers and the kiddies playing football in the street. You're not a noggin that we can't just put all this in that beautiful building here some steps away and not half-a-way across the country?"

The lead bartender said, "Asaf, he's right you know. Why hump all this back to the bar when we can just put it in this abandoned building right here, five steps away. There's no one living in this town. Maybe some rats. But I think even they are gone since there's nothing left to eat. It seems the buzzards have taken care of that."

They unloaded the first two pallets and sure enough, there was another set of pallets. The thug said this corresponded with his assumption of a standard load. Nothing out of the ordinary. They had taken off two layers of the next pallet. When the lead bartender lifted the first case off of the third layer, music began to play. They all jumped in fright and surprise.

"Wazza, wazza?"

Asaf said loudly: "Everybody stop."

Asaf recognized the tune of 'Happy Trails.' He smiled and shook his head in disbelief. He said to the thug: " I know this song, but how is it coming out of the shipment? Take a look at what's going on in there."

The thug waved his finger at Asaf. "Asaf. A word. On the side."

They got down and went to the side of the container. "Asaf. I ask you. What is this? First, I get intructions for bringing this away from the village. Now, all spooky, you have me unpack. What? Coca-Cola? Why?"

"I don't understand this shipment. Let's keep going and see if this is part of the plan or just an order of Coke that got mixed up somehow. It's more than I've ever ordered."

They went back and the thug politely elbowed the waiter to the side and motioned for him to back away. "We're needing the light." The thug said: "There's more than Coke in here. The music is what you call: a booby a trap. Who makes this booby, they know their skills. You see here, you lift the weight of the Coke, and it completes the circuit and the music, it plays itself. Simple in the knowing and learning, but not always so simple in the doing to make it work right. Simple is the light thing. A book, a shoe. Like that. This Coke case is heavy, so harder to get just right. I see that."

Asaf was excited. He said to the thug, "I know who sent this, and it's a good thing. But still, be careful. I think we're ok, but — I'm just not completely sure. Let's keep looking."

They carried away the last four cases, one by one. The thug stopped them when the music device was traced out. He lifted it out and showed them the triggering mechanism, some fine wires, a well designed weight-sensitive switch, and an old cassette player. "This tape player is the old. The old. But this switch is nice. Like I said, the skill, it is in the know-how."

The next layer of cases was different. The thug held up his hand. "Here are the cases, the different. This is where we are interested. Asaf, look."

Asaf looked at the next layer on the pallet. The thug said, "Lookie at the inside of these. They are not like the company they come out from the package storehouse. See, they are being opened. And they are being shut by tape. See?"

Asaf looked down between the cases. The outside faces were lined with real bottles of Coke. The rest of the case, facing in, had been repacked. The tape over the cuts in the plastic shrink-wrap was done with care. If someone wasn't looking for it or was trying to find something out of the ordinary, they would not have noticed.

Asaf said, "Let's take one away from the rest of the layer. But be careful. Make sure there's not some monkey business."

"Monkey business? Wazza?"

"Never mind. Just look at it closely."

They turned the case so that they could see the edges clearly.

"What do you think?"

The thug said, "We have a look and see where it leads us." The thug carefully lifted out one of the taped-up cases. They all climbed out of the container. They found a pile of rubble with a flat piece of a blown-out wall on top for a table.

The thug began to move his fingertips all over the case, then very carefully at the seams of the tape. No one spoke. The thug murmured very softly and nodded his head slightly. "I think ok to take some tape away. I do not feel any suspect wire or mechanical something."

Asaf nodded his consent. The thug found the end of the tape and pulled it away slowly. He looked into the gap where the plastic separated. He took his finger and felt inside. He sniffed his finger, then put his head close and sniffed at the opening. Everybody watched in silence. He took his finger again and poked with purpose in the gap, applying more pressure and adjusting the angle of his probe. He looked up at his comrades, each in the eye, and nodded at them with a confident look. He removed the rest of the tape and unwrapped the whole top. Behind the bottles, there were blocks, like small bricks, wrapped tightly in heavy wax paper. The thug nudged one of the bricks at a corner and pushed it out some, so he could see it from the side facing in. Seemingly satisfied with his examination, he took a brick in his hand. The others involuntarily stepped back. The thug sniffed the brick. He then took a fingernail and dug into a crease. He smelled his fingertip. He turned to Asaf and smiled.

"Tell us, tell us."

The thug answered with confident satisfaction, "Explosive material. High the grade, highest the quality. Not fake. The good. Only the specialist comes at this. The specialist on the inside. The very good, it is not dangerous. Here!"

He tossed the brick to Asaf who jumped but caught the brick. He juggled it a bit in his hands.

"You see, you see?" the thug said with a laugh. "It is good because not being volatile and shaky to go off. Stable is the way it is safe. And of this category of explosive, this is the one most desirable."

He smiled broadly and spread his arms wide as if to reach out and hug the container. "Only the best … And we hazza lot of it."

33

THE FOUR OF THEM BEGAN taking the tampered pallets apart. The thug instructed them to put the Coke on one pallet and the explosive material on another. As they made progress, the thug came up to Asaf quietly and tipped his head indicating that they should go outside.

"It is proper to show you my honor, to bring this to the light of your own eyes, direct."

Asaf looked with worried curiosity at the thug and the packets in his hands. "What is it?"

The thug showed the two packets, which looked similar to the other bricks. "These not the same alike the others. Two only like this. This one is too light, this one is too heavy. Here is my honor, like I say. I explore them and stop. Here we are, they are in your hands now. However, you like to go ahead, that we will go ahead."

Asaf looked at the two bricks. The thug handed them over. Just as the thug said, one was light and one was very heavy.

"Too heavy, no? I have idea, but we will see. One thing, if it is what I think, it is not to explode. No."

"What do you think it is?"

The thug shrugged his shoulders. "Lead. Because of the atomic property. Heavy. Some reason to have a protection. Maybe."

Asaf set the light brick down and took the covering completely off the heavy brick. It was more of a flat black rather than the dull gray of lead. They each handled it again, feeling its weight. The thug asked one of the men in the container to hand his knife down. He made a few scrapes on the brick. Asaf saw a brightness under the flat black. The thug scratched some more. With wonder in their eyes — a brick of gold.

The thug threw up a hand. "Wazza wazza? In here? I sure don't understand."

Asaf looked at the thug but said nothing. The thug set the light brick down and carefully took off the wrapper. It was a simple cardboard box, hand-cut out of a larger piece of cardboard to the size of a brick, taped together at the edges. He peeled off some tape to look inside the little box. There was a folded sheet of plain white letterhead and a package, wrapped in more paper. The thug just shook his head and waved for Asaf to make his own inspection. Asaf looked at the thug and shrugged his shoulders. The thug shrugged back. So the thug took out the package and unwrapped it. It was a double bobble-head of Roy Rogers and Dale Evans. Asaf pointed to the folded paper. The thug flicked it with his finger. Not sensing anything unusual, he handed it to Asaf.

Asaf was confused. He opened the paper, it was a handwritten note.

Like all good mystery notes let me start with the classic line: If you are reading this Dot Dot Dot.

Then you hopefully got what I sent As far as the souvenir — I like the way their heads wobble I think what you are going to do will make heads wobble too!

The gear — I guess your buddies are asking why so much?

My best answer is — it's like making Pancakes. 20 is just as easy or Easier! than 10 so I sent 20. Also, I believe that if you are going to do what you are going to do, you should do it Big One and Done in One. Explain that to the henchman that does the rigging He will think its Too Much — but you tell him its gotta be that way.

I understand your uncle. I would be on his side if I were him but I'm not, you're not we all have to follow a path.

Maybe you'll settle the score for all these ragtags once and for all and nobody will be left over to come after you— I doubt it but

If you have the other surprise everything will be alright. The brick is just for him to do it Big and do it Right! The excess gear is a big temptation to take down the street and flip. So the brick is to keep that from happening. You will have to work that out between yourselves

It's all Dangerous work! I have thought about different ways to do it — but this should be ok if you can keep your man under control. Best of luck!

PS The whole Roy Rogers thing is a complete lark don't read anything special into it. It could've been a turtle or red leather … I just thought the sentiment matched our acquaintance of each other — and the lyrics are my True Wishes for you!!

There was no signature, none was needed. Asaf knew for sure, that if they ever crossed paths again, crossed trails, he would know it. Turtles, red leather, counrty singers or the next thing your left-hand touches. He would know it.

Asaf pressed the button on the bobble-head. It played a not-too-bad rendition of Happy Trails. A lonesome tear ran down Asaf's face.

Asaf took the gold bar in his hand, tipped his head to the thug that they should go for a stroll. Down a rubble-strewn back ally, Asaf looked the thug in the eye. "This gold bar is yours. It is yours to keep and do with what you want."

He looked down at the gold, then back at the thug. "After you complete our mission."

The thug looked steadily at Asaf. He looked at the gold bar. He nodded.

Asaf said, "What we are going to do is very serious. Just as this amount of gold is serious. I will need your full cooperation and I am asking for your expertise. So far so good?"

The thug nodded.

Asaf continued, "From what I understand, there is more than enough explosive stuff here to completely destroy both the bar and the tea-house, as well as the basement."

The thug listened. He found a place to sit on a broken-down wall and lit a Marlboro.

Asaf waited. Seeing that the thug was biding his time to speak, he continued, "I want to make one hundred percent sure both are destroyed to the ground. I want the basement destroyed. I want to make sure the nuclear material the Prophet is hiding in the basement gets blown-up somehow so that the whole area becomes a radioactive wasteland. I am not concerned how wide or far the wasteland goes. It will spread as far as whatever amount of plutonium he has down there that is completely blown up will spread. I don't care. And I don't care for how long it is a wasteland. It will be a wasteland as long as the radio-activity lasts to make it uninhabitable. I don't care about who is or who is not around when the bombs go off. There may be many, there may be a few, there may be none."

Asaf stopped. The thug did nothing.

"Are you my man for the job?"

The thug did not say anything. He stood up and stretched. He walked a few paces. He came back and sat down. "Can I ask a few questions?"

"I think I know, or I think I have some ideas about your questions. Before we go there, let me ask you in another way. If you knew nothing about the village. Nothing about the two buildings. Nothing about the basement, the plutonium, or the Prophet or the General or the Soldier or me. If you knew nothing about the war, the foreign mercenaries or the religious sectarians. And, if I could guarantee you your safety, that is, you would be able to get away before everything goes up in smoke, only leaving out anything done by your own hand, that is, a mistake or something … all of this, are you my man for the job?"

The thug took a few more moments to smoke then started to answer.

Asaf cut in, "I do not want to offend you. But I am not looking for hesitation here. I know, as plain men, there is room for discussion, and right and wrong. I understand that. But right now — right now — I need the best answer you can give me."

The thug nodded. "You are right. You need an answer. This all very serious. The concerns. I have mine — you have yours. I see more than just the gold. I have the plans too that I can bake into your pastry," the thug concluded with a gleam in his eye.

"I don't want any sideshow. No games. It's the job and the gold. You get away if you don't make any mistakes on your part, which I don't have control over. I don't want to begin bargaining about pastries and pie slices."

The thug laughed. "Is not pies. I am thinking out loud I am. You got the tickles about right and wrong. I got the code of honor. The code of honor is on the top. Under the code of honor is the right and the wrong. Whatever happens beneath the code of honor is not for the talking about. Maybe I ask you, 'Hey Asaf, where you get all this gold? Hunh? Hunh? Hey Asaf, Where you get all this fancy gear? Hunh?' No. I don't say my mouth and questions at nothing. Because, before the gold — and before the gear — and before you and me — is the code of honor already. And you like it or not, the ethical theologian have to choke and spit and a cough on it. We all get up, we all eat, we all do the plop, we all go a sleep again. Nobody knows for sure the morning what is coming in the life that day. That is why I keep the code. Is like the white road stripes. Here is a line, there is a line. Betwixt the lines I don't fear to veer. Is the moral failings in the code? Go find old rock and lick. Our word is gold and it is on the coin of our brotherhood. Honesty is one side of the gold coin. The other side is loyalty. The coin has two faces. Honesty is a angel of Vengeance looking down on the corrupt souls. Loyalty is the face of mister Death. He looks at a man, and the man looks at him. Death he stares at your face. Eye to the eye. This the code. The honesty and loyalty between the brothers of the code is, ever, until the death. The other is most deep, the deepest of the code. If ever a brother of the code kill a man; ever the knife, the gun, the car, whatever, however the killing happen, even until the number one murder with thinking ahead — it is under the code of loyalty to the death. No code brother never says nothing. It is the code. We don't pay the tax. We don't use the bank. We don't let political tell us what to do. And if the tenant, the tenant is too poor from the tax and bank and broker and political — we are his brothers who help the kiddies and uncle and gran-mama. And everybody else the bank kicks in the behind, for not paying the ferry wheel with blood, sweat and tears. We save lots of money for the poor and those not from the special expensive school, by no fault of their own. So the code is something, which is better than the nothing. Is better than being a slave to the men with the nose so brown and so high in the highest cloud that cannot smell his own fly-speck moral emptiness. Better than the ethical fig-for-brains and his big, bad, gods who demand just as much money out of the pockets of the poor, as the king's bastard sons. Stealing out of the pockets of the poor with one hand, they take the other hand and put it under the clothes of the neighbor's wife, or the little kiddies, and feel around and say, the gods are liking this to be done. These better-than-thou, they send the men in front of the bullet, they send the women to the harvest and bread-making, they divide the kiddies into two. The one group of kiddies, born like all the rest, except for their address and phony titles of their bastard papa, raised up on an empty meal of ethical nothingness, come up and inherit and take over when their father princes and uncle sultans go to the grave. And the rest of the little ones, born in the back of the shed between the morning shift and the evening shift, their momma going back to work the same day, they grind with the mill the hands like brown sandpaper in the slavery. Slaves to who? To the sons of aristocracy with brains just above the monkey, but holding the sticks and strings of others who came from a woman's vent like any human ever brought into this fig of an unjust world. The dangling puppets, they build and build the walls and pavements, eating the dust and the dirt, so the bastard sons of kings can put little diamond-toe-capped shoes on the next dainty generation who never actually plant their perfumed feet on the soil of the earth, our common mother. So, young and clever man, I put your tickles asleep. First: Yes I can do the job. Two: I am the man. Third: Sure, I am having the moral qualms and that. But — I have the code."

Asaf was at a loss just what to say. He didn't expect a long answer. He just wanted to be able to move forward with the plan. "Ok … these thoughts and ideas are good and interesting. But I don't need to talk about them right now. I'm sure you have thought about this, I'm sure you are right about these things. I understand. But can we just do the job according to plan? And when it is all over and we are either alive or dead or our soul is saved or damned we can sit and split hairs over the lines in the road and diamond shoes. I am feeling that our time is short. Can we do the work that we have to do?"

"We can do the work. One last thing. Then, the job." The thug stubbed out his Marlboro and began counting on his fingers. "This job. A very serious, yes? And the dangerous. And the illegal. Ok, you follow? And nobody else wants to do, right? So, it is all the hardest of work. The hardest. Serious, dangerous, illegal, nobody else … Now, this gold. This is the most of all the money I have ever held in my hands. This job, it is also the most compelling. Not the car, stealing a whole or the parts, or to break the hand or feet of a wife cheat, or shoot a fly-stink. All that. So, I put the family jewels, for you and this secret container to make a nothing of the village. Also, I see my own eyes clear, that where there is a one bar of the gold, there is the second bar of gold too. In the illegal and the dangerous, the one payment before and the one payment when all is over. I know two things. First, this is asking a lot and I am grateful just the one. But … second, I know if he can arrange this — all this gear — he can arrange the next gold, he can. But for me — hoofta — one last job maybe, if I go on living. Under the code, the honest and the loyal, can you be obtaining for me the last gold payment, from your container-man? And I will be the receiving of it only after you and me are both having our own legs for the running and family jewels for the keeping and some place far and away for the passing the last gold from the secret spot, to me."

Asaf answered, "I am not a man of the code. But I understand — maybe — your value system. I haven't even thought about the possibility of more gold. I didn't even know the gold existed until now. So I don't know the answer. But if you think there is more for you to get, I will ask. I don't know how to ask, but if you think I can learn or understand how to get another gold-bar, I will do it."

The thug crooked his finger at the gold bar and Asaf handed it over. The thug felt the weight in his hand again, then returned it to Asaf. "We both feel the heavy, no? Ok, Asaf. This, the gold, and the next gold, is not for the carrying in the pocket or shoe or by the family jewels across the border or to buy a ride on a ship or train. Like this, it is not much better than a big rock. The man digging the underground of the construction. Remember?"

Asaf wasn't sure, but nodded his head, trying to recall the face of the excavator operator.

"That man is nothing between us. This is the trusting of this you and me ... and your waggle man. He will understand this what we are to do. You bring this to him. At his home. Quiet and private, not the wife or kiddies knowing and looking and hearing. In your educated own words you tell him the manufacturing of this hunk of metal into common pieces. That means one troy ounce. Each piece. Whoever he is finding to do this, one ounce gets. The digging man, for his wife's happiness, one ounce gets when he brings you all the ounces, properly made by a smithy. Can you accomplish this task, for us?"

They walked around the broken block and came out a ways up from where they had been working. Asaf looked again at the gold. He looked down the sad and lonely road at the container, their helpers, the stacks of Coke and explosives, then at the thug. "I can do it. We can do it. We will do it," he said gravely.

The thug nodded and made a small smile. "Hoofta, it will be a thing made. Let's get to the job — our own hands doing."

They made their way back to the container. "Asaf. Let's bring waggle the head over here some ways." The thug took his knife and rapped on the heads and the base. "Now Asaf, for the taking apart? Maybe the not putting back together? Ok?"

Asaf nodded yes.

The thug took the heads off and examined them, then the bodies. He shook his head. He looked at the switch on the base and actuated it. It seemed normal. Music on, music off. He took the screws out with the tip of his knife. He opened it up carefully. He examined the circuit board. He looked at Asaf and pointed to what he saw. "This, is ok. The tune, single circuit, here the itsy bitsy speaker. But see these coils, the copper? This, notta needs to be here. No tourist shopping needs these. And lookie at this. For tiny speaker, just one itsy bitsy battery such is needed. Inside waggles, three bigger sized. This also not for tourist."

Asaf grew nervous. He tried to stay as natural as possible. "What is it? Is it dangerous?"

"Not the dangerous, no. For this we are opening up. The copper is not for the music. The copper is for the signal receiver."

"Signal receiver? What's that about?"

"Not for your concern. We just need the knowing from the music box that we are not blowing up all over before all is ready."

They went to work on the last two pallets. Once again, the cases had been altered. Two cases were complete. Three cases had two rows of bottles, the inside rows had been replaced with materials that were well packaged and fit perfectly within the size of each case. The thug stepped back and pointed out how it was well thought out and ingeniously designed. "In my head, wondering how all this was to be setting-off, now I see. Here is the detail of the bomb setting. "

According to the lessons he had from the spy, Asaf thought he knew what he was looking at. Asaf had not let the thug know what the spy had taught him … he hoped. But now, uncertainty bubbled up in his mind as to how well he had been playing the role of 'bumpkin', as he thought of himself sometimes. He was trying to get a better look at the rectangular packages but trying to act as if he didn't know what he was looking at, or looking for. All of this was going on in his head while still trying to figure out all the pieces of the puzzle the spy had created for them.

The thug looked around at his companions. He reached for a package. He drew his hand back and slowly stood up. He looked around at the container, then went to the door. He jumped down and walked back from the container and the broken buildings. He looked at the container, the pallets they had moved and the adjacent rubble. He walked back to the container. The others came over.

"Sorry, not to the worry making. Just thinking. Asaf, men, have your own eyes the seeing anything of the electric? the wiring, lighting bulbs, the power pack?"

Asaf immediately mentioned the battery-powered bobble-head. The thug nodded in agreement. "Anything else?" They looked at each other one by one. Everybody shook their heads or shrugged their shoulders.

"And the bricks? The different seeing? The heavy, not the same? Color? All, all?"

Nothing from the crew.

"Ok-dokie friends. Here's the going forward a little. First, you two, once the more look at the genuine Coke. Not the bottle every one. But look at the case each, see that it is the genuine case. Not for the being opened and 'monkey' like Asaf calls it. Asaf, we go and lookie close again at all the explosive the bricks. Each one. I tell you how it goes."

The waiter and the lead bartender jumped down and walked over to the Coke. Asaf and the thug went over to the pallet of explosives. The thug instructed the two crews to grab empty pallets and pass everything from one pallet to the next, one unit at a time: a case of Coke, a brick of explosive, a case of Coke, a brick of explosive. Each hand-off must get four eyes on it, two handing and two receiving, the thug explained. Anything weird or unusual and everything comes to a stop.

After double-checking everything, the thug said, "Ok. Here we take a lookie at what is the Coke from the factory looking like. One by one. Then not from the factory. Two things. One and then one. That is two. Ok?"

The thug and the waiter pulled out the normal cases of Coke one at a time and handed them to Asaf and the lead bartender. What remained were the half-case sized packages. The thug looked at the one nearest him. He felt it, then nudged it out to get a look at the hidden sides. He held it up to get a good look and nodded his head. "Ok. We call this package A."

The thug picked up a package from the opposite pallet and did the same examination. "Is the whole sense making of it," he said with a smile while tapping the side of his head. "Now we can be calling these B. Now, we go and find all the number A and the number B that is the same same and all go apart together."

The lead bartender leaned over and whispered to the waiter, "Same same and all go apart together?"

The waiter glanced at the lead bartender and made a small frown which meant, "I know it's hard to take, but stay cool bro, and we'll all get out alive."

The container empty, the thug called them together. "Each one, we each make the circuit of all our eyes in and out before we do more. We all have the making certain nothing is escaping notice."

They all walked in and out and around, each looking at the container in their own way. Nothing unusual.

The thug walked to the middle of the street in thoughtful silence. He stopped and looked at the Coke. Then he shifted his feet and gazed at the explosives. He turned around and looked at the A packages. Still silently thinking, he looked at the B packages across the street.

He walked back. "I am having the good understanding — but not all. Asaf, the waggle again."

The thug examined the disassembled souvenir once more. He shook his head.

"What is it? What's wrong," Asaf asked.

The thug walked to the middle of the street and lit a Marlboro. He waved the others over to join him. He pointed with his cigarette. "Is the old rule from the first of the beginning. Not to blow yourself and the building in smoke and thunder. The bombs their parts separate to the keeping. When I see the packages, I am expecting the both. Cord and caps. We are setting aside, there and over there, right?"

Asaf interrupted. "So what's wrong? What are you looking at?"

The thug gave Asaf a glance showing his irritation. "I am explaining. So, we have the things here. And here. And here," poking the Marlboro at each pallet.

He picked up the bobblehead parts. "And here."

He looked at his listeners, expecting another interruption. "What is wrong, issa the missing electrical for the whole of the explosion. In their order: the transmitter, the receiver, the detonation switch, the caps, the cords, and the explosives. We have the explosive, we have the caps, we have the cord, and we have the receiver from waggle. The one missing, is the detonation switch. And the two missing, the remote trigger." More cigarette pointing. "Explosives from the Coke. Packages A, caps. Packages B, cord. Waggle receiver. No detonation switch. No transmitter trigger."

Asaf was stuck. His feet were stuck to the ground. His brain was stuck in neutral. His mouth was stuck shut. He had learned enough from the spy to understand what the thug was talking about. He also understood enough to see that there were missing components to the remote detonation he wanted. But he didn't understand why the parts were missing, and he didn't want to let the thug know he had this knowledge. At least not yet. Or did he? So he was stuck. Asaf's mind began running and helped him get un-stuck. But only to move him from a standstill, to a quagmire of what to do, or not do, what to say, or not say, and all the twists and turns and permutations of the spy the thug and the plan. Who's on my side? who's an enemy? is my confederate trusting in my guts? were there enemies? does the waiter know? has the spy duped me? can I trust the thug? can I trust anybody? fork one, fork two, route Sixty-six? where's the missing parts? …

Asaf didn't know what else to do, so he said, "I don't know what to do."

The thug interrupted Asaf reveries. "Well, something is needing to make this right. Maybe we don't find here, or lost, or forget. But I don't think so. No. Asaf, I am knowing this here, is the business the dangerous, the illegal — and also the difficult. Somewhere in this these, the friend yours, he knows all this. But where he is sticking his finger in the pie is not for the knowing. Or not just yet. Too, too much clever for this, I am sure he is. This is not for the forgetting, or the monkey, as you say. If you are not knowing, and I am not knowing, then we wait. We wait, the looking, listening. Your friend, he has the know-how of these jobs. He will have the gear in his own way of having it. He is not leading us to the water for a camel, then not for the drink. You don't worry Asaf. Let's get the gear we have, all of this in good order in the safe place, and wait for your man with the waggle heads. He'll do it right."

Intermission

Skip this chapter to continue.

It is included only to take a break to stretch or get a coffee or fresh air. Thank you, The Author.

The lead bartender said to Asaf, "I've noticed since our acquaintance, that you have struggled with, bumbled through and stumbled upon a variety of idioms, analogies, sayings, twists of phrase and such, including culinary terms. So now, I ask you: What kind of pickle or jam or hot water have you gotten us into … and who's goose is going to be cooked in all this?"

Asaf looked at his lead bartender with a scowl. "Hey! I never liked all those sayings and ways of explaining things, you know that. So why foist it upon me now?"

"That's the whole point. To get a rise from you. We've been close in all this bar business, but I think now is the time for taking the pulse or checking the hat at the door."

Asaf balked. "Checking the hat at the door? Not sure I've ever heard that one. Is it a thing? or do I have to google it? as they say?

[Sound of screeching halt, smell of burnt tires and brakes] Wow, that was terrible.

"Ok, ok. It's bad enough around here without you piling on. Ok? We're in this together at some level, so just stay focused until we get our bearings."

The lead bartender asked, "Get our bearings? Not even sure how to contextualize that. I don't want to jump on your back, but shouldn't we have our bearings gotten before now?"

Asaf went from irritation to frustration. He lowered his voice and said in an even tone, "Look, I know this is crazy. We all know it is. But it is what it is. I'm moving forward. You know that. You also know I don't know what I'm doing. So I need help. And you're one of the few characters in this whole plot I can rely on. So help me out and let's get this thing done. Ok?"

The lead bartender looked around at their surroundings which hadn't been described by the Author yet. So instead of walking or sitting, he chose to be riding a horse, side by side with Asaf dressed in old Western cowboy outfits.

"Say Pard..." the lead bartender began.

Asaf looked down and around. "Hey! What the blazes? How, what? Hey!

"Don't you worry Pard. I think these are what they call 'nags.' They're docile and old and calm and easy to ride. Just enjoy the moment."

Asaf was not enjoying the moment. "Enjoy the moment. What moment? Where are we? How did you do whatever you did?"

"I just thought about it. I looked around and saw that we were not in a scene yet. So before the Author could make one up, I did! I mean, come on Asaf, how many scenes can the Author toss out there. Let's count them up. Right? Ok. One. They were walking along in the street. Boring. Been there done that. Two. They stood or sat around in the bar. Ditto. Boring, done. Three. They sat around the cafe. Ditto. Tea-house. Four. All of those settings are fine and dandy, but they're tired. Tired and worn out."

Asaf interrupted, "Worn out? How can they be worn out? There aren't too many choices out there so what are we supposed to do? Plus you forgot the spring and the water stand. And the compound."

"Well, I wasn't in those, so they don't count. Anyhow, we do what I did," the lead bartender said triumphantly. "I made up my own scene. Ha ha. Now that I think about it, the only thing tired and worn out in this scene are these two nags."

"But I don't want a new scene. I like my tired and worn out scenes. They're comfortable or homey. No, not homey. Familiar. I like my scenes. They're familiar. And what's with all the Western again? Didn't we already have a Western conversation way back in the old club?"

"Well, what about Roy Rogers? The King of the Cowboys?"

"That was the spy's doing. He told me in the note it could be red turtles or small birds or something like that. Don't ask me about Roy Rogers. Well, you can ask me, but it won't get you very far. I had nothing to do with the whole music box. Anyhow, I don't know what any of this has to do with the plan to blow up the village and here we are riding some sort of nags in where-ever-land. I get fed up with these highways and byways in this book. Everybody is always going off with the most lame-brain notions... The spy ... What, why, and wherefore did he come up with Roy Rogers?"

"Uh, Asaf ... Uh, I think it was because Roy Rogers' theme song was Happy Trails to You ... until we meet again. And, all those lame-brain

highways have mostly been edited out. The lost lot, buying the lot with the girl and her bloody earrings, the bureaucrat, the whole Daughter, Husband, Wife cycle. All on the cutting room floor. Someone would have to find an early semi-edited version of this book."

Asaf pulled his nag up and came to a stop. "Oh. Yeah. Happy Trails. That's... that's right. Hmmm... maybe I shouldn't be so agro over this. Plus if those birdwalks are gone, maybe I shouldn't be so harsh. What about the 'witness' scene? That was lame."

"I would refer you back to Dan Rinnert. Plus, did you say 'agro'?"

"Yeah, I guess I did. Pretty corny. Like a lot of sayings around here. We might have to throw in another screeching tire. You thought I wasn't paying attention, but I overheard you talking about Ric Flair."

"Hey, the thug started it. You asked him if it was fair, and he said Ric Flair. We just jumped on the bandwagon he started, that's all. And you can't go throwing the waiter and me under the bus because we have a certain appreciation for some vintage WWE guys."

"What do you two know about WWE? What is WWE anyhow? How come I'm the only one around here who doesn't know all this stuff everybody talks about? WWE, cowboys, Dick Francis, James Patterson, The Pep Boys, The Three Stooges. I think I even heard mention of Fredrick Forsythe. I'm sure there's more. Oh speaking of more, what about Roger Moore? Hunh? Hunh? Didn't think I had it in me, did you? First, the spy gets all clever with Pierce Brosnan, then you toss in Timothy Dalton and George Lazerby. At this point the reader will be completely lost because your Dalton Lazerby chapter hit the cutting floor, [BTW so did Pierce Brosnan, I think] but who cares? We can heap-pile it up in some post- post- epilogue errata along with the movie scene crap and the General punching me in the stomach. And the way this is going, this scene is going in there too, so nobody will know how clever I was — for once — in throwing down my own external reference, even a James Bond one, which should count like the red squares on that Scrambling board."

"Uh, Asaf...? I think that's Scrabble. And, not to kick a dog when it's down, but I think the whole WWE scene is in a future chapter, not this one."

"There it is! Even when I try to poke myself into the external references I get it wrong. Instead of WWE it should all be WTF! Scramble Scrambled Scrambling. What do I know from cooking eggs? I gave all that work to those two guys and they run that part of the bar and the General the Soldier and I just take a cut."

"Asaf, Asaf. It's me your talking to. Me. I run that whole program. I make sure the cooks do their job. I tell them to stop bringing in stuff that doesn't sell because Asaf will deduct the amount if it's not selling because of your own not

paying attention to your inventories. And I'm chasing the kids out if they are just looking for mischief or trying to get some angle on stealing guns or this type or that type of military hardware. I make sure the money is right. I make sure to remind you to count the money. You tell me to count it for you because you're busy. I count the money for everybody and dole it out. Somebody from the tea-house gets in my face 'Where's Asaf? Where's Asaf?' and I'm all like — Hey — take a number — I'm busy here counting his money because he's over with you counting your money. They say 'No he's not. One of the councilmen was asking for him to count our money and we were told he's here with you.' Where are you anyhow when everybody is looking for you at the same time? And scrambled eggs are not a word board-game. And a big up to you for the Roger Moore. Well done."

Asaf appreciated the compliment and nudged his nag forward. "Well, to be honest, I don't know James Bond from Bondo glue, which the spy was all jazzed about, from St. James Compostela, even if I walked there. Not sure if that was luck or some random memory fragment that popped up out the quantum foam in my brain and surfaced just for that moment."

The lead bartender came up alongside. "That's pretty deep. I wonder … maybe we'll never know. What about the Prophet's crazy campground? I thought he was all about different worlds and chemical voodoo. You could ask him? You're one of his groupies. Ask him if he has an angle on quantum foam and snippets of memory. Like those snippets that Bumbledorf tossed into that birdbath. Remember? It was like pulling dental floss out of his brain or ear or something and he threw it into a magic birdbath and somewhere the dental floss turned into a dream or fantasy or nightmare-vision. I don't know. But you said his campground was nice and there were peacocks in it. Maybe he's got a birdbath with that mythical lady and the jug of water. HA! Knowing him he's got that one with the little kid pissing in the water. Just like the old stink! A kid peeing in his bird fountain. Where does he get off with that in his line of work? I mean, look at us. We serve beer all day long. You think we don't have guys peeing left right and center from sunrise to sunset? But do we have a fountain with a half-naked kid peeing in a pool of beer in the bar? Of course not! What kind of outfit would we be if we did that? I mean, come on man, we're in the business of providing quality food and drink to a respectable clientele: soldiers, mercenaries, guns-for-hire, spies, counter-terrorist operatives, hit-men, snipers. Probably some undercover agents of one kind or another. And those women that the soldiers hang around with. Have you seen how they all have big knives either strapped to their waist, or in their boot?? Ouch!"

Asaf dropped his reins down so his nag could nibble some grass. "I am of two minds, lead bartender. One, to correct all your erroneous musings, or, to continue one or another train of thought that appeals to my interest. Let's start with the former. I wouldn't refer to myself as one of the Prophet's groupies. Even if I knew what that was, I shouldn't know because it doesn't fit in with my character in this book. I am barely up on what's cool or modern. Groupie is way too hip for inclusion in all this writing. The Prophet is my spiritual father. I can't really argue with the chemical voodoo though. In fact, I wish I could have come up with that phrase. Kudos and back atcha for that apropos the Roger Moore complement."

The lead bartender nodded his appreciation.

Asaf continued, "I have no idea what this dental floss is all about. I'm afraid to ask because whatever explanation you give will be even further afield than the original reference. So, let's skip the dental floss. The bumble-bee, the birdbath, and peacocks … we're on a bit more solid ground here, my friend. One at a time, maybe. First, the peacock. I think it was the staffer who was observing the birds in the campground — I mean compound. I was going to correct you about the campground/compound reference, but it's not worth it and it's all six of one and half a dozen of the other by me. I can tell you it's not a campground, but that's beside the point. It could be thought of as a type of campground, but nothing like you would imagine. So, let's leave that aside. But, I don't recall ever telling anyone about seeing any peacocks, even if I did see some. And I didn't see a birdbath. Or a statue. Or a birdbath and a statue. Especially the statue part. I am pretty sure the sects don't like statues. I'm not sure why, but somewhere in my quantum foam — I mean my memory — there is some negative something about statues. What about you? You know as much or probably more about the sects and their weltanschauung than I do. What's up with their not liking statues? And last, I have seen those big knives and I don't want to know more. They're scary enough just looking at. I've never even brought it up with the Soldier."

The lead bartender was watching Asaf's nag chew on the grass. "I'd like to make just a few comments and/or observations. But first, I'd like to ask, did you just use the term weltanschauung*?"*

"Yes, I think I did. It's another quantum fragment of foam. I think it's ok in the context I used it in, but it's kinda weird having me say it, right?"

"Right. Why doesn't the Uncle say something like that in one of his rambling speeches? He's all lottie-dottie about things like that."

"That's probably where I picked it up. Anyhow, it's there, and there it is. Not much to do about it now. Seems ol' Unc' isn't around to claim or defend it."

The lead bartender nodded his head in agreement. "I can go along with that. I mean, we put that to rest pretty quickly. I was thinking there would be a whole kerfuffle over it. But I guess we're ok. Now back to the sects. It might be true, at least for the sake of argument, that I am more acquainted with their folkways and mores than you are, but not by much. All I think I know is that there is a really old belief, which has evolved into style, that you shouldn't have statues because the old pagans did, and the old pagans were old pagans and we're not old pagans anymore because our one god is better than their animistic mythological panoply of angels, angles, circles, demons, drives, divines, demi-gods, ethers, essences, forces, fonts, flows, lines, sources, sprites, spirits and so on. And lest the demi-gods and sprites feel lonely, the pagans also truck in all the good old half-baked weirdo creatures like trolls and dwarfs and that goat-guy pan something and that doll with the tall pointed red hat."

Asaf clicked for his horse to move along. "Not to dump water on your head, but I think you stuck an old Greek weirdo creature in there. Does that fit with there guhnomes and hobbilies?"

The lead bartender was resting his hands on the pommel, which drew a frown from Asaf. "Asaf, I can only give so many answers at a time while also attending to some comments I have to make as well. So here we go, in no certain order … First, back to the sayings and turns of speech. I think 'rain on the parade' is what you're looking for. But dump water is ok too. Just not as catchy. And it isn't really a saying is it? It's just a statement of fact. So much for that. I'm not going to split hairs with the inclusion or exclusion of the Greeks. They have a corner on the market with half-breeds. If the pagans want to corral them into their spiritual barn, who am I to stop them? I don't want to further step on your toes, but I think the word is 'nome', but spelled with a 'g'. And the 'g' is silent. Why? Why not? Don't know. This scene is running on fumes anyhow. Getting long in the tooth. Can't go there. Same with hobbilites or how you said it. Hobbits maybe? Trademark maybe? And I'll finish with troll dolls, Smurfs and Rainbow Brite. All old, all pagan, probably some trademarks going on, I'm sure there's some Greek influence in rainbow bright with Aurora and Pegasus. I don't eat sweet cereal for breakfast.

And while we're at it, I'd like to toss in the Bard easter egg… …

The Uncle was observing their surroundings. "The words Shangri-la and El Dorado come to mind."

"What did you say?"

"Oh. I was saying, that those shaggy goats over there must have a hell of an odor."

Asaf looked at the goats. "Well, ok … maybe, Nuncle."

"Did you just call me 'Nuncle'?"

"Uh … I guess so. Why?"

"Well, I'm a little leary of that appellation."

"Why so? Seems harmless. Uncle of mine. Mine Uncle. Nuncle. I thought it was kind of clever."

"It's just that once I was wandering aimlessly out in a wet and windy storm. I thought I was a goner, I was so ill. I only wanted to re-gain my inner strength, my core, to deal with such foolish behavior."

Asaf wasn't sure how to answer his Uncle's tale of storm and sickness, so he summed up his travels and return. "... After that, it was time to come home. I wanted to see you and get your side of the story of the Prophet's men."

The Uncle smiled. "Ah yes ... The Prophet's men. All the king's horses ... " ...

Asaf was lost by the lead bartender's answer. Instead of trying to sort it out, he moved on to another question. "Well then, what about the heathen? Don't they fit in somehow in all this mess?"

"Myself, I don't think it's too complicated. The pagans are peasants and farmers, and all those guys who look to the rain and sun and dowsing and throwing hay in the air for luck or a curse, or the hair of a goat to cure a sore throat. I think heathens are those outside the circle of a formal religion. But that doesn't get my question answered. What kind of pickle have you gotten us into?"

Asaf nudged his horse with a heel and clicked for it to stop eating and start walking again. "Well, lead bartender, that's a right, a down-right, good question. I reckon, I do reckon, we'll just have to keep on reading to find out. Ok, Pard?"

"I'm not sure if it's ok or not. You see, the reader turns the page and finds out. Right? And guess who's there for them? Me and you, the bar and the tea-house, all the other characters, the village end. Right? But why can't we flip this on its head? Instead of the reader being the one to keep following the plot, what if we, the characters, took over the plot and changed it as we saw fit, or change it just for the fun of it? The reader could flip the page and, BOOM, it's a scene from when you're dying or something."

Asaf was not happy. "Dying!? Why am I dying all of the sudden? I don't want to die. I'm still young. I haven't even got to the end of this book yet and you're all killing me off already. Not cool bro, not cool."

"Ok ok ok. Not dying. Bad example. Well, what about this? As it is now, each reader reads us and has his or her mental image of what we look like. I mean, this has been addressed somewhere else in this, what I'll keep calling a book, although it continually digresses from what is commonly called, or thought of, like a book. That is, there's no description of anything. Is Asaf

really tall with blond hair or really short with black hair? Nobody knows. It all has to be made up in their minds as they read."

Asaf interrupted, "Or is the lead bartender on drugs, or is he just whacked out, just because?"

The lead bartender did an Asaf and ignored his friend. "As I was saying. Is there a way for us to mess around with the reality of the book, so that each reader finds a different plot? Why are we, here inside the book, the victims of pure fate? We're put down in type and DONE! No more changing Asaf from a water boy to a bar manager to something different. Everybody gets the same treatment. Water-boy to bar-guy. Water-boy to bar-guy. Over and over and over again. Why not something a little more interesting? Like, Asaf, from a crippled polio kid with flies in his face to the CEO of some robotics conglomerate. You could be a zero to hero, as per above, but each reader would read something different. Check it! The readers all get together with tea and biscuits to blah blah about this book, number one-gazillion on the best seller list. They nibble and say 'How's little Kelly?' And 'Oh? So she did get accepted to [insert fancy school name here, like St. Gaudens on the Marsh] how nice.' And 'Oh I know last year's model was a classic, but Aunt Flurby said the insurer would give a premium reduction if I kept dunking this Oreo in my coffee.' And 'Oh Deb, how do you like your new Cayenne? I heard its carbon footprint was a carbon pinkie-fingerprint! Ha ha ha. Not.' And other such conversations. Ok? Finally, they get around to talking about this book. But they all get confused because the plot and the twists and turns and, heck, even the scenery, like right now, is all random and bizarro-world. First, they would just start correcting each other or asking simple questions. 'What was that dearie? Page forty-two?' 'Now Maude, I don't think it happened that way.' Soon it would devolve into chaos and a food fight. 'He did not turn left! He went straight. Look it says so right here!' 'What do you mean he got her pregnant? He had his manhood blown-off in Chapter Two.' Each reader would be reading her own version of the whole story. Hunh? How about them apples?"

"Did Dan put you up to this? It sure is sounding a lot like how he would manage a book that was supposed to be really cutting edge and cool and on-guard and all that too-chez lingo."

"Do you mean avant-garde and touché?"

"I mean — let's get back to the book. This book, not another book, or some hair-brained whatever that the Author has bouncing around in his brain. But the village, our people, our plot. Our book. I'm getting tired. I'm in the lead role most of the time. So, now it's time to stop with all the nonsense and get back to work."

Intermission Finished.

34

ASAF AND THE THUG WALKED up the lane to the tea-house and bar. The thug asked casually, "Ok Asaf, you point out the placing of the gear, where you want it to go."

"I thought this was your job? I don't know how to make these things work. That's why you're in this with me."

They both fell silent, mutually and simultaneously realizing that there was a big hole in their plan. Both thought the other had figured out how the explosives would be put in place.

"Hoofta! I reckon we are reading not the same book. I can hook these particulars. Is the pork for brains. But what do we tell all the eyeballs and all the listenings? They see and hear, then think: 'Not every day Asaf is fiddling with making the bombs in clear viewing of every man and bird that passes along.' Hoofta! The mercenaries. Punch your train ticket for that! — and call the conductor. The train — it stops on the spot. I am in the thoughts that we need to have a talk. Maybe away from the eye and ears of birds, and especial, the mercenary."

They walked a distance away and sat on a low wall, left from what was a poor dirt farmer's front garden. They observed the buildings. Asaf asked: "How about the simple old way of doing things in secret? Do it in the dark of night? Is that too simple?"

The thug sat thinking, ruminating. "Yes. And maybe some, not yes. Time. We have to make time — time to get it laid to the bone. Even in the dark, the night, we need to have us a cover parable. A plot to say this and distract from what we really making happen. We found this here already. Or, we are practicing. Or, the General is telling us to build to guard from the enemies. Some something to tell the eyeballs and the listenings, all is ok. Not a thing to see, not here. Just following the lead partridge and do what he tells us."

Asaf wasn't sure about the trains and birds. "Ok. I guess that makes some sense. I don't have a better idea. You need to tell me how much time you need to get all of the explosives laid out and put in place. I need to know if there are stages, or parts, like part one and part two or whatever. Like getting the material from where we stashed it to here on the side of the buildings — in a truck or something — to having everything in place and wired."

Asaf was struggling to keep his thoughts in order, or even to make some order out of all the thoughts coursing through his mind. "Everything just where it needs to be for me … And set up so that I can walk away. And walk far enough away to set off the bomb … Whether I set it off or another … that's not my concern … our concern … So, how long? How many hours of darkness? Remember we need to blow up everything and make sure what remains is a big radioactive pit."

The thug looked around the neighborhood. "I can give a best good answer if we walk the buildings again. We walk and look. Then we know."

They walked early in the morning so they could take as much time as necessary without having anyone wondering what they were doing. They slowly went around the entire perimeter of both buildings; stopping here and there as the thug thought, taking in all the information he needed to calculate his answers for Asaf.

When they finished their stroll, the thug said, "I can take stones and rocks — and I put the rocks where each hidi-hole needs cut in. I will show these rocks for you for the help of the others digging.

"Lessee. One … two … three … Here is a plan that is workable. Everything as it gets going on the night, the first and the second, maybe the third. In the one night, we bring over the gear. You must be having the camouflage in order. Nozza the explosives all laying about like eggs fallen out of a nest for a vulture or fox to see and explore. I give this camo for you to think about. I pre-arrange the gear, side by side, side by side, side by side. Where each brick goes, by each rock. Bit by bit, we make a layout, so we can put the cord right. Right first time, every time.

"Next, we have long night and sweat and churn. We need time for all this. Is the making all the hidi-holes. We do it one time, first time, every time. We dig, then even more, for the cutting the ditch all around. We do it careful ways. We do the half, then the half again. Two nights."

Asaf stopped and looked up and down the sides of the building. "I would rather have one long night than two shorter nights. I don't want to drag this out or make it more complicated than it already is. Can we get the digging done all at one go?"

The thug thought about the project some more. "You are having the money. Money ready at hand?"

Asaf said he did.

"The money, it helps, whether the one night or two nights — same as three days, but I answer you your question. Are the two nights and not right first time every time and no explosion or half only? Or the three nights right, right first time, every time and a success make? I think I am knowing the answer. But, to do you the best, either two nights or the three, the money is always a scoop of grain on the hay for motivation. Also, you will be letting me tell the lads how it is going for the money. I will explain that they will get the whole month extra, like the thirteen month, for three days the working. I will tell them it is hard work. I will tell them arrival when I say. When I say. Not the before or after. And the leave only when I say. Not the before or after. And only the month worth of money if everybody together a success of this project makes. If the one or the other not to work coming, or coming late, leaving early — not even for the mama's funeral no — or arguing with me. No money for nobody. That means done in time and all the rules and what I say obeyed like the strict mama or papa or school teacher. Whatever the most strict, I am twice that. Everybody goes in. Everybody does just as told. Everybody finished, goes out. Everybody gets paid the one month value of work extra. Can you do this? Is there the money, real money in the hand, in the hand at the finishing of the project, to afford these workers this much?"

Asaf said he would make it so.

35

After counting the money that week, Asaf told the Councilman he wanted to talk about the two businesses with the whole council.

The Minister of Justice, the Councilman, the Plebe and Asaf sat at a corner table in the tea-house and ordered tea. "Gentlemen, thank you for this little meeting. We are all busy. I would not have asked for this time together unless it was important."

The others nodded, waiting for Asaf to continue. "We all know things are not going well for the Prophet. He spends more and more time at the fruit shop with the General. When he is here he is disgusting. I don't know if he goes out to the compound or not. The cafe owner has banished them to the back alley. This effects the tea-house more than the bar. But as the bar manager, anything that is bad for the tea-house is bad — maybe more important — maybe less important — for the bar. In this case, since it involves the General too, it effects all of us. I know I am not a member of this council. I know I am not involved in your underground affairs."

At this, the Minister of Justice shot a sideways glance at his two fellows and frowned. Asaf put up his hand. "I see that, Minister. Don't worry. I know just enough to know I don't want to know more. I've got my hands full enough next door and don't want to get involved in gun-running and drugs and political assassinations."

"Well, I never!" the Minister cried out, jumping to his feet. He began to shake his finger at Asaf. "Young man ..."

The Councilman intervened. "Minister, Minister. Sit down. Sit. Sit. It's ok. Asaf is just generalizing. He's not pointing fingers at any one of us. Asaf, the Minister takes the umbrage too easy. Go on, then the Minister can have his say. His say you know."

Asaf glanced around at each of them. "Well, it wasn't really pure generalization, but that's not what — what I mean is, bad things happen, bad for business, bad for us. Seems like I've tried to make this speech before. Anyhow, one of my partners is out of the picture and your leader is out with him. I'm not here to discuss if I'm serving vodka on ice or straight, and not here to ask if you're running missiles or just rifles. I'm here to tell you things are bad with these two."

Asaf looked straight at the Minister. "Fair enough Minister? Would you like to say anything; ask me any questions?"

The Minister of Justice looked at Asaf, then at the Councilman. "Councilman? What do you think?"

"Thanks for asking. We're fine, Asaf. Fine. Minister? Ok?"

The Minister nodded. "Go on. What is on your mind with this reprehensible situation?"

"Thank you, Minister. I will try to keep what I have to say real simple. As you three know, better than anyone else, I am in a unique position here in these buildings. What you may or may not know, or might suspect or are curious about, is my spiritual status. That is, with the Prophet."

Asaf paused. The Minister of Justice was paying close attention, ready to pounce should the need arise. The Councilman knew the most about what Asaf was talking about and stayed relaxed. The Plebe was glancing all around the table looking for clues as to what was really happening that he might not know about and how to decide which way to bend with whatever wind might blow through their confab.

"Tell us — about your — spiritual status …" the Minister whispered slowly with a hint of conspiracy in his tone. He lifted his eyebrows up and down as if indicating that the gathering was ready for the goods to be laid on the table, be they welcome or disagreeable.

Asaf took a quiet deep breath. He looked at each of them, one at a time. "I will say this in two parts, so as to not create a scene. One, I am the Prophet's successor. His spiritual heir. Two, this is not a thing done, final, once and for all. That is, I am not the one and only heir and if I die tomorrow, it would not be the end of what the Prophet was all about. But I am the direct successor. If nothing else happens this thing or that thing, I am the successor. Back to number two. If I do not take up my succession, it will move on to whatever the next thing a succession moves on to. There. Said it. I think I said that in plain enough words for us to talk about it."

Asaf was expecting one of the councilors to jump up and slit his throat for saying what he did. But no-one did. Not even the Minister of Justice. The Councilman looked at the Minister, then the Plebe. Seeing nothing, he pulled out a pack of Marlboros, lit two up and passed one to the Minister. Even though they knew the Plebe didn't smoke, he delicately waved off the non-offer to be cool.

"Well, what about us?" the Minister asked blowing out a great stream of smoke.

Asaf looked at him with a blank face. The Plebe decided to join in and follow the Minister's lead. "Yeah. What about us?"

As there was silence at the table, the Councilman also asked, "Yeah. What about those two. And me too?"

Asaf didn't know how to answer because he was not sure what an answer would be and didn't know the answer anyhow. So he said: "I'm not sure how to answer. Could you be more specific?"

The Minister cleared his throat and tapped his cigarette in the ashtray. "Dear Asaf. It's quite simple. We, we here, we, are the Prophet's council. As his successor, we would like to know from you the direction we, all of us, we all, will be going in. The agenda. The mission. Where we will be going, the direction that is."

The Plebe nodded his head with as much gravitas as he could muster. "Yes … the direction."

Everyone looked at the Councilman. "Uh … uh, sure. I wanna know too. Do I? I do, right men?"

Asaf's mind was a muddle of confusion mixed with befuddlement, with a pinch of disbelief, a dash of perplexity, wonderment, and surprise. "Uh, direction? What direction?"

"Yes. What direction?" the Minister repeated.

"I … ah … I. Well, how does one find direction?"

The Councilman lifted his hand. "Hey, Asaf. It's ok if you don't know. None of us all know everything. This prophet thing. It has to grow on you. It just doesn't come overnight," hard snap of the fingers, "you gotta work into it. Work into it, you know."

"Yes, your Dignity. Work into it. We know it becomes you," the Plebe added, secretly hoping he was not over-fawning with the titular address and assumptive finish.

Not to be out-shined, the Minister quickly butted in. "Your Dignity, take heart. This is rash, to be sure. But we, the council, your council, are at the ready. The beck and call. The summons and notary of your officialdom. Why, we, we here, are the glad tidings of what we all show forth. Show forth to the world in darkness. Trust us your Dignity. Trust in us. With us." He finished with a look over at the Councilman.

"Yeah. Like he said, your Dignified. We know how to do these things. To carry out, you know. Sure."

Asaf was dumbfounded. Then incredulous. Then baffled. He started out hesitantly. "Uh, ok. I mean, is that what it takes to become the Prophet's successor?"

The three looked at each other, shrugging shoulders, nodding in agreement. The Minister spoke for them all. "Your Dignity. It is not too hard. Let us speak plainly, as you have done. May I?"

Asaf nodded, inwardly hoping there would be some clarification.

"Plainly then. The Prophet is not perfect. None of us are. But he is gifted. He is a leader. He speaks grandly of paradise and spiritual things. And he is a visionary. But he is not a miracle worker. He may or may not even be God's voice for this generation. We all get along. We take his mannerisms with the proverbial grain of salt. I think I can speak for us all," nods all around, "that it is not far-fetched at all to see why the Prophet chose you as his successor. You're young, bright. A natural leader. Not overbearing. Not too much spiritual gobbledegook in the way you speak. Right men?"

"Right," the Councilor answered. "Look, Asaf ..."

"Ahem!" the Minister reminded his fellow.

"Ok. Asaf, your Dignified, look I know you pretty well, you know me. Ok? So you know we all roll with what we got in front of us. I really agree with the Minister here. You're a good guy. It's time for a change. The Prophet, come on guys, you're calling for plain language, ok, the Prophet lost it. He lost it when he started dallying with the lads. You can't be a respected prophet and fiddle with the boys. Right?"

No comments.

"So there you have it. No dallying with the lads. But sure the Minister is correct. It doesn't have to be a big deal like Moshe and the Sinai. You're here. We have these businesses. Now that the Prophet has got nothing but mush in his cranium for brains, we can use a stand-up guy like you. In fact, I think maybe the one thing the Prophet has done right lately is to name you his successor."

Asaf looked around the table. They each nodded at him when he looked their way. "Well, ok ... I guess. So, what do I do? What should we do?"

The Councilman leaned forward and put his elbows on the table. "Asaf," (sharp glance from the Minister. The Councilman ignores him.) "We got a lot of things we can do. A lot. Right fellas? Right now we have these businesses. Now, I know, or I think I know that you are not too fond of these things. Not too fond. Well, that's ok. Remember the Minister's advise, grow into the job. Good advise."

The Minister nodded his smug approval.

"So we can continue these businesses. It's easy to do. Carry on, you know, and we talk about our future."

Asaf was still uncertain. The Plebe, being the youngest, ergo closest to Asaf's age, saw a window of opportunity to advance his standing in this brand new order, leaned in and got Asaf's attention. "Your Dignity, we know there is the old and the new. The generation the Prophet was addressing is already moving toward their ancestor's sacred plot. A new generation is coming up, nay is already here, to turn an ear to the clarion voice of what-is-to-come on the planet and its inhabitants. Gather yourself. Muster your resources and lead the way. Do not feel that you have to step in the perfumed feet of our predecessor. We can strike out in a direction and form of modality which suits and befits this turning of the page. It is yours to take up the whip and rein and steer the steed of destiny to its teleological guerdon."

The Minister of Justice was impressed. He even allowed a tell of widened eyes. A stream of thoughts ran through his mind in quick succession. "Well said. Damn, maybe I could have said that. Upstart! We'll see where that gets him. Maybe he should be the new prophet instead of this Asaf guy. I know, I'll bring him under my wing even closer. What's that saying? An enemy closer is like a good shower? No that doesn't sound right. Keep your enemy as close as an undergarment? Hmmm ... Shower your enemy with Close-up toothpaste? Close-up toothpaste?! I don't even think they make that anymore. For the love of Petra! What am I thinking about? I'll have to break out my old Godfather videos and review my tactics and strategy."

Then aloud, "Ahem. Well stated young Plebe. Well said. And I put my silver and gold pieces upon what you have expressed. I believe my impartation unto thee of worthy skulldomnesses is bearing fruit. We shall make note and endeavor to further cultivate such advances. If it suits the council and the prophet. Ad hic salutus et adoptionae fortuitas nostrum. Eh?"

Silence.

"Look, your Asafness, don't get too sucked in with these guys having a religious pissing contest. It's ok. We all have our own way of expression. But the Plebe is right. Turn a new page. Or peek under the current page and see what's coming. Here's what I recommend. You know the etymology, having been around the Prophet. To-speak-before or the-speaker in-front-of, and so on. Well, take a good look around. Around this province. This country, other countries. See what's going on. How are the people doing? What do you see in their lives that we can make a difference in? Give them help and support. You can show them how to live well. Good water. Cleanliness. That sort of stuff. Show them the way to God who wants us to do well. The way of righteousness. Point out the currents of culture and history and contextualize it in a meaningful way that leads to a better, wholesome spirituality. A wholesome spirituality leads to a better life because the inner man feels goodness and light. You take what you see going on in the world and interpret it for the people in light of their actual circumstances. We can even help out with those subsidized NGO loans for small businesses. That's a prophet's job. You're young. Not real religious. Not being too religious is an advantage. It allows a fresh perspective on the life of the average household. And we here on the council, we're just a beginning. The Prophet has many followers. All over. We can leverage that to your favor. Leverage you know."

Asaf looked around the table. The council looked back, calm and cordial. Asaf smiled. Then shook his head. Then started to laugh. And laugh. And laugh pointing at the men at the table. When he saw their reaction, not humorous or funny or farcical or hilarious, — not even a smile — but grave and scowling and puzzled and questioning — he knew he made a misstep somewhere. "Sorry. This is a joke, right?" Looking around. "A joke. Prank. You know, pulling the goat by the beard?"

No smiles. Fermenting resentment.

The Minister slowly, very slowly, getting everyone's full attention as he stood up. Rising to his full height, he took a deep breath, taking time to put his thoughts in order. He looked down at Asaf. "Young man, if you think this is a joke, then we are all badly mistaken here. You can't come in here; declare yourself our Prophet's successor; acquiesce to our acceptance; listen to our sage advice and wisdom, then step on the entire proceeding with jest and selfish frivolity. I'm very sorry if this is where we have come to. We are men of faith and morals. We accept what you claim and we embrace our new leader. The time is ripe for such a thing, as my brother councilor has pointed out. Now this. Laughter. We can be sarcastic or make fun of the

Prophet behind his back, which is merely human. But we don't eschew our vocation in this. He knows we poke fun at him once in a while. But we all go on with our business. Our business! If you think this is a prank, as you say, then we owe each other an apology and we will part ways. I, myself, would lean towards sterner measures, but that is not beneficial nor conducive to what we have at this table today. Gentlemen, what say you? Asaf, what say you? Where are we at with this? Is this a misunderstanding or just getting used to each other's company? Please express yourselves. And let's be civil. I take my seat now. Thank you."

The Plebe was about to speak, but the Councilman put his hand up in front of him. "Thanks Plebe. Just sit there for a minute. Asaf, as sober as the Minister is, I have to tell you what he says nails it. I have seen him flare up at lesser things. He has remained calm and collected here. You know? So tell us, tell me, your friend of sorts, what's going on here?"

Asaf put his hands on the table in order to stand. He looked at the Minister. "May I?" The Minister nodded. Asaf stood. "Gentlemen," looking at each one in turn, "I apologize, as you have suggested. I never ever thought or even had any notion that I would — would, could? be or become the Prophet's successor just — just in an instance. Or today. Or now. Don't you have to go to school or be in charge of a religious group or something like that? I … I think there might be something wrong. Or not? I'll sit down now. Tell me what's going on."

Asaf sat. There was silence as the council members waited to the other to speak. The Councilman broke the silence. "Asaf, for the Minster's sake, your Dignity, I saw — just enough — I saw what went on between you and the Prophet. Out in the compound and here. Here, you know, when we were new. So this announcement of yours doesn't surprise me. No, let me re-phrase that. I saw the Prophet give you the succession. What surprises me is that you have come to it just at the right time. For me, it confirms that what the Prophet bestowed on you is real. Real, you know? We've talked. You know I'm a regular guy. You know too I have spiritual light too. So, seeing that there's no rejection from the council here, I'm in. I am witnessing God's hand right here at this table. Someday, maybe there will be stories told of how all this — all your future ministry started. They'll say: 'It was in a cafe in the corner of the country.' This cafe in this corner. Go ahead Plebe. I stopped you. I don't want to be rude. Just keep it straight. You're on the council. That's good enough for us. No need to grease the goat on the spit, right?" This last he said glancing at the Minister.

The Plebe attempted a sage air. "Very well. Following your advise, I do not have much to add that is substantive. I follow in the Minister's footsteps as he promoted me to the council. I am grateful to God to be present at this historical event. Your Dignity, I do not wish to grease the goat. But I would also remind you, if you can accept it without it seeming like I am reprimanding you, you started this conversation. You called this meeting. You revealed to us your spiritual status as the Prophet's successor. We have taken that at face value. Don't laugh at us or doubt us if we accept it. Otherwise, it makes us out as evil, taking you for a marionette or stupid, being duped by you."

"Hey!" Asaf retorted, "I'm not here tricking anyone. I'm just saying I didn't know becoming a prophet was this easy."

"Not easy," the Councilman said. "No. We all have been saying that it is something you grow into. Haven't we?"

The Minister held his hand up. "Everybody, let us stop. Asaf, Plebe, my brother councilor, let us take a step to the side. Let us split this in two. First, Asaf here has got our attention. Second, the pros and cons of a spiritual calling can be addressed separately. Well, maybe. But let us at least go back and let Asaf continue where he left off. Asaf, I believe you prefaced your reason to have this meeting with the successor announcement. Setting that aside just for now, what is it you would like to discuss? Ok, gentlemen?"

Nods all around.

"Thank you. Listen, councilmen, you all know me. I'm not here to argue. I'm here to ask for help. Maybe I got started on the wrong foot. I wasn't expecting to become the successor so fast. But we can work on that as the Councilman has wisely recommended. So, I have asked to meet with you because I have a plan that I need your help with. I know each one of you is assigned to one of the sects. I know the sects are being looked at carefully for elimination or assimilation. I want to do the one thing that actually might give the Prophet's vision for peace a chance. I want each one of you to bring your sect leader here. Here to the bar and tea-house."

Silence.

"And … so … that's ok?" Asaf asked.

"Sure, Boss. When …"

"Ahem!"

"Oh. Right. Sure, your Dignified. When should we plan on this get-together?"

Asaf was caught off-guard again at the lack or absence of being second-guessed by the council. "Oh. Yes. When. Uh. The new moon. Either this one or the following one."

The Minister raised a finger. "Dignity, how do you propose, or how should we keep these rascals from fighting in here. One hates the other and the third hates either the first or the second."

"Good question Minister. I've thought about that. There are three places here. Here, the tea-house. The bar. And the basement."

Asaf addressed each in turn. "Councilman, bring the leader of the Radicals to the outside entrance of the basement. Plebe, bring the leader of the Fanatics to the bar. And Minister, you can bring the leader of the Zealots here, in the tea-house. It won't be perfect. If there is a big group of them, we can't keep them from getting in arguments. But we can try."

"And, what should we tell them," the Councilman asked.

"Tell them a palatable version of the truth. The Prophet going away and he wants this meeting."

"Won't fly Dignified. Can't tell them the Prophet is going away. This will fuel their lust for power. We have to have a better cover."

The Minister nodded.

"Ok," Asaf said in a lackluster tone. "What else can there be? He's sick? He's passing on the torch to the next generation? He got lost in the desert?"

"How about he's fiddling with the lads so much he's gone blind?" the Councilman said with a big laugh.

"Oh! I know, I know," the Plebe cried out. "How about he was in the desert with a torch, it went out and he was blind — then he got sick."

"Wait, wait," the Minster joined in. "He took two of his boys on a field trip in the desert, one of them got sick, one of them went blind and the Prophet is out there saving them and, and … and something else …"

"Ok, how's this. Right. Boys, desert, sick, blind — ok. And he is making a brand new foundation for blind and sick lost boys of the desert. The missionary charity is so compelling, that he needs the full cooperation of the sects to make it a viable thing. A thing, you know?"

The Minister nodded. "Ok. I think so … Plebe?"

"Blind, lost, sick, boys. Of the desert. Wow. That's pretty good. Councilman, you've earned another level of respect from me."

"Thank you."

"Well then, your Dignity," the Minister concluded. "I think that will do. What else? You mentioned the new moon I believe."

"Uh … Oh, yeah. New moon. The new moon. How long do you need to know … how long will it take to get … That is, how much time do you need to know from me when I want everybody here and how long will it take for everybody to get here?"

"That's not a problem," the Plebe answered confidently. "We have pull with these guys because we're tight with the Prophet, even if they think they don't like the Prophet, they like us because they like power and they think the Prophet has power. So just give the word, your Dignity, and we'll bring them in."

Asaf was trying to appear normal and congenial. But inside he was astounded how the council operated and their casual acceptance of him as the new prophet.

"A word."

"What?" Asaf asked the Councilman.

"A word. This thing has to have a word attached to it. A code word. You know? So we can go into operation."

"Ah. Yes, of course."

Asaf slowly stood, then looked at his council one by one. "Snakehead."

36

Asaf called a meeting with the thug, the waiter, and the lead bartender. He told them the next step in their plan was to close the two buildings to get the bombs in place. Asaf explained that they would close for a complete inventory and a deep cleaning. "Everyone is to be notified and made aware ahead of time that the tea-house and the bar will be closed for at least three days sometime during the next few weeks for inventory, and the day after that for cleaning, and the day after that for re-opening. If anybody asks about this undertaking they are to be told that it is required by new regulations that govern us in this region since the province was being upgraded. This is now to be done every year to make sure the businesses are done by the books and that the establishments are clean. Tell them we will re-open later in the week after everything is clean and all our food and drink are re-stocked and our inspection complete. This will make up for any disappointment for our regulars, that we're doing it for the common good."

Asaf looked at his three comrades. "Questions? comments?"

Everybody was paying attention. They all looked relaxed and ready to keep listening.

"Each of us will have three or four lads under us. The lead bartender knows these boys and has told them what we need and the money is good. These will basically be small teams. The thug and the waiter will run everything on the tea-house side. My lead bartender and I will run the bar. We need a person on the inside of the buildings who is in charge, and a person on the outside who is in charge. Between the four of us, that spreads us thin … but I think we can go like this … The thug and I will be in charge of the outsides. You two will run the inside. You two on the inside must send everything out to the thug and I. Out there, we will tell the lads where to put everything. We'll do the front of the house first. Furniture, tables, chairs. Small goods, large goods … Dishes, salt and pepper, condiments … We will box up as much as possible to keep it clean and orderly, and for maximum efficiency."

Asaf looked at his three comrades. "Questions? comments?"

Everybody was paying attention. They all looked relaxed and ready to keep listening.

"Good. The back of the house will come next, after the floors and front of the house are cleared out and everything is outside. It will be important to remove everything from under and behind the bar and counters and all the cooking areas. Because some back-stock is in the basement, we will get as much out as we can without invading the Prophet's apartment. We are better off leaving the apartment alone if we can. Someday, we can get that clean — another time. This cleaning has to be a short turn-around. Ok?"

Asaf looked at his three comrades. "Questions? comments?"

Everybody was paying attention. They all looked relaxed and ready to keep listening.

"Each one of us has to discern who and how our team members think and operate. We want to play into their natural skills. Strong, weak, smart ... shy, too loud ... all that stuff. Little things that can help make things go smoothly. Make decisions as you go and change jobs as needed. If one kid can't lift, have him do something he can."

Asaf looked at his three comrades. "Questions? comments?"

Everybody was paying attention. They all looked relaxed and ready to keep listening.

Asaf continued, "Once everything on the floor and back-stock is out, we will send the lads back inside to start cleaning. The thug will stay outside. I will send the waiter out to help him there. The lead bartender will come over to me. He and I will coordinate the cleaning. We will do it with all the lads. At this point, all the lads will be inside with me and the lead bartender. Only the thug and the head waiter will stay outside. We will start with the tea-house cleaning, then we will clean the bar."

Asaf looked at his three comrades. "Questions? comments?"

Everybody was paying attention. They all looked relaxed and ready to keep listening.

"Ok. This is important because it's why we're doing all this work. The thug and I have looked carefully at the walls where all the bricks will go. There are rocks we put there to mark the spots. You two, take a look at these spots for your own knowledge. But do it in a simple way so someone doesn't get all curious about what you're gawking at. When all the boxes and the other stuff is brought outside, we will place this junk around the rocks so it will act as a cover. This thug and the waiter can point out where this or that can go and they can shift stuff if necessary. We all need to know where the rocks are if something goes sideways, and can continue to stage stuff in the right spots. After everything is scattered around outside, everybody but the thug and the waiter will be inside cleaning."

Asaf looked at his three comrades. "Questions? comments?"

Everybody was paying attention. They all looked relaxed and ready to keep listening.

"Speaking of cleaning … Do you need extra hands out there to rig the gear?"

The thug nodded. "It was on my thoughts, yes. If the waiter and I each have a lad, one for the one, one for the other … the job progression improves good."

"Good. I like that. Ok, time. All this planning and who does what and when has to be spread over the time we have to do this which will be, hopefully, two days. We won't know for sure until we're up to our noses in the thick of things. The thug is running the lads' work days. So we'll have to rely on his progress to take each step. Ok. We've covered a lot … I think it makes me less nervous than I already was and should be. Is that right? I'm nervous now … and will be? I will be more than I am? I was … and now … Help me out here lead bartender."

"Well," the lead bartender began pensively. "Let's start by examining and or assessing how nervous you are right now. Also, how many more times in this scene will that paragraph up there be copied and pasted? How nervous are you — right now?"

Asaf looked at the small group. "Right now? Well, I guess I'm not too nervous. I mean … in compared to what?"

"Uhh … compared to how nervous you felt before now. Or before right now."

The waiter joined in. "Wait. I think I remember back in school, they taught us to establish a baseline — for whatever comparison is being made. And with the baseline, you can track, or gauge how up or down or sideways you are from where you normally are, or in Asaf's case, where he was — maybe … "

"Sure," the thug chimed in. He turned to the waiter. "If we can like a line in sand the drawing. And, like, step one over. It is one step over the line, and back is one back, and the line is the even. Normal nervous. Not too much the nerves. Maybe not too less the nerves. Yes?"

"Well, in school we made the baseline on a chalkboard. I don't remember any lines in the dirt except out doing football in the street or in a field somewhere."

"There everybody goes with the fancy schools. Just because I'm not the fancy school-making-boy, like you three figs, don't mean I cannot know from the nerves here and the nerves the other side. I've got the nervousness million more than all you."

The lead bartender tried to reel in the conversation, "Hold on, hold on. Let's get back to what we're doing here. We're not comparing schools and athletic equipment standards. We're here to assess how nervous Asaf is. Or was, or will be … right, Asaf?"

"Don't 'Hold on hold on' me. I know from the looking in the nerves. Asaf!"

Asaf jumps and looks at the thug.

"Asaf. How many the bad nerves year ago?"

"Umm … I … When a year ago?"

"A year — a year . Not know from the year? Januaries Febbuaries Marsh Abrril. How the nerves then?"

The lead bartender cut back in, "Hey wait. It doesn't make sense to ask how he was last year. Without first the baseline making. I mean, we need to make a baseline, so we can compare how nervous he was years ago and how nervous he has been since we've known him these years. Right?"

The waiter answered, "I don't know if that's quite what I mean. A baseline is sort of an independent standard to measure against. I'm not sure if how many years Asaf has been nervous is part of that."

"Well isn't a baseline time dependent? Or at least some variable? I mean, you can't just say 'I'm nervous' without some time frame, can you?"

Looking around for some support, the lead bartender asked again, "Can you?"

The thug said with a touch of compassion, "Asaf, I didna know you the nerves for so many years. It is not good like this. Look at you. Smart guy. The big Uncle. Soldiers all around — even if theys but a fly-stink fig-headed sons of Beelzubaal. You don't need the bad nerves — and all those years. Hoofta! Maze, Joonz, Yoolio …"

The waiter protested, "How did we get years into the equation?

Asaf, have you been nervous for years? or just recently?"

"I don't know if years really says it. I think I'm thinking … maybe a while, since I've been thinking more and more about the plan. Yeah, I guess since thinking about that."

"Good. Now we're getting somewhere. Ok. Think Asaf. How long have you been considering blowing this village apart to millions of bits and pieces?"

"Hey!" the lead bartender objected. "Don't make him even more nervous by reminding him how many tiny shards of shrapnel will be flung out in the whole area. That's not going to make him less nervous. You're all Mr. Baseline. How can you establish a baseline by jacking him up with talk about how much extreme damage he's going to inflict on the entire area? Holy radiation batman!"

The lead bartender turned his attention to Asaf. "Asaf, now listen to me. We all understand blowing the holy hell out of this place is your primary goal. But now we have to step back a bit. Step back from the tension and anxiety of it all. You need to sit back and relax."

Asaf sits back and relaxes.

"There that's good. Now breathe. Breathe evenly. Good."

The thug joins in, "That's right, Asaf. The breaths of breathings. Good."

The thug breathes noisily and heavily. "Nnnngggshhh — ooogghhhhhh — nkkkkkerrr — oooggggghhhh …"

The waiter shook his head. "You know, I was going to protest all this folderol. But I think I won't. I really think I won't. I think we're actually getting somewhere. The breathing. Lowering the blood pressure. Maybe some alpha and theta waves going on. Heart rate. This might be ok."

Asaf breathes. "Huuuhhhh — hoooohoo — huuuuhhhh — hoooohoo …"

The lead bartender leans in, "Ok, Asaf. Tell us, on a scale of one to ten, how many fingers am I holding up?"

The waiter rouses himself from his nascent meditations. "Fingers! What's that got to do with breathing?! What do you mean fingers? Asaf. Asaf, listen to me, not the lead bartender. No, keep breathing. Yes. Just like the thug, but not as loud. That's it. Ok. Now, Asaf, on a scale of one to ten, how much louder is the thug's breathing than yours? No, no — that's not what I meant. Let me rephrase that. On a scale of one to ten, how nervous are you right now? One, being you don't have a care in the world, (except you're trying to blow this whole building up.) And ten, that this whole thing is going to collapse on your head any minute now and the Soldier is going to come in here, blast us all to eternity, and the eternity may be the bad one, depending on your theological take on the matter of the afterlife and such."

"What the fig!? You fly-speck! You canna tell the Asaf to be relax like the whole world entire not a thing he cares about and then parenthetically slip in that whoops, 'cept that you're cracked in the head-skull for your belove' plan. How the relaxing when you dump the energies all bad on him like that?? Asaf, Asaf. You to me be listening. Keep the breathes. The breathes. Ok, ok. Not the ear turning to waiter boy here. Ok now. Asaf the scale, the scale. One, you are float the floating the cloud and pillow and a big hookha of poppies. And the ten, in the big pit with scorpions all running up and down the feet for nervousness. How nervous are you? The one and the ten. Poppies and snakes and things. The nervous? How do you feeling it?"

The waiter waved his hand in the air. "Whoa whoa whoa! You can't make a baseline by telling him he's up to his eyeballs in scorpions and snakes! And it doesn't make any more sense than if he was high on opium. We need to interpret how nervous he is on any given day, — really we need more than any given day — we need to establish some sort of time frame, a representative pool of time, to sample from, which can be used to extrapolate into the greater months and years — that is, a time-frame reference from before he decided to completely annihilate all the innocent people around here, to a pool of time since he decided to commit genocide. Then, once we have random samples from before and since, then we can put the one-to-ten scale test overlaid on the two time-pools and establish a true sample, from which, the Asaf-nervousness-quotient can be derived."

The thug and the lead bartender's eyes were glazed over.

Asaf broke the silence. "Hey! Let's move on from breathing and nerves. I appreciate your concern, but maybe we can go back to that some other time. Ok? Where were we? Choosing up helpers and cleaning I think. Well, anyhow — you two each get to pick a lad. Make a good choice and all that ... I don't need to lecture you, just do the best you can and let me know if there's anything I can help with. Otherwise, pick your own lad at will. Ok? Meanwhile — here's what we plan for the outside. The thug and the waiter, along with their two lads, will begin the rigging process for the bomb gear. The cover of the boxes and stuff will allow them to dig proper holes and cut-outs and trenches. Since we are operating under extreme time constraints, we need to be able to move boxes and other junk in concert with the digging and bomb-making as the thug directs."

Asaf directed his speech at the thug, "Sorry about the lack of technical lingo in all this. I actually don't know the parts of a bomb well enough to make a meaningful set of sentences to explain all this. I practiced like I knew what I was talking about … but I was only fooling myself. Now, I just say bomb for everything that makes the bomb. The caps and the cords the what hooks to the other and back again. I'll just say bomb-stuff. Fair enough?"

The thug nodded his head. "Izza Ric Flair."

The lead bartender whispered to the waiter, "Did he just say Ric Flair?"

The waiter whispered back, "Yeah, I think so. Weird. Isn't that Nature Boy Ric Flair?"

"Yeah. How did the thug get off with that?"

"Talk about bombs. He let go a WWE bomb."

The waiter paused to think. "Maybe he's just a wrestling fan. Those guys hang out downstairs and watch sports. Makes some sense. The brothers of the code and all that. Even thugs need some sort of entertainment. Might as well be professional wrestling. They probably have some brothers in there they use for muscle. Who knows?"

Their whisperings caught Asaf's attention. "Everything ok?"

The lead bartender answered, "Oh, sorry. We were making a checklist. Go on, we're done."

Asaf went on, "I'll just skip over the technical. So as the digging progresses, we need to be flexible to move inventory from spot to spot while making some attempt at erasing our tracks and still give the thug the time he needs to put all the bomb parts in place. Right?"

Asaf finished this sentence looking at the thug for affirmation.

The thug nodded.

Asaf looked at his three comrades. "Questions? comments?"

Everybody was paying attention. They all looked relaxed and ready to start with the plan. *Just like that.*

37

THE CAFE PROPRIETOR TREATED HIS clientele equally respectful and equally dour. But when the General and Prophet were not at the fruit shop, they became noisome to the other customers. So he managed to move their repartees to the back of the back, that is, in the abandoned alleyway behind the back of his cafe. There, they were out of the front where they were an embarrassment, but he could still sell them his goods. He also figured that since they were prominent figures, it would not be good for business to be known for kicking them out altogether. The proprietor sold them the whole idea, appealing to their pride, insinuating that since they were big-shots, it was better for all that they have their own private "veranda" where they could pretend to conspire in private. The base was tired of the General who was considered a danger to others — and himself — if that mattered or anyone cared. When his absences grew longer and more sporadic, the dreary, bedraggled, remaining troops and officers were glad of his AWOL, which they called Absent With OUR Liking. They knew if it was something important enough, they could drag him out of the alleyway or the fruit shop.

The General and the Prophet sat in the alleyway, a "Neutered Zone", as the General called it where they would "stratergize". The Prophet had let his hair and beard grow long. It was greasy and stringy. His former look of calm self-composure had degraded to a shaky nervousness. He had huge, dark circles beneath his eyes. His fingernails were mangy, along with his dirty, stained forefinger and thumb which were dark brown from the use and abuse of various smokable substances. He occasionally wore sandals, but mostly went barefoot. He had not trimmed his toenails for weeks at least. They twisted and curved in all directions and in shades from ugly yellow to brown to dark blue. Two of the fingernails on his left hand were encrusted with blood, from fresh red to old, scabby purple. He habitually inched and scratched and scraped at his groin and crotch with these fingers. He then magnified the putrid stench by wafting about his bloody and pus-greased fingers as he spoke. He wiped his hand on a tattered silk robe, which was all he wore anymore. For a long time, he was self-conscious of this disgusting habit but then gave in to it out of laziness and unabashed, dead shame. He was usually consuming some mind or body altering substance or another: coffee with speed, any form of tobacco, hashish, opium, khat, and a broad pharmacopeia of "natural" hallucinogens. When he was on speed he would pull and tug at his hair like a lice-infested ape. When he was on hashish and opium he would space out and not be able to carry on any sort of conversation save for the expressions of his glassy eyes. When he was high on mushrooms or any variety of psychotropic plant alkaloids, his behavior and vocalizations would swing from raging theological exhortations while stomping about, to a blubbering pile of human parts slumped in a corner. He was mad with the power of a self-proclaimed Prophet: scornful, demanding, self-righteous, imperious, glowering, unmerciful, disdainful, and conceited. He was imbecilic in his self-degradation and slavery to the lowest in human nature: jealous, petty, craving, bawling, crawling, hissing, barking, biting, drooling and passing-out. In all of this, he was completely self-indulgent and insatiable.

The General made a good try of holding himself together. He was less haggard than the Prophet because of his station and standing in life. His career straightened him thus, and to fall below the Prophet's low bar, would reduce him to a rabid animal. He was a general soldier, and there were limits to how far down the sluice his outward appearance could careen towards homeless-bum-hood, while he himself butt-slid (downward-bound) to the swampy slough of sloth. What military garb he still donned, when in the mood, or for duty's sake, was unwashed, unpressed, unbuttoned and unzipped. He still shaved — weekly at least. Showers became movable feasts. He was still rather happy-go-lucky, but in a different way; more like bitter-sweet-stumble-cursed. The fine cigars, formerly relished for their fragrance and long ashes, had slowly but surely been reduced to stinky stubs stuck in the side of his nicotine-stained gob hole. More often than not, there was brown ooze dribbling from the corner of his mouth.

The General sported a few old random medals like cheap jewelry.

They had neither rhyme nor reason for being there, other than some delusional idea that wearing them showed the world that he was somebody important.

His heart still pumped but like an irregular 5/4 waltz. One of his eyes watered, so he was always wiping it with a sleeve or hand, making it chronically red and swollen. He had long since ditched his flask. It became a burden to reach in and out of his pocket to avail himself of it. Now he just walked around holding a bottle of Jack by the neck, sucking on it casually.

The General said to the Prophet, "Come see, come saw, the Seer and the Law. Might obliged ah meetin' again."

"Yes, you too," the Prophet answered without emotion.

The proprietor came through to the back, deposited two ice-cold Cokes on the table and left without a word. The two ignored him.

"Exalted One," the General said, chasing his Jack with a sip of Coke, "I am a plain-spoken man-o-war. Like an Ironsides ship or a jellyfish. No the nippin' and tuckin' chuckin' and jive. So I lays it to ya on the bone, straight as George Strait hisself: We need more money. The bi-valves, shekels, el dinero, moo-lah-lah and any otter overused pseudopods."

"Yes," the Prophet replied.

The General stood, a little shaky, and extended a hand to the Prophet. The Prophet unenthusiastically shook the General's hand with his own grimy paw.

The General sat back and waited for the Prophet to say something.

Nothing.

The General leaned forward, hoping to draw the Prophet into the conversation.

Finally, the Prophet asked, "Why do, or did, you think I would say 'No' to your mention of our mutual pecuniary needs?"

The General smiled, glad the Prophet was engaged, even if just a bit. "You have a misdemeanor of arranging your galavantin' before the lucre-izing. It's just that …"

"Just what?" the Prophet asked with a slanted eyebrow.

"Well, just that … that … gol darnation! Git it, git it gone yer skeeterizations o' the wig!"

The General started waving his hand all around his head and face. "Sick 'em Seer Son, sick 'em! Hellified floosicums foisted!"

The Prophet slowly, slowly rose to a three-quarter stance, braced himself with one hand on the cheap table, and with the other hand, hit the General as hard as he could on the side of the head, without falling or tipping the table over. This seemed to bring the General out of his apparent battle with an invisible host waging war in his head.

The Prophet scowled at the General and asked, "What did you say? I didn't catch that last remark."

The General paused to take a slug of Jack and another sip of Coke. He breathed heavily after his attack. The General rolled his cigar stub from one side of his mouth to another, lathering it well with his brown salvia. He inhaled through his nose, then spat the stub out. It bounced and rolled up near one of the cafe's refrigerators which the proprietor kept out back. He was not yet in the clear. His eyes were out of focus, he was not fully present in the moment and his surroundings. "Snuff. Snuff! Gottyee any snuff yer Profit?"

"Hunh … ?" The Prophet was still in the process of re-taking his seat.

"Powdered tobakkie. Talcum and minty in a can. Snuff stuff luv a puff."

The Prophet finally sat down. "What? You want talcum powder in a mint can? Afeared, I am dear soldier, but the foggiest notion I do not have … foggiest … Where was I?"

The General was regaining his equilibrium, the seizure had ebbed away. "I said. Do you have any tobacco snuff? There. Aint so turrubles iss'r?"

The Prophet didn't hear what the General said. He was fumbling in the folds of his pajamas. After a bit, he hit some form of pay dirt. "Aark and vark! Here, Big-n-Dirty in big and dirty green. Here's your oh-so-precious talcum powder. I was not sure if it was on my person. And actually don't know how I found it, but there it is."

The Prophet tossed a snow-seal envelope across the table to the General. The General looked down, then picked up the snow-seal. "Oh. Whaa isser Sir?"

"Talc. Special blend. The boys over at the tea-house give it to me, thinking they are currying favor."

The General opened the snow-seal and looked at the white powder. He looked up at the Prophet, shrugged his shoulders and asked, "Now what? The jan-ewe-wine snuff box is pre-implemented with a dainty despensing hole. This … uh … talc … I don't see no straws."

"Lick."

"Whaaa, Imma … I …?"

The Prophet nodded, reached out for his Coke. "Big lick. Forget a straw. Just lick the paper clean in one big lick and rid yourself of your floosicums."

The General looked at the crank, up at the sleepy Prophet, then at the crank again. He held the paper wide open and licked up contents, about two grams of powder.

The General sat back, allowing himself to swallow, and waiting to see what would happen. Then he slapped his knee and said, "Glockenspiel and Master, the lunar force majeure aquaciferous end-run it is! Noggin and lumberjack's salty Adamic curse! House it said? 'The voracious shall merit the mirth'? Or some cast-iron farinous Fahrenheit foible. But Pan's land trip and lose a leg. The duck walk and a honey maker?"

The Prophet sat back and seemed to be thinking. He closed his eyes in deep thought … deeper and deeper … … deepest thought … … … he fell asleep. His hand fell off the armrest and his head lolled over, hair drooping over his face.

The General fished a Marlboro disposable lighter out of a pocket. He held it up to the light and shook it a little to see if there was any fluid in it. There was. He grabbed the bottle of Jack and took a pull. He lit the lighter. He took a deep breath through his nose then expelled a massive spray of whiskey out of his mouth and over the flame. The alcohol burst into flames and flew violently into the Prophet's face. His hair caught on fire, being readily flammable from all the grease and grime. The Prophet moaned and rolled his head back a bit. The General then took a swig of Coke, inhaled deeply again, and blew a huge spew of wet fizz at the Prophet, thus extinguishing les homme flambé.

The Prophet moaned again and waved his hand around his face. He muttered something indecipherable, blinked his eyes, and began to brush the stinky smoldering hair out of his face. He shook his head, clearing his face further, rousing himself out of his stupor. He blinked some more and said, "Hunh, what happened?"

"You fell asleep."

"Oh. I think that was some powerful stuff I smoked last night."

"Well, don't get all dozy on me your Worship. We've got business to do. Money matters and the like, so snap out of it. Since I am a succinct vocalizer, you turn an ear sidewinder, at whosyadaddy. I am agleanin' the harvest of golden ripenesses afore my baked egg and bacon hatch. So couldersnatch yer jitternibbers. Burl Ives a longhouse's worth of body parts to parlay into the nakedness grape fizz goodonyas and salty peskatario nugs of bard's perchance to. It's yer own gummified self who got this hitch in the getalong of guns for bovine excrements and on to the Tide and Joy ever fresher printed sheets of legal tender cotton. Like a gnat in the warming season seen through the fly fisher's feathery festooning of a Mustad number fourteen, I dun my parts. Now seems like afore mentioned Tides have turniped into the drought of demand from your frizzle-frazzle fellows of fearsome fighting. All urine war n rumors of wars are drying like a codfish in the Negev. The meanings wile, the iron trains and smoky snakes that ought be motorizing hills dales and arroyos are ferrizizing and paint peeling. Line up s'mores a ragamuffins to flog the gear like hot cakes in a winter whyemseeay and an owl unner a heavily limbed timber flop his glop snort and shoot smack flaccid attack vertebrae. No sir!"

The General pounded his fist with a bang on the table that made the Prophet's ears pop. The loud noise reverberated in the Prophet's inner ear. The ear was stuffed up from wax and an excess of microscopic lice. Since such a viscous matter cannot be readily compressed, the energy from the sound waves was transferred through the water-and bone-ways of his head and impacted a vein between his eye and his ear. The bulge in the vein impinged on the local nerve ganglions. From that moment on, the Prophet's lower left eyelid quivered when he heard loud noises.

The Prophet retorted, "First. You suck at how long you think it takes you to get to your point. Not succinct — suck. Second. You stink at trying to not beat around the bush while beating around the bush and thinking everybody is impressed by your chain of logic. Suck and stink. Just so we are clear. Third. I am glad, of a fashion, that you have finally come full circle on what you know is a clear path of financial rewards. Having acquired a taste for the filthy lucre, you come back to its source, not hat in hand, but with a determined bravado and appropriately downward scowl that befits your vocation, pretending that you were the brain-trust behind this whole arms-scam-money-game, and have overcome your psychological, moralistic scaffolding which has blocked your path to true freedom. Your ethical structure has straightened you into an unhappy, unrealistic personal quagmire of thinking you know right from wrong. But you're not able to scratch that nagging itch, tucked away somewhere in your ur-psyche, that gives you uncomfortable hints that you're not quite clear about all this. Well, now I give you the keys of knowledge to unlock the chains which have held your structural scaffolding in place, yea these many, too many years. True freedom is opening yourself to the possibilities of any- and everything that has been is or will be. Be it paradise or consignment to the pit … in any possible lifetime. I know this is not only unfathomable to you but even if it were fathomable, could not fit into your being. For, it is fate, General, fate. You have no embracing of fate. Fate is the embracing whatever may come in life, including the personal realization that fate cannot be understood but must be held — in whatever form one's self-actualization that is existential at any given passage of time-life-line — and not only as any possible combinations or singularities of destiny, but also as a current of reality no different than electricity, gravitational attraction or the speed of light. Look at you. Look at us. A mere shuffling of our spent legs and feet from tipping into the horrible chasm of beastly madness and derangement. And here you are, worrying about your cash-flow. To the wind with your money-grubbing. Even the wind from your stinky behind. Better than the foul wind of your smelly breath which is only good for the furthering of the gagging stomach of anyone near enough to whiff it, unto the completion of the heretofore only approximate act of vomiting. At least your nether-wind is suitable for an entertaining puff of flame. To the winds I say! The wind which flies in the wake of the hounds of horror, the wind kicked up by the hooves of the pale rider's steeds, the wind which whipped poor Dorothy into that place ruled by witches and terrible wizards. Terrible in the complete dearth of self-esteem and confidence, not terrible in the real meaning of the word: causing terror. You grope and grasp at phantoms and fleeting shadowy ghosts of whatever slip or purchase is left of anything that was ever fastening you to your over-confident, haughty sense of good and right. I piss on it all. I open my breast to come what may. And in so doing, am not only experiencing the truest form of freedom but am evolving into freedom itself, even such a form as it may take, that is not yet known."

The General took a nip of Jack and a sip of Coke. "Seer Son, allow me to respondicate 'ton your jawbonin'. Firstin's, I'll allow for the long-windedness of my speechifying. But you have to spend a time spying in the speigel yourselfuns. Nary mind that four now. Although you may reckon that the ol' General's noggin maybe can't absorbify yur attempts at philsoftical pontiffications, let me assure you, it can and I can. You see, Seer Son, you might ways have …"

The General stopped speaking. His one-man audience was not listening. The Prophet had casually watched the flight of the mouth-turd. During their back and forth, out of the corner of a droopy eye, he had been watching a cockroach explore, then capture the cigar-butt. It came out timidly when the butt landed. Then cautiously tested and tasted the fumes and fragrances emanating from the gob of tobacco. It approached and probed it with its antennae. Finally, deciding it was worth taking home, the cockroach seized upon the slimy butt and began to tug it towards its crack in the wall. But once the blob shifted, the roach's feet got stuck in the goo. It br'er-rabbited itself to the butt. The Prophet then played the insect himself by doing a praying mantis on the cockroach and cigar-butt. He leaned out and over the poor little tar-baby, snatched it up and gingerly popped it into his mouth. It was a moment to remember, for it left the loquacious General speechless … for a few moments.

After letting what he had just watched sink in, the General asked in plain, simple, words, "Well, how was it?"

The Prophet leaned back and leisurely munched the unusual snack. "General, Sir, there's the dried, or jerked. There's the stir-fried. And the fresh, or crudo, like some sushi or tartar. This particular delectable … is an acquired taste."

"May I say, Seer," the General began, "that in all my awarrin' years, yea these many, hither and skither and yon, memories many there be. Eggersizing my scintillific speech patterns, I'll just lay it down as: That was memorable."

The Prophet suddenly reached over and patted the General's shirt pocket and felt that there were indeed a few Panatelas still stashed in there. He quickly snatched one out, and before the General could launch a protest, the Prophet did his own imitation of the General having a smoke while in a tizzy. He bit off the tip, spit it on the ground and fired it up with a Marlboro disposable lighter, flames burning the end of his numb nose.

The General was disappointed. "After all the cauldron-stirrin' hexagons that the wooded slurry affords me, yon Seer of nephesh in the pecuniary booted country of a sandwich, and looks to be the pretzel of prize. Hooky ho. Takin' the Goya and the vaporous mineral distillate which should only be that ligneous combustiblity of what sounds like a diminutive capon. Like a denuded vat of lanolin is full of it."

The Prophet exhaled a mighty cloud of wonderful smelling, pure Cuban tobacco smoke. "Ok, ok. Let's get on with it like you said."

The General decided since the Prophet was so enjoying one of his purloined Panatelas, he might as well join in. "Two things. What planopliac crest would succumb? And emperor emporium euphorium. How's that littoral lunar lance?"

The Prophet was enjoying his cigar so much and getting a bomb nicotine high that he lost track of what the General was asking him. This annoyed the General since he was trying (albeit ineptly) to have a real business meeting, so he kicked him hard in the shins under the table. The Prophet jumped and fumbled the cigar onto his lap. It burnt through his clothes and gave him a start. With the kick to the leg and the burn, he jumped up and turned the table over, spilling their drinks on the ground with a crash.

The proprietor came out scolding them. "You two nincompoops! what are you doing!?"

The General and the Prophet both started talking excitedly at once. The proprietor waved his arms. "Stop! Everybody stop. One at a time. Between the two of you, it's a wonder the planet still spins on its axis."

"Well, to the calcified bird baby, your shopkeepness, it's a double dozen and a negative nickel on the proceeding warble," the General inserted.

"That's right," the Prophet chimed in. "At twenty-three and a half or so degrees, it does not spin well on its axis. But I must make a slight objection to my friend's vocabulary. Warble is fine, as it follows from the avian reference, and we all know the General always wants to be oh-so-clever. But by compounding his astronomical observance with the word 'proceeding', he has missed the exact target. For the verbal allusion ought be to precession. Precession, in this context, is directly related to the wobble of the axis of the planet and describes the ray or vector extending out into the far reaches of the galaxy. This vector acts like a galactical pointer and has been useful in marking where the axis points to as it slowly sweeps through the zodiacal plane. My favorite use of this phenomenon is to exculpate all sorts of shenanigans under the guise of — it's this or it's that — because we're in the Age of Aquarius. Now, astronomers are not in agreement as to whether we have been, will be, or are pointed to the constellation of the water-bearer. But it's still cool to drop the reference to it at cocktail parties and such."

The cafe owner took a bar mop out of his back pocket and wiped his face. "Look here you two. Maybe … maybe, if we're lucky, you two numbskulls will boink together and the Earth will gain your twenty whatever degrees. For now, let's clean all this mess up."

38

Asaf came up to the Daughter as she was finishing her shift waiting tables. "You and your family have been very supportive of the bar and tea-house."

The Daughter smiled and nodded for Asaf to continue.

"Now there are serious changes coming to the bar, the tea-house, and the whole village."

The Daughter showed concern. "How serious. What changes?"

"Very serious. And very soon."

The Daughter narrowed her eyes in doubt and uncertainty.

Asaf tipped his head toward the door and they walked outside. He explained that he was not able to answer some questions. He told her that it was in the family's best interest to get ready to leave the village. Leave forever. She asked him when this might happen. He told her he wasn't sure, but to keep an eye on the phases of the moon. It could be sooner than later and told her again to make plans to get away.

"Why the moon? That's odd."

"The religious sects are odd. It's their agenda." Asaf was in a difficult situation. He had his plans, but he didn't know exactly how the details were going to come together. He wanted as few people involved as possible, but the closer he got to one of the new moons, the less control he had over how his plan was going to happen.

"We need a place to talk. But not here. And not in public."

The Daughter remained puzzled. "I don't know. We could go to my house, but my parents are there. And my little girl."

Asaf didn't respond.

"We have a garden shed behind the house. We shouldn't be seen going in there together, but it's certainly private. I'll go, you come after five minutes."

In the shed, Asaf told the Daughter his plan, finishing with his request for help in the snakehead. "My soul is sick. Sick of the evil over there that I cannot talk to you about. I don't want you … I don't want any of this blood on your hands …"

Asaf trailed off, choked up with conflict and incipient guilt about dragging the Daughter into his plan.

Quietly, but seriously she said, "Asaf, you have given my family a chance to earn money in this retched village. This home is all we have. I hate the hypocrites over at the tea-house. Because of your help, I serve in the bar over their stupid objections. The soldiers treat me well because I am not a threat to their social ways. I think … I don't know. I think your plan is extreme … I've never heard of anything like this before, but I have not been in the wars. They have visited me, us, here, but I have never participated in the fighting. Our village is already bombed-out. Maybe blowing up one more building isn't as horrible as it sounds. I don't like hearing myself say such a thing, but when I look at my little girl, I cry for her future …"

The Daughter began weeping quietly. Asaf stood by in silence.

When she composed herself she looked up at Asaf and nodded sincerely and seriously. "I will help. I will help if it will help my future, my little girl's future. Tell me what to do."

The proprietor beckoned to Asaf in the bar. They went over to the cafe. "I have this unusual parcel. It has your name on it but it came to me. It was sent registered, return-receipt, authorized by the cafe only."

Asaf looked it over. Brown paper. Standard postal marks and registered tags. He shrugged his shoulders. "What do you think?"

The proprietor shrugged back. "Open it and see."

Asaf unwrapped the package. "It's a carton of cigarettes. Camel Filters. That's strange. And way too heavy. Where did you say you got this?"

He told him again.

Asaf carefully opened the carton. Inside were two hand-cut cardboard boxes, fabricated to fit inside the cigarette carton. Asaf pulled them out and set them down. He looked at the proprietor. Neither of them having anything to say, Asaf opened the smaller of the two. Neatly packed inside was a Zippo lighter. The lighter was engraved with the head and mane of a fine horse in expensive tack, with its name below in the same fancy script as Asaf's other lighter.

Asaf looked on the other side. It was engraved with an Ace of Spades. "Will you let me look at this in the back? I think it was sent here and not to the bar for a reason."

Seeing his consternation, the proprietor said, "There is curious meddling going on in this village. I usually use plain ways of speaking. But there is a saying that comes to mind. It seems to me you all have brought a tempest in a teapot into our village. And is the storm rising? Is there a tornado or a whirlwind for us from these businesses? In the books, there are the mythological or metaphorical characters who struggle with that which is or becomes, too much for them to handle. The hunter and the beast. The sailor and the monster fish, and so on. Maybe at the outset, the beast and the fish seem tame and manageable. But now, they have achieved their true stature and nature. Putting these metaphors together, are we all now wrestling with beasts in a storm? I hope you will think of me as a friend for whatever is going to happen."

Inside the second box, two objects were wrapped in plastic. Asaf set them down side by side. He looked at the things in front of him and thought back on what the spy had taught him. If he surmised correctly, the two things in plastic ought to be a detonation switch and a transmitter. They already had the third component, the receiver, from the bobblehead. Asaf unwrapped the largest and it turned out to look like what the spy had described as a detonator. It was heavy because it was mostly a large battery with an initiator switch attached. The switch would be actuated by the receiver which had its own small power supply from the bobblehead batteries. The detonation switch would deliver the big charge to the first cap, initiating the whole explosion. But instead of a transmitter, there was another — apparently a second — receiver. This made Asaf think a mistake had been made and the spy had inadvertently shipped two receivers and no transmitter.

The Zippo looked like a regular lighter at first glance but had been modified very carefully. The top cover was an on/off switch when flipped open and closed. Upon rotating the knurled striker wheel, instead of grinding against a diminutive flint, it actually generated a small electrical current. Asaf prized the case and the innards apart. Where the butane fuel tank would normally be, was a small, extremely well crafted, transmitter. So by making the same thumb action to create a flame, the holder was sending out a radio signal.

Thinking back on the cases of Coke, Asaf took the carton and looked it over. Sure enough, it had been opened at the seam and carefully taped back together. He opened it and immediately recognized the spy's handwriting.

I suppose this might be silly to write inside this box but it is an easy step — to avoid just one puzzle piece from fitting — Wrong hands/Finding the det/ Finding the lighter At least this note might not be found I know you'll be wondering what the extra receiver is. It's a layer of deception in case your confederate goes south on you.

Keep Trigger and this second camel receiver. Only give the big det switch to your man. If things take longer than his patience he will try to build a transmitter. I know his pride in this if he's capable of being your side-kick.

This receiver has a seven-minute delay built-in. Once you install it, then trigger it, it will detonate in seven minutes. This gives you a chance to get away as far as you can in seven minutes. In the left-over intel gear in the secret closet is a small booster to amplify trigger's signal. I don't know which escape path you will take but don't go too far away — even with the booster left behind — it's on low power, but will still work.

SO — pay attn. This zippo is NOT tuned to the bobblehead. NOT!

It's tuned to the rcvr' in the camel box. The one in your hands now!

There are several things

1) your man can't get HIS hands on trigger zippo AND the camel rcvr' If he does — things might go sideways depending on his personality and the gold and so on ... speaking of AU, he might be a half now/half later guy?

2) I'm sending a bogus transmitter That tx won't be tuned to jack squat but he won't know that becuz he can't test it — becuz if he does everything will blow up. If he thinks this thru even for a moment he'll understand this. I don't believe for a minute he won't believe anything other than the 2nd tx — Mr Bogus — goes to the bobble becuz (hopefully) — he won't know about the zippo in your hand.

3) This is getting longer than I hoped. I hope there's enuf space on this carton. Somehow — someway — you have to get the camel rcvr' attached/ replaced to the det switch.

It's the only det sw so your boy won't have any other choice than to put the bobble rcvr' there. He'll have the bogus tx I'm sending. He MAY or may NOT offer it to you —

That's why you have to put THE CAMEL BOX rcvr' attached to the DET SW

Take a good look at it. How he made the connx. It's either for you to swap out OR bypass. Remember: milk-pitcher handle milk-pitcher spout Just like that - handle spout - look at bobble / look at camel / look at handle / look at spout. It has to be one of these two connx (If it's not your confed is all con man not knowing ass/hole in the ground) in which case be ready to escape plan one or plan two and so on.

Just to make sure we're all straight here. IF your man gets his hands on trigger zippo — don't install camel rcvr' Or disconnx if you can, becuz the zippo in HIS hands AND camel rcvr' to det is FUBAR and RUN!

Asaf took the detonator over to the bar and hid it away. He needed some time to think about a story of how it came into his possession. When he felt he was ready, he sent for the thug.

When the thug saw the detonator he was thunderstruck. "Asaf! My own wagglehead! You are not showing this part to me? Wazza wazza? The fingernails all the biting up until now. When where how this is coming?"

Asaf explained that a delivery boy had brought it a day or two ago. He delivered it to the family a lot over by mistake. The Daughter saw it on the table, asked her mother about it and then brought it over to the bar the next day.

The thug took the detonator in his hands gingerly. He looked at it from each side, mumbling as he inspected it. When he was finished, he asked, "Ok Asaf, where is the transmitter being? Not for the pork-head does all this gear going without the transmitter, if there ever was one."

A kid on a bicycle rode up and rang the bell on his handlebars. Asaf and the thug watched casually while the lead bartender went over. The lead bartender and the delivery boy chatted. The lead bartender took the package, tipped the kid as always, then walked through the bar heading out back. Asaf called to him, "Anything special?"

"No, not much. The large coffee machine in the tea-house has a part that broke. They ordered a replacement. The delivery boy dropped it off over here because I always tip him and the tea-house sometimes does and sometimes doesn't. I'm walking it over there."

Asaf and the thug finished their talk, concluding they would have to keep watch for the transmitter. Asaf expressed to the thug that he was uncomfortable with the missing piece and was concerned about the timing of the plan. The thug told him they had to continue to wait for the spy, and that he could begin work on his own transmitter in the meantime, just in case the correct transmitter never came. He told Asaf not to over-worry himself, that a pairing of the parts was possible, it was just a matter of taking the time and effort to get it right. Asaf said he understood, but that time was not something they had a lot of. The thug asked why their time was so short. Asaf told him that parts of the plan were only known to one or the other involved, but not everybody knew everything. For some of the sects, the new moon was "an auspicious celestial occurrence" which was also the darkest night possible. The next new moon was about a week away and was understood practically as the night before, the actual night and the night after. Different groups had their way of judging just when the exact new moon was because of the old observational techniques and maybe traditions. But in any case, the new moon was really only new from one side of the earth to the other so the exact new moon was not exact. This also allowed for devotees to adjust their busy modern calendars to one of several possible new moon dates. The thug was ho-hum about this explanation. He mumbled to Asaf that religion is for figs and flies, but gold is good everywhere and always and is worth its weight before, after, and on, any given phase of the moon or a fig's behind parts.

The waiter took the package from the lead bartender. "Great! We've been hampered in our coffee sales because of this. This is an expensive machine. It does everything anybody in the solar system could want in a brew. It's never malfunctioned before. We all looked at it and found one part that undergoes high pressure and temperature — there was a small drill mark in it where it developed a crack that allows the boiling water to leak out and it makes a mess. We figure it was a mistake when it was made. It can't be used for everything now because of that, so it's been reduced to making simple drip coffee. Fortunately, the manufacturer stands behind the machine and supplied the part for free. They asked if we could do the replacement work and if not they would send a technician out to service the machine. I told them we would have a go at it and let them know. So, how did it come over to your side?"

"No big deal. The kid likes my tips. Well, good luck with that machine, hope the part goes in ok." The lead bartender went back to the bar.

The waiter opened the parcel. He took out the replacement part. There was something still inside the carton. He shook it and looked inside, then tipped out the second small box. It was a boxed deck of cards. "Whoa, now. I … well I'm not sure …"

He looked around. Nobody was near. He took the card deck box out and opened one end. His eyes widened. Still talking to himself, he said in a very low voice, "This, I've got to show the thug."

39

ASAF CALLED HIS COOKS OUTSIDE. "Get together some lads you like. Ones that don't mind doing errands for money. Ones that will do what you tell them. Tell them whatever you want, but I need them for a day or two. The pay is good. It comes from my own pocket, so no-one has to worry. Get together behind one of those buildings over there. Come find me as soon as you're ready. If you can't find me, ask the lead bartender to find me."

Asaf explained to the cooks what he wanted, "Two of you will go out to the Prophet's compound. I don't know who will be there. It doesn't matter. You must explain, you must explain with seriousness and earnestness, why you are present. Tell them I sent you. Tell them you require the green paper and the incense of the missionary blessing. If they are willing and able to help, have them help. They have resources that take us longer to arrange. I have already sent a message to one of the printers they use explaining everything. Hopefully, the compound will anticipate your request by me and the Prophet, and your work will go smoothly. I think it will."

The cooks and their companions came to Asaf. "We have done what you asked. The compound was very helpful. They are nervous. They know things are changing. They are unhappy that the Prophet is sick. They tried to get information from us. We gave them answers that helped. We told them we were on a mission from God for you and the other sect leaders. When they asked questions we didn't know, we told them we were merely humble servants of God and needed what you asked for to further God's will. All that you have asked for is in a house across the village where it is safe."

Asaf was pleased with their report. They went to the house. Asaf looked at the green papers. He was satisfied. He gathered all the lads around him.

He commissioned them, saying,

"Take these leaflets, and take this incense. These leaflets are the leaflets of freedom and doom. This incense is the incense of life and death. The leaflets can be read and believed and will lead to freedom and life. The incense can be burnt as a thank offering, or to stifle the stench of death.

"Go forth through the streets, lanes, and allies of the village and give these leaflets with incense folded in them. Give them to all who will take them from your hand. If anyone asks what it means, tell them the message is written on the green paper. Tell them they can read it for themselves and decide what to do on their own. Then go on, until you meet the next person, or come to the next house. Do not waste time in long discussions or arguments.

"When you run out of paper and incense, you are done with your mission. You can return here to ask for your money, or to ask for more to deliver. If there is more, we will give it to you. You will continue to be paid for your work. If there is none, you will be paid and you are free to go on with your life. By the time the leaflets and incense have been completely given away, it will be the time of God's judgment on this village. As my friends, I encourage you to heed what the leaflet says."

Here is what Asaf had printed on the green leaflets:

Citizen!
Take heed! This is the hour indeed.
Wake up! The spirit is beckoning
to reckon with the reckoning
of the evil in our village.

Citizen!
Flee the coming wrath of God.
From the rooftop to the sod,
every life will be under the sword.
Flee, you are forewarned!

Citizen!
Do not stay to gossip and be curious.
The village will become injurious.
Pack up and leave, leave!
at the new moon's eve.

40

THE THUG HAD CONVINCED ASAF they needed to spread the digging out over two nights. Asaf then calculated two nights for digging, a day of fussing around moving the bombs and putting them in place, then one extra day to bring the sect leaders into the buildings. So, one week before the new moon, Asaf put out the word that the businesses would close in a few days. There were mixed responses, but there was nothing anyone could do about it, so the plan to close went forward.

On the first night after closing, they hauled all the explosive materials from the bombed-out building to the back side of the bar. The lads had begun the cleaning process and were directed where to put the furniture and boxes. The thug and the waiter placed all the explosives, the det cord and the caps in position, while furniture and boxes were moved out and around the buildings hiding all the bombs. Before dawn, everyone except Asaf and the lead bartender went to their dwellings to rest.

Between coordinating the inventory and cleaning, Asaf made sure the leaflets were being distributed. He made sure the snakehead was in place with the cooks and that it was understood and being implemented. He made sure there was food and drink for everybody around the clock and cash enough for him or the lead bartender to use for any unseen problems.

Asaf was extra careful to see exactly where the thug placed the receiver and det switch. They still had a day and a half until it was time for Asaf to detonate the bombs and there was still no bogus transmitter from the spy. Asaf asked the thug about it when they were together between work shifts. Asaf was anxious but didn't want to arouse any suspicions. The thug seemed too calm about the missing transmitter, which did not sit well with Asaf.

41

The Soldier had no interest in cleaning the bar but felt that he should show some modicum of involvement. He was bored with drinking beer alone while the bar was closed and was tired of spending time with the other junkies who hung around the goat barn. As he approached the bar in the late afternoon on the second day of inventory and cleaning, he looked up and saw some unusual activity. He was curious. He walked over to the shadows for a look. The thug was occupied checking a section of det cord that was difficult to tell how it was buried in the dark. The Soldier, even through the fog of his chemical cocktail, was roused. He went up to the thug and confronted him.

"What in the heck are you doing down there? Stand up. Stand up now. No sudden moves. Keep your hands where I can see that there is nothing for me to worry about."

The Soldier unholstered his gun.

The thug knew he had to show all the respect he could to the Soldier, otherwise, things could get bad very quickly. He stood up slowly and kept his arms spread.

The Soldier brought the gun up and pointed it at the thug.

"What are you doing?" the Soldier asked.

"I am here the making a defensive perimeter."

"A defensive perimeter? Move aside."

The Soldier waved the thug off, motioning with his pistol. He made sure the thug was well away, then knelt on one knee, took out his knife and dug where it had been disturbed. He saw what appeared to be det cord. He was surprised. He stood back up. He looked sternly as the thug. Neither of them spoke.

The Soldier took his boot and nudged the det cord. "Is it going to go off?"

"No."

"Ok. Let's do each other a favor and keep this all safe and sane — as they say. Down on your knees. Fingers laced on top of your head. You probably know the drill."

The thug complied.

The Soldier pushed the dirt away with the side of his boot. He looked back at the thug, no movement. The Soldier loosened enough det cord for him to be able to grasp it with his free hand. He pulled up on the det cord and saw that only a few yards further on it was connected to a brick of explosive. He dropped the cord to the ground. He took a step backward, made a slow half-turn, stepping back again, and said quietly, "Somebody's got sum splanin' to do." Then he quickly spun all the way around, took two more steps, and with a precision blow with his pistol, dropped the thug unconscious, face-first, into the dirt.

Unbeknownst to the Soldier, the waiter was lurking in the shadows. Seeing all this was unsettling, to say the least. Not knowing exactly what to do, but knowing that having the thug taken prisoner was not the way forward, he picked out a good-sized rock, walked stealthily up behind the Soldier and brained him good and hard.

Now there were two unconscious men in the dirt.

The waiter ran off to find Asaf.

42

ASAF WAS LYING ON AN old sofa in the corner of the bar, trying to get some rest, pretending to himself, and hopefully others, to be asleep.

The waiter ran up to him, stooped down, and recounted what had happened. Asaf sat up. Apprehension, surprise, and fear swirled around in his drowsy head. He asked the waiter to quickly go over the story again. Asaf was not sure what to do, but he knew that action was better than inaction. He called out for the lead bartender. Asaf asked them if they could take the Soldier into the opium den and leave him there.

The lead bartender asked for how long.

"I don't know. Is there anybody down there who can sit on him for … for at least a day. Do you think that will work?"

The waiter said, "We don't have enough time for the den. If we hustle him into the tea-house, we can give him a special brew to keep him quiet. And soothe his aching head."

"Do it," Asaf said. "Do it now. Make it strong. Take one of the lads. One of us will come over and get him. Then you stay in the tea-house. There will soon be visitors who will need food and drink."

Asaf turned to the lead bartender. "Let's go bring the thug inside. We'll hide him somewhere out of sight. Maybe under a blanket or behind a stack of boxes. If someway, somehow, the Soldier makes it known that explosives were being put around these buildings, we're done. We might as well all get out of town for good. Right now, he has no direct connection or evidence that you and I are tied into this insanity."

When they got to the thug, he was just waking up.

"We've got to get you to a safe place. Can the Soldier get into the basement?"

"Safe is the far away. But if you have want or need of me, then closer is the better. But I don't wanna be under the feet of the Soldier surrounded by four walls."

Asaf and the lead bartender looked at each other. "Ok. I don't have any better ideas, so we're going to the garden shed behind the Daughter's house. Let's grab some rugs for you to wrap up in."

They put the thug in the shed. "We're going on some errands. You're on your own. We'll try to have the Soldier out of there. But be careful."

Asaf and the lead bartender went out into the lane. "We have to put the snakehead into action tonight, and tomorrow if we have to. We have to act fast to stay clear of danger. Here's what you need to do. I'm going to add on to the thug's thirteenth salary and give you a fourteenth out of the thug's gold. You'll probably have to split it up with the cooks. You've got plenty of that mountain-juice crap over there?"

"It's there. The cook has them well oiled. In fact, we'll probably have to toss a bucket of water to bring them around … if they're alive."

"Go to the tea-house. We've got to get the Soldier out of there. The place will be crawling with sect members soon. If he's asleep … I don't know. I guess it depends on what kind and how much medicine was in his coffee … If you can get him inside the fruit shop. Then go find the Plebe quickly. Tell him Snakehead RIGHT NOW. Tell him to get the Minister and the Councilman. Snakehead RIGHT NOW. No questions. Tell him his prophet says so. The new moon is here. Actually, it's not until tomorrow, but who's counting? Tell him all three councilors are on tonight! Tell him to bring the leaders of the sects down to this end of the village. Make sure they all are in the same page. The Councilman and the leader of the Radicals get down to the basement. The Plebe brings the Fanatics into the bar. The Minister gets the Zealots into the tea-house. Right?"

The lead bartender nodded. "What about you?"

"I have to get the Daughter coached and ready. I'll send her to the fruit shop as soon as I can. Then I want to make sure that the sects are coming down here. If you can get the Soldier moved before I come over, move him. Then I'll see you in the fruit shop — to put the snakes in the cage — if we can … I guess we'll see."

Asaf paused. He looked around. He looked at his lead bartender in the face. "You know where to meet. You know who to get. You'll spread out some gold if you need to. Ready?"

The lead bartender nodded at each of Asaf's questions. His face was grim. "Ready."

43

ONCE ASAF SENT THE LEAD bartender to the Plebe and council, he knew his time would be short. He got the Daughter outside, went over the plan and sent her to the fruit shop. He went to the detonator and bobblehead receiver. He looked closely at the installation. Just as the spy predicted, Asaf could replace bobblehead with the Camel/seven-minute timer using the milk-pitcher method.

Asaf switched the receivers, then hurried off to the snakehead. As he went, he replayed in his mind: milk-pitcher handle, milk-pitcher spout … milk-pitcher handle, milk-pitcher spout … coffee and coffee … sugar and sugar … milk-pitcher. He got to the point where he had doubts about the installation he had just done. It was dark. He was in a hurry. Now he wasn't so confident that his installation was correct.

44

THE MINISTER OF JUSTICE DIDN'T like being roused out of bed, but when he heard the word snakehead, he got up and put the kettle on for a quick cup of tea while he got ready. "Who knows," he thought to himself. "If this Asaf fellow is the new prophet, I'm in good with him by doing what he tells me. If he's just an imposter, it won't do any harm being with the Zealot in case things go sideways."

In the Zealot's vestibule, the Minister was explaining his visit …

" … Not to worry. The young man runs the bar. The tea-house is not under his control. If we arrive in good time, and keep our wits about us, this might be a good thing for the Zealots. And what is good for the Zealots, is good for me. And as a council member, what's good for me is good for those in the good graces of the council. This whole boys-in-the-desert thing will suffice for now until we can steer a new course."

"Fair enough Minister. But I still am not clear why I want a tea-house."

"It's not just a tea-house for us. It is a base of operations for this region. Whoever holds that corner of the village can leverage influence along the foot of the mountains. Do you want the Fanatics to control the mountain pass? Of course not. So let's go. We'll find out soon enough what this is all about. One thing for sure, if we're not there tonight, whatever happens, will happen without us."

After Asaf's council meeting on the snakehead, the Plebe spoke with Asaf in private. "I think there is talk about gold in these new enterprises. I think I can use some — just a bit — to entice the Fanatics. They're crazy. And if something special, like gold, was waved in the leader's face, they would more likely be willing to go along with our plans."

Asaf was suspect that the Plebe needed gold to get the Fanatics, but reminded himself that he wasn't a sect leader. "These are all one-ounce bars. Take one. Take two if it will help … … or three," he mumbled at the end. Asaf shook his head wondering what he had got himself into.

The Plebe told the Fanatic that a new mission had sprung up somewhere in the desert to rescue boys from slavery. But the slave traders there put a bounty on the Prophet's head because he was hurting business. At the new moon, the Prophet would be giving out blessings in the tea-house. "I know your followers are the only ones who will carry out the bounty deed. Here is the earnest." He placed the gold ingot in the Fanatics hand. "Don't go into the tea-house. Go to the bar. The soliders are gone. That is where you can muster for an assault when the opportunity presents itself. This gold is yours for the effort. Tell each of your men, ten bars are his — in exchange for the Prophet's head."

The leader of the Fanatics did not exercise much control over what the adherents of the sect did. As long as they were against the other sects and against the Prophet taking control of all the sects, they could do whatever else they pleased. They saw the gold and pledged to decapitate the Prophet.

They were already wild-eyed when they arrived. Some drank freely from a jug of high-mountain moonshine. Others passed spliffs of tobacco and hashish to one another. Several came naked, but the leader told them to have at least some decency. So they went out, killed a few farm animals and returned wearing the bloody hides over their heads or around the waist. There was a small pack who only babbled in mystical tongues, addressing no human in particular.

45

THE THUG HEARD MEN'S VOICES in and about the village end. He snuck out of the shed and made his way over to the tea-house. The Soldier was nowhere to be seen. The leader of the Radicals arrived with his cohort. The Councilman met them outside the rear entrance to the Prophet's apartment. As the thug anticipated, they were well-armed agitated and curious all at the same time.

"Hey! All you clowns. All the iron to the side here you are laying. We don't know who and what of the fig mercenaries is doing the surveillance. The figs see you with those pipes in your hands, not for the music-making are those, and hoofta, you know the Swiss cheese, all hole-y like. You be looking through your own personal gut-hole before you drop, anna next round a third eye is carving into your forehead to help you fall even faster. Everybody stay cool, and living for another sunrise our eyeballs to see we will."

In the basement behind locked doors, the Radical leader was puzzled. "Just what the heck is going on around here? Where is this so-called snakehead training compound in the desert for new recruits? Why all the tumult and secrecy?"

The Councilman nodded and looked at the thug. The thug raised his hands, gesturing that all would be ok and explained in due time. "Is the Asaf and the Soldier. Big trouble. Asaf has the idea, the stupid, to destroy these buildings. The Soldier, he discovers the bombs. The stupid Asaf, somehow he rings the whole place with explosives. Too much and too many."

"What do you mean bombs?! Why are we here on such a short notice? This is unusual and unexpected. Why are we in the Prophet's basement? I don't like it. Tell me. Tell me what's going on here." the Radical shouted.

The Councilman was disturbed by this news. It confused him, left him with many questions. He had to think fast if he wanted to stay relevant in this unexpected situation. He had understood that if he followed the snakehead, he could win the tea-house for his possession. He also knew that the leader of the Radicals must participate in the takeover. Now he realized he used the code-word with the Radical by mistake but wasn't sure if that mattered or not. But hearing this talk of bombs was not good. The Councilman knew the thug, so he could imagine him going two ways. He could be telling the truth, aiming to participate in the future businesses run by the tea-house. Or, the thug was spinning one of his webs that served him first, and everybody else second, even those in the code, even if the code-brothers were second above everybody else. He didn't know where he stood in the code hierarchy, or even if he counted. The more he thought about all these possibilities, the more his thoughts ran over each other and got jumbled up. He also knew Asaf was trying to prophesy that the Prophet was to die or move away. He wasn't sure exactly how that fit in with the need to bring the Radical into the basement for some snakehead. He was afraid of the Radical, had shaky trust in the thug, couldn't imagine Asaf behind such an unhinged set of circumstances, so he tried to pretend to be calm, but still serious.

The Councilman decided to go along with the Radical. "Yes, tell us. What are we going to do with these bombs? What has gotten into Asaf's head?"

The thug answered blandly. "I don't know all these the answers. The Asaf, he is gone crazy I guess. I call you here because the Soldier is going to kill everyone. And he will do it too. You know this, Councilman, right? Like a fig I think you know."

The Councilman nodded, continuing to think. He knew the Soldier was unstable and didn't like the tea-house. He knew all the mercenaries would side with the Soldier if things got bad. If what the thug had just told them was all true, the Councilman understood the predicament. He decided to redirect the attention away from himself. "Do you have a plan? I am thinking you brought us here for a good reason."

The thug took a few moments to answer. "I am thinking of plan and plans. I have other ideas where to go. But today, I am here under the code, until I see how the settling of why Asaf these bombs is needing. Who knows what the gods have ventured? To live, to die, or to carry on in business."

The Radical said firmly, "God. Not gods. There is only one God."

The thug nodded outwardly. But inwardly he didn't care, one god or one thousand.

The Councilman asked, "How are you on the inside of this? You serve me. My hand deals with the Radicals. For me, the Radicals are the best choice for future peace."

The Radical nodded smugly at this.

The Councilman continued, "How is it that you claim to know what you are telling us? And why should we listen?"

The thug looked at them both, the one, then the other, then again, back and forth, sizing them up. He took a deep breath and said with a hint of insider knowledge that had been a burden for him to keep secret. "Is all the spy."

The Councilman asked, "What spy?"

"The spy for the foreign mercenaries." The thug spat on the ground.

The Councilman and the Radical looked at one another, then at the thug waiting and expecting a further explanation.

"I know a nobody I am. I know I work for whatever I'm told. I know I'm not a religious. I serve — I am loyal — to my brotherhood of the code."

The thug stopped, as if giving a short reverential moment to the brothers, wherever they may be. "All this circumstance is only because the spy, only him. He is lonely. He is not the friends to having. His whole life is spent on the outside looking in. He maybe from a good school and a good family. Yet on day to day, month to month, year to year, he lives outside. Me and my brothers of the code, we are on the outside too. Maybe the spy sees this. Maybe a kindred spirit there is going him and me."

The other two remained silent.

"You know the Soldier. Well, you know him," he said to the Councilman. "He is the pie fallen on the ground. No good but for the pigs and dogs to eat up. He is away from everything he is. No family, no friend. What and where is the home? The spy — I think he is the same. The more or the less. The Soldier, he hates me and my kind. We are the enemy to him we are. The spy, no enemy he has — only opportunity. Opportunity to make more the spy games."

The Councilman looked at the Radical seriously. He then turned his attention back to the thug. "What did you learn from the spy that has brought about all this confusion?"

The Radical added, "And how — if there was anything to learn, for I am not sure there is — did you learn it?"

"I know you two little faith in me have. But here the truth is. Is all in the alcohol. Maybe for your upbringing, you are not knowing the power in the alcohol for the telling all in the mind, but especially in the heart. The truth, it comes out by the alcohol spirit. The spy, he's all the drinking always. And the drinking, he's all the talking. He's a nice guy, so I'm all the listening. He talks about the wars on every-side this and every-side that. He is observing the men and women coming and ..."

The Radical cut in, "I don't care about your alcoholic — maybe homosexual — stories with your friend of the ungodly mercenaries. I don't want to hear about alcoholics. They are a shame to the whole planet. He's not a nice guy. He is representative of evil and the evil one — in whose house he will mourn forever."

Without rebuking the Radical for his vehemence, and desiring to understand the thug's story, the Councilman held one hand up toward the Radical and pointed at the thug with the other, "Just get on with it. Skip the friendship. What did he tell you?"

This irritated the thug. He stood up and glared at the two of them. "You nozza point the finger at me! You are both the sons of the evil one thousand more than me! If I was no gentleman, I strangle you here and now with these hands your throat until you are blue the face and dead like fly-speck. If ever a man the men loving, is you and fly-speck the Prophet!"

The Radical stood up, matching the thug's aggressive pose. He was on the verge of shouting back but checked himself. He said with a low hiss, "I could have you whipped for saying such things and acting out this way. But — I will not. Not now. Not here. I am in possession of my human nature with dignity. The last thing we need is a stupid quarrel among ourselves."

He sat, smug with his sense of self-control and full of selfish pride, secretly congratulating himself for rising above the fray and being a mature man.

The thug stood his ground, his eye was sharp and piercing. His spirit was alive with fire and hatred for these overly religious.

The Councilman said, "Enough — sit, sit. Everybody sit."

He was still trying to make sense out of these unexpected events. He turned to the Radical and said, "Now is not the time to throw stones. There is a lot of evil that goes on in these buildings. A lot. Evil. I don't even want to think about half of it. So for you — stop grousing about the devil and God and gods and eternal punishment. We're here for the work in front of us. We all — someday will have to work out our own salvation — who knows? maybe that will happen faster than we think. I am a follower of the Prophet, but I am not a blind man — either physically or spiritually. I know he is human — and shares in humanity — in many, or all ways. Just like all of us. Being a follower of the Prophet does not make me a marble statue. I retain my own volition, opinions, volition and opinions, you know, and the natural need to circulate in many realms of society. If — the Prophet's time — if his ministry, his mission — is coming to an end, or displaced, or replaced — or eclipsed — or some combination of all this — it is what it is. I am not here to be swept aside by the tides of change but to change and adapt accordingly. Obviously, something very disturbing is afoot this very night. Let us settle down and see where it takes us."

He then turned to the thug and said, "Tell us what is going on. Skip all the details that we don't care about. We are not interested in what the spy stirred in his drink or what kind of shoes he wears. We want to know what is going on with the Soldier, these businesses upstairs and these explosives."

With reluctance, some hesitation and with untarnished pride on open display, the thug slowly sat and took his own time, gathering his thoughts, making calculations of what, and what not to share with the Councilman and the leader of the Radicals.

The thug leisurely lit up a smoke with his Zippo. After a few puffs, he began again, "Ok, I tell you what I think the telling is worth important — and not important. All the behind the telling, how the spy, he confide in me. How we smoke together. Maybe play the cards the gambling. The cards, the alcohol, the secrets, maybe? But, if you are not interested, is ok by me, is only fly-speck — for your virgin daughters ..."

The Radical jumped halfway up again, but the Councilman reached over and touched him, gently reminding him that everyone needed to stay calm and not let the thug bait him into another argument. The thug feigned to ignore their reactions, puffing away nonchalantly.

The Councilman knew when to pivot, and said politely, "Ok, ok. We get the point. Our pride and masculinity are not on trial here. And don't get uppity. You dragged us in here. We can leave just as well. Now we're going to sit here and listen. You talk, we'll ask genuine questions if we have them. Civil everybody, civil. Sheesh ... too much testosterone around here."

He then added, in a poor imitation of the thug's accent, and in an equally poor attempt to alleviate the uncomfortable atmosphere in the room, "Wheese bringga ze Prophet's an' heez boyez down here, yess?"

The thug showed zero reaction. The Radical rolled his eyes and slightly shook his head. He extended a hand toward the thug with his index and middle finger raised a bit. The thug met his reach halfway with the pack of Marlboros and nudged a cigarette out with a blip of the hand. The Radical still couldn't reach the pack and hesitated, anticipating that the thug would lean forward to assist in passing the cigarette. The thug held the pack steady, so the Radical, just a little begrudgingly, leaned some more and extracted the fag from the pack. He couldn't summon the humility to ask for a light, but glanced around and spied a plastic Marlboro lighter. He tried to light his smoke, but the little disposable lighter only gave off futile sparks — no butane inside. He sighed, rolled his eyes again and turned back to the thug with a disgruntled exhalation of his lungs, and leaned over again with the cigarette in his lips, ready to accept the thug's light.

It was a perfect chance to further humiliate the Radical by demonstrating the infinite superiority of the Zippo — the full sound and flick and flash that can be made with experienced hands. Instead, he merely opened the lid quietly with the side of his thumb, gave one modest roll of the striker, lit the cigarette and quietly closed the Zippo and re-pocketed it without any flourish.

The Radical accepted this subtle display of truce. He sat back in a calmer mood with the light rush of nicotine and the thug's little gesture of peace soothing his nerves.

The Councilman observed this petty game and said with resignation, "Alright, give me one too. I'll turn the kettle on. Might as well get comfortable, it could be a long discussion."

The thug still didn't know all the story but was confident enough to parcel out good information and see where things went. He weaved a mostly true tale about what he had learned from the spy over coffee and cards and cigarettes.

According to the spy, the big mountain range above the village had attracted the military-strategic planners. It separated two distinct areas. One side was already burnt out by the wars, but the other side had not been touched by war, as it was remote. They reasoned it would be wise to create a socio-economic political presence there. They took note of a pass in the mountains. The pass was little used, but not treacherous. It was not big enough for a motorized military campaign, but maybe suitable for infiltration, reconnaissance or other military leverage. He said they needed a place from where they could explore the area. They mapped out where the military bases were in relationship to the pass. They found one base that had once seen a lot of action but was no longer in a hot zone, yet still had some officers and troops maintaining the place. So they made a plan to insert themselves into the local society. They found a village that was close to the pass. It was bombed out, but not demolished. It had poor infrastructure. The population had not only been decimated but was discouraged and broken-spirited. They came up with an idea to revitalize a part of the village by building an outpost.

The thug told his two-man audience that he was only relating what the spy said. The truth behind it all was open to question and not readily verifiable. He went on to tell them, that, according to the spy, the plan-makers ginned up all the major actors involved in their scheme to reconnoiter the mountain pass: the General, the Prophet, the Soldier, and Asaf.

At this point, the Councilman and the Radical objected. The thug held up his hands and said he understood their objections, but he was only the messenger, relaying what the spy told him.

Then the thug told them that someway, somehow, and for some reason, Asaf had taken delivery of a shipment of explosives. At this, the Councilman and the radical tried interrupting the thug, but he waved them off. He was insistent on finishing what he had to say.

He concluded with a version of the run-in with the Soldier, hiding for a while, and Asaf disappearing somewhere.

When he was done talking, the Radical stood up. "This is — is crazy. I don't know where to start … First let me speak for me, myself."

Turning from one to the other, he pointed as he spoke. "I don't know about you and you … or even the Prophet. I have a respect for the Prophet, but we also differ much, too. Now — what I want to know is what is with these bombs?"

The Councilman threw his hands in the air. "The bombs! The bombs! Asaf! What is Asaf doing with explosives? Where is he!? Where!? … The Soldier! Where is he? He's going to kill us?! Where's the General? We're going to die! Die!! Where's the Prophet? This is his apartment! It's the devil! THE DEVIL!!"

The Councilman jumped across the table, grabbed the thug and started biting on his arm. The thug sprang up and tried to shake the

Councilman off, but he had a good grip. The biting was painful, so the thug landed a huge hammer chop to his head. He stopped biting and staggered away. The Radical saw how the thug hit him and thought it was a good move. So when the Councilman staggered near enough, the Radical hammered him on the top of the head again. This time he fell down. The Radical thought to himself … good for the nanny, good for the kid … and kicked him hard in the side. "You're the devil if you don't get ahold of yourself. Idiot!" He gave him another boot and told him to get up and get a grip on himself.

The Councilman got back to his feet. He was shaky. He sat down and blinked. When he had gathered his wits, the ire rose up inside of him. "Leave me alone. Maybe you're the devil." He grabbed his teacup and threw what was left of the tea in the Radical's face. The Radical jumped up in rage, and was about to go for the Councilman, his hands poised to choke him by the neck. "How dare you!" he said loudly.

As he moved towards the Councilman, the thug stepped forward and gave the Radical a swift and accurate kick between the legs. The Radical yelped, covered his groin with both hands and flopped to the floor headfirst.

The thug yelled, half angry, half laughing, "Now I'm the devil to both you! Everybody the trap shut and clapped! I nozza give a fly-speck fig the both you. I'm go. Bye."

The thug half-turned toward the stairs to go.

The Councilman said loudly with nervous anxiety, "No, No! Don't leave me here with this devil … No. Leave! You are the devil … No, wait. The devil is inside me. I feel him! — The bombs! The bombs! — Tell us about the bombs!"

The thug turned back, calmly reached over to the Radical's teacup, picked it up and threw both the cup and the tea in the Councilman's face. The cup hit the Councilman on the bridge of the nose splashing the tea in his eyes before falling to the floor and shattering. Even though the tea had cooled to room temperature, the Councilman put his hands to his face and yelled, "My eyes! My eyes! Blind! I'm blinded! Blind! Ahhhyy, blind!"

The Radical, who was just recovering from his pain, stood up, took a full swing and batted the Councilman on the back of his head. "You're not blind you, idiot. The tea wasn't even hot. Do as the thug says. Shut up and get a grip on yourself."

Finally, the three settled back down and sat. The thug told them that he did not know the back story to the bombs. Even more unusual, it seemed like Asaf was unclear about it too. The thug told them that Asaf had asked him specifically to come to his aid in the matter. He explained how Asaf didn't know how to use bombs whatsoever.

"So, here we are," pointing to them in turn, "Dumb, Dumber," and thumbing his chest, "and me, Dumbest. These whole two buildings surround with powerful explosive all around. All linked with high quality the cord, and professional caps the exploding, and det devise, very nice. Hoofta, wadda life we lead."

He stopped talking. The Councilman and the Radical remained silent until it was clear that the thug was done talking, at least for now.

The Radical said, "Before Dumb gets all ants-in-his-pants over here, allow me, Dumber, to talk. We both are uncertain about these explosives. We both have questions. For me, I would like to know about danger. Are we in danger? If so, what kind of danger? And, what can we do about it? Do we have long — or is this whole place going to go to the devil any minute — like it probably should," he added as a sarcastic rejoinder.

The Councilman was uttering, "Yes, yes … yes," as the Radical spoke. But before he could get going more than that, the thug kicked him in the shins and waggled his finger at him to remain quiet.

"All questions, the good. Not so sure answers. The Asaf, for me knowing, has no reason these buildings to destroy. I like him. He likes me. He rescued me from devil mercenary fly-speck Soldier. Councilman here, he knows the truth of Asaf, yes? He's the money count, the beer and Coke bringing. He's looking at the waiters and others the staff. Working the always hard. Like I'm the telling, he knows from nothing the explosives. So, we, the dummies three, we are asking: Any reasons here? If some crazy double the cross, what for? And, why he's me all bringing in and make like a partner with the explosives?"

The Radical and the Councilman reflected on these questions quietly.

The Councilman cleared his throat a little bit, as a precursor to asking permission to ask a question, maybe. The other two looked at him showing no emotion one way or the other.

"I still would like to understand more about the bombs. Specifically: how will they go off, if they go off? And by what means? There has to be somebody or something that sets these bombs in motion. So to speak …"

The Councilman trailed off, not knowing exactly what else to ask.

The Radical was looking at the Councilman as he spoke. When he was finished, he nodded and looked at the thug waiting for some answers to reasonable questions.

"Like I said, the explosives all the high quality. Military-grade. I installed all. No shortcuts. The Asaf, my word, my code of honor I give him for all this. I answer you, Councilman, because of your insight in the setting off the explosives. I have been the wondering of the double-cross. This is the reason. As you are knowing, the explosive, it needs the detonator and how to trigger the switch. Asaf, for all his high-grade gear, as for the trigger, it is missing."

"Missing?!" the Radical asked with surprise. "What do you mean missing? First, we're all preparing for martyrdom — each in our own mind I might add — and now you're telling us there's no trigger to set the bombs off?"

The Councilman joined his fellow. "Yes. First, it's military highest grade. Now they won't work?!"

The thug smiled, sipped some tea and had a smoke. "My men. My fig-headed fly-speck friends. Yes. Military-grade. But maybe or maybe not, going off. All the time Asaf is having me set the explosives, I know of certain there is a trigger missing. I think the Asaf knows … but I'm not one hunnert percentile. But, for all the questions, questions not answered, and for having answers, I have been wondering how the Asaf is bringing all this to an end. Also, how is the …"

There was a loud banging and shouting up in the tea-house. All three men sat up straight.

"Wazza wazza?"

"What's that noise?! What's going on here now? Who's upstairs?!"

"The Soldier! He's here to kill us … Or the judgment. The judgment is coming! Run! Where? Here, no — this way. Wait!!"

The noise grew stronger upstairs and the three ran up into the tea-house.

46

During the long hours of the night, the Zealots, the Radicals and the Fanatics filled the bar and tea-house. Drawn to the rumpus like Asaf's mystical moth-vision, was a legion of sectarians. Coward warriors, make-believe emissaries, male-only pimps, dealers of every sordid type, slave boys, eunuch masseurs, lazy dope-heads, and other such flotsam and jetsam were sucked into the vortex of vice. They sparred and parlayed over the great and grand, the minuscule and minutial in prolix philosophical, religious and ethical arguments and grudge matches. Accusations and counter-accusations sailed through the air in verbal bombardments. Threats and counter-threats were an evil hiss in the ear. Promises were made by the lips — broken simultaneously in the mind. Real and fake diplomatic overtures, mock-regal gamesmanship, nation-building, revolution and war, all had their moment as the most important idea at hand, only to be overthrown a sentence or two later, by the next diabolical scheme of power.

These intense deliberations were rudely interrupted by the bashing, ear-grating cacophony of a trash-can lid band. A three-person ensemble trudged into the tea-house. A cook and two kitchen workers were dressed in filthy rags that a bum or hobo would not have donned. One of the boys held up a trash-can lid, while his partner banged on it with a gnarled, desiccated branch. The beat was modest, not unlike a death knell. The cook banged two lids together, like cymbals from hell. They shouted in turn, "All Hail! All Hail!" and "The End is Near! The End is Near!"

Mind-boggling and ear-grating, the display made jaws drop, eyebrows contort, and eyeballs bulge.

The little parade gave no regard to anyone. They marched slowly as if they were only practicing; as if no one was present to witness their dirge. They wended their way through the tea-house, then outside, around the back of the building.

The stupefied crowd in the tea-house began milling about, no one knowing whether to stay, leave, follow or flee.

47

IN THE BAR, ALL THE men suddenly stopped their talking and shouting and whispering and gesturing. The strangest noises were coming from outside. No one knew what it was or what it meant. What had been the background noise of the men arguing in the tea-house, was silenced.

Then, an outlandish parade came into the bar, led by the noisy band. "All Hail! All Hail! The End is Coming! The End is Coming!"

Everyone looked up, startled and amazed. Those who were sitting jumped to their feet.

Behind the harbinger hobos, Asaf entered on a litter carried by the cooks' helpers. The litter and the stool were cobbled together from old, dismantled wooden pallets. Asaf sat straight, wearing plain clothes. The Prophet's ceremonial miter sat on his head, creating a striking and auspicious visage.

Behind the litter, came the Daughter, holding a fierce-looking sword. Behind her, she towed the Prophet, the General and the Soldier. They were shackled and manacled. Behind her, the lead bartender wielded a shepherd's crook. He wore a very large ring around his neck with three simple keys, dangling out of proportion to the size of the ring. The mock prisoners walked uneasily and dragged their feet. It was clear they were not in their right mind. The Prophet was a slovenly, putrid piece of humanity. Sweaty and smelly, he hung his head as he was pulled along. He let out a 'yip' when the Daughter tugged his manacled wrists, then spat viciously over his shoulder, when he was prodded by the lead bartender who acted as flanker and rear-guard. The General was a dirty, filthy, shadow of his former self. His shuffling gait was jerked with irregular spasms. His eyes glared and raged in his head which twitched out-of-sync with his bodily tremors. His tongue rolled in and out of his mouth like a tortured tortoise. He made grunts and grimaces. If he saw someone look at him, he made a short lunge and snapped with a slobbery mouth. The Soldier was subdued. He was unshaven, unshowered and looked tired and plain worn out. He seemed unresponsive to what was going on around him.

The train came to a standstill. Asaf waved his hand gracefully and the trash-can band was silenced. The home-made palanquin was set on the bar. The Daughter stopped and made an about-face, scowling at the prisoners, keeping her sword at the ready. The lead bartender moved up, taking her side at the bar.

Asaf stepped off the palanquin onto the bar.

He cast his gaze over the assemblage. In his mind, he saw a degenerate coterie. Human in form alone. Worthy only of extirpation.

Someone began to speak. Before he could get half a phrase out of his mouth, the Daughter slapped the broad side of her sword on the bar, making a resounding crack. She did not speak, she simply pointed the sword at the man and waggled it. The man clamped his jaws tight.

Now, the only sounds were the slight shuffling of feet, some clothes rustling, and a few throats clearing.

Asaf continued to look the crowd over. He was nervous. He was not certain if he was doing the right thing. His resolve, which had been so strong, was wavering.

Then the chains rattled. The noise shook him out of his moment of doubt. He looked at the three and regained some resolve. "You are all here tonight either by accident or by design. If you are here by accident, no one knows what fate has in store for you tonight. Maybe some are here just because they were in the wrong place at the wrong time. Maybe the tide of history has swept you in here. Only time will tell. Others are here tonight because the will of God has decreed it to be so. You also have an unknown fate. And there are those who have been brought here by design. All who have been brought here by design will pay for their wickedness this day. Then there are these three special ones. They too will pay. But first, they will undergo the trial. Then the judgment!"

First, there were murmurings, then normal conversation, then raised voices mixed with shouting. The crowd was at each other before Asaf had arrived. But now they had a new target for their anger — and he stood on the bar.

Asaf grew nervous again. He sensed he was losing control of the situation. He raised his hand, pointed to the Solider and yelled in a commanding voice, "Release the Soldier!"

This distracted the men. Some looked up at Asaf, others looked at the Soldier, all wondering what it was all about.

Asaf said to the lead bartender, "Unlock him! Take off his chains and let him stand there."

Everyone watched the lead bartender set the Soldier free. The Soldier did nothing except rub his wrists.

The murmurs began again and some were growing restless. Trying to maintain some direction and control, Asaf said loudly, "But leave the General and the Prophet in chains."

Asaf continued in a loud voice, "This is the Soldier. He is the founder of the bar. He is guilty! He is guilty for bringing alcoholic drink into our village. And the alcoholic drink brings the poison of life with it. He is guilty of indulging his lower-self. His fantasy of having a club where sin is allowed has brought him to this day of judgment. He is a man under orders. He violated his orders and flaunted the authority of his superiors by establishing the club. Even though he is an evil foreign devil mercenary, he was still under orders in his situation and circumstance. For, as despicable as the mercenaries are, they have their ranks and orders. For him to go against those ranks and orders makes him a coward. It makes him a traitor and a deserter. In all militaries, for all time, the traitor and the deserter are executed. He has fully earned this treatment — this fate — this sentence."

Asaf paused, and again grumblings and vicious chit-chat rippled across the bar. Asaf observed this and realized that he had better keep up his speechifying, to stay ahead of what could be a dangerous crowd scene.

Asaf threw an arm in the air and continued in a proclamatory voice, "Nevertheless! Nevertheless — I have just set him free of his chains. These are the only chains I can relieve him of. The chains of sin and damnation are left to God and the devil to work out among themselves. For I cannot carry out his judgment — his punishment. The weakness — the frailty which caused him to create this place. That is, the place before, the club — that led him to build the club — is the simple desire to be with your friends. It was the need for friendship which made him want to open a club. He wanted time with his own kind: the warrior class. All of us here," Asaf waved his hand before him at the men below, "have the basic human need for fellowship. And even though a mercenary is evil — a mercenary is still human. He has been thrown into this world somehow, someway, so that fate digs into his soul, and makes him a solider for hire. And I cannot carry out his just punishment ... for I am as guilty as he is ... in another way ... I too need and want friendship. I was young and looked up to the Solider. I thought I had a friend — or could have a friend — in him. Maybe. But it was not meant to be. The Soldier could never have a friend like me, for I am his enemy. I am the one he is here to fight — to kill. I was stupid. How could I have ever thought that helping the Soldier would ever turn out good? When the club was bombed, I saw the true nature of the mercenary. The Soldier turned on me like a serpent on a rat. It broke my heart and emptied my soul. I saw that I was not, and never could be a friend ..."

Asaf paused, trying to swallow and get some air in his lungs. "But by then, the club was already in existence. It was something — and, I guess, once something is something, for the warrior class, the military, and the mercenaries — it must always be something. I do not understand it. But I know that I share somehow in the guilt of the Soldier — so I cannot set judgment upon him. I ... I set him free …"

Asaf was moved to tears. He then said, "But! Let us also not forget, that the Soldier is not without feelings. He too has suffered. Suffered much. His turning down the dark road of drugs is only a symptom of the evil life all around him. The torture of the way of war is a torture for him — inside. His pain is the pain from war. He suffers. He suffers. I suffer. We all suffer because of war ..."

Asaf knew he had much more to say, but his rambling, wandering, discourse became laborious and his throat dried up.

The whole bar was awash with men who were upset, tired, confused and now even more befuddled. There were ripples of discontent, which could become waves of violence any minute. The Daughter saw all this instantly but knew well enough the precarious position she was in, so she hesitated to do anything rash. She pointed her sword at the lead bartender and shouted in a commanding voice, "Bring forth the General!"

The General was in front of him, just a few paces away, so the lead bartender was not sure quite what to do. The Daughter made eyes at him. She nodded in Asaf's direction, then moved her eyes toward the crowd. She made subtle gestures, nodding slightly and twirling her finger, suggesting that he do something, anything, to keep the whole schtick moving.

The lead bartender stepped over to the General and grabbed his chains. He rattled the chains and shouted, "The General!"

This aroused Asaf who had been choked up and mentally drifting.

Asaf raised his head, then his hand. He pointed at the General and commanded, "Leave his chains on!"

Then in a tone of sorrow and self-pity, he continued, "Forgive me, men. Forgive me for my weakness. I was not born to greatness like these two," Asaf swept his hand in front of himself, "and some of you. I am a just plain man. Born not far from here. Nobody here would know anyone's name in my whole family. The path which has brought me here today is one that started when I was young. I was young and stupid. The Soldier had an idea which developed into this place — although much different then — this place where we all stand now. But fate or destiny — or just plain stupid decision making — has brought me here this day. It all started with the Soldier. And although he has been brought here in chains, I release him. For, he is guilty of founding this evil place but has never done me true harm. Or I believe has never intended to do me wrong. I have suffered at his hands though — but it is probably just as much my fault as his. So — I release him."

The lead bartender and the Daughter were worried about Asaf. He was faltering badly. He had talked them into this whole event with courageous words and a deep conviction of what was right and wrong. Now, he was going in circles and it was becoming dangerous for all of them. Asaf broke out in a cold sweat. He put his hands up to his face and head. The stench of cigarettes, bad breath, and unwashed men had made him nauseated. He was dizzy from tiredness and stress. He was touched with vertigo from standing on the bar looking down and around the bar.

"I am done with what I can say for now. There is so much more I would like to say. That is ... I have thought about this day for a long time. I have rehearsed so many lines and statements and pronunciations. So much anger and frustration have built up inside me ... But, to be honest ... I am out of breath for fear. For fear and — how should I say it ... Misgivings? So let me say this, then I shall leave. Maybe coming here was a mistake. I look at what I have done with my friends here with me — and part of me is ashamed. How I brought them here, with, I guess, what might be called — delusions of grandeur. Should be more like illusions. I chose these for a symbol or image of your wretchedness."

Asaf suddenly and violently kicked the palanquin off the bar. The cobbled planks clattered on the floor and fell apart. Everybody jumped in surprise. The lead bartender was confused. The Daughter was apprehensive.

All of this happened quickly. The crowd, all along puzzled and filled with confusion, was now growing angry. Asaf said, "I know what you are thinking. I hear your voices of anger and discontent. I will not detain you any longer. I am sorry that I have jumped up on this bar and tried to make a speech."

Asaf addressed his followers, "To you, my friends, please, you can go now. We will leave this place. We will leave others here to determine their path. They can make what they will of the tea-house and this bar."

Asaf turned his attention to the angry men, "And to you, I say this. I am a fool. We will leave you. I renounce this bar. Take for yourselves what you want with it. We will leave the General and your Prophet here with you. Only I will not give you the keys to their chains. That is being too generous. Most of you do not know what is going to happen here shortly. What I am about to tell you, you will not believe anyhow. Just a few days — or maybe a week or so ago — I gave out slips of the Prophet's paper to this village. That is I used the Prophet's paper. I wrote my message on the paper. The message was simple but serious. I told and warned the people of this village that the judgment was coming and it was time to flee this place forever. Maybe no one here knows anything about this. My own Uncle, who raised me, has forsaken me in this thing I am going to do. Others have done the same. Perhaps the Daughter here understands and is still at my side. That stands to reason, for she, more than all of you idiots put together, has two things that you don't have: a mind and heart that is not full of your own evil selves, and a true basis — a foundation, genuine reasons — for real revenge and real justice — to rain down on all your heads!"

Asaf was feeling bolder as he began to harangue the men. "So hear this and hear it well — it is the last thing I am going to say to you reprobates! Here it is! Soon, very soon, this whole building — including the tea-house — including the whole village — which is why I gave them a fair warning — this whole place will be blown to dust and completely destroyed! And not only that, but this entire area will become uninhabitable for generations to come. There will be nuclear waste here which will ruin this place for a long time. The evil that was spawned here will be exterminated forever. I tell you all this truth to at least lessen the blood on my hands. But I am sure most of you do not, and will not, believe me. In a perverse way — and I confess I am not happy with myself in this — but in a strange way, I hope most of you will stay here and let the destruction take you as well. All I can say, for now, is that the destruction will come! Leave if you can. Or stay, and DIE!!"

Asaf was about to climb down and make his way out of the bar. Suddenly the thug yelled out, "Wait! WAIT!! Juzza minute here!"

Every eye turned his way. Those who were already flummoxed were even more so now.

The thug said in a loud voice, "Everybody — everybody listen. To me the listen!" He confidently made his way to the bar and climbed up, where Asaf still stood.

"All the men, quiet down. Quiet down! I am telling you now the telling real of the truth! This here Asaf, I know him pretty well. For the time, the good while, I'm working side on the side in the tea-house. He comes to me, not I go to him. He goes to recruit me for this crazy, the mixing up in the brains, idea, destroying the bar. I'm listening, the ears all the listening, I hear the plot, the plan here the destruction. I think: Wazza in all this? I'm thinking: I don't understand what the fig he's talking all this? But he's more the boss than me, so I keep listening. He tells me of the bombs, the explosives, all. This Asaf, I say, right now, here — now I know is crazy, all. From a fig-filled fly-speck head, all to the toes, a stinking the fly-speck stinking feet!"

As he was talking, the thug was inching his way closer to Asaf. By the time he insulted him about his feet, he was next to him. When he finished his rant, he quickly ram-rodded his elbow into Asaf's face and jaw. Asaf's knees buckled in shock and pain. He lost his balance and went down on one knee. The thug kicked him in the ribs. Asaf fell. He grabbed the edge of the bar as he went down and lessened the hard landing. His miter tumbled off his head and flopped to the floor as if imitating the humiliation. He sat up, shaken. The thug looked down at him and laughed derisively.

"Now who is making the big speech, eh fig-boy? All you to know the truth? The truth Asaf doesn't know himself the knowing? First, the one, is true, the bombs. The bombs are here! All around, the buildings surrounding!"

At this, a wave of chatter and foot shuffling went across the gathering. Nervous eyes darted at the walls and roof. Everyone was looking for either a way out, or for someone to conspire with, or someone who looked extra guilty to point out — or even wrestle with.

The thug said loudly, "All you fly specks! The mouths shutting! Listen, the ears, here to my mouth speaking now! Sure, the bombs are all surrounding. But to be nervous? Not a fig for it! A FIG!" He laughed at them and gestured profanities in their faces.

Still laughing, he said, "Hey you fly specks! What are you going to do with the big bad bomb? Hey, you Asaf! On the floor still? You Asaf, big fig! Where the explosives? Not exploding?"

The thug cupped his hand around his ear and turned this way and that. "Oh no? Why? I'll tell you why. I am in charge the bombs! I make the det cord. I make the cap. And I string together all the explosives, them stringing all around."

The thug pointed and gestured at the four sides of the building as he raved on. "Soldier put me face-first in the dirt as fast when he was eyeballing the explosives. It's because he knows what his own eyeballs were telling him. Big trouble. He saw and knows for a fig they are good the bomb, the cord, the cap, the explosives. And dangerous, the most dangerous!

One of the men shouted, "We're all going to die!"

The thug grabbed a heavy-glass Marlboro ashtray, took good aim and beaned the man in the face with it. "You be shutting your useless hole or the next ashtrays I come over and personally fist it your gullet down like who laid the rail. Hoofta, no more hunger for you ever. Now, back to my explain you fly-specks why the bombs are not the dangerous. Look!"

The thug reached in his shirt pocket and pulled out a boxed deck of cards. He held it high. "For all the eyeballs in this bar is now, look who is in control of the explosives that can take over half this village to the devils. This is the piece Asaf fig-for-brains doesn't have. Why?, Because he doesn't know from the bombs. All the gear rigging and no explosion without this: The transmitter talks to the remote switch. And the transmitter is in my pocket. Not the fig Asaf's pocket."

Looking down he addressed Asaf. "So, my friend Asaf. Where is the fire for lighting the bombs now? Is there a transmitter in your pocket? Well, if maybe there is, we make sure no mistake in blowing up the whole village by the accident. Here you go! We put the fire out for you."

At this, he let down his pants and urinated all over Asaf, who was still sitting dumbfounded on the floor.

The thug turned back to the men. "I am now telling you that those who come to my side of the bar, we will take over, this very night! Take away from the pig mercenaries and from the boy-love, even worse than fly-speck, Prophet, these businesses. We take them and run them for ourselves. We drive out the pig mercenaries and we drive out the boy-lovers."

When the thug stopped his speech, the whole crowd began talking at once. The thug was hoping the revelation of the transmitter would bring the men to his cause, but it was not to be. The drama between all the disparate groups was too much for any sort of cohesiveness. The three sects, already distrustful of each other, the crazy parade with their costumes and antics, and the sudden appearance of this barbaric lone wolf, made it impossible for the groups to rally around any particular cause whatsoever.

As bad as Asaf felt, he still had his wits about him. He ran his eyes over the men in the bar. He looked at the broken litter and the bedraggled prisoners. He looked at the litter-bearers. Then he looked at the lead bartender and the Daughter. He saw that the Daughter met his eyes with the same animation as his own. She was on fire with passion and a sense of urgency to do something, anything. But he also saw that she was out of her element, and was waiting for him to do something first, and she would readily and willingly follow.

All the others who had come with him remained distracted. The Soldier was not chained, but his mind was so fogged up that he was unable to make any real decisions on his own. Asaf didn't care about the fate of the General and the Prophet. He did not have the chance to preach all the condemnation sermons that had been brooding and weaving and patching together in his head. It was too late for that. Asaf had given the lead bartender ideas for escape one and escape two. Asaf's heart let his friend go — his life was his own now.

Trying to attract as little attention to himself as possible, Asaf gathered the miter in his fist, got up and went over to the Daughter. He whispered to her quickly. She listened and nodded. She, in turn, whispered to the lead bartender that she was leaving with Asaf. Asaf waited and watched until he saw the Daughter get out the door. Then he moved to the door and motioned for the lead bartender to come to his side.

Before they slipped out, Asaf took a few quick steps and grabbed up a fallen trash can lid. He banged it loudly on the wall next to the entrance. "Listen once more to me!"

Everyone stopped their talking and bustling and gawked at him.

"I thought I had more to say, but fate has it, that I am done here with speaking. Now, I wash my hands of you all! I can assure you that the day of judgment is here! Everyone who remains here will die this day! You have been warned! This is now the tea-house of death and saloon of doom!!

Asaf turned through the doorway and ran.

48

ASAF SAT DOWN. HE WAS out of breath from running and walking. He knew he had to get away from the bar, but he wasn't sure how far away he needed to go. He was not sure if he would have been killed or not, but the odds favored getting killed. There were not enough reasons for him to live. He was no longer necessary. He wondered if he had ever been necessary. But that was grist for future ponder-mills. Whether or not the men would have killed him was minor compared to why he fled. He ran to escape the detonation of the bombs. He had to go far enough so that he could get away from getting blown up or blown away. But not so far that the signal from the trigger would not be received by the booster.

For now, he just had to stop, catch his breath and think.

He looked back at the way he had come. He stood on the slope above the village. He could pick out the route he had taken between the rubble, low buildings, small houses, dusty roads, and lanes. He wanted to see whether or not there was movement or some indication that he was being either followed or chased. Nothing.

At first, a subtle prick of pride made him frown. Then, as he let reason take over, he realized that it would almost be absurd for anyone to chase him. Why? Why would they want him? To make another silly, stupid circus show?

Asaf reached into his pocket and took out the Zippo. He carefully opened the top. He pulled the innards out of the case. No-one knew, certainly not the thug, not the lead bartender, or even the Daughter, that for the transmitter to function, it was not enough to spin the striker wheel. There was a micro-switch in the bottom of the lighter, built into the butane receiver-port. The only way to make the transmitter send its signal was to turn this switch on. And the only way to do that was to take out the whole assembly, flip the micro-switch, then replace the transmitter into the case. Only then would the current from the striker wheel go through the circuit to the transmitter.

Asaf put the lighter back together and made his way further up the slope until he came to a spot where he had a good view of the village. Once again, he surveyed the village and retraced his exit. No one was after him, he was sure now. He could not see the bar directly, but he could pinpoint where it was, from the roads and little neighborhoods he knew so well.

He found a boulder to perch on. Took the lighter out of his pocket. The spy had explained the details of arming the transmitter. Take out the whole coffee pot. Turn the coffee pot upside down. Since this is a magic coffee pot, nothing will spill out. In the bottom of the coffee pot is where it is plugged into the electrical socket. The coffee pot has to be turned on to brew coffee. Asaf turned over the internal assembly, flipped the micro-switch with his fingernail and re-inserted the guts into the Zippo's stainless shell. Trigger was armed.

All of the long months and weeks and days and hours of Asaf's vengeful planning had finally come to this moment when he would remotely start the timer's countdown. The timer would let him move further away from the village — seven minutes further. Only seven minutes. He did not fully understand the configuration, but the spy said that was how it had to be. He told Asaf that he must use his judgment as to how far to go.

He looked around. He looked up the slope. He tried to imagine how far the blast would reach. He looked back and wondered if the transmitter's signal would reach all the way to the bar. He thought about his options. First, how far, going uphill, could he get in seven minutes? He had made the walk up to the spring many, many times. But his route was always from home, never from this end, on the opposite side of town. He knew the direction to get to the path leading to the spring but did not know where seven minutes of walking would get him. If the signal was too weak, he could walk back towards the bar and try over again. But this wouldn't work because he would always have to wait seven minutes to find out, then his seven-minute escape window would be useless.

He looked along the hillsides, picking out pathways that would lead him toward the pass trail. If he went straight up, he would be higher. If he went along the grade, he would be further away. Carefully weighing each route in his mind, Asaf made a complete circle, trying to come up with the strategy that made the most sense to him. He wished his Uncle was there to counsel him. They could talk about terrain and distance and calories and water intake and the sun and wind and ... and could not talk about the most important thing at hand: how to run from a powerful explosion.

His head started to hurt. All the calculations were too much. He secretly hoped, too secret to admit to himself for fear that his conscience would berate him for being childish, that he would be given a sign. He looked here and there, in one instant calculating his escape, in the same instant searching for a bird or snake or hare. Then his will could attach itself to the animal and follow the trace of it to salvation. The sign would serve as an out, from the foreboding that he knew was coming. The overhanging shadow that darkened his day of vengeance was the premonition that if he did not have some real external sign that would exonerate him, he would have to shoulder the entire plot alone — in his mind and memory, heart and soul.

Here a breeze, there, a slight rustle in the dry grass. Then a lone vulture far away — almost too far to see. Is that cloud morphing into something? No, nothing. Just a small cloud. No snake. No rabbit or mouse or squirrel. No eagle or dove. Just a human heart beating; human lungs inhaling, exhaling. Genuine sweat — sticky, salty. Dry mouth. Itchy eyes. Sadness. Emptiness. Alone.

Asaf dropped his head and sad, empty, lonesome tears dripped onto the dry dirt. A single ant happened to be near a fallen teardrop. It stopped. It twitched its antennae. It found the tear to be rich in salts and trace elements. It drank from the teardrop and swelled its abdomen enough to offer samples to other ants. Slowly but surely, a few more, then a few more ants, came and partook of Asaf's tears.

In Asaf's mind's eye, he began to see the ants as beings. He began to see the globules of water as worlds. He began to see the sharing of the worlds, with the beings, as their salvation. He imagined that if there were no worlds, then these lonely beings would perish from existence. Oh, that the watery worlds that emanated from him would not only save these little ones but give them a reason to live. They would share and care and thrive. The tears. The water! The SPRING!

The thoughts of the spring revived Asaf's fatigued body and flagging spirit. He stood up and wiped the tears from his eyes. Then he knelt on the ground. He looked at his little subjects. He spoke to them, "Truly hath the sage written: 'Go to the ant, thou sluggard, and consider her ways.' I thank thee, my little subjects, for ye have drunk of the sorrowful spring of mine face. And in thy imbibing, hast vivified my soul, so cast down from the weight of such an undertaking as I have set my face toward — and subsumed all as my fate."

Asaf, in this moment of quiet reflection, realized that he still had the Prophet's festal miter. He held it in his hand and looked at it thoughtfully. He solemnly fitted it on his head once more. His mind and spirit were stirred up. The feelings of sorrow and anguish were now tossed in the tumultuous sea of his soul with the newfound joy and hope that his little kingdom had given him.

He did not know for sure what his next step was, so, for the time being, he threw reason and care and pity and embarrassment aside, and decided to make a strange sort of sacrifice to the assembly. He was not sure whether or not he was losing his grasp on reality; whether or not the craziness of recent events had infected his brains, or he if was just fulfilling some unknown divine plan. He came to the point where he didn't care. "Maybe it's all three," he said to himself.

Addressing the ant colony, he said with proper gravity suiting the moment, "My dearest six-legged subjects. I, thy new-found benefactor cannot stay with you long now. For although ye have pleased me, by accepting my gift of sorrowful and shameful tears, I must needs continue on my way. For, I am pursued by the hounds of hell and driven forward by the steeds of the spheres. To tell the telling of it all, I have not the strength. My kidneys and spleen leak their vitality. My brow is moist from anguish and worry. But ye have given me hope. The hope that, although I forge ahead with the most ponderous of plans, a plan quickened in the fires of fury — that — that I will not be totally lost and cast away because of my willfulness in exacting judgment on the wicked. I feel my head spinning and have knelt down to thee not only for ye to hearken to my voice; but also because I am weak from ordeal. Now, my humble host, accept my offering. It is not much. This offering is easy to make. Here it is. This is the celebratory headdress of the so-called Prophet."

Asaf unceremoniously dropped the miter on the ground. He scooped up the dirt with his hands around the hat, and with funereal words, began to bury it …

"With this burial, I solemnify the sacrifice we are all to undergo.

"I bury the Prophet and all his kind.

"I bury the indolent who have not harkened to my warnings.

"I bury the innocent. May God have mercy on me for raining destruction and death on their poor heads.

"I bury thee, my disciples. For the poison which will follow, will not treat thee kindly.

"And I bury myself. My ignorance. My sanity. My fateful pride which has brought me to my knees this day.

"Now, I set my face like flint to fulfill my fate.

"Now, my hand shall not be stayed in this deed of destruction.

"Now, I set loose the sentence of death upon the wicked.

"The time is now."

Asaf stood up. He was numb in body, mind, and spirit. He no longer weighed the pros and cons of what he was doing. He no longer felt the burden of guilt. He felt no guilt, no remorse. He felt no joy nor fulfillment either. He lifted the Zippo out in front of him. He flipped open the top. He put his thumb to the knurled brass wheel and spun it, sending the signal to the timer for the seven-minute countdown to detonation.

He looked at the Zippo. He was about to put it back into his pocket where he was used to carrying it. He thought about how he had done his calculations on what to do if the trigger did not work. The considerations of these thoughts, swirling in his mind mere minutes ago, seemed like another time and place to him now. The other-Asaf thought like that. The now-Asaf cared not for such petty selfishness. He knelt back down and buried the lighter next to the miter. "What is done, is done. What will be, will be," he thought. "If it goes off, it goes off. If it fails, it fails."

Then aloud to whatever or whomever in any world that could perceive it, he said, "Now, I resolve to go to the spring and from there, to my new valley, regardless of the bomb's success or failure. Likewise, I yield up my success or failure in my new life, to the powers that be. I cannot do otherwise."

Asaf briefly pondered his little, hand-made grave. The ants went about their business; disturbed by the digging, but still calm, as it was a chilly morning and they were moving slowly.

Asaf stood. There was still no movement other than the light breeze. He turned and began walking in the direction of the trail which would lead him up the pass to the spring.

49

ASAF WALKED AT A NORMAL pace towards the pass. He knew the general direction and was not concerned about intersecting with the path which led up to the spring.

Out of the corner of his eye, he caught the light of a flash.

He turned to look. Any other person would have been in awe of such a great and powerful fireball. But Asaf was unmoved. Only his eyes involuntarily widened. Shortly after watching the huge flash, the sound and shock wave rolled up the slope, flattening the grass and bending the shrubs. It hit Asaf. He felt his ears pop, then was knocked to the ground.

After the shock wave passed, Asaf slowly regained his sensibilities. He sat up. He was dizzy and his head ached. The back of his head was traumatized. Blood trickled from his ears and nostrils. He was stunned physically and mentally at just how large and powerful the explosion was. He recalled how the thug had told him that the explosives were the highest grade and there was more than double to do the job.

Asaf knew it was not safe to stay put. He turned his attention now to getting up and out of the valley before the spread of deadly radiation reached him. He looked at the spreading smoke and dust, turned and walked briskly up the hill, knowing that he would never return to the valley.

50

THE DAUGHTER AND HER GIRL stopped to rest. They had hiked and hiked through the mountain pass to the far side and were tired and thirsty. As they rested, they took in the wonderful beauty of the trees and bushes and birds and mountain vistas and all of the nature surrounding them.

The Girl saw a shimmer. She heard water. She softly went to the sight and sound and found a little spring. The two quenched their thirst with the spring water.

They found an old bottle near the spring. They washed it well and filled it up. The Daughter told her Girl that she had an idea. They would go back to the top of the pass to meet Asaf and present him this new water from the other side of the mountain range. It would serve as a gift and a token of the turning away from the old and turning toward the new.

When they came back over the pass, the Daughter looked down and saw Asaf below looking at the village in the distant valley. It was about half destroyed. A great pillar of smoke rising from the scorched earth, marked where the bar, the tea-house, and surrounding neighborhood once were. From afar, it reminded her of a giant, squashed black bug or spider. The sight gave her a flood of emotions ...

Grief — over the lost village she knew from childhood.

Loss — from knowing the family home was gone forever.

Disappointment — in the human race, for allowing this to happen by their own hand ... not a storm nor flood nor drought nor fire nor volcano nor earthquake.

Sorrow — for the poor lost souls ... the gullible and the stupid.

Pity — for even though they were wrong and guilty and vain and egotistic and self-aggrandizing, the self-righteous religious leaders sparked a feeling of pity in her because they were so blind and so lost and so ignorant.

And anger — she held deep, deep anger at the self-serving religious oppressors of her gender, and war-mongers in the name of God.

Asaf had arrived within sight of the top of the pass and stopped again to rest. It was morning and he found a spot on the path to look back. For him, the stark reality of the aftermath of the destruction was bitter-sweet. It was a Pyrrhic victory; accomplished, but empty. It was not satisfying, as he had imagined it would be, to bring down vengeance upon the wicked.

He came to understand — why his Uncle did not join in the plan.

He came to understand — that proclaiming divine justice was much easier than carrying it out.

He came to understand — why the wise men from all ages teach that only God is the one who metes out justice, judgment, and vengeance.

He came to understand — that the oft proclaimed 'wrath of God', was much more mysterious than was commonly supposed.

The vessels of wrath were the preening peacock preachers and prophets.

The substance of the wrath was their vain and vile teachings.

The fruit of the wrath was burdens of guilt and shame.

And the victims of the wrath were the innocent, the ignorant, and the gullible.

Absorbed in the view before him, Asaf did not notice that the Daughter and the Girl had come down from behind. Not wanting to disturb him, they remained still until he finally felt their presence and turned to look at them. He gave them a small smile. Without saying anything, they walked down and stood at his side.

After a while, the Daughter said, "The Girl and I have found a lovely spring on the path to the new valley. We gathered this water in a bottle we found. We rinsed it out. Here it is. Fresh water from a new spring on the other side of the mountain pass for you to drink and quench your thirst."

Asaf looked at the old bottle. He held the bottle up and looked at the water inside. He saw that it was clear. He put his nose to the opening and the smell told him it was potable. He took a sip. It was good water. Very good water. He turned and looked at the Daughter. "Thank you.

It is good water." He looked down at the Girl and said, "Thank you."

Asaf took another sip and savored the water's taste. Without saying anything, he walked back, assuring himself that he was on the downward slope of the pass, the slope leading back to the valley of his birth.

He turned, held the bottle aloft and saw that the Girl was watching. He nodded at her and smiled slightly in thanks once more for the gift of the bottle of spring water. He then turn back around and faced his valley. He held the bottle out so that the Girl and the Daughter could see it. Then he slowly poured the fresh spring water, which had been brought from the other side of the pass, onto the ground. When the water hit the ground, it slowly trickled down the slope towards Asaf's valley. When he was finished pouring out the water, he turned and rejoined the two who had been watching him from up the slope.

The Daughter asked him, "Why did you do that?"

Asaf addressed them both in his answer. "I have left the valley of my birth and home. Just as you have. I have nothing left there. What I have done there, I was compelled to do because I could not bear such evil in my little village and because I was tired and weary of all the wars. But what I have done also makes me sad. I am not sure what I have done is right. When you brought the water to me, it made me happy because I was thirsty. It was good water, and it is from the side of the mountains where we will go and live. Because I brought about the destruction of life and property, and have nothing left from the village, and will never return, I poured out the water as a small sacrifice, a very small sacrifice, for myself and for those, alive and dead, who are still in the valley of many wars."

The Daughter and the Girl came up and stood side by side with Asaf.

The Daughter said, "It too, was my valley since birth. I am not sad to leave it. It was a valley of pain and shame for me. Their traditions made me a second class citizen. Death came to our house. After the birth of the Girl, her father was taken away by the wars and never returned. My life as a second class citizen was reduced even more, to a third class citizen if such a thing exists. I was looked down upon as a single mother of a female child. People did not think of me as a widow since I was still young. Since I am proud by nature, I did not make a show of being a war-widow. There are so many factions in the wars, that being a war-widow could be taken as a victory by one group; a pitiful loss by another, and scorn by yet another. Each would presume

I got what I deserved by being on the wrong side of God's will.

"So, the sorrow from the loss of my husband turned to bitterness. I secretly vowed I would never let my Girl be raised as a second class citizen. I did not have a plan for this, but I knew it was what I would do. Now I know fate has destined us to become full-fledged members of society in the new valley."

Asaf, who was listening intently to the Daughter's sad story and her description of how she was treated, asked her, "How do you know you will succeed in this noble goal?"

"Asaf, I have known you — or, I have known about you — for a long time. You don't know this, but I have watched you. Watched you in your life. I have watched you interact with people. I have watched how you do business. You are smart. You are honest. You can do business with many different types of people. The young and old — our own people and the foreigners. And you are not rigid and tradition-bound. This is good. These are all good things. I also know that you have remained busy with life and work and fighting injustice these years. You have not taken a woman into your life. Now, we are on the path, both literally and in our lives, toward a new place."

She turned around, took the Girl's hand and silently returned up to the top of the pass. When she reached the top, she called back, "Come."

Asaf walked up the slope to them.

She said, "It is time to turn around and face the new valley."

The three of them turned and the Daughter said, "Here." And she took Asaf's hand in her own and relaxed it there, looking at his face as she did so. Asaf did not anticipate this, but once he felt the warm aura of her hand in his, it felt good and he clasped her hand in his with gentle lovingkindness.

Asaf looked at her and calmly said, "You're right. I have been busy with life and work."

He looked at their joined hands, then at her face, then back to their hands. At his look, the Daughter began to wonder if she was too forward by putting her hand in his. She tensed. Asaf immediately sensed this. "No," he said. He brought his other hand around and laid it on top of their joined hands. "It's ok."

The Daughter smiled.

Asaf said softly, "I was just looking at our hands, wrists, and forearms. The way they are joined together. They form a new valley too, right here." He gestured with his eyes at their hands together.

They both looked at their hands, then at each other and smiled warm and lovingly.

The Girl tugged at her mother's clothes.

"Yes, Little One? Do you have to tinkle?"

The Girl shook her head.

"What is it then my child?"

The Girl hemmed and hawed, thinking and swaying back and forth.

Asaf said softly, "What is it? What can we do for you?"

The Girl was quiet for a few moments more, then said, "In my short life, I have seen that war and religion, and religion and war, can be bad when they are put together.

We should not fight wars in the name of God.

And we should not say God has told us to make a war.

War for religious reasons, and religious war, are not good."

He sat nursing a Jack and Coke on the rocks, a Marlboro in the ashtray sending up a wisp of smoke. Deep in thought, setting his words down carefully, he trolled through his memory the calamity of the poor village and those who participated in its demise …

The Soldier. A fun place at first
To sit and quench your thirst.
But things went really wrong.
Tired of plodding and plotting,
He plops down his weary bum on the stool,
Pops open another Bud,
And wonders who's the fool.

The General, half a pickle
Has earned his nickel.
The finger of fate, being fickle,
Has suborned his senses.
A stumbling man,
Non compos mentis.
Along and beside, stalks
The shadow of the sickle.

The Prophet debased
His righteousness erased
A hypocrite from the start
Eyes piercing like a dart
Peace was his motto
Desolate as a grotto
No man of God was he
Upon no bended knee
Was he ever found
His forehead to the ground
Swift will come his end
No ministry to extend

Asaf, the only one herein
that made any sense
of the true nature of man.
Humble, willing, able.
Yet happiness lacked a din
in his troubled soul.
Fraught with thought
He was caught
Between two worlds.
At last he brought down
Trouble on the trouble and troubled.

Thank you for reading.

There is more at

http://www.timbonner.net

You can email me at
tim@timbonner.net

Comments, suggestions, praises and pans, reviews, etcetera are welcome. You may leave a review on Amazon.

I'd like to acknowledge,

Sonia, my wife. Always allowing me time in our busy schedule to work on this book, originally titled: *Bud, Coke, Jack and Marlboros*. Her understated support and encouragement in my writing efforts never flagged. I managed to get her on the back cover somehow.

James Fisher, editor-light of *Bud, Coke, Jack and Marlboros*. I gave him a 950 page paper copy in a box. He went through it line by line marking the punctuation and grammar with a pencil, along with comments here and there.

My friend, Patty, who went through the first printed book with a pencil and reminded me of Rob Dircks' first rule: Your stuff must be bulletproof.

T. R. Harris and his *Human Chronicles* series. The first four, which were all that was out at the time, were the first ebooks I bought through Kindle.

Rob Dircks of Goldfinch Publishing for his positive attitude and simple motivational email to me: "Go Tim go!"

Derek Crane, (born Coburn) lives in Pasadena, CA. He faired poorly in Hollywood *writ large*, so he turned to what had attracted him next-most: Theoretical physics.

He works at JPL and is an associate professor at Cal Tech.

Because of his Hollywood upbringing, he consorts with, runs into, engages with, celebrities such as: Telly Savalis/Kojak, Tony Shahloub/ Adrian Monk, Peter Falk/Lt. Colombo, George Clooney/himself, Jack Lord/ McGarrett, St. Julian Perlmutter/Clive Cussler, Ben and Jerry Stiller/themselves, and more, too many more.

Derek lands in the hospital having been seriously wounded in a LA driveby shooting which took the life of his royal-blooded mailman in exile from Ethiopia.

Look for:

Ant Crane

Medical Crane

Mexico Crane

Golem Crane

Jorge Luis Borges Crane

Made in the USA
Middletown, DE
08 March 2021

35054269R00182